# DOUBLE VISION

*The creak of the door opening. The boy looking straight ahead not seeing the figure lurking back there in the shadows, his blood throbbing and pounding, his hands, incongruously, clutching a bouquet of chrysanthemums.*

The hospital.

Steven hung on to this vision—he could not call it anything else—desperately, before it faded. He stared into the storm, into black nothing, telling his legs to run, eat up the ground, get there in time . . .

*Also by Owen Brookes*

# DEADLY COMMUNION

## OWEN BROOKES

PINNACLE BOOKS  NEW YORK

DEADLY COMMUNION

*Copyright © 1984 by Owen Brookes*

A Pinnacle Books edition. Reprinted by arrangement with Holt,
Rinehart & Winston.

Holt, Rinehart & Winston edition/July 1984
Pinnacle edition/August 1985

ISBN: 0-523-42574-0
Can. ISBN: 0-523-43524-X

*Printed in the United States of America*

PINNACLE BOOKS, INC.
1430 Broadway
New York, New York 10018

9     8     7     6     5     4     3     2     1

I am more than usually
grateful to Rosalind Belben,
Giles Gordon, and Paddy Kitchen
for their support, criticism, and for
seeing me through.

# DEADLY COMMUNION

Waiting was no hardship to him, even though the night grew increasingly cold and his purpose demanded that he keep still, be invisible in the shadows. All his life he had been waiting, wearing out the interminable years with a secret guilt and a dreadful longing. He had spent a lifetime waiting for his freedom, his flowering, this night—which would bring the culmination of all that was strong, fine, and unique in him.

He waited in the shadow of some bushes, behind a bench set back from the busy main road. It was a place designed for people to sit and watch the world go by, for heavy-laden shoppers to take their rest, a little semicircle or crescent stolen from the park that joined it. If he stepped back just a few paces, he could feel the park railings pressing against him, sense the dark acres of it stretching away to the river, smell the dead and dying leaves, the bonfire smoke, autumn turning into the first winter of his freedom.

It was no longer a nice place. Lovers left the sordid remains of their illicit couplings here. Children and tramps dropped food wrappers, beer and soft-drink cans on the ground. He had observed winos and down-and-outs here, sleeping off their excesses, picking at their scabs. Dogs urinated here, as well as young men from the nearby pub and amusement arcade, so that this intended haven stank and the bushes gradually died. It was a place brought low, demeaned by the falling standards of a world that no longer liked and respected itself.

Perhaps for these very reasons it was an ideal place for his purpose. He had picked it out years ago, studied it, kept a watch on it, knowing without ever admitting it that when his freedom came, it would be from this spot that he would launch himself into his new life, his ecstasy. There were also other

1

such places, all of them more or less public, that he had noted over the years, certain that one day he would wait here or there, silent and watchful for the instrument of his destiny.

A bus passed, a red ship lumbering through the night. There was a stop nearby, and so the buses passed more slowly than the cars, and their brightly lit windows pierced his shadowed place. He shrank back, his ears pricked for voices or footsteps. The one he awaited might arrive by bus. It was a good place precisely because there were so many possibilities: the pub, the amusement arcade, the buses, even the busy road itself might offer up to him the one for whom he waited. He was infinitely patient, had all the time in the world tonight. He could wait.

Two girls went by, laughing, their voices rising to a screech of delight or shock. An old woman, bent with arthritis, followed them, shuffling painful feet on the pavement. He observed lovers holding hands, a group of noisy boys finding safety in numbers, and then for a long, unmeasured time, there was only the rhythmic whoosh of cars. Then suddenly, he heard the pad of feet and felt his throat tighten with excitement.

The boy paused for a moment directly in front of him, paused and looked back over his shoulder, toward the amusement arcade, as though waiting for a friend to catch up. Then he pulled down the elasticized welt of his bomber jacket and set off again. At the first intersection, where the park railings formed a right angle, he stopped again, perhaps hesitating as to which route home he should take.

It was an ill-lit, tree-lined road he chose, bounded on one side by low blocks of old mansion flats, on the other by tennis courts and a miniature golf course. The pavements were covered by the plane-tree leaves, which a recent wind had blown into drifts and banks. The boy, acting younger than his years, waded and kicked through these, unaware that he was observed and followed.

Or was he? Beside the tennis courts, approximately halfway down the road, was a telephone booth, which spilled dim light into a pool confined by shadows. The boy stopped there, teasingly displayed in the light, and glanced back to the main road. The man following him pressed his trembling body against the trunk of a tree, gathering its shadows around him. The boy stooped to pick a leaf from the leg of his trousers, and then went on. The patter of his running shoes against the pavement joined with the footfalls of his pursuer and the dry crackle of dead leaves.

At the bottom of the road, the ornate gates of the park stretched up into starless darkness. There, the road made a right angle, then ran straight on for a quarter of a mile beside the park. Beyond that, when the park ended, were old and lonely wharves now in the first stages of development for new housing. But the boy did not get so far.

He stopped at the gates, aware that it was very dark, but failed to see the man materialize out of the shadows or hear his quick, sure-footed approach. He only felt the man's gloved fingers clamped to his windpipe, cutting off air and the screams that rose within him. He felt his own nails break and slip from the smooth leather of the choking gloves. Then he was propelled and kicked forward. His head struck the railings, making them shudder. Once, twice, three times his head was crashed like a battering ram against the railings.

The boy's weight dragged at the man's hands. His legs had gone and when the man lifted him, limp as a puppet, they dangled and swung harmlessly against his assailant's body. Blood ran from his split forehead and mashed nose. Released, the boy slid to the ground and flopped against the railings, bleeding onto the leaves he had scattered himself.

That should have been enough. The man could have walked away then, mission accomplished, but something gave him the idea for the finishing touch. Beyond the park gates the railings were low and viciously spiked in compensation. He stooped and lifted the boy, lifted him as though he weighed nothing, and carried him past the gates to where ornamental trees overhung the railings. Then he raised the limp, warm body above his head and, with every ounce of force that he possessed, hurled it down onto the railings.

One sharp spike snapped the boy's backbone, and lodged in the soft flesh of his side, from which fresh blood flowed, staining his clothing and spreading, spreading. Another gouged his left thigh and pinned him, one leg dangling. A third found a vulnerable gap between the bones and gristle and tendons of his neck and hooked there so that his disfigured head lolled, and blood ran down the railings to form a pool on the cold and glistening pavement.

At the very moment that the boy's body struck and became impaled on the park railings with sufficient force to set them humming, Steven Cole turned from his window and hit his wife, knocking her to the floor.

"You bastard!" Georgia Cole hissed as soon as the shock of the blow and the impact of her fall permitted. "You bastard." Her voice rose and cracked.

Ashen-faced, her husband took a step toward her, his arms automatically held out.

"No." She flipped down the hem of her nightgown, slid along the floor away from him. She turned, pulled herself up onto the large sofa. As she did so, part of her mind screamed that she was courting danger. She must not leave her body unprotected, must not sit. Sitting enabled him to tower over her, trap her. She stood up and, with a jerky, nervous movement, touched the left side of her face where he had hit her. The prominent, high cheekbone throbbed.

"I'm sorry," Steven said. "Jesus Christ, I'm . . ." His voice shook, sounded very small. He let his outstretched arms fall to his sides.

"You're *sorry*. . . . You're sorry. . . ." She advanced on him, her right fist bunched. She did not feel very brave, but something urged her to take the initiative. Steven turned, not really to avoid her but because he could not bear to look at the red weal on her cheek, the hatred in her eyes.

"Mum? What's going on?"

Together, they turned. Mark, their fourteen-year-old son, stood at the top of the two shallow steps that led down into the living room. It was this room, with its long window overlooking the park, that had made Steven and Georgia decide to buy the flat. For some unaccountable reason, this was all Georgia could think of as she stared at her son. He stared back, his eyes flicking from her face to his father's.

"It's all right," she said. "Go back to bed. Come on, I'll tuck you in." She seemed to waver a little, take a second to find her balance.

"What's happened?" Mark asked. "I heard a crash. You were shouting." As she entered the square of brighter light that fell into the room through the open door, casting Mark's shadow with it, he saw her face clearly and caught his breath. Georgia wanted to go on, keep moving, take charge of the situation, but somehow she had to pause, avoiding his eyes but letting him see.

"You hit her," Mark said. "You creep, you hit her."

She looked at him, shocked by the low whiplash of his voice, and saw that he was no longer a little boy. He was an angry and impotent young man, frustrated by his slim boy's body. He started down the steps. Georgia thrust out her hand, pushed hard against his chest.

"Do as your mother says," Steven said, but his voice lacked weight and authority.

"Come on, Mark," she said firmly, and made him back up into the hall.

Steven sank down onto the sofa. He was trembling. His thin robe—when had he put that on, for God's sake?—was inadequate against the cold night. The central heating was on an economy time switch, would not click on until six in the morning. What time was it? His watch had stopped. He put his head in his hands. He knew that he ought to prepare something, rehearse an apology. What the hell had happened? He winced as pain, electric, stinging-sharp, shot through his head, searing. He had gone to bed, then he had been standing at the window and felt Georgia's light touch on his arm:

"Steve?" she had said.

He looked at the window, a black rectangle, reflecting back the glow of the hall light. He got up again and went to the window, saw his own uncertain silhouette against the darkness. Why this window? What had he been looking for—at? The pain again, like a needle, white hot, passing from one temple to the other, pierced his brain. He clapped his hands to his head, and when the pain receded, he cupped them to shut out the light, pressed his face against the glass. He saw lights twinkle on the distant gloss of the river before his warm breath misted the pane.

He heard a soft thud behind him, turned around, guiltily.

Georgia stood on the steps. The spare quilt lay in a heap on the floor.

"You can sleep in here. I don't want you near me, understand?"

"Georgia . . ." He moved swiftly, with something like his old certainty. He stopped when his bare feet hit the softness of the quilt. He should bend over, pick it up. Such normal, everyday actions would reassure her, would make him feel that his world was not irreparably damaged. "I'm sorry."

"I'm not interested. I just want you to leave me alone. Do you understand?"

"We must talk."

"Not now."

He gave in. His head hurt, not with the piercing pain, but much like a bad hangover.

"Okay," he said, and picked up the quilt.

"And don't you ever do that to me again. Never."

He saw her hurry up the hall as though afraid of him, her long, silky nightgown swinging about her legs. She closed their bedroom door and locked it firmly.

He lay in the dark, his head throbbing dully, the quilt pulled up to his chin, and tried to remember. Was it a dream? Sleepwalking? He could recall no dream images. A sound then, waking him, tugging him to the window? He remembered no sound, and if there had been one, it surely would have woken Georgia. She was a much lighter sleeper than he. He tensed as he heard Mark pad into the corridor, go into the bathroom. He did not know how he would face his son in the morning, ever.

He had gotten up and he did not remember getting up, had put on his robe, evidently, walked down the hall into this room, opened the curtains. His wife had followed him, spoken his name with concern, even alarm in her voice, and he had hit her, knocked her to the ground. Why? He could not remember. He could remember nothing, not even what he had felt at the moment of striking. Blind rage? A kind of pleasure? Some men did take pleasure in hitting their wives. But surely things were not that bad, and anyway he wouldn't. He wasn't violent. Was he? If anything he was too soft. Georgia had always said so, except the night she'd agreed to marry him and during the first few happy years of their marriage. But what about the strange headaches, the bad temper, the loss of concentration, this sudden, frightening violence?

He heard Mark flush the toilet, pause at his mother's door, return reluctantly to bed. Steven thought that he might as well get up, take some aspirins, make a cup of tea. He would in a minute, when he could face the cold, make the effort, when he had worked out how to put his life together again.

A West Indian bus driver found the body of the boy just as dawn was streaking the sky over the river. He almost slipped on the frozen pool and rivulets of blood, almost knocked the lolling head with his shoulder. He started back, stumbled off the pavement. The heavy frost had given the boy's body a glistening, ghostly appearance. For a moment, Winston Cleave thought that he was seeing a ghost, but the dead child was too solid, too dead for that. He felt sick and then was seized with fear. If anyone saw him standing there, they would think that he . . . He began to run. He ran to the telephone booth in Park Road and wrenched open the door, snatched up the dead receiver. A cold gust of wind blew through the vandalized windows. Dead leaves shifted and drifted against the foot of the booth. Winston saw an old man coming slowly down the road, clapping his mittened hands together.

He pushed out of the box and ran toward the man, shouting. Alarmed, the man tried to cross the road, look the other way, avoid trouble. He was old and chesty, and these cold mornings gave him trouble enough without some black lunatic having a go at him.

"Clear off, you," he said as Cleave seized his arm, babbling.

"No man. There's a boy down there. Him dead. A boy on the railings. Oh man . . ."

"What you talking about? My railings?"

Winston Cleave repeated his message, dragging the old man along as he did so, until he could see for himself.

"Jesus Christ," the old man said, staring at it, his breath a puffball. "Silly young bugger. Got shut in as like as not and fell onto them spikes trying to get out. Or hid in there, I suppose, for a lark. Bloody vandals."

"The police, man," Winston Cleave urged him, dancing in agitation. "The phone back there doesn't work."

"All right, all right. You'd best come along with me."

"Where? Where we going, man?"

"I'm the park keeper. There's a phone in my office."

"I gotta call the garage, man. I'm late for me shift."

"Well, you'll have to hang on till the police get here. You found him," the old man said accusingly, fumbling with his mittens, the heavy keys chained to his belt. He'd known it would come to this or something like this. Bloody kids today. Hadn't he said so, often enough? And now there'd be questions and inquiries and God knows what else.

"Hurry it up, man. We gotta get help."

"He's beyond help," the park keeper said, glancing back at the boy, whose blood was frozen like red wax to the newly painted railings. He shook his head. At last the big lock snapped open. "Come on then. Let's get on the phone."

When Steven awoke, Georgia was standing at the big window, craning her neck toward the corner of Anchorage Road. For a moment it seemed like an action replay of last night, with the roles reversed. If he went to her, spoke her name, would she hit him? The thought brought home the full awfulness of what sleep had temporarily suppressed. He rolled over on the sofa, sat up, and was surprised to find a cup of tea standing on the floor beside him. A peace offering, a signal that she was prepared to forgive him? Gratefully, he picked it up, drank.

"Thanks," he said.

In fact, Georgia had brought the tea out of habit. After all, she had been doing so daily, five mornings a week for more years than she could bear to contemplate. It appalled her, chilled her that domestic habit could be so strong, so limiting, more powerful even than her hurt and anger. She pressed closer to the window, ignoring him.

"What are you looking at?" he asked.

"I don't know. There must have been an accident or something. There's a police car, an ambulance, and they're cordoning off part of the road."

Straightening his robe, Steven went to the window. Georgia, as though to avoid him, moved away. Her face was lopsided from the swelling, the effect exaggerated by her stiffly drawn-back hair. The knob of her cheekbone was livid red. The rapidly forming bruise spread upward to the delicate tissue beneath her eye, which was itself a little puffy and bloodshot. Steven stared at her, unable to speak, his heart tripping.

"Yes," she said, her eyes cold on him, "have a good look. Proud of yourself?" She lifted her head and twisted the damaged cheek toward him, defiantly.

"Oh Georgia, love. I don't know . . ." He reached for her and at least she did not pull away. He stroked her arms, which she held stiffly at her sides, then, stepping closer, embraced her. She did not respond but she did not resist either. She was like a hard, dead thing in his arms, a statue of her former self. "I'm sorry, so sorry," he said, resting his forehead against hers.

"Sorry's not good enough," she said on a sigh, and broke free of his arms. "Don't ask me what else you can say. I don't know. That's just not good enough, that's all."

"What are we going to do, then?" he asked, feeling as lonely as she looked, stranded in the middle of the room, her shoulders defensively hunched.

"I don't know. I've got to think about it. I just don't want to talk now, okay?" She moved toward the door at the top of the two shallow steps. "I'll tell you one thing, though," she threw at him over her shoulder, "I'm not covering this with makeup. I'm not going around in dark glasses. And if anyone asks me, I'm going to tell them you did it."

"All right," he said miserably. Then: "What about Mark?" he added, facing his other dread.

Georgia stopped at the bottom of the steps but did not face him. She shrugged.

"He's all right. I suppose you'd better talk to him. Tonight, though. I don't want him late for school."

"All right. Whatever you think best."

She turned around, then, her face tight with anger.

"What the hell was wrong with you? What were you doing?"

"I don't know. Perhaps—did you hear anything?" He looked at the window, remembering what she had said about an accident.

"No. I just woke up, half frozen because you'd thrown the quilt back and I found you in here, standing at the window."

He went to the window, looked up toward the park gates, which were still shut. A policeman was looping white tape around a row of traffic cones standing in the gutter. The ambulance she had mentioned had left.

"What was it?" she said, her voice softening a little, containing something beside anger.

"I don't know. I can't remember."

"Well, you'll have to do better than that for Mark," she snapped. "And for me."

He knew it. He leaned forward, his toes curled around the lip of the hospital swimming pool, at the deep end, tempting gravity, waiting for that moment when balance would desert him and he must plunge, slicing cleanly through the blue water, his ears soothed by its comforting roar.

Mark had only grunted at him before sloping off to school, his back giving off almost visible waves of sullen resentment. Georgia had only spoken once more, to demand that he leave the car. So he had walked to the hospital, where he worked as an administrator. There had only been one policeman standing by the cordon as he passed, and he averted his face when Steven looked at him, as though to nip curious questions in the bud. At the hospital, Steven immediately heard all about the killing.

"I wonder you didn't see or hear something," his secretary, Gwen, said as she made him a cup of instant coffee. "It must have been right outside your flat."

"Not quite," he said. For some reason he did not want to hear any more about it. But it seemed the obvious explanation.

Had the boy cried out, woken him? Had he gone to the window to see what had caused the noise? So why hadn't he done something, why could he not remember? Had he fallen asleep again, at the window? It was true Georgia often said she woke him in the night because he was hogging the quilt or snoring and he had no memory of it. But that didn't explain why he had lashed out at her. Had she startled him, scared him? Was he really living on his nerve ends, sufficiently so to make him hit out just because someone—not someone, his *wife*—startled him? Had things really gotten that bad? He did not think so. All right, then. Was he really so hurt and angry at what Georgia was doing, *might be doing*, he corrected himself, that he was ready to beat her?

If his nerves were so shot, he should do something about it. If he was being driven to this pitch by suspicion, he should seek help. He worked in a hospital. The place was crawling with doctors and psychiatrists and counselors, many of them his friends. He only had to ask.

There had been the headaches of course, and, yes, they had been getting worse. Headaches was a misnomer. It was more like a shooting pain. He thought suddenly of old Frankenstein movies, the moment when a jagged zigzag of white current fizzled through the monster's bolted skull from one giant electrode to another. It was like that, exactly, like that would feel if it were possible, imaginable. They had started, what, a week, ten days ago? Just the occasional jolt at first, easily dismissed, quickly forgotten. Then two or three at a time, building up, until yesterday they had been almost regular, leaving, by the end of the day, a constant sensation of soreness in his brain itself, making thought difficult. Erasing memory? A sort of blackout, which would explain why he could not remember?

He touched the side, flipped over, started back across the pool in a slow and more graceful crawl.

He tried to remember, back, way back, to when life had been good and seemingly easier. It had been exciting, coming to work in this brand-new, ultramodern, magnificently equipped building. They had been lucky, finding a flat they really liked so close, with its magical view of the park and the Thames. They had been happy then, that first year before Mark started at elementary school. Surely he was not fooling himself?

Georgia had always wanted to space their children. Even if it did lessen her chances of getting a career together, she did not want to cope with two toddlers at once. They had only wanted two, which was not a lot to ask, and they had celebrated Mark's first day at school in the oldest and best way, by trying to make another child. They had tried for an ironically symbolic nine months, until the crippling pains started and Georgia had been rushed to this very building, suspected of having acute appendicitis. If only it had been. They found instead a raging infection of the fallopian tubes, which had to be removed. There would be no more babies, at least not of their own making.

Had that been the start? Georgia had been devastated. He understood. But she had slowly pulled herself out of it, and when she got her job, voluntary at first, working for the borough council's adult-literacy scheme, she had seemed fully recovered, busy and accepting. All right, so maybe she was filling a gap, an almost immeasurable emptiness in her life, but what was wrong with that? They were lucky, as everyone said. They already had Mark. Thousands of childless couples would envy them.

Georgia was a good teacher, good with people, but she had more valuable skills and had soon been taken onto the payroll as an assessor, matching pupils to teachers, devising special courses where required. They had been happy. Search his memory as he might, he could not recall anything that had disturbed their happiness, no black rocks beneath the calm blue surface, no festering sores that could have burst into the violence of last night.

Dull? Georgia said it was dull. That's why he couldn't remember anything specific, hadn't noticed anything. He'd become soft and fat and prematurely middle-aged, she'd said. He'd settled. He only thought about his job, promotion prospects, the ordered routine of their dull lives. The life she ordered, the routine she found stifling yet was forced to maintain for him.

Dull enough for her to take a lover?

If he had to date the beginning of their present difficulties, it would be at the arrival of Roger North, a whizz-kid brought in to coordinate the many schemes started by the council—Roger North, who was Georgia's boss and perhaps her lover.

Secretly, somewhere at the back of his mind, he suspected that she referred to much more than his body when she had said he had gone soft. That's what she had said to him before—had taunted him with—all those years ago when he had been crazily in love with her, certain of her, only to discover that she was seeing another man. The broken dates, the excuses, all in order to be with another man.

When he had charged her with it, begging her to marry him, she had said, "I can't. It wouldn't be fair. Really, you're too soft for me."

It had stung then and it stung now. He had thought that he was going to die or go mad with grief and shame. He had become a little mad. He waited for her one night, half-drunk, half-crazy, waited until the other man brought her home. He had grabbed her arm, hurting her, pulling her away. He had shouted into the astonished face of her new boyfriend, told him to get lost because Georgia was going to marry him. And she had. He had proved something to her that night, something about which he still felt uncomfortable. They had often laughed about it. The boyfriend could have made mincemeat of him, but he was too surprised and then completely devastated by Georgia, who had said, "Yes, that's right. Get lost. I'm going to marry Steve."

In his heart of hearts, Steven had always felt like a phony about that night. Oh, he had done it, right enough. He had taken her, more or less by force, from his rival, but it was not his way, and he had never thought that he would be required to do it again. Was that what she wanted, for him to take a swing at Roger North? It would be a pleasure.

He was shocked to find his fingers bunched into fists, the knuckles staring white, his bones cracking and hurting. He opened his hands slowly, spreading his fingers. The wave of violence that had seized him, the flash image of North's smiling face—what he had wanted to do made him shudder.

That was it, then. His nerves were shot. He was acting out of character, like a maddened bull. He needed help.

True to her word, Georgia wore no makeup, made no attempt to conceal her injury, and, as she stood at the bar, she saw curiosity, concern, embarrassment in the eyes of strangers who looked away, heavy with their own conclusions. Except the young barman, who, she thought, smiled to himself as he turned to reach for a bottle of red wine from which to fill her glass. Georgia braced herself to challenge him, ask him what was so damned funny, but his expression was bland when he placed the brimming glass before her, and he did not look at her directly when she paid him. She carried the glass to a less-crowded spot near the entrance and stood there, sipping her drink thinking.

She had called in to the office saying she wasn't feeling well but probably would be in after lunch. Then, on impulse, she had asked her best friend, Marion, to meet her for lunch. The truth was she did not want Roger to see her like this. It was simple vanity, she supposed. Roger was scheduled to be out of the office that afternoon, attending a meeting, and she wanted to get Marion's questions out of the way before she faced the rest of the staff. Marion would be her ally, encouraging the others to speculate in silence. Beyond that, she did not know what she was going to do. Steve's hitting her brought things to a head, faced her with choices she'd been avoiding for months, had hoped to avoid for much longer.

She saw Marion heave through the heavy swinging doors, loaded as usual with bags, her coat flapping, an air of bustle and busyness about her. Georgia waved, turned fully to face her so that Marion would have time to adjust before she had to speak. She watched her friend's smile fade, a sharp frown crease her eyes. Anger and worry mixed, Georgia thought, but when Marion stopped in front of her, dumping her bags on the floor, her grin was ironic, her eyes concerned.

"Steve?" she asked.

Georgia nodded. For the first time she felt tears well up in her, but she quickly choked them back.

"Hang on. I need a drink. Another for you?"

In a flurry of activity, Marion located and extracted her purse from one of the bags and set off for the bar, her coat flapping behind her like a windswept cape. Georgia smiled, and the smile hurt her face. Marion almost always made her feel better. She bent and collected up the bags, ranged them against the wall, and by the time she had balanced them, Marion was coming back, a gin and tonic in one hand, another glass of red wine in the other.

"Cheers," she said, toasting Georgia, who emptied her first glass in acknowledgment.

"Don't let me get drunk," she said, reaching for the full glass.

"In your shoes I certainly would." Marion pulled a face at her own glass. "In fact, I think I may."

"Oh Marion . . ." In spite of all she was feeling, Georgia laughed.

"Well? Want to tell me about it?"

"There's not much to tell." Briefly, Georgia recounted what had happened. Marion looked doubtful, as though she thought Georgia was holding back on her.

"No row? No civilized discussion that turned into a brawl?"

"No." Georgia shook her head. "Nothing like that."

"Well, he must be feeling pretty nasty about things if he's started thumping you without winding himself up first. My beloved ex always needed an hour of verbal abuse before he got physical. Perhaps that's what was lacking in our sex life. There's a thought. Maybe I should have talked him into it first."

"Bit late now, though, isn't it?" Georgia said. She'd heard about Marion's marriage and divorce over and over, and right now she had her own problems.

"Sorry," Marion said, fishing a packet of cigarettes from her coat pocket. She lit one. "So, what did you say? What are you going to do?"

"He said he was sorry. I didn't say anything really. I was too angry, too confused. God, Marion, who the hell does he think he is?"

"A cuckolded husband, perhaps?"

"That was below the belt," Georgia said.

"It's the truth."

"He doesn't *know*," Georgia protested.

"He knows. He just hasn't got any proof."

"Oh that's nonsense."

"No, Georgia. That bruise on your face proves it. That says he knows."

Georgia stalled, fiddling with the stem of her glass, avoiding Marion's eyes. "Okay," she said at last, sighing. "I've been trying to tell myself it wasn't that but . . ." She shrugged.

"And what does Roger say?"

"He doesn't know. That's why I didn't come in this morning. By the way, is he still going to that meeting?"

"Yes. He left just before I did. *And* in a foul temper."

"I'll come in this afternoon, then."

"But you can't go on avoiding him, if that's what you are doing. He'll have to know," Marion pointed out.

"Let's get some food," Georgia said, knowing Marion was right again but not wanting to admit it. "This is going to my head."

Marion finished her drink and followed Georgia to the counter where two hot dishes and a big selection of salads were set out.

"Oh to hell with dieting, I'll have the moussaka," Marion announced. "And roast potatoes, and we'll have a carafe of wine."

"To celebrate?" Georgia asked ironically.

"Either that or to drown your sorrows. It comes to much the same thing, I sometimes think. Come on, we'll go Dutch."

Seated at a table near the bar, Georgia stared at her salad without appetite while Marion went to retrieve her bags. Marion was right, and she did not want her to be right. What Steve didn't know couldn't hurt him. But knowing could hurt, she reminded herself; and anyway he *did* know now. Why else would he have hit her?

"So, what's all this about keeping it from Roger?" Marion demanded.

"I'm not. I just haven't had a chance."

"At least it explains why you called me this morning, not him. I thought it was odd."

"All right. I need to think. I don't know what to do."

"Well, you're going to look a mess for a week or more, so you'd better make up your mind pretty quick."

"Thanks a lot. The thing is, I'm scared."

"To tell Roger? *Of* Roger?" Marion looked incredulous.

"Yes."

"I would have thought Steve was the one you should be frightened of."

"I mean that Roger'll push me into something."

"Do his knight-in-shining armor bit, you mean? Rescue you from the violent husband and whisk you off to the safety of everlasting happiness? And all that jazz."

"I wouldn't exactly put it like that. . . . Christ, Marion, he loves me. What do you expect him to do?"

"I don't know. Does he?"

"You don't think he does."

"You know me. I'm a legendary bad judge of men. It's my only known claim to fame."

"I'm scared that he'll see this as a crisis, a reason to change the way things are."

"And isn't it?"

"I don't know if I'm ready."

"Ah, good old lack of commitment. Now with that I am familiar. What about Mark?"

"We never talk about Mark. He saw this last night. I think he wanted to hit Steve. He didn't say anything to me this morning."

"Don't worry about him. Paul and Fiona saw me get much worse, and they survived. Kids do, better than us."

"I can't decide anything now. I just can't."

"If you feel like that then you mustn't let Roger pressure you into anything."

"Why don't you like him, Marion?"

"I do like him. He's a nice guy. I'm just not sure he's right for you."

"Is Steve?"

"He seemed to be."

"You mean Roger's just a last, desperate fling?"

"You said that. Oh, look, Georgia, I know I'm the last person to talk, but, well, Steve's okay. You've got a nice home, nice kid, steady marriage. Why throw it all up? God, I sound like my mother, a senile sentimentalist. Ignore me."

"It's dull," Georgia said flatly. "Not enough. I don't care about furniture and cooking nice meals. I mean, I do care, but . . . Oh, it was fine to begin with. When we first moved into the flat I enjoyed choosing things, looking after them. I liked recipe books. I liked sex and being with him, but somehow it just got too settled. It was like I woke up one morning and thought, that's it. We never need to buy another table or sofa. We'll never have another child. We'll just go on, wearing each other down. I am too young," she said, raising her voice, "to get settled, to start thinking about retirement."

Marion said nothing. Georgia pushed her plate away impatiently, helped herself to more wine.

"Besides," she began again, defensively, "I wouldn't be throwing it all away. I'd be exchanging it for something better, different."

"Different I'll buy. Better, maybe. But if you feel like that, your mind's made up. And the sooner you tell them both the better."

"My mind is not made up," Georgia protested. "I don't know what to do. I don't know what I want and . . . oh Christ, Marion, I think I'm going to cry."

"Go ahead. You've been wanting to ever since I got here."

"It must be the wine," she wailed, searching for a handkerchief. "I can't cry here."

"Yes you can. Or shall I take you to the ladies' room?"

"No. I'll go by myself. I'm sorry." She got up, banging against the table, making the wine slop. Heads turned to follow her as she hurried across the foyer to the ladies' room. The barman caught Marion's eye, a look of amused exasperation on his face. Marion stuck her tongue out at him and decided to eat some of Georgia's salad.

"And that . . ." Leigh Duncan paused. She had almost added, out of habit, "ladies and gentlemen," but there were no women present. Indeed, she thought, there was hardly anyone present. Twelve bodies, all male, scattered through the first three rows of the vast lecture hall, which could easily accommodate several hundreds. "That concludes my address, gentlemen," she went on, stressing the noun a little, "but I'll be happy to answer any questions you may have." She collected her papers, not expecting the desultory ripple of applause. She felt sure it was the two who were obviously students, shiny-faced, eager young men, who led the applause, such as it was. Certainly they were the last to stop, and Leigh directed her smile of acknowledgment to them. The coolness of her reception just might be because of that famous English reticence she'd heard so much about, but the looks of boredom and, in a couple of cases, open, patronizing disbelief in what she had had to say made her doubt it. They were bored. They thought her work, her precious work, was trivial and fanciful, not scientifically kosher. Leigh knew all the arguments. Well, to hell with them. She had a year, attached to the psychiatric unit here at the hospital, to change their shut minds, and she would.

She walked around the lectern-like desk, dragged a chair forward, and sat down, crossing her long legs. She did not bother to hitch her skirt down. Let them look, she thought. If that was all they were interested in, that was their hard luck. She waited, cool and unembarrassed, a polite smile fixed to her face.

"I'd just like to say . . ." It was one of the students, blushing slightly, ". . . how very interesting and . . . er . . . stimulating that was."

"Please sit down, and thank you," Leigh said. Obviously relieved, grinning broadly, the boy sank back onto his bench. "Are there any questions?" she said sweetly, looking at the larger group of older men. One, a very neat little man with wisps of hair slicked down below a bald and shining dome, cleared his throat, shifted in his seat. Leigh fixed him with her eyes.

"Did I understand you to say, Miss . . . er . . . Duncan, that the U.S. government seriously believes there is military potential in these psychic phenomena you have so . . . um . . . lucidly described to us this afternoon?"

"Not exactly, sir," Leigh replied. "Obviously I can't speak for the government of the United States. What I can tell you is that the Agency I work for is partly funded by the government, and part of our task is to consider the possibility of applying the sort of powers we are examining to what could broadly be termed military use. The main purpose of the program, however, is to verify, chart, assess, and try to develop the abilities of those individuals we broadly term *psychics*."

"In what fields would *your* government," the big man said, emphasizing the pronoun as though to indicate a gulf between them, "plan to use these so-called abilities?"

"Well, we're not in the business of making human bombs, if that's what you mean," Leigh answered, and was grateful for the burst of laughter from the students, "but I think it's obvious that the sort of powers we're dealing with would lend themselves to information gathering and possibly espionage work. But this is only a very small part—a spin-off you might say—of our work. The program is concerned with exploring, researching, preserving, and developing the powers these people happen to possess in the general context of their overall psychological health and social integration. Ours is an affirmative and supportive approach. As I told you, the possession of these powers often causes great distress and mental imbalance. The suicide rate . . .''

"Clearly such persons are generally unstable?"

"Absolutely not," Leigh corrected the questioner. "Our findings show no correlation between the possession of so-called 'abnormal' powers and the mental stability of the possessors. The very high incidence of mental distress is entirely due to social pressures, a feeling that may be summed up broadly in the phrase I quoted to you earlier: 'I am different, therefore I must be mad.' And that attitude is one, gentlemen, I would have expected you to have encountered many times in your own more orthodox work. Thank you."

She gathered up her notes and left the rostrum. They made her so goddamned mad! She pushed through the swinging doors, ignoring the murmurs of surprise, the guffaws of laughter that rose behind her. She was going to find Dr. Page and tell him exactly what she thought of him. Not only was he supposed to supervise her work while she was on attachment, but he was also supposed to be present and attend her lectures, to introduce her. Instead of which she'd had to cope with those morons all by herself. It was not good enough, and she was not going to let him get away with it. She'd had her baptism by fire. Now she wanted a little support and courtesy around here.

Leigh was still unfamiliar with the layout of the hospital, which in certain areas resembled a Hampton Court maze of identical, anonymous corridors. In her anger and preoccupation, she had forgotten to check the signs and now realized that she was hopelessly lost. She swore under her breath. It made her feel foolish and incompetent. She made for the nearest door, tapped on it, and walked straight into him.

"So sorry," he said. "Excuse me."

For a moment his hands touched her upper arms to steady her. It was like a burn on her flesh. Leigh shrank away from him, cringed back against the wall. There was a smell like sulphur in her nose, a scream sounding at the back of her mind. She could hardly bear to look at his retreating figure. It was surrounded by a dancing double aura. The scream grew louder. Her eyes dazzled, and she squeezed them shut, leaning limp and sickly against the wall.

It was about three in the afternoon when Tracey, the youngest of the typists, popped out to buy some cakes for their tea. She brought back a copy of *The Standard* with her. The boy's death was blazoned across the front page. There was even a photograph of the road in front of the park with the white ribbon of the police cordon showing clearly.

"Here," she said, looking up from the paper, "isn't this where you live, Georgia?"

Georgia twisted her head to look at the paper, saw the headline BOY SLAIN, and snatched it from Tracey's hand. Before she had scanned half of the brief article, something like a moan of panic and danger had started in her head.

"Oh my God," she said.

"What is it?" Marion asked, peering through a cloud of smoke.

Georgia ignored her, hurrying across the room to where her coat hung from a peg.

"It's this young boy," Tracey explained. "Murdered, right outside where Georgia lives."

"Where are you going?" Marion asked Georgia.

"To get Mark. School'll be out in half an hour. I'll come straight back."

"Georgia, you can't go—"

"Don't you see?" Georgia shouted. "There's a maniac out there somewhere. Oh, why am I trying to explain? I'm going to get Mark."

Marion looked at Tracey, shrugged.

"Well, I don't blame her," Tracey said. "If I had a kid, I'd be worried sick. And right on her own doorstep, too."

"Hmm," Marion muttered, doubtful and enigmatic. She

22

was remembering what Georgia had told her about Steve staring out of the window, and wondered . . .

"What's that supposed to mean?" Tracey asked, reluctantly returning to her typewriter.

"It means that lightning doesn't strike in the same place twice and that Mark won't thank her. He's old enough to look after himself."

Because she did not know what to do, Heather dithered. She wished Dr. Zimmer were in. With a worried expression, she looked at the tall, shaking young woman she had persuaded to come into her office to sit down. Should she ring somebody, get medical help? Oh, if only Dr. Zimmer were here. Perhaps she should get a nurse at least. Leigh was like a statue, sitting there, eyes blank, mouth open, all color washed from her face.

"Would you like a drink of water?" Heather said, bending a little to look into Leigh's glazed eyes. She made no answer. "I'll get you some anyway," Heather said, and went to the small sink in the corner of the office.

Perhaps she should ring down to the Emergency Room? It seemed ridiculous to be working in a hospital and not know what to do. The trouble was she couldn't be sure the woman was actually ill—perhaps she was having a fit of some kind. But Heather associated fits with thrashing limbs and foaming mouths. This woman was disturbingly calm. A heart attack? But she wasn't blue around the mouth or anything.

"Here, try a drop of water. Come on. Please? Or shall I call a doctor? I don't know what to do unless you can tell me . . ."

Leigh's right hand lifted slowly from her lap, reached for the paper cup of water.

She was "tripping back"—her own private phrase for it. You tripped out, you tripped back. She felt queasy. All shapes were insubstantial, indistinct but becoming sharper. Okay, come on, Leigh. Get a hold of yourself. Count. She started counting. The mechanical recitation of numbers always soothed her. She closed her mouth. She seemed, to Heather, to shake herself. A light of some kind drained into her eyes. They were the most extraordinary blue, Heather realized, almost navy. And her hair was completely gray, iron gray and not dyed, either, although the face it framed was that of a young woman. She couldn't be a day over thirty. Heather could not decide whether she was odd or beautiful.

Leigh raised the cup. She could see clearly now, or almost so. She tried to smile at the woman who stood anxiously before her.

"Feeling better?" Heather asked.

"Yes. Thank you. I'm so sorry . . ."

"You gave me a nasty turn, I don't mind admitting. Would you like a doctor or a nurse?"

"No, that's not necessary. I'm really . . . perfectly fine now." Leigh prided herself on the speed with which she could get back, get herself together. She kept herself on such a tight rein anyway that she hardly ever tripped out. And she had not let her guard down. But it was him, that man.

"Did you want to see Dr. Zimmer?"

"Who?"

"Dr. Zimmer. This is her office. I'm her secretary."

"Oh, no. Fact of the matter is, I'm lost. I'm new here and I haven't gotten my bearings yet. I just came in to ask where Dr. Page's office is."

"Oh, I see. You work here?"

"Sort of. I'm on attachment to the psychiatric unit for a year."

"American, are you?"

"Yes, that's right." Leigh stood up.

"Are you sure you shouldn't rest for a bit more?"

"No, really, I'm perfectly fine. Thanks for the water." Leigh put the cup down on Heather's desk.

"Do you often . . . I mean, have you had a turn like this before?"

"Oh sure . . ." Leigh laughed. "I just felt a little dizzy. It's nothing. I skipped lunch." The lie seemed to satisfy Heather. "I'm really sorry I scared you."

"Oh, that's all right. No harm done."

"Now could you direct me to Dr. Page's office?"

"It's over on the other side, the last wing. This is the west."

"Of course. How stupid of me. I never was any good at geography."

"It's quite easy once you get the hang of it. My last office was like a rabbit warren. Took me months to find my way around."

"Well, thanks again."

"You take care of yourself, now."

"I will," Leigh said. "By the way," she added, trying to make it sound casual. "That man I bumped into, do you know who he is?"

"Mr. Cole?"

"I guess. Cole . . . Is he a patient of Dr. Zimmer's?"

"Well, yes. I suppose he is. I mean, he came in here to make an appointment, but he works here, too, in administration."

"Oh," Leigh said. "I must have seen him around, then. I thought I recognized him," she lied again. "Thank you for your help."

Outside in the corridor she realized that she had been hoping he would be a patient, a casual visitor to the hospital, someone she would be unlikely to see again. The fact that he worked there depressed her and made her afraid.

Georgia parked by the school gates and sat there, fidgeting. She hadn't thought, hadn't stopped to think. There was nothing to think about. She had acted on instinct. Realizing what she had been watching that morning with only vague curiosity was terrifying to her. Something inside her kept insisting that it could so easily have been Mark. She did not consider any of the facts, only that someone had killed a boy about Mark's age, had killed him brutally, and she was frightened.

She saw him at last, and relief flooded over her. He had never been more precious, more loved. His tie was askew, his top shirt button undone, and he was whirling his schoolbag around, trying to hit another boy on the back. She leaned on the horn, called to him, her head thrust out of the passenger window. His face showed surprise, then fell. The boy he had been trying to hit, two others she recognized as special friends, stood on the pavement, staring at her.

"What are you doing here?"

"I came to give you a lift."

"I don't want a lift. I'm going to walk home with my friends."

"Well, 'Thank you very much, mother dear, for bothering.' Come on, get in quickly. I've got to get back to the office."

"I told you, I'm going—"

"Mark," she said, not meaning to yell but unable to stop herself. "Get in the car, now."

He rolled his eyes toward heaven, sighed.

"I've got to go," he called to his friends. "See you tomorrow."

"See you, Coley."

"Yeah, see you, Mark."

He got in, sullen, and fastened his seatbelt.

"Why did you have to come here looking like that?" he grumbled.

Georgia had forgotten about her face. Instinctively, she touched it.

"I didn't think," she said, and then wondered why she was almost apologizing to him. She'd been frantic with worry for him.

"Showing me up," he muttered.

"Well excuse me. If you find my face a problem, I suggest you discuss it with your father." She ground the gears, could feel his silent criticism of her driving fanning her anger. "If you must know," she said, "I was too worried about you to consider that my face might embarrass you."

"Worried about what?"

Her instinct was to keep it from him, keep him safe and unsullied by such horrors, but it would be on the TV, in all the papers.

"Look, I don't want *you* to worry, but there was a murder last night and—"

"Oh that," he said dismissively. "Some kid from Compton. What's that got to do with me?"

"I don't want you out alone at night until the police catch whoever did it."

"Oh, don't be stupid, Mum. I can look after myself."

"Don't you be stupid. Nobody's safe when there's a maniac—"

"How do you know he's a maniac? How do you know the police haven't already collared him? What makes you think—"

"Shut up! God, sometimes I just don't understand you,

Mark. You make the simplest thing so difficult. I love you and I don't want—"

"You can't pick me up from school like some little kid. I'm fourteen."

"I know you're fourteen and I know you think you're a man already, but the fact remains that you are very young, and I just want you to be careful."

"I will be."

"Good. Then let's not argue about it anymore. I'm going to take you home, and I want you to stay there. I've got to go back to work for a while, but your father'll be home about six-thirty."

"Why have you got to go back?"

"Because I didn't feel up to it this morning and I've got a lot to catch up on," Georgia explained, averting her eyes as she turned into Anchorage Road. A tarpaulin covered the spot where the boy had been found and there were flashing warning lights on either side of it.

"Look at that. That must be where he got it." Mark twisted excitedly in his seat.

"Are you completely heartless?" Georgia snapped, easing the car into the curb.

"I was only saying—"

"Go on. I'll wait here until I see you at the window. And remember, don't go out."

"All right. I won't. I've got loads of homework anyway."

"Just make sure you do it, then. Go on," she said, softening her tone a little. "I'll fix something nice for dinner."

"Mum?"

"Yes?"

"Can I ask you something?"

"What?"

"Your face . . . Does it hurt?"

"Only when I laugh. Go on now."

Did she fuss too much? Was she in danger of becoming an overprotective mother, hanging on to her child because there was nothing else to fill the yawning emptiness of her life? She shook her head. No, she was not like that. Such women did not lie about going back to work when in fact they were going to see their lover. Oh no, Georgia Cole was not like that at all.

She looked up and saw him at the window, one hand raised in a joking salute. She felt guilty then, really guilty that she was leaving him. What would he feel if he knew? She sounded the horn twice and drove away.

"Ah, there you are, my dear. How did it go? So sorry, by the way, to have abandoned you at the starting post, but something rather interesting came up." Dr. Page was a roly-poly man, a lot shorter than Leigh, and was made to look as benign as a cuddly toy by a thick growth of beard and twinkling eyes.

Her anger had gone anyway, had been subsumed into the shock she had received. She still felt a little reeling, disoriented from that. Leigh Duncan had seen some strange and peculiar sights in her time but that . . . She blinked, suppressed a shiver, and realized that she had not been listening to the doctor, who was gazing at a corner of the room, talking and finger-combing his beard.

"Well, actually he's Rathbone's patient. I don't think you've met Rathbone. Sound man. Very. You'll like him. And he'll like you." Appreciation, warmth crept into his voice as he gave a sideways, almost sly glance at Leigh. "There's nothing definite yet, but if you would be interested . . . What do you think?"

Leigh said, "I'm sorry. I'm rather tired. I wasn't listening properly. You want me to help with this assessment?"

"I think you'd be invaluable. Rathbone's keen to have a second opinion. Normally of course I would automatically oblige, but since we have you here . . ."

"If it's okay with Dr. Rathbone, I'd be pleased to help."

"Good, good, well I'll speak to Rathbone."

"If I could just have my schedule for tomorrow, Dr. Page, I think I'd like to call it a day, if you don't mind."

"Of course. Lecturing can be very tiring. Good turnout, was it?"

"Not at all."

"Oh dear . . ." Page shuffled through a tray of papers. "You've got your seminar, of course." He pulled a sheet of paper out of the tray and handed it to her, upside down. "Not a heavy day, though, so perhaps you could fit in Dr. Rathbone's patient."

"Thank you," Leigh said, glancing at the sheet. "I'll do my best to fit in with Dr. Rathbone's schedule."

"And we must set a date for you to come and have dinner. Mrs. Page would like that. I'll consult with her tonight. You must think us very lax in our hospitality."

She did, but it hardly seemed tactful to say so.

"May I ask you something?"

"Of course, of course." He leaned back in his old-fashioned swivel chair, his stubby arms held out expansively, inviting.

"Do you know a man named Cole? He works here, in administration, I think."

"Cole. Let me see . . ." He turned, the chair protesting loudly, to consult a photocopied list of internal telephone numbers. "Oh yes. Steven Cole. He's one of the assistant administrators. Said to be a bright man, in line for promotion. I know him slightly. Why do you ask?"

"Oh, no reason. I was just curious. I sort of bumped into him."

"You'll soon get to know everyone, I'm sure," Page said guardedly. "Everyone will be most anxious to meet you, of course."

"Well, I'll see you in the morning then."

"Good night, good night." He picked up a paper clip and began to straighten it. Leigh opened the door. "He's married, our Mr. Cole."

Leigh stopped. Her hand tightened on the doorknob. She looked back at Page, who had the grace, she thought, not to look up at her.

"That was not my interest, Doctor."

"Oh no, no, of course not. I was simply— Since you seemed to want information about him— I was just offering what I know."

"Good night," she said, and closed the door sharply behind her.

Well, that was one woman she did not envy, not Mrs. Steven Cole.

He knew as soon as he let himself into the flat that Georgia was not home. There were no cooking smells, no light in the kitchen, and the television set was playing at a volume only

Mark could tolerate. Steven was not really surprised by her absence, was even a little relieved. He put down his briefcase and hung his coat on a peg. Probably her absence was deliberate, designed to give him a chance to talk to Mark alone. Probably she was also avoiding him.

Mark got up as he entered the living room and switched off the set.

"There's no need," Steven said. "Just turn it down a bit."

"I was just going to my room anyway."

"Homework?"

Mark nodded. Steven stood on the lower step, blocking the doorway. Mark brushed the hair out of his face nervously.

"Where's your mother?"

"At work. She had to go back."

"Did she say how long she'd be?"

"No."

Steven moved into the room. Mark started immediately for the door. Steven put out his hand, caught the boy's arm, stopping him.

"I think we have to talk, Mark."

"I've got homework."

"It'll keep. I don't think this will take long. Sit down? Please?" He made it gentle, not a command. Mark slouched to the sofa, sat.

"Do you know why your mother went back to the office?"

"She said she had a lot of work to catch up on. She didn't go in this morning."

"Oh, well . . ."

"I wish you'd talk to her."

"About work?" Steven looked at him in surprise. Why should that worry him unless he, too, suspected—

"No. She came to fetch me from school. She's going on about this kid who's been killed. I'm not a baby. I don't want her fetching me. You tell her."

"She's bound to be worried, Mark." The boy's death, about which everyone had been talking that morning, seemed an age ago.

"Everyone'll think I'm a baby if Mum comes and fetches me. I can look after myself."

Against such logic Steven could find no argument.

"I'll speak to her," he said. "Now, what about last night?"

Mark said nothing. He hunched his shoulders, pushed his hands into his pockets, and stretched out his legs, crossing them at the ankles. Steven wanted a drink. He went to the old restored marble-topped washstand where they kept the liquor.

"I'm very sorry and ashamed for what happened last night," he said, speaking quickly to get it over with. His hands shook as he mixed gin and tonic water, clattering bottles and glasses.

"Why did you do it?" Mark asked.

"I don't know. That's the truth," he added quickly. "I know it sounds like a cop-out, but I've been trying to puzzle it out all day. Apart from you, I have to explain it to your mother, and the simple truth is, I can't."

"Do you hate her?"

"No, of course not. I love her very much. But, okay," he admitted, seeing the doubt on Mark's face, "we are going through a bad time just now. Married people do. You've obviously noticed." Mark pursed his lips, tapped his foot on air. "That wasn't the reason, though. At least, I don't think it was. All I can think is that things are getting on top of me. I've been having headaches. Anyway, I'm going to have a checkup."

"But being ill wouldn't make you hit someone, would it?"

"Possibly. If a person's tense enough, unhappy, sometimes pressure just explodes into violence. Anyway, I mean to find out so that it doesn't happen again."

"Then it's all right, isn't it?" Mark stood up, hunched and gangling, his eyes lowered.

"Is it? I wish you'd tell me."

"I don't know what you mean."

"How are you? How do you feel about it?"

Mark shook his head as though denying the question, pushed his hair back again.

"I don't think you ought to hit her, whatever she's done."

"Done?" Steven's heart seemed to stop. "What do you mean?"

"Nothing. I don't know. I just thought— You'd have to have a reason, and I don't think you should have done it."

"Well," he said, lying, "apart from what I've told you, I know of no reason. Can you believe that?"

"Sure. You should know."

"I don't want this to upset you, Mark."

"All right."

"Well, I . . ."

"I'll get on with my homework, okay?"

"Yes. And I'll get us something to eat, shall I?"

"Yeah, great. I'm starving."

Steven nodded, thought that he would finish his drink first. At the top of the steps, Mark stopped.

"If you really want to know, I think she went back to work because she's scared of you. I think you'd better ring her."

"I will. Thanks." It was a good idea, and he wondered why he had not thought of it. Perhaps he had been afraid. Of what? Of Roger North answering? Of Georgia refusing to speak to him? Tears? Recriminations? Those he expected, deserved. But if she was really scared of him, she might not come back at all.

Steven hurried out into the hall and lifted the telephone receiver.

He had said that he would be back just as soon as the meeting was over. When everyone else had gone, Georgia waited in his office; the phones were switched through. She started when the telephone rang, feared that it was Roger calling to say the meeting was dragging on, that she'd better go home, he'd see her in the morning. She snatched at the receiver, leaning across his desk, and a little breathlessly said, "Hello?"

"Georgia."

"Oh. It's you. Is Mark okay?"

"Yes. Fine. I just called to see when you'd be back."

"I'm not sure." She looked around the room, searching for an excuse. She felt as though Steve could see that she was not working. "I've got a couple of things . . . er . . . assessments to finish off. They're needed for the morning."

"You could bring them home?" Steven suggested.

"No . . . I need files and things. Eight," she said nervously. "I won't be later than eight."

"All right." He sounded disappointed. "I'll get supper. Any suggestions?"

"Oh, there are some hamburgers. They'll do for Mark. I'm not very hungry."

"Well, I'll fix something in case."

"Okay, thanks."

"Are you all right?"

"Yes. Look, I really must get off."

"All right. Take care."

She put the receiver down. She had unfastened her hair and now she pushed it back with a gesture that was almost identical to Mark's. Was he checking up on her? Roger kept a bottle of Scotch whisky in the bottom drawer of the filing cabinet, and suddenly she wanted a drink, something warming. She opened the drawer and helped herself to the equivalent of a double in a paper cup.

Roger's office was no more than a cubicle partitioned off from the main office. The door and one wall had glass panels in them, and she could see into the dimly lit larger space. Roger was trying to get them more and better accommodation. This was noisy and inconvenient, only ever intended to be temporary.

Oh, what did that matter? Why was she thinking of that? She drank some whisky, shuddering at its sharpness. Because it was easier to think of mundane things like that than what he was going to say, what she was going to do. She looked at her watch. Where the hell was he? She had lied her way into an hour and a half. If she did not want another black eye she had better not be a minute later than eight. Unless she put an end to it all tonight. But there was Mark to consider. She couldn't uproot him at a moment's notice, squeeze him into Roger's one-room flat. What kind of mother was she anyway, leaving him alone in the flat when there was a killer out there? Suddenly she realized that he had not been safe. Their flat overlooked the scene of the crime. Didn't murderers always return? Supposing he had been there, watching from the park, had seen her drive off, leaving Mark alone, defenseless? She had not even told Mark to bolt the door and let no one in. Was there someone now, skulking in the shadows, watching Mark through the uncurtained, brightly lit window? She reached for the phone feeling sick and guilty, remembered in time that Steve was there. Steve had said he was all right. Oh God, she thought, drinking more whisky, this was crazy, impossible. She was tearing herself in two and she was failing everybody. Perhaps she even was failing herself.

She was freshening her drink when Roger came in, the bruised side of her face turned from him.

"I see, pilfering my booze, Mrs. Cole," he began, but then she turned around and shook the hair from her face. She saw his smile fade and something she had totally not expected take its place. He looked embarrassed. She had imagined anger, shock, pain, tenderness, but he stood there looking like a schoolboy about to blush.

"Well?" she said. "Do you want one?" She raised the bottle.

"Yes," he said quietly. "I rather think I do."

It was all right while she was pouring the drink, listening to him put his briefcase down, remove his coat. Then he touched her, gently, his hands on her shoulders, and with a feeling of intense relief and safety she leaned against him, smelling his familiar but still-exciting smell, spicy aftershave, pipe tobacco, his skin.

"What happened?"

"Oh, I had a quarrel with a door, fell down the stairs, all the usual sort of things." She twisted from his hands, thrust a cup of Scotch at him.

He took the bottle and the cup from her, set both aside. Then he pulled her close, holding the back of her head so that her face was pressed into his shoulder.

"It's all right. It's all right," he soothed her.

"No, no it isn't."

"You're safe now. I love you." He kissed the top of her head, and she tilted her face back, offering her mouth, reaching for his. They kissed hungrily. "See?" he said, cuddling her. "It's better now."

"Yes." She nodded, butting his shoulder with her forehead.

"So let's have that drink and you can tell me all about it." He pressed a paper cup into her hand, lifted his own.

She heard herself repeating in a flat voice a story that had already become lifeless with repetition. Roger cleared a space on the desk, sat on it, holding her hand loosely in his. He asked

the same inevitable questions that Marion had, and she
answered by rote, without thinking.

"Do you think he knows about us? Is that it?"

"That's what Marion says. I think she must be right."

"Marion? You've discussed this with Marion?"

"Well, of course, she's my friend. I had to talk to
someone."

"Marion knows about us?"

"Yes, of course. Don't look so bloody incredulous. What
did you think?"

"I suppose I assumed they all suspected—"

"Why shouldn't I tell Marion? Am I supposed to be
ashamed of us or something?"

"No, no, of course not. It's just that, well, business and
pleasure—"

"You should have thought of that."

"I'm sorry. Okay?"

"I don't know why you're making such an issue out of it."

"I was surprised, that's all. We've been so careful."

"Yes, haven't we?" She tossed back her drink. "Well, I
think I'd better go."

"Georgia, don't be stupid."

"I don't need this. I don't need to be told I'm stupid, that I
should be discreet, not talk to my friends. I just don't need it."

"I know. I'm sorry. Please, come here."

"No. I don't need that, either."

He let the arms he had reached out to her drop.

"What do you want? What can I say?"

"Something," she said miserably. "Even Mark asked if it
hurt. Well it bloody does, and so do I. I look terrible and I feel
worse and you . . . I want you to say something."

He stood up and pulled her against him.

"Let's go somewhere, talk about it."

"No, I don't want—"

"Will you tell him then, have it out with him?"

"What for? What good will that do?"

"It will at least clear the air. If I were him, I'd want to know.
Especially if I suspected—"

"He knows. Of course he knows. What difference will my
admitting it make?"

"We'll all know where we stand."

"But *I don't know* where I stand, Roger. That's just it."

"With me, you mean?"

"Who else?"

"You know I love you, I want to be with you."

"I have a son, remember?"

"Yes, Georgia, I do. Look, I'm not going to make a great speech, full of promises I might not be able to keep. You know my situation. I know yours. We'll just have to work something out, but you'll have to decide."

"Then perhaps you'll schedule it for our next meeting, if you can squeeze it in." She wrenched free of him, crossed the small room, and picked up her coat from a chair.

"Don't you see that we can't talk calmly now? You're upset."

"That's just what I was saying. I'm glad you got the message."

Roger turned away, rearranged things on his desk.

"You think I've let you down, but when you're calmer you'll understand."

"I thought you'd make it all right, I hoped . . ." She pulled the door open, rattling the handle. Roger started after her.

"Please, at least let me take you home."

"I've got the car, thanks."

"Then let's go to my place, just for a bit, until you feel better."

"No. No I really must get home. I didn't arrange to be late."

"All right." He sounded resigned, defeated. "You go on. I'll lock up."

She nodded, walked slowly across the main office, knowing he was standing there, watching her. She didn't want to go like this, leave it hanging, fragmented.

"Try to remember one thing," Roger said. "I want you to do whatever makes you happy."

"Thanks," she said stiffly. "I'll remember." But his words did not comfort her.

She did not want to go home at all. She could have sat in the car, watching the warning, flashing lights and trying to name what it was she had wanted from Roger and why he had failed to give it. But the spot outside the park, eerily lit by the flashes of amber light, was horrible. She could not bear to think what had happened there. And that made her think of Mark and how, in a way, she had betrayed him. But even though she was eager to get away from the associations of the street, her feet dragged up the four flights of stairs to the front door, and she stood there for several moments, the key clutched in her cold fingers, not wanting to use it.

"Georgia? Is that you?"

"Yes." She felt resigned to it now, now that she was inside. She pulled off her coat and hung it up feeling tired and listless.

Steve stood in the kitchen doorway, a silly little frilled apron someone had given Georgia for Christmas tied around his middle.

"You got through quicker than you thought, then?"

"Something like that," she said ironically, picking up her bag and walking past him down the corridor.

"Would you like something to eat?"

"Later, maybe."

She did not want him to smell the whisky on her breath, and yet she wanted another one to give her courage. She drew the living-room curtains first, to shut out the bleak night and the knowledge that a boy had died out there, violently and for no reason. At least none that she could understand.

"Does it hurt?" Steven asked, watching her as she poured her drink.

"What?" She saw his eyes fixed on her face. "Oh, it throbs a bit. I'll take some aspirins later."

"You should eat something."

"Stop fussing, Steve." She flopped down into a chair, eased off her shoes. "What about you? Have you eaten?" She asked only because he was still standing there, looking at her, irritating her.

"I've finished. Actually, there's something I want to say to you about Mark first, while he's busy with his homework."

She had not been expecting this, and the slight loss of tension she felt at the mention of her son's name reminded her how much she dreaded facing up to the other subject.

"He said," Steve went on, coming into the room and sitting

on the edge of the sofa, "that you fetched him from school today."

"Well, of course I did. Haven't you heard what happened?"

"Yes, of course. Everyone at the hospital was full of it. They took him, the body, there."

"Oh God." The thought of him dead, lying on a cold slab, was awful.

"Anyway," Steven resumed, "I don't think you should make a habit of it. You know how kids feel at that age. Independence is very important to them, especially boys, and with their friends."

"Important enough to allow them to be killed?" Georgia said, her tone a parody of sweet inquiry.

"Don't be ridiculous. Mark's not in danger."

"Oh no? Don't you understand there's a maniac out there, someone who kills young boys, presumably for kicks?"

"But you don't know that he'll kill again. You don't know that even if he does it will be around here. He could have been in a car, passing through. He could be anywhere by now."

"Yes. He could be next door, or out there in the park, waiting his chance."

"Georgia, you're overreacting. I'm not suggesting Mark should be allowed to roam the streets late at night. When has he ever? But going to and from school, with his friends, in full daylight, along busy streets—"

"It's almost winter," Georgia said bleakly. "It gets dark earlier and earlier."

Steven stood up, his patience stretched dangerously thin.

"In this mood you'll find any excuse. There's no point in arguing about it. I'm asking you not to do it. Don't foist something on Mark you'll regret later."

"And if I choose to ignore your directive, what will you do then? Hit me?"

The blow was deserved, he knew, but it was calculated to do the maximum damage. Her eyes did not flinch from his look of pain. She merely raised her glass and drank as though making a mocking toast.

"Yes, well, we'd better sort that out as well while Mark's busy."

"For God's sake take the stupid apron off, first," she said.

Fighting to control his temper, Steven untied the strings, bunched the apron in his hand, and thrust it down the side of the sofa. He sat down again, tried to marshal his thoughts.

"I still don't know why I hit you," he said, knotting his hands together. "I haven't got an explanation. I've been getting these funny headaches lately, and I do feel on edge. I've made an appointment with Sonia Zimmer to have a checkup." Georgia was staring at him, her mouth a little slack, an indifferent glaze in her eyes. "I don't know what else to say or do," he said, his voice cracking, "except to repeat that I'm sorry, that I bitterly regret—"

"You know, don't you?" Georgia said. She remained quite still, her stare unwavering. Even her lips barely moved.

"Know? What am I supposed to know?"

"Oh, don't pretend. Please don't let's go through a whole rigmarole. You know that I'm having an affair with Roger North. That's why you hit me. Why pretend?"

He waited for the knife to slice open his heart, his belly, any soft, unprotected area. He waited for the rage, the jolt of one of his electric headaches, for tears. He felt completely blank, empty, wiped clean.

"Aren't you going to say anything?" Without his having noticed that she had moved, Georgia was standing at the liquor cabinet, freshening her glass.

"I thought, of course, wondered. I didn't actually know. I didn't want to."

"Well . . ." She forced air from her mouth in a pant, a sort of irritated sigh.

"That's not why I hit you. At least, not consciously why."

"What does it matter? You did and now you know and I don't think I want to talk about it anymore."

"You can't just leave it there. I mean, what are we going to do? Is it serious? Are you going to continue it?"

She shook her head fiercely.

"I don't know. I don't want to talk about it. I'm confused. I can't think straight."

"Well you'd better start," he burst out angrily. "You can't just drop a bombshell like that and then withdraw."

"Be fair. It wasn't a bombshell. You admit you suspected.

All right. Talk. Talk all you want. Only don't expect me to contribute anything."

"Now just a minute, Georgia." He was standing over her, his hand raised, not clenched, his finger wagging. He saw the wince of fear cross her face and felt his anger vanish with it. "Oh Christ! I'm sorry, so sorry." He knelt down beside her chair, reaching for her clumsily.

"Don't, please don't," she said, making herself small, squashed into the corner of the chair.

"Do you find me repulsive suddenly?" he asked, looking at his useless hands, lying on the arms of the chair.

"No, of course not. I just don't want to be touched. I want to be left alone." Steven stared at her. Habit told him that there came a moment in all rows when it was possible to relent, retreat, or meet the other person halfway at least. This was such a moment. He was sure of it and he willed her to soften, try. "I really mean it," she said.

He felt foolish kneeling beside her, in the pose of a penitent and pleading husband. He pushed himself up.

"All right," he said. "If that's what you want." He waited again, thinking that it was still not too late, but she said nothing. He went to the door.

"If it's all right with you, I think I'll have a bath and go to bed. It's been quite a day."

"Sure." He heard her get up, swallow the remains of her drink, and clink her glass down on the marble table.

"I'll just say hello to Mark first."

He went down the corridor, to the kitchen. There were dishes to be washed, to occupy him.

Behind him, Georgia paused at Mark's door.

"What will you do?"

"Oh, I was thinking of doing the dishes. I don't know. Does it matter?"

"I'm sorry," Georgia said, and tapped on Mark's door, opening it simultaneously, as though the room and her son offered refuge from Steven.

Leigh was brushing her hair, the thick iron-gray hair with curls of pure silver in it, which still startled people. Because it had been like that since she was twelve, Leigh was entirely accustomed to it, could barely remember it being any other color. Long before her hair turned, she had developed the art of secrecy. It went right back to kindergarten, where she had first discovered that she was different, that everybody did not see as she saw. She could still remember Miss Frank stooping over the table where she sat drawing with three other children, could still smell the teacher's flowery scent.

"Why do you draw people like that, Leigh, with all those funny clouds around them? Are they clouds or flames?"

"Sometimes clouds, sometimes more like flames," she had answered with complete honesty.

"Well, I'm sure it's very imaginative, dear, but let's try to do it properly, shall we?"

"But they are properly," she said, forgetting her grammar in her frustration and the first twinge of anxiety. "That's you, Miss Frank."

"Well yes, dear, I can recognize my blouse and my spectacles but—"

"That's how you *are*!"

"Now Leigh, get hold of yourself, please. There is no need to raise your voice. Now you just look at me. You take a good long look at me, and you'll see there are no clouds around me. Are there, Leigh?"

"No, Miss Frank."

Which was the simple truth, because the clouds had changed then, become more like flames, jagged and dancing. That always happened when people got cross or upset about something.

"So draw it again, Leigh, properly this time."

"Yes, Miss Frank."

The other children giggled, but Leigh ignored them. She started over and debated long and hard with herself whether to crayon in the flames dancing around Miss Frank's head and shoulders. She decided she better not: teacher's bite was much worse than her bark. But she felt miserable when she handed the drawing in: it was a rough, incomplete, half-done thing.

She puzzled about it because Miss Frank had been so certain, and Leigh was at an age when all adults appeared to have the wisdom and knowledge of gods. Was it perhaps because Miss Frank wore glasses, which were a remedy for defective eyesight, she knew, that she could not see the clouds and flames around people? She asked her mother, who stared at her with the mingled anger and incomprehension that was her basic feeling toward her strange daughter, and snapped that Miss Frank had myopia and not to bother her with stupid questions. Leigh had persisted, but the shutter came down in her mother's head, sealing off her thoughts, leaving Leigh feeling anxious and uncertain of her grasp on the world. Her mother lectured her instead on the absolute necessity of being a good girl, an obedient and quiet girl, a girl who did not ask questions and bother people. Any other course led to hell and damnation.

But Leigh's mother did not know what she meant by hell and damnation. The words came easily and often from her mouth, bringing with them a dark undertow of horror and awe. Leigh thought that these words might have something to do with the bad and horrible things the man who was her father had done to her mother, the things that had caused her to grow in her mother's stomach. Yet she knew too that her mother had not always feared and loathed those things.

All this little Leigh knew because she could "read" her mother's mind, could enter it, become a part of it, share even her memories. Once, when she was very small, that had been Leigh's favorite place. Curled, metaphorically at least, in the safety of her mother's mind, Leigh had effected a virtual return to the womb. There had been happiness there, delight in the world even, until the reality and the hardship of being a woman alone with a child had turned so bitter that Leigh did not want to go there anymore. Sometimes it happened involuntarily, when she was afraid or grazed her knee or got the chicken pox, but she practiced to control the tug, to close her mind to the pull of others. But she could not cut out entirely. She practiced to become adept at what, later, was to be called "dual listening," hearing at the same time the spoken words and the thoughts that leaped from her mother's mind to her own.

Slowly, gradually, through incidents like that of Miss Frank and the drawing, Leigh learned that other people did not see clouds and flames, did not see people as pretty and colorful, as she did, and that though they sometimes mentioned that they could read so-and-so like a book, these were lies, properly termed "figures of speech." It seemed to her that this inability to see the world as she saw it, this careless use of language that was literally true for her, was all part of the disparity between word and thought that was her daily experience, such as when her mother said how glad she was to see a neighbor while her mind snarled that the woman was a vicious gossip and an ugly sinner. Leigh concluded either that she was more truthful than her mother and other people, or different. But different was wrong; she had a disadvantage every bit as great as a club foot or a harelip. Besides, the world her mother inhabited was indeed a terrible place, as was that of most of the other people she knew, and Leigh was glad to keep her clear-eyed distance from it.

In every other respect her difference was indeed a disadvantage. It required constant vigilance. She had to school herself, with more strictness than Miss Frank could have imposed, not to blurt out that someone was lying, not to try to rescue timid friends who, faced with a choice, asked for the thing they did not want in order to please some adult. She had to remember not to repeat the bad thoughts, the mysterious, ugly longings that oozed from the minds of the best and most respect-worthy men and women. Above all, she had to discipline herself not to hear, to switch off or at least reduce the noise of her mental world to static.

The effort often gave her headaches, and so she became known as a sickly child. Her difference, which she worked so hard to conceal and control, was everywhere commented upon as her "strange ways."

"She has such strange little ways," people said of her. "She's such an odd little thing. I quite wonder what is going on in that pretty head of hers." They did not say it with affection but as though suppressing a shudder. She was grateful she was pretty in a style that adults liked and approved, for it softened her oddness a little, enabled people to pin a smile on the shudder and leave her be.

Leigh's protective prettiness was taken from her, at least according to the narrow and strict standards of the society she lived in, when the first streaks of gray grew in her hair. It began shortly before her first menstruation and increased with the regular monthly flow. Her mother connected the two phenomena into some mythological network of curse and sin, of shame and punishment. Leigh's changing hair was a mark of God's displeasure, a warning to her innocence.

"Nonsense," her principal said. "It's probably hormonal. When so many changes are occurring in a young girl's body, who knows what might be affected? Take her to a doctor, Mrs. Duncan. They can work wonders these days."

Oh, what wonders they had already worked, Leigh thought bitterly, laying down her hairbrush and pushing her fingers through the gleaming but flattened mop of her hair. What a freak she had thought herself, her graying hair cropped short and hidden under a kerchief when Mamma took her to the first doctor, but little she knew then of the freak she really was.

The doctor's routine tests showed nothing. She was referred to specialists her mother could barely afford. The first one said it was just some weakness in the pigment, the explanation of which might lie in her medical history or even her mother's. They were passed on, bewildered and frightened human parcels, to another specialist and yet another. One prescribed hormone tablets, which helped to relieve the monthly cramps she had come to dread, but did nothing to remedy the color of her hair.

Finally they reached a man who said, frowning, "I see, Mrs. Duncan, that you were prescribed Anactreon-b for nausea when you were carrying Leigh. Did you take it regularly?"

Well of course she had. Just because she had conceived a child out of wedlock, which she knew to be a sin, entirely counter to the strictures of her good Christian upbringing, she was not by nature disobedient, not devoid of all respect. She had, indeed, the greatest respect for the medical profession, and by golly if a doctor told her to take something she took it, religiously. And she had brought Leigh up the same way.

"Well, the thing is, Mrs. Duncan—and I must warn you that I don't personally know too much about all this, and there is absolutely no cause for alarm—Anactreon-b was withdrawn shortly after Leigh was born, but there is still a lot of interest in it. It just might be that Leigh's condition is in some way connected with the side effects of the drug."

"But I took it, not Leigh."

"But while you were carrying Leigh, Mrs. Duncan. While she was living inside you."

At which, Leigh remembered, her mother had pursed her lips in disgust and waved her hand at him to shush him for talking so dirty in front of a child.

Then a nice man had come to see them at home, a man from the drug company that had developed and marketed Anactreon-b. The drug, he said, as Mrs. Duncan herself could verify, had the most beneficial effects, and a person only had a look at Leigh to see that there was no connection, absolutely none, with Thalidomide. Such indeed were these beneficial effects, not to mention the potential of the substance, that his firm was still working on Anactreon-b, and a major part of this very important program was to check up on the offspring of women who had taken the drug during pregnancy. It was just a little routine thing, a few ordinary medical tests, possibly some long-term monitoring. But it was all absolutely free. In fact, the company offered a sort of package deal: in return for cooperation, Leigh and her mother would receive free medical care until Leigh came of age, partial payment of medical insurance premiums for the rest of their lives, and a sizable cash bonus. All this in return for a thorough medical and psychological checkup.

Leigh knew, even before the nice man had finished his spiel, that her mother would be totally unable to resist. While she feared and despised charity, she was greedy for freebies. The house was crammed with free plastic flowers, money-off vouchers, free glasses and ashtrays, even though Mrs. Duncan neither drank nor smoked. Free was good, in some mysterious way, her due.

For a while Leigh felt that she had been sold, but as she slowly understood that with these people, the doctors and the psychologists, the nurses and the chemical researchers, she need not fear her difference, she began to be glad. She still did not regret it. That visit from the man had opened doors, changed her life, made "different" bearable.

At first, of course, she had been afraid.

"Have you ever noticed anything different about yourself, Leigh, anything odd? Can you do things other girls can't? Or see things, perhaps, that other people just don't notice?"

In the face of such questions she withdrew, practiced hard to deceive.

And then it was just weird and silly.

"Now, Leigh, you see that rock on the table? Yes? Good. Now I want you to move that rock from here to there without touching it or leaving your seat. I want you to think it to move, Leigh. Will you do that for us?"

She thought they were completely crazy. She could not think-move a heavy rock, nor even switch a light on and off by thinking about it. Nobody could. So they brought a strange, waiflike little boy into the room, and she saw the rock move, the lights go on and off with no more visible effort than the clenching of the child's fists, the screwing up of his eyes. She was impressed and scared.

And, of course, in time they trapped her.

"Do you know what I'm thinking, Leigh?"

A dirty blow, right under her guard.

"Sure. You're thinking I'm the exception that . . . may not prove the rule."

"Excellent, Leigh. The star of our program. That's how I think of you now. Don't I, Leigh? You can check it out for yourself."

Following hard on the horror of having been tricked into betraying herself had come relief, a collapse into tears.

She had been luckier, so much luckier than most. She had not minded the special school, set up by the drug company, because in her case there was no wrench from the bosom of a happy family. She did not resent the tests and the examinations, because she wanted to develop what she had, what was uniquely hers. She was no longer a freak who could read other's thoughts. Or if she was, at least she was surrounded by her own kind. She was tough, they said, tougher than most. Perhaps she had learned tenaciousness in the womb, for many women on Anactreon-b had miscarried in the sixth and seventh month, which was another reason why she and the others who had been safely born were so precious to the company. In addition to their abilities, of course.

Special. Yes, Leigh had begun to feel special, to be pretty again, and if her adolescence could never be completely normal, it was happier than many. She had been shown a way to flee her mother's narrow, bitter-tasting world. Leigh had the chance to develop, grow, become herself. The company educated her well, and it seemed entirely natural to Leigh that she should use her talents to help others. She chose to do so through psychology, and, as soon as she graduated, she had joined the Agency, working with and for people like herself. She still felt ambivalent about Anactreon-b, but she truly believed that she could be of more use within the system than as a critical outsider. Finally, the chance to come here, to London, to compare her work with that of others, to preach her own small gospel had seemed to crown the best period of her life so far. But the man with the double aura complicated things.

Cut it out, she told herself. She had her own business, her own life and work. There was no need to go looking for problems. By a controlled effort of will, she pushed Steven Cole and the whole penumbra of doubts, questions, and feelings that surrounded his name, out of her mind.

After driving Mark and three of his friends to the local ice rink, Steven dawdled toward home, then parked the car on impulse near Chiswick House and went for a stroll in the grounds. He would not say that he was avoiding Georgia: she would probably be out anyway, having arranged for one of the other parents to collect the boys from the rink later. She was still obsessed with Mark's safety, the supposed danger posed him personally by the uncaught killer. The rows and tense silences had all centered on that and the restrictions she wished to impose on their son's freedom. Steven knew that he had colluded with her to use this rather than her affair with Roger North as a channel for their miserable energies, conflict. It was probably cowardly of him—another example of his softness—but he was too tired and too lonely to care. He walked in the wooded part of the grounds, following paths at random, unappreciative of his surroundings. The occasional jogger passed him, men and women walking their dogs, a pair of lovers, arms snaked around each other's body. These penetrated the insular fog of his preoccupation, filling him with bitterness. That was the easy part, he thought, curling his upper lip involuntarily: ahead of them lay horrors. He neither pitied nor envied them. They made him angry.

Sonia Zimmer had given him a complete "overhaul," as she called it, approving his loss of weight and arranging X rays, a cardiogram, an encephalogram, blood tests of every kind. The results would come back in a few days. He had admitted to being listless, *down* was the word he had used, but despite an opportunity he had said nothing about his relationship with Georgia, he was not sure whether because he did not want to admit it or because he was afraid where such a confession might lead. Anyway, Sonia was no psychologist. He told himself it was only sensible to check the physical facts and conditions first. Part of him hoped that one of the machines to which he had been wired, one of the samples he had given would yield something positive, provide some explanation for the headaches, at least. Sonia had been very interested in the headaches, but she had, quite properly, jumped to no conclusions, given him no clue of any suspicions she might harbor.

The headaches had, in fact, ceased, yet he felt sure that they were only dormant, not cured. He could not explain why he felt this. It was just a certainty that they lay coiled somewhere in his head, resting, recovering their strength. They would come again as sure as . . . as sure as once he had been of Georgia. He faced again the fact that they must talk about it. He had already considered moving out, leaving the affair to blaze, burn itself out, if it was that kind of affair. He had speculated on divorce, trying to order his mind so that, if it should come to that, he would not be caught napping, would know what he wanted, what he was prepared to give up. He thought that it must be shock, or a stubborn refusal to take in and comprehend her infidelity, that made him so cool and clinical about it all.

He came out of the trees and walked along by the fenced-off lake where a young woman helped a little girl tear and throw bread to the greedy ducks.

He crossed the bridge and turned toward the house itself. A group of boys were playing noisy and inexpert soccer on the pale grass. Suddenly, Steven felt very tired. The car seemed a long, long way away. He needed to rest before making the return walk.

Wrapping his scarf more warmly around him, he sat on a bench. He looked up the slope to one of the big cedars of Lebanon that dotted the old carriageway to the house, but his tired eyes were tugged back and down to where the boys chased and yelled, where a black-and-white ball alternately spiraled in the air and skidded on the grass. He felt numb, observing these events as though he had stepped aside, outside. The thought bothered him by its strangeness, and he tried to get back, to get control of himself. The effort, the mental effort seemed to trigger the pain. It cracked across his skull, and he felt himself powerless, frozen in its sickening aftermath.

Waiting was intense pleasure, as was the sense of being invisible. He saw the flash of limbs, lithe, powerful, young bodies crisscrossing, merging in pursuit of the ball. The wintry sun was already low, and what had been a crisp nip in the air became an insidious, shivering cold. The game slowed, lost impetus. The boy guarding the improvised goal clapped gloved hands together, his breath puffing. People began to walk purposefully through the grounds, calling dogs to heel, collecting their children. There was a drift, an exodus toward the various gates, marking the dying of the day, the twilight time. He tensed and waited, savoring the pleasure.

The boy wore royal blue shorts and the zippered jacket of a black track suit. His legs were very white in the graying light. As though he knew that he had been chosen, he was reluctant to cease the game. Even as the others gathered together, put on their jackets, prepared to leave, he dribbled the ball, calling to the others. He sent a long ball curving toward them, and one of his friends, impatient now, thinking of the warmth of home, booted it high and wide. The boy chased it, saw it bound and fly away again toward a stand of trees and shrubs.

"What d'you do that for?"

"Serves you right."

"Wait for me, then."

"You can catch up."

The boy ran after the ball, his eyes fixed on the spot where he thought it had landed, had been lost to sight.

The ball lay on the edge of the man's hiding place. He moved forward, bent and scooped it up, retreating into the shadows, holding it against his heaving chest. The boy came closer, closer, skidded to a halt, searching for the ball. He

50

walked now, eyes fixed on the ground, pushing long grass aside with his feet, moving inexorably into the bushes, ducking under branches.

The man held out the ball to the boy, smiling, and saw with gratification the start of shock on his face, which was as pale as his legs. As he reached to take the ball it was withdrawn, teasing the boy deeper into the shadows, his smile melting like wax. Then the ball was dropped onto the soft and silent soil.

The handle of the car door was icy on his palm. The streetlights were on. He tried to open the door, then remembered that the keys remained in his pocket. He dug for them, bewildered, and realized that he could remember nothing. He had sat down on a bench, his back to the lake, and now he was standing by the car, in the road, with the high walls of Chiswick House behind him. Traffic passed. The knowledge that he could not remember made him afraid. How long had he . . . ? He got into the car and looked at his watch. It had stopped. He shook it impatiently, listened for its sluggish tick. His memory could not be a complete blank, he reasoned, fighting the fear his mind's emptiness sparked in him. Even if he had dozed on the bench—he remembered at least the feeling of tiredness that had made him sit down—he must have woken, chosen a route back to the car. He must remember something. He knew the grounds well, and his memory offered him a choice of routes, but it was the memory of other visits. There was nothing at all left of this afternoon, of how he had gotten from bench to car or what had happened in the interim.

He felt unfit to drive, imagined himself blacking out in the car. Accidents flashed across his imagination. It was one thing to walk across the traffic-free grounds of Chiswick House without knowing you were doing so but quite another to risk driving through the heavy Saturday-evening traffic of Hammersmith and Fulham. But he wanted to get away from the place. Darkness was thickening all around him. Any minute now the gates would be closed. Before he knew what he was doing he had started the car and eased it out into the traffic.

Georgia tried to hang on to the tingling, glowing sensation that diffused like a slumberous drug through her body, to use it as a

bulwark against the cruel realities of her thoughts. She felt
good, replete, warm, and she wanted to stay that way, floating
free of troubles. The room was sealed off from time, the blue
blind drawn, her watch abandoned with her clothes. She
wanted it to stay that way, but immediately the longing was
dashed. She had to be aware of time. Mark would be back at
six, and she hadn't bothered to check with Steve that he would
return by then. She hadn't needed to, for she had not planned to
spend the afternoon in Roger's bed. She had thought that they
might talk, argue. She twisted toward him, grasped his up-
flung arm and turned his wrist toward her.

"Mm? What?" he said drowsily. His eyes flickered open,
smiled at her.

"I've got to go."

"No."

"I must. It's a quarter to five. Can you run me part way
home?" She was already out of the bed, too quick for his lazy
reach. He admired the flow of her hips, her buttocks, even as
he thought that there was nothing worse than having to drive
your lover home afterward. It snapped the natural rhythm of
such encounters, which should wind down and then up slowly,
giving the body and the heart time to recover. His imagination
leaped forward, conjuring the slap of cold air on his face when
he would leave the cosiness of the flat to take her home. He
shivered, pulled the quilt closer round his shoulders. He felt
her warmth and scent still on him and realized that he wanted
her again. He wanted to sleep and then make love again.
Without that the night stretched emptily before him. But she
had changed, he saw. The soft roundness of her had vanished
with anxiety. She was all sharp planes and angles, crackling
with tension as she hauled up her jeans. Even her breasts
seemed hard and pointed, rejecting.

"Please, Roger. Mark will be back."

"All right, all right," he said, unable to keep the irritation
out of his voice. He sat up, threw the quilt from his body,
swung his feet to the floor, all in one brusque gesture. It was
like removing sticking plaster. If you had to do something that
hurt, best do it quickly.

"If it's too much trouble . . ." Georgia began, her voice as
sharp as he had seen her body.

"It just negates what we had," he said, raising his voice to quell her. "And I don't much relish the prospect of a lonely Saturday evening. Another lonely Saturday evening," he said, snatching open a drawer, looking for clean underwear.

Georgia paused, her sweater half pulled down, looking at the pale knobs of his backbone, the neat curves of his buttocks. She had not thought of him being lonely. Worse, she had never considered that living a bachelor's life he was free to go anywhere, meet anyone, someone else. She saw how sickeningly easy it would be to lose him.

"You could go to a movie. You've got friends."

"Who haven't invited me. And a movie isn't much fun alone."

"Well I'm sorry. It's not exactly going to be a fun evening for me either."

"I'm not blaming you, Georgia."

"It damned well sounded like it," she said, using his comb to smooth her hair. Marion had been wrong about the staying power of the bruise. It had already reached the gray-and-yellow stage and the swelling had gone down. She looked merely unwell, tired, not beaten.

"That's because you're blaming yourself," Roger said, zipping his trousers.

"Me? Why should I?"

"Oh Georgia, don't let's have a postmortem now. I'll drive you. It's okay."

"You blame me. Steve blames me. It's all my fault. Even if neither of you say it, I can see it in your eyes."

"You see and hear what you want to," he contradicted her. "You didn't feel anyone was blaming you half an hour ago, did you?"

His face appeared in the mirror before her. He adjusted the collar of his roll-neck sweater.

"No," she admitted. That was why it had been so good, why she had wanted to prolong not spoil it.

"Then don't spoil it now."

"I already have," she said. "You can't deny that."

"Oh Georgia, love." He turned her to him, embraced her. He spoke so sadly, hopelessly, that she wanted to cry. And she wanted to rest against him, stay in his arms. If only, she

thought, it was possible to make love in isolation, without
words or contact afterward.

"I really must go," she whispered. "I have to."

Steven's fear that he would black out again increased as he
drove, so much so that by the time he could see the hospital
towering on his left his hands were shaking on the steering
wheel. With relief, he pulled the car out of the heavy traffic and
into the restricted parking lot, which, this being Saturday, was
all but empty. He leaned back in his seat, willing the panic to
flow from him. After all, nothing had happened. He had made
it. What he needed was a drink, something to steady his
nerves. Then, as he got out of the car, it occurred to him that
his panic may have been caused by a subconscious dread of
returning home to Georgia and their unresolved conflicts.

He reset his watch according to the hospital's reliable
electric clock and saw that the staff bar would not be open for
another fifteen minutes. Perhaps a drink was not such a good
idea anyway. What he really needed was time to think or
someone to talk to, he thought, his sense of loneliness
returning and biting deeper into him. The possibility of finding
anyone he knew well enough to confide in at the hospital on a
Saturday night was highly unlikely: the bar would be given
over to medical students and off-duty nurses. A swim would be
better. The physical activity often aided thought and calmed
him. He could have a drink afterward, if he still could not face
going home.

He rode the escalator to the first floor and turned into the
empty, echoing corridors of the administration wing. From his
office he collected his trunks and towel. Then he crossed the
deserted concourse, passed the closed Tea Bar, and turned into
the east wing, the ground-floor side entrance of which provided
a shortcut to the recreation building. These corridors, identical
to those he had just left, were also unfamiliar, with Saturday-
night emptiness. His footsteps sounded too loud, as though he
were stamping, and he made himself walk more lightly, on the
balls of his feet. Ahead of him, around the right angle of the
corridor he heard a door shut and the rattle of keys. He
stopped, surprised that anyone should be there, and almost
immediately he heard the approach of rapid and distinctly

feminine footsteps. A tall gray-haired woman turned the corner and stopped as though startled. She stared at him, with one hand fluttering to her throat. Steven stared back, trying to place her. She wore no white coat, and there was nothing else about her clothing to indicate her position, if any, in the hospital. He even considered that she might be an intruder. But as she began to move forward again, her pace steadier, suggesting caution, he saw that the keys looped around her finger bore the official hospital tag, to which would be fixed her identity pass. The tag bounced against her lavender sweater, and, raising his eyes, he remembered colliding with her outside Dr. Zimmer's office, and he saw that she was extraordinarily beautiful. At least that was his first impression. Almost at once, he saw that *extraordinary* was the operative word. She had moved close to the wall, as though to creep past him, and Steven, feeling suddenly foolish, veered toward her, unaware that from her point of view it would seem a deliberate attempt to cut her off, block her path. She stopped again, pressing one shoulder against the wall and raising the folder she carried like a shield in front of her.

"Yes?" she said. "Can I help you?" Her tone was wary, the voice itself firm and melodious.

Steven realized that he was still staring at her, with an intensity that must look rude.

"I'm sorry," he said. "I heard a noise. I didn't think anyone would be in, not on a Saturday night."

"I just dropped by to pick up some notes." She removed her shoulder from the wall but seemed unable or unwilling to continue on her way. "Are you all right?" she asked, frowning.

"Yes, of course," he said, too quickly. "Look, I don't think we've met." He put out his hand. "I'm Steven Cole."

She stared at his hand. Very slowly, shifting the folder and keys into her left hand, she reached out and touched it briefly, as though she found something repugnant about it. At the same time she said, "Yes, I know."

"Oh?" Steven looked surprised and felt a little flattered.

"I saw you the other day. Somebody mentioned your name."

"But I don't know yours," he said, smiling.

"Leigh Duncan."

"Ah yes, of course. You're on attachment from America."

"That's right." She glanced behind her, then looked back at Steven. "I'm in a hurry. Please excuse me."

"Yes, of course," Steven agreed, automatically.

He was surprised by the intensity of her stare, the battle that showed on her face, as though she was struggling to say something or prevent herself from saying something. He did not want her to go, so he remained there, passively returning her stare.

"You're not all right, are you?" she said at last, and her voice had a chilling note of defeat in it.

"I had a rather disturbing experience this afternoon . . ." Steven said, unable to help himself. "I was scared to drive home. I thought I might have a swim," he added apologetically, indicating the rolled towel he carried.

"You wanted help, to talk to someone," Leigh said. It was not a question.

Steven continued to look at her. She made him feel better, made his blood race a little.

"Do you want to tell me about it? My office is right here," she said, gesturing to the sharp corner of the corridor. "I could even manage a cup of coffee."

"I'd like that very much," Steven said. It seemed the most natural thing in the world that he should talk to this strange and strangely beautiful woman.

"Okay," she said softly. "This way."

Leigh had been given a narrow, rectangular room next to Page's office. Steven recognized at once that it had been intended as a nurses' changing room. Shorn of its lockers and pegs, equipped with standard hospital-issue desk, chairs, and filing cabinets, it looked coldly institutional and unused. Leigh Duncan had done nothing yet to stamp her personality on it, and he wondered whether this was because of lack of time or interest.

Leigh was aware of him and his thoughts as she filled the electric kettle, busied herself unnecessarily with mugs, and impatiently told herself that now was not the time to puzzle over it. It was sufficient that he had presented himself—now it seemed that she had always known he would—and perhaps her motive was simple curiosity. Certainly she was curious to know why his aura was so faint and ordinary tonight, almost faded, even though she sensed a great trouble in him, something that cried out mutely to her. She knew one thing: she could have walked away from him in the corridor and she had not.

Watching her, Steven savored her attractiveness, the spare lines of her long body under loose winter clothes. He wondered about her gray hair and her strange, dark eyes. She attracted him deeply, and the awareness of this gave him a jolt of pleasure. It was a welcome sign of normalcy, of cheer in his bleak world. He began to speculate how she would look without clothes, how it would be to touch and arouse her.

"Stop that," Leigh snapped, turning to face him.

"What?"

"What you're thinking."

"I wasn't . . ." He looked at her, perplexed. "I assure you, any stray thought that may have crossed my mind was purely complimentary," he said, deliberately flirting with her.

"It's not that," she answered, waving her hand at him as though to disperse a cloud of smoke. "It just gets in the way."

The kettle began to steam, and she turned away again, switching off the electric power and pouring water on the coffee.

"How can you be so sure of what I was thinking anyway?" Steven asked, settling himself in a chair. His tone was still bantering, trying to draw her into the ritual game he was pleased to discover he still knew how to play. He would enjoy sparring with her, for she would be a stylish adversary.

"Oh it's not difficult to know what men think in situations like this," Leigh replied lightly. She knew she was being as deceitful as he was. If he challenged her, she could always fall back on good old "woman's intuition." It never ceased to amaze her how readily men would accept so vague and meaningless a concept as an explanation of so many things. She put his coffee down on the desk, careful to place it sufficiently far from him so that he could not "accidentally" touch her hand. "There's no milk, sorry."

"I prefer it black," he said quickly, too quickly. He smiled at her. "Has anyone ever told you you're a very attractive

woman?" he asked, letting the smile stretch into his voice so
that its tone became warm and slightly sensual.

"Lots," Leigh said. "Now, why don't you tell me about
what happened this afternoon to upset you?"

"Oh that . . ." He was not feigning. It seemed irrelevant
now, something to which, at best, he had ludicrously over-
reacted. But he saw from the quick hardening of her expression
that he would get nowhere with Leigh if he avoided the
subject. "I lost my memory," he said, still smiling. "It was as
simple as that."

"Oh? But you know your name. You knew to come here,
where you work. I'm sure you remember your wife, Mr.
Cole," she could not resist adding.

He did, with a start of guilt that made him look away
quickly, turn his coffee mug around on the desk, drawing it
toward him.

"How did you know I was married?" he asked, truly
curious.

"Somebody told me. You do remember then?"

"Oh yes, yes . . . What I meant was that I have no
memory of a certain passage of time. Like a blackout, you
know?"

"No," Leigh said, sliding into the other chair, with the desk
between them. She cupped her chin in her hands. "You tell
me."

So he told her about sitting on the bench near Chiswick
House, the sensation that he was standing outside himself,
looking with other eyes when he watched the boys playing
soccer. And then he told her about standing by the car, trying
to open the door with the keys still in his pocket and his mind
blank.

"I suppose I panicked," he went on. "I was scared that I
would black out again in the car. I was trembling pretty badly
by the time I got here, though I was completely aware all the
time. I decided to stop off here for a drink." He looked at the
neatly rolled towel on the desk beside him and thought that she
would think he was mad or lying. He took a sip of coffee.

"Has this happened to you before?" With surprise, Steven
saw that she had been making notes. She looked at him now, a
pen in her hand, poised over a block of lined paper. Her eyes

seemed to compel him to answer even as he thought how beautiful and strangely disturbing they were.

"Yes."

"Tell me about it, everything you can remember."

He did so, omitting only that he had hit Georgia.

"And that was all?"

"Yes. Not very much, is it? Certainly nothing to worry about."

"You've done nothing about it, consulted no one else?"

He told her about Dr. Zimmer and the tests. He felt uncomfortable. Put into words it sounded like such a fuss about nothing that he really did not want to go on talking about it. Leigh made one more note and then capped her pen with an efficient click. Steven wondered if she would have a drink with him, dinner perhaps.

"I'd like to see the results of those tests when they come through. Would you permit that?"

"Certainly."

"Then perhaps you'd tell Dr. Zimmer when you see her."

"Of course. Does this mean that I'm your patient now?"

"Absolutely not. I'm on attachment here in a teaching role. I can't take on patients of my own, or only at the direct request of Dr. Rathbone."

"Oh, that's a pity."

"I'm sure one of the other psychologists would see you if that's what you want?"

"Would you advise it?"

"I can't say."

"You won't tell me your conclusions?"

"I have none. Temporary, local loss of memory such as you describe is often caused by stress. I suggest you rest and try not to worry, but that's a personal not a professional opinion." Leigh stood up and put her notes into a drawer, which she locked.

"Well, I'm very grateful to you and I must apologize for taking up so much of your time. Look, can I buy you a drink? I was going to the bar anyway . . . or dinner?"

"I'm sorry, but I can't."

"You have another date?"

"As it happens, no."

"Well then, surely you have to eat? I would like to thank you."

"You have."

"I hope you're not turning me down just because I'm married, because—"

Leigh shook her head impatiently, picked up the folder she had been carrying and her keys.

"You needed someone to talk to, Mr. Cole, and I happened to be here. I don't think anything would be gained by socializing with you, and there is no reason for you to feel indebted to me."

"Oh, but I do, and surely dinner isn't against the rules, is it?"

"It's against my rules." She held the door open for him.

As he moved slowly toward her, Steven said, "One thing intrigues me, in the light of your present attitude. Why did you bother to find out so much about me?" He thought for a moment she was going to blush. Certainly he had pierced the armor of her professional manner, and that pleased him.

"All I know about you is your name, profession, and marital status—the sort of thing one always learns about one's colleagues in a new situation. Don't make too much of it, Mr. Cole," she said, nodding him through the door.

"Steven, please."

She said nothing, locked the door, and set off down the corridor.

"That's strange, because I get the feeling that you know a lot more about me. The way you knew what I was thinking, for example."

"Why? It's very common for men to mentally undress women they find attractive, especially when they've just met them. Put it down to experience or women's intuition, and don't feel too bad about it. It's normal as well as common."

"Oh, I don't feel bad about it at all," Steven said. "On the contrary . . ."

She paused. They had reached the concourse. A solitary nurse, her rubber-soled shoes squeaking on the highly polished parquet, glanced over at them, then moved on toward the elevators. Leigh turned her finely chiseled face to look at him.

"I was just a shoulder to cry on, Mr. Cole. Glad to have been of help. Let's just leave it at that."

She set off across the concourse, moving quickly and purposefully. Steven let her go. There was no point in chasing her, and besides, he wanted to preserve some dignity. But she was wrong, he vowed. He would not leave it at that, and he felt confident that she would not fight him off forever.

The conclusion that emerged from Leigh's long deliberations, which carried her through into the early hours of Sunday morning, were so preposterous, exciting, and frightening that she would have given anything to be proved wrong. Such ideas were not new, of course. She had heard them discussed during her time at the special school, and as a student she had often debated the hypothesis with her contemporaries. Even at the Agency such things were not dismissed out of hand. However, the topic remained on the wilder edges of research where fact and science fiction dangerously overlapped. That night Leigh applied all her training, mustered every mote of her professionalism, but she could find no other explanation and no proof of it either. On one point she was satisfied: she had tried her damnedest to avoid *this* conclusion, and she had failed.

She leaned back, easing her shoulders, which were cramped from sitting hunched over her makeshift desk too long. Among the litter of papers before her were her own notes about what she had experienced when she had tripped out, the first time she had seen Steven Cole and his double aura. She tended to be a visual person, a "seer" in the parlance of the Agency and mythology, yet the aural and emotional input of that trip had been much stronger. She was not sure whether this told her something about herself—powers such as she possessed were likely to mutate and change—or the transmitter. The visuals she recalled were jumbled and dark, sharp-pointed shapes, an impression of movement that was a kind of swirling force. Aurally she had noted rustlings and scufflings and, strongest of all, screams. There was no mystery about them. They were the unalloyed expression of terror, of a fear so strong Leigh did not even want to imagine it. It was a sound she had never heard before and guessed it to be a sound of people only heard or made once in their lives. *It was the sound of violent death itself*. What she had felt obviously stemmed directly from that noise: a tremendous fear, yet mixed with it a species of excitement, a sense of almost joyful fulfillment and release. All this she had picked up from Steven Cole much as, earlier, she had sensed the bleakness and the fear lurking behind his simple accounts of loss of memory.

But was it "loss" in any true sense of the word? she asked herself, getting up from the table and wandering into the kitchen. Was it not more likely suppression? Her stomach rumbled loudly, as though answering her, reminding her that she had skipped dinner. She inspected the contents of the refrigerator and set about making herself a tuna-fish sandwich. Latents were good at suppression. Most latents, unless catapulted by some stimulus outside their control into a full realization of their powers, kept these well battened down. They were adept at explaining away the isolated moments of precognition that managed to break through their shuttered minds. And because they were usually and understandably scared by these flashes of knowledge, they worked hard to prevent any further occurrences. In effect, all this usually amounted to was an ability to ignore the signs or a failure to make the connection between external evidence and mental power: they "lost" their memories of these events. The question was, she thought, as she bit into the thick sandwich, whether Steven Cole was so scared by what he "knew" that he had suppressed it to a dangerous extent. She wished she were back home—the taste of tuna, mayonnaise, crisp heart lettuce was powerfully nostalgic—with the backing of the Agency where she could discuss such matters without fear of encountering hostility or looks that declared her obviously insane. She could all too easily imagine Page's face if, on Monday morning, she should lay her theory before him. It made her laugh and feel despair all at once.

There was another complication, too, one her training and professionalism had enabled her to put aside but which, ultimately, they were powerless to resolve. Steven Cole was a very attractive man. She had wanted to have dinner with him. She wished it were possible to have dinner with him without being aware of him as a special case. She sniffed disaster. If she were to follow up, investigate what was happening to him—and her conscience already told her that she had no choice in the matter—there was no basis for a relationship outside the professional. She could not split herself in two. Even if she could she doubted that he would be able to handle it. And if she permitted herself to know him unprofessionally, as an attractive man to whom she felt drawn, then every time they got close, what was happening to him would intrude and distract her. It was for such reasons that one never, ever got involved with a patient. But Steven was not a patient, not even yet a friend. For once, it did not feel good to Leigh to have a choice, to know that it was entirely up to her. Most of all she could not afford complications, professional or emotional, at this stage in her career.

Leigh had been in love twice. The first time, when a teenager, with a boy who was all athletic muscle and no brain. She had suffered for him with a passion that still made her tremble. What agonies she had borne waiting for him to see her strange eyes and prematurely gray hair as an attractive and viable alternative to the ripe blonds he favored. When he did at last notice her, she had felt positively grateful to him. She had given herself totally and with a kind of animal joy. She had even convinced herself that she could be comfortable with a man whose head was stuffed with batting averages, athletic training programs, a passionate concern with junk food, and fast, selfish sex—nothing else. She had not even seen that where there is no feeling there is no prohibition to hurt. To this day, she would be prepared to bet he had no knowledge that he had hurt her. He had the devastating simplicity of the truly unintelligent. He spoke his feelings clearly, mashing the language that would always be an alien tool to him. He dumped her, just like that, without grace, apology, or regret, and now she wasn't even angry at him. At herself, yes, but for that poor ox she felt only pity.

And she had done better for herself the second time around. Spike was one of her own kind, a young man as talented and dedicated as she, a man with whom she could communicate with that closeness poets fantasize when writing of lovers. If only the poets knew how sharing one heartbeat, living inside one another's thoughts, could destroy. For their abilities had destroyed their relationship, or at least rendered it intolerable.

It was, in the simplest words, too much. In the end, neither of them could bear it. Separation had been essential, the only way either of them could survive intact. It was when she had finally acknowledged this that Leigh had applied for the year's visiting professorship at a London hospital. Spike left for Canada while she was waiting to hear if the Agency would grant her request, and she still crossed her fingers and hoped that the move had not damaged Spike's career.

And now there was Steven Cole threatening to screw up her "recuperation" period. Not that she was in love with Steven Cole, she reminded herself firmly as she began to undress for bed. It was just that she was good at recognizing the signs. All the signs were there, had probably been there when she had first set eyes on him—empathy was a common cause of involuntary tripping out—but she had been too scared and bemused to recognize them. Now she did, and it was time to run or risk.

She forced him out of her mind, made herself sleep. She succeeded, but the sleep was light and fretful, plagued by dreams. Many of these were hauntingly erotic, and all of them centered around Steven Cole. Often, too often, the images of languorous eroticism exploded into those of violence and death. Splayed bodies, open to pleasure, became corpses, victims. Death and Eros melted one into the other, like something horrid glimpsed below the surface of a lake, darting dark and mysterious.

She awoke after only a few hours, her mind made up. As she bathed and dressed, drank coffee and ate cinnamon toast, she firmly rejected all the excuses that offered themselves. The need to clear her head, the desire for fresh air were all-consuming. She accepted the professional in her and let it be for the moment, uneasily hand-in-hand with the woman. As she ate, she studied a London street map and worked out a direct route to Chiswick House. As she stood on the elevated platform, well wrapped against the crisp winter morning waiting for the train, she wished she could feel like a tourist setting off to see an eighteenth-century folly and explore its spacious grounds. But the reality was too strong. She was a professional, undertaking an investigative mission that she earnestly hoped would fail, but feared would yield horrors.

After leaving the subway, she walked up a wide, tree-lined avenue and crossed a humming highway by means of a tunnel. Once inside the pale walls of Chiswick House's outer grounds she found herself on another avenue, bounded on one side by a mellow brick wall and overlooked by houses on the other. She had to walk nearly the whole length of this undistinguished avenue before entering the grounds proper through a narrow archway set in the high wall. She followed the most obvious path and found herself on the edge of a knot garden, an intricate arrangement of beds hedged with miniature box, with evergreen plants arrayed in strict patterns within, formally laid out before the ethereal Victorian fantasy of a bulbous greenhouse. On the far side of the garden she saw a stretch of white tape and the blue overcoat and helmet of a policeman. Any vestige of hope she had nursed that this might, after all, turn into a pleasantly fruitless Sunday-morning stroll died. She passed along the front of the greenhouse, the sound of her boots causing the policeman, a fresh-faced young constable, to turn toward her. As she approached the tape he said, "You'll have to go round that way, Miss."

"Oh, fine." She treated him to her smile, let her looks—she still did not think of herself as a beauty—work their peculiar magic on him. "What's wrong? Has something happened?"

He hesitated, had obviously been told to say nothing. Without even trying, she could perceive his shock, his nerves jumping from what he had recently seen.

"It's very unpleasant, Miss. If you'd just go along that way." He smiled back.

Leigh nodded and took the twisting path that meandered through, became a feature of the curlicues of the knot garden, aware of the coppice of evergreens that stood directly beyond the little boundary hedge. It had happened in there, she knew. The path led her through a natural break in that same coppice where the spicy smell of pine needles mingled with leaf mold and loam. Dimly, through the screening vegetation, she could see men moving cautiously, as though searching. The path led her to the side of the gray-washed house, and she focused on the vista before her. The old cedars of Lebanon were mighty and magnificent; the broad sweep of grass led down to an ornamental lake with a little temple on its far bank. She saw all this, she even took it in, but it was the cordoned-off coppice and the uniformed policeman guarding it that held her true attention. She became aware of a knot of people huddled together in the lee of the house, many of them with leashed dogs that fretted and whined for their scampering freedom. She went toward the little crowd of people, who, though chatting one with another, kept their eyes fixed on the coppice.

"What's happened?" Leigh asked.

"Been another one of them murders," a woman said, certain of her facts.

"We don't know there's any connection," a tall, military-looking man corrected the woman, who glared at him. "They found the body of a young boy," the man said directly to Leigh.

"Oh, I'm sorry," she said.

The woman pressed close against her, jerking at the mongrel dog who tugged her in the opposite direction.

"They haven't taken him away yet," she confided. "He's still lying there, poor little lad."

Leigh moved away. She did not want to know that. She needed to be alone to try and make sense of what she had come here to discover. Behind her, the woman's voice rose, loudly sounding the rallying call for all who supported capital punishment. There seemed to be no voices raised in dissent. Leigh crossed in front of the house, not looking at it, and started down the steep incline toward the lake. There were three benches down there on which Steven might have sat, but she fancied that he would have chosen the first, the one closest to the bridge, which, he had told her, he remembered crossing. She sat on the bench herself and looked up the hill to where the coppice, though distant, was clearly visible.

She closed her eyes and concentrated, holding her body tense, trying to see what he had seen, to catch some trace of it on the air, the bark of the trees. The only image that offered itself to her was one she was sure Steven Cole had not seen. It was of a body, lying on its side, cushioned by pine needles, dead leaves, and soft earth. The skin was very pale, almost luminous in that shadowed place. The hair was dark and matted, matted, she thought, with blood as well as soil. He wore a black zippered jacket and bright blue shorts, which had been pulled down low, below the crooked knees.

She stifled a moan of anguish and pity, opened her eyes, blinking at the morning's contrasting brightness. What she had just seen, could still see if she permitted herself, was what the policemen up there were guarding, which they would not disturb until measurements and photographs had been taken. Then the ambulance would arrive and— Leigh stood up quickly. She did not want to see the body removed, not even shrouded on a stretcher.

She walked quickly toward the bridge, her eyes fixed on the ground, and crossed it without glancing back. She slowed down only when she had entered the protection of the wood on the far bank. With her hands thrust deep into her coat pockets, walking with a slightly dragging step, she tried to figure out what was the true connection between that boy's body and Steven Cole.

Georgia answered the phone, its shrill ringing setting her already-raw nerves jangling.

"It's for you," she yelled, rattling the receiver down on the little wooden table that, apart from the telephone, held a jumble of keys, notepads, pens, and circulars. She went back into the kitchen and stared resentfully at the dishes piled from their separate breakfasts, their tense and almost-silent lunch. She did not understand how such simple, thrown-together meals could produce so much cleaning up.

She had picked a row with Steven last night when he finally returned at eight-thirty. She had done so because she was angry and felt safer when she was on the offensive. She had demanded to know where he had been and had paid little attention to his story of going for a walk at Chiswick House then to the hospital for a swim. But she had pounced again when he had said that he did not think she would be in anyway. How could she go out? How could she leave Mark? And who had the car? That had developed into another stand-up fight about her supposed neuroticism concerning Mark's safety and his equally supposed lack of care for their son, the one decent thing, she had shouted, this rotten marriage had given either of them. Steven said it was just her guilt talking, the guilt she felt about betraying Mark as well as him. The row had gone on and on, circling back on itself, dying down briefly, only to flare up again. Twice she had said yes, she did love Roger, did intend to go on seeing him. Yes, their marriage was over, and Steve had better face up to that. Twice, also, she had retracted, insisting that she did not know, needed more time to think and evaluate.

She heard him say into the phone, "Yes, yes I can. Of course I will. No, really. I'd like to."

It hit her then, like a slap that sent her mind reeling. He had been with her last night, that soft, husky-voiced woman on the phone who had asked for him by his full name. She did not know the voice, but she knew it to be pleasing and utterly female, and that suddenly explained where he had been last night. His hair had been damp from some illicit shower, probably taken with her, not from the hospital pool. She began to slam crockery about, shifting dishes from one pile to another. She had *known* there was something funny about him. He had seemed on edge, tired out yet somehow more alive than she had seen him for months. Exhausted but excited, like a lover. She heard him hang up the receiver, walk down the hall, and go into their bedroom. The extraordinary thing was that she minded. Her uselessly busy hands suddenly grew still, lay trembling on the rim of the sink. All last night, in between rounds of their fight, and long after, when sleep continued to evade her, she had imagined Roger out on the town by himself, picking up some younger and more attractive woman. And now this. Now Steve. She was damned if she was going to stand for it. She whirled around, snatching up a cloth to dry her hands on as he appeared in the doorway, zipping up his old parka. At least he didn't think her worth dressing up for, Georgia thought wildly. That was something.

"I have to go out," he said.

"To see her, I suppose."

"Who? What are you talking about?" His eyes widened in surprise, which looked very much like guilt to Georgia.

"That woman on the phone."

"Well, yes, as a matter of fact."

"And you were with her last night, you bastard." She bunched the cloth and hurled it at him. It fell short and harmless, making her even more angry.

"She's a colleague," he said calmly. "A psychiatrist at the hospital."

"And since when have you been interested in psychiatry?"

"Always, as you perfectly well know."

"And what about me? What am I supposed to do?"

"You can do what you like. You have been for months anyway."

"I can't leave Mark," she hissed.

"That's your problem," Steven said, and walked into the hall.

"If you leave now," Georgia shouted, following, "you needn't come back."

He scooped up the car keys, opened the front door, and walked out slamming it behind him. Quivering with rage, she ran back into the kitchen and snatched up the nearest dish, flung it at the wall, then another and another until she saw Mark staring at her white faced, from the doorway. She dropped the dish she held onto the floor and burst into uncontrollable tears.

Leigh's rented flat occupied the second floor of a small terraced house in the back streets of Barons Court. The street door was painted a cheerful orange, and since there was no intercom Steven had to wait for her to come down and let him in. The hallway was dark and cramped, having been divided off to provide two separate entrances to two separate flats. Leigh's front door opened directly onto a steep flight of stairs, up which Steven followed her, his heart thudding like that of an adolescent calling on a girl for the first time. He realized that they had not spoken except to say "hello" and now he felt tongue-tied, wondered how it would be possible to begin. The stairs led to an L-shaped hallway, off which four doors opened. Leigh moved down the hallway to a room at the front of the house. Steven was momentarily dazzled by the light that streamed into the room through three wide, sashed windows. Against the glare, Leigh's outline was diffused and seemed to be on fire. He could not make out her shadowed face.

"You'd better take your jacket off. I keep it hot in here. I feel the cold."

"Do you?" he said, unzipping his parka and thinking of all

the other things he longed to know about her. She held out her
hand for his coat; he gave it to her and looked around for
somewhere to sit that would enable him to keep his back to the
light. Beneath two of the windows was a plump, old-fashioned
sofa covered with pretty multicolored rugs. He sat there, not
knowing what to do with his hands, waiting for Leigh to come
back. She stood in front of him, and he regarded her face with
relief. He had not imagined it or its beauty. Even her little
frown of worried concentration could not mar it.

"Will you answer some questions without wanting to know
why I ask them? Questions that might seem completely mad to
you? I promise to explain later."

"Yes," he said, and nodded to seal the bargain. Because he
did not know how to approach her, because her very presence
overwhelmed him, he would have agreed to anything. Like the
awkward adolescent he had forgotten he had ever been, he
needed time to collect his thoughts, to comprehend that he was
not dreaming. She had called him, and he was sitting in her
flat, looking at her.

The intensity and gentleness of his gaze unnerved Leigh,
threatened to melt her resolve. She shook herself mentally and
crossed to the table she used as a desk. She sat down, her chair
deliberately turned away from him, and had difficulty uncap-
ping her pen.

Her face alone could destroy him, he thought. If ever he
should get close enough to stare deeply into those navy-blue
eyes he would be sure to drown. He knew now what Circe
must have looked like and why men went so willingly to their
doom.

"This first blackout or memory loss," Leigh said briskly, her
voice too loud due to nervousness. "When was that
precisely?"

He screwed up his eyes in thought. It was not difficult to
remember, though it seemed an age ago. Her words had a sort
of banal irrelevance, which threatened the vision he had partly
conjured for himself.

"Tuesday," he said and had to clear his throat. "Or early
Wednesday morning."

"You're sure of that?"

"Yes. It was the night that boy died. What's his name? I

can't remember the time because my watch had stopped." He felt for his watch hidden under the cuff of his gray sweater.

"A boy died?" Leigh asked, her voice dropping to a whisper.

"You must have heard about it. Everyone at the hospital was talking about it. As a matter of fact he was killed almost right outside our . . . where I live."

"And your watch stopped?"

"Yes."

"It stopped yesterday, too," she reminded him. Leigh started to write something, then gave it up. She lay down her pen with a sigh and linked her hands together.

"What's the matter?" There was no mistaking the concern, the gentleness in his voice. He did not speak like a man bewildered, a patient who felt that he had failed.

"You promised not to ask questions until I'd finished," Leigh said.

"I just thought . . ."

"Please . . ." She held up her hand and fixed him with her eyes. There was a strange light in them, a light that was also a mist that made their full expression unreadable. "Have you ever undergone hypnosis?"

His lips twitched with amusement as he shook his head. "Never, no."

"Will you permit me to hypnotize you?" she asked, leaning toward him, her eyes still on his.

"I think you already have," Steven replied, his smile growing wider while his throat and mouth were dry with excitement.

"Stop that," she said, but it was not the impatient command of yesterday. Her voice told him that she understood, but that there was a time and a place for everything.

"Why do you—?"

"No questions. You promised."

He wanted to laugh but feared to offend her. Did she want to hypnotize him in order to make love to him, to have him in her power, so that she could rob him of memory? It was a sweet temptation, soon destroyed.

"In order," she said, as though answering his unspoken question, "to demonstrate something to you. In hypnosis I

think you'll be able to remember what happened during those
blank times."

"Oh, I see."

"Hypnosis is widely used in psychiatry. I assure you it's
perfectly safe."

"I'm sure."

"Trust me." Leigh smiled and held out her hand. It was
against all the rules. She was using her body, her looks, her
charm to persuade him, and she knew she was doing it. What
made it even worse was that she was enjoying it, too. He took
her hand.

"All right."

She gave his hand a slight squeeze before pulling hers away.
Steven saw that she was indeed a magical creature. He saw her
transform herself before his eyes from a soft, bewitching
woman into a remote, detached professional.

"Lean back, get really comfortable, and fix your eyes on
some point or object over there."

"You for example?" Steven said, settling back on the sofa.

"I said over there." Leigh pointed to the opposite wall as
she stood up and moved to stand at the side of the sofa, out of
his line of vision.

"All right."

"Got it?"

"Yes."

He had chosen a dapple of sunlight on the glass of a cheap
flower print. The light wavered, obscuring the print so that he
could not identify the flower, and, as this occupied his
conscious mind, the light flowed and dazzled, seeming to
smooth all the wrinkles from his mind. He felt drowsy, wanted
to tell her that this was crazy, that it would not work.

He heard her voice but could not make out the words. It
became a humming in his ears, a throbbing, and the little spots
of light grew and joined into a cloud that seemed to spread
throughout the room until it engulfed and carried him away,
far, far away.

Sailboats idled on the Thames, their canvases limp for lack of
wind. They, like the cold sunlight, seemed to mock Georgia as,
with Mark either darting ahead or lagging sulkily behind, she

walked through the park toward Putney Bridge. Her eyes were red and swollen, her nose as pink as a seasoned drunkard's. She was ashamed of her outburst because Mark had seen it and she knew it to be hysterical. Not that there was anything wrong with being hysterical, but it did suggest that she was losing her grip on the situation. As soon as she had realized that, Georgia had pulled herself together and taken action. First she had telephoned Jane Cadwallader, the mother of Mark's current best friend, who had agreed readily enough to have Mark over at her house for a few hours. Then, making as sure as she could that Mark did not overhear, she had called Roger and asked him to come to the flat in an hour. He'd balked at first, she recalled, until she assured him that Steve would not be there. And if Steve returned? She didn't know. She'd think about that later.

She turned away from the river toward the tunnel under the Putney Bridge approach and hovered, looking back to where Mark hung on the railings, watching two men on the opposite bank lower a light racing skiff into the water.

"Mark," she called. "Come along."

A passing elderly couple stared at her face, obviously reading the signs of recent distress. Georgia tilted her chin a little, stared them down.

"This is far enough," Mark said. "I can go by myself now."

"Please don't start that again." Georgia made a beeline for the mouth of the tunnel, Mark at her side.

"You promised," he whined like a child half his age or less.

"To leave you at the bottom of Braham Road, yes."

"And when we get there you'll think of some other excuse to come to the gate and to the front door," Mark said, a sneer in his voice. Georgia fought an impulse to slap him, right there in the park, with people all around them.

"You needn't worry," she told him, when she'd gotten the impulse under control. "I don't want the Cadwalladers to see me looking like this any more than you do."

Whether from relief or embarrassment, Georgia could not tell, but this quieted him, at least until they emerged from the tunnel into sharp sunlight again.

"What shall I tell them if they ask? Ian's mum's very nosy."

Georgia's mind was a blank, one that quickly filled with the sickening realization of what she was doing to her son.

"Just say . . . say I had to see someone from work . . . something urgent came up . . . and your father had to go out."

"So they'll think I'm a pathetic little kid who can't be left alone even in the middle of the day? Thanks a bundle."

"Oh Mark, please, try to be helpful."

"I am. Why can't I say that you and Dad had a row and you want to be by yourself for a bit? That's the truth, isn't it?"

There was a lump in her throat that made speech impossible for a moment.

"I didn't think you'd want them to know," she said. "Fine."

"That's all right then. Look, you can see the corner from here. You go back now, okay?"

She did not have any fight left. She stopped, nodded her head. A broad, cheerful grin split his face.

"Thanks, Mum."

He set off at once, paused at the pavement's edge to check for traffic, like a bird poised for flight, Georgia thought, so eager to escape the cage.

"Mark?"

"What is it?"

His grin was gone.

"Have a good time with Ian."

"Sure. See you."

And he was off, dashing across the road, along the opposite pavement, around the corner into Braham Road. Georgia watched until he was out of sight then forced herself to turn around, go back. She took the direct route home, her pace quickening.

Once inside the flat Georgia pressed a face cloth, wrung out in cold water, to her face. The effect was soothing. She did this several times then patted her face dry, made up her eyes and mouth lightly. She considered changing her jeans and sweater—they were the ones she had worn yesterday to visit Roger—but she had no heart for it. Instead she brushed her hair until it shone and fell springly to her shoulders.

She stood by the big window, looking down into the road. A

group of youths played football in the park opposite. The sailboats still idled on the windless river. She saw dogs romping, a child roller-skating along the pavement, people out for a Sunday stroll, taking advantage of the dry bright weather. At last she saw his car, a red Maxi, draw into the slot usually occupied by their own car, saw him get out and glance at the fanlight over the double front door where the flat numbers were displayed in faded, art deco–style glass. She moved away from the window suddenly, not wanting him to see her watching and waiting. She hurried to the front door, opened it, and stood just inside, listening to his footsteps on the echoing concrete stairs. As soon as his head became visible through the iron bannisters, she said, "In here."

He did not answer but smiled at her. As soon as he was inside, he closed the door and embraced her. Georgia resisted the impulse, powerful as ever, to rest in his arms, let her body speak for her. As soon as she could without seeming to reject him, she pulled away and said, sounding, she thought, like a maid in her own house, "This way."

At the end of the corridor she warned him about the steps down into the living room. He stood just inside the room, admiring it.

"So this is where you live. I've tried to imagine it, but . . . It's not what I expected. It's a fabulous room."

"We like it," Georgia said, sounding stiff and awkward. She regretted the pronoun immediately.

Roger went to the window, took in the view.

"Let me take your coat," Georgia said.

"I'm expected to stay, am I? Isn't that a bit dodgy? The marital home and all that."

"Steve's gone," she said. "I told him not to come back, though he probably will. I'll bolt the door if you like."

"Don't be ridiculous." He shrugged off his sheepskin coat and handed it to her. "You've reached a decision then?" he asked, looking at her levelly.

Something in his tone, perhaps because he was ill at ease, made it sound as though any decision of hers would only be of academic interest to him. To hide her disappointment, Georgia carried his coat across the room and folded it over an elegant little ladderback chair she and Steve had bought together in the

Fulham Road, before antique prices soared. And because she
was scared to answer him directly, yet, she said, "Would you
like a cup of tea, a drink or something?"

"No, I'm fine."

She walked slowly back across the room and sat in her usual
chair. Roger, taking what he thought was a hint, sat on the edge
of the couch. He looked out of place in the room.

"You haven't answered my question."

"Not really. We had a blazing row. I think he's got a woman.
That's where he's gone now."

Roger waited, hoping that she would say more, give him
some clue as to how she wanted or expected him to respond.
The important question, it seemed to him, was whether she
minded Steven's supposed infidelity, but he felt uncertain of
that ground and asked instead, "And you told him not to come
back?"

"Yes."

"And if he doesn't? But of course he'll have to. He didn't
take his clothes or anything?"

Georgia shook her head.

"Well then . . ." He shifted his weight, glanced toward his
coat. Georgia saw this and knew that he wanted to get away,
avoid Steve at all costs. Was he afraid of him, a confrontation?

"The point is," she said, waiting until he looked at her,
"that we can't go on like this. It's not fair on any of us. When
he does come back I want to be able to settle it with him, once
and for all."

"Oh I'm all for that," Roger said, perhaps a little too
enthusiastically. "Definitely."

"But I need to talk to you first. Don't you see that?"

"Of course. And here I am. Shoot."

The muscles at the sides of her mouth tensed, drew her lips
into a compressed, angry line.

"You never help me. You never give me an opening."

"Darling, look, don't let's start that again. Tell me what the
options are, then we can discuss them."

It sounded reasonable, and she hung on to that even though a
voice in her head still cried out that it was unfair.

"There's Mark to consider. I have to put him, his welfare
anyway, before everything. I can't leave him." Her eyes shone

as she said this and her hands clenched into fists on the arms of her chair.

"Of course not. I understand that," Roger said easily.

"Do you? You left your child, after all."

"That was different."

"Why? How?"

"Oh Georgia, really. How could I have looked after a toddler, a little girl at that? Besides, Lynette wanted her every bit as fiercely as you want Mark. It's only natural."

"God, it's so easy for you, isn't it? The good old sexual stereotypes. They make life so . . . so . . . black and white for you, for men, don't they?"

"No, as a matter of fact they don't. And that's not what we should be discussing now. It's irrelevant to—"

"Oh yes we should. If you could leave your own kid, why should I think you'd welcome mine?"

"I accept Mark's existence. I know he's part of the situation. What more can I say?"

"I don't know. But there has to be something."

"I'm sorry." He stood up, considered going to her, touching her, but knew that it would do no good. He strolled to the window, put his hands in his pockets, and stood there looking down, rocking back on his heels a little.

"Well," Georgia said, "that rules out one option, anyway. Thank you for that, at least."

"I don't know what option you're talking about."

"There's no chance of moving in with you. So, Steve will have to go."

"That's not fair," he said, turning around to face her. "You know there isn't room. You couldn't even contemplate moving an adolescent boy into a flat like that. Where would he sleep? What privacy would we have?"

"There are other flats, Roger. Even houses. The market is full of them. But okay, let's not get into that. What I want to know is, if Steve goes, leaves here, would you come here?"

"Well, of course I would. You really don't have to ask."

"Would you move in?"

"Well I . . ." He went back to the sofa and sat down again. "Not at first, of course. We'd have to see how things went."

"You just want to be my part-time lover and that's it?"

"Yes, I do, very much, even when you make it sound disgusting. I want to be your lover and give us both time to develop, but you've got to think this through, Georgia. This is Steven's home—all right, half his home. You can't just move another man in. He'd have every right to be angry. And what about the effect on Mark? I'm a stranger to him. What are you going to tell him? His father's gone and I've moved in to take his place; just get on with it?"

Georgia did not answer for several moments. When she did, her words were preceded by a sigh.

"Why is it that when you are reasonable and sensible, I always feel you're slipping out of something, rejecting me? Why do you always make me feel that I have no future with you?"

"I don't know. That's your problem, not mine. I think it might be because you can't envisage any future for yourself and won't accept that any future we have is going to take time and will always be compromised."

"Because of Mark?"

"Partly, yes."

"What else?"

"Our pasts. Me and Lynette, you and—"

"Why did you never marry her?" Georgia said, changing tack.

"I've told you . . ." He saw from her expression that she would not be fobbed off, needed, perhaps, to hear him tell it again. He shrugged. "All right. Neither of us wanted it. We wanted to be together but we didn't want a public commitment, all the complications you're facing right now, just because you got married, legally tied to someone."

"You think it would be any easier if I wasn't? Would Mark suddenly cease to matter, like your child?"

"Christ, you can be a bitch sometimes," he said, shaking his head as though weary. "No, of course Mark would not cease to matter. Probably you'd be even more attached to him. As for me . . . I never wanted a child. That was Lynette's idea, and she had good reasons, sound arguments. I loved her enough to give in. It seemed the right thing to do at the time. It was just bad luck that I realized too late that I didn't want a child because I was scared it, she, would ruin our relationship. And she did. But she was right for Lynette. Bad for me. So we split up, and yes, that split was a damn sight easier than yours is going to be."

"So you don't like children. Now we're getting somewhere. You don't want Mark."

"For God's sake, Georgia, I'm not in love with Mark."

"He's just one of the complications. That's what you're saying, isn't it?"

"Yes. I am. Just one. One that I can accept, given the time. I'm willing, given the chance, to get to know him, like him, even live with him. But neither you nor I can just move me into his life and say, 'This is it, like it or lump it.' And he has to like me and want to live with me as well, you know. That's going to take time."

"You're right. Why are you always so damned right?"

She wished then that he would come to her, comfort her, but he remained where he was, his eyes moving restlessly around the room as though weighing it up.

"I'll try," he said again. "I'll come here if Steve goes. I'll see as much of you and Mark as we can all manage. I can't promise any more than that, Georgia."

"I know." She sniffed. "And I still have this feeling that you're leaving me."

"In that case," he said, standing up, "I think I better had."

"No, please . . ."

"You've got to think it through, Georgia. I'll see you tomorrow."

"Oh . . . I thought you meant . . ."

"When I don't want you anymore, Georgia, when I don't love you, I'll tell you. I don't lie about my relationships. At least, I try not to."

"And I suppose I ought to be grateful to you for that? Was Lynette, I wonder?"

"I don't know. Why don't you ask her?" He went to the chair in the corner and picked up his coat. "Frankly, I don't care. If you want more from me than I've got to give . . ." He shrugged. "I'm going now. You think about it."

She wanted to stop him but she did not know how. She wanted him to make love to her, make it all go away, but it was impossible to ask or suggest. She was terrified that he would push her away, see her as cheap or clinging. She heard the front door close behind him. Well, that was it then. She knew where she stood. Roger had drawn the parameters very neatly and clearly. No doubt, she thought, Steve would do the same if she gave him the chance.

"And what about me?" she said, hurling her voice into the desolate emptiness of what had once been her happy home.

"Where are you now?"

Leigh spoke in a low voice, little more than a husky whisper, but she projected the words with purpose and determination.

"Can you hear me? Will you tell me where you are?"

She had drawn the chair from her desk up close to him and now leaned toward him with tense urgency. His eyes flicked but did not see her, returned always to the chosen spot on the wall. His hand moved, but not in any alarming way. Otherwise his pose was relaxed: a man sitting on a sofa, with a preoccupied, contemplative look to him.

"Steven . . ."

Before she could frame the rest of her sentence, his eyes closed and his lips moved, seemed to be trying to smile. His name was, she guessed, the key. It roused him or prompted him. Excited, she said it again.

"Steven, please answer me."

"Yes."

He spoke quietly, in his own, recognizable voice, but without expression, as though tired.

"Where are you, Steven?"

"Waiting. He's waiting."

Leigh caught her breath, clasped her hands together so that each gripped the other tightly.

"Who is waiting, Steven?"

He frowned, shook his head.

"Is it you, Steven? You are waiting?"

"No. He . . . is . . . He is waiting."

She was afraid of this confirmation, afraid and excited, too. The two halves of her, professional and woman, were already pulling at each other.

"Where is he waiting, Steven?"

"In the trees."

"Where are these trees?"

"Here."

He shook his head impatiently, as though the question was foolish and therefore irrelevant.

"What is he waiting for, Steven?"

"Him."

"Who is that, please? Who is 'him,' Steven?"

"No . . . him."

"Describe him. Tell me what you see."

Nothing. No answer.

"Is it dark or light under the trees, Steven?"

"Light. Going dark. Dark. Light going. Shadows. They've got to stop playing now. They must. Oh, come on, come on, come on . . ."

She saw sweat break out on his face, form a gleaming moustache on his upper lip. He was moving his body restlessly, rolling his head from side to side. His fingers clenched and opened in poorly coordinated spasms.

"Steven, try to tell me what it is."

"Oh no, no, no . . ."

He tried to rise from the sofa, but it seemed that he could not control his own body. His arms flailed wildly. Leigh had to draw back to avoid being struck. Then, quite suddenly, he fell back, his body limp on the sofa, his hands palm-upward beside him. His stillness was shocking.

"Steven?"

Nothing.

"Where are you now, Steven? Please answer me."

Leigh heard the panic in her own voice and forced herself to be calm. Experience told her that his trance had deepened, that he had slipped away from her not into sleep but to some deeper level of unconsciousness. If this were so, she had to be calm and patient. To wake someone suddenly from such a trance could be dangerous, but then again if he stayed too long . . . She stood up and bent over him. His skin was damp but warm, his eyes disturbingly still under closed lids. She raised one gently, saw only the white of his pupil, a shining crescent. His pulse was slow, his heartbeat steady. She realized, as she straightened up, that she had enjoyed touching him, that his body felt good and familiar to her.

"Steven?" She spoke more loudly, partly against her own thought, partly in the hope of reaching him. He did not stir. She looked at her watch. She would give it five minutes. Every thirty seconds she would speak his name. Five minutes and then, if he had not responded, she would have to go after him. She stared at her watch, at the slow crawl of the second hand. She hated putting herself into a trance. Although she could control it pretty well, the other side was always dangerous, scary. It was like the bad dark places of her childhood where monsters lurked. But she knew when she spoke his name for the last time and still there was no flicker of response that she would have to do it. The watch would serve. She concentrated on it, emptied her mind.

He was lying on his back, staring at a faint crack in the ceiling. The place in which he lay was filled with a strange greenish, underwater light. He had been dozing and he felt uncomfortable. Guilt tugged at his mind. He moved his hand and touched something, paper, which crackled under his touch. His clothes were undone, pushed awry. The air was cold on his groin, cold and shameful. He started up, heart hammering with panic. The room swung out of focus, blurred. He had to put everything away quickly, before Mummy came in. Then pain exploded through his head, seemed to leap in a single sizzling arc from one temple to the other, and he cried out at the agony of it.

Steven was standing in a strange room, his hands clasped to his temples. The force of the pain receded as quickly as it had come and left his senses reeling. He dropped his hands, stared around him. The light behind him threw his shadow across the unfamiliar room, up the wall toward a picture of flowers on which sunlight dappled.

"Leigh?"

He turned his head and saw her sitting bolt upright in a straight-backed chair. She was quite still, staring ahead of her. For a moment he thought she must have fallen asleep or was lost so deep in thought that . . . Then he saw that her very immobility was unnatural, seemed to be caused by a clenched and dreadfully controlled energy.

"Leigh?"

He touched her shoulder, felt it hard and resisting under his fingers. He moved around so that he could see her face properly. Her eyes glazed and did not flicker as he stooped and then knelt to stare into them. Her face was ash white. The skin looked dry and dusty. How long? He looked at his watch, panic rising in him. The bloody thing had stopped again. Why had he ever agreed to play such a stupid game? Was she having a fit, in a coma of some kind? He reached his hands to her shoulders, grasped them and shook her.

"Leigh? Leigh, for God's sake, wake up."

Her whole body resisted him. He shook her but he could barely make her move. She was like an effigy of herself— frozen life.

"Leigh, please . . ."

He threw his arms around her, working his hands down between her back and that of the chair, pulling her terrible stillness against him, pressing his face against the softness of her breasts.

"Leigh, please wake up. Please, please . . ."

Then he felt it, although he could not describe it. It was as though life returned to her body. What had felt chill, became warm, he suddenly realized. What had been rigid and stone-like became soft and pliable. He felt her become human again, living. Still kneeling, he drew back from her, his arms outstretched to support her. Her left hand, lying in her lap, twitched then moved slowly, a little jerkily, like that of an automaton. He watched it, fascinated, his mouth open. He saw her hand rise and hang in the air then move toward him. After a long while, her fingers touched his cheek. Gently, she stroked his skin. Her eyes were dark and sad, as though washed with grief, and in a strange, exhausted voice, she said, "Oh Steven, I thought I'd lost you."

He turned his head and kissed the palm of her hand, almost weeping with relief and happiness. She let him help her to the bedroom. Every joint in her body felt as though it had been stretched until the bones had cracked. Each muscle protested at the slightest movement. Without his help she would have been forced to lie on the floor, lacking the energy even to crawl. The back of her neck felt bruised and sore, as though it had been grasped in some monstrous vise. From there a dull, throbbing pain crept up the back of her skull to unfold its tentacles right across her scalp to her eyes. She could not see clearly, and her only thought was that she must rest. She let him help her onto the bed and had no energy to protest when she felt him stretch out beside her. His head lay so close to hers, on the same pillow, that his breath ruffled her hair. His arm encircled her stomach, clasped her. He was trembling with emotion or shock, possibly desire, she thought, but she could not form any words. She could only lie there with him, trusting him and fate.

Steven watched her. He did not think that she slept, but she was not fully awake either. Somehow he knew that she was going to be all right, or so he told himself later when, with a feeling of guilty panic, he realized that never once in that long afternoon had it crossed his mind to call a doctor or seek any kind of help. Somehow she had reassured him, told him that she would be all right. He wanted to believe that, to savor the intimacy it suggested. He kept her warm and he watched over her. Although she did not speak or move, he knew she was very close to him. He watched her face change with shadows as the light faded and died. He listened to her regular and gradually stronger breathing. He watched her and slowly realized that he was completely happy.

She stirred, stretched, pulled from under his arm, and suddenly flooded the bed in a pool of amber light. Steven snatched his arm away from her body and shielded his eyes with it, wincing. He felt her move beside him, the bed tremble, shaking his own body. When he removed his arm, she was sitting up, her knees drawn up, her arms clasped around them. It was the endearing pose of a child. With the intimacy and confidence of a lover, Steven touched her curved back, tracing the line of her spine.

"Are you all right now?" he asked.

"Yes. Thank you, Steven."

"You scared me."

"I'm sorry."

"It doesn't matter, not now you're all right." He tried to sit up, embrace her. She twisted quickly toward him and pushed him down again, her hand strong and commanding on his chest.

"I think I'd better tell you about myself," she said, and wished that she did not have to.

When she had finished, when her voice no longer masked the rapid ticking of the clock on the nightstand beside her, Steven thought that he had been right. She was his Circe, a magic woman. Not a witch or really a sorceress, but some amazing otherworldly creature. His Ariel, spirit-free and magical. His mind was whirling. By some effort of will, he had bitten back every question, each challenge as it came to him. And now he believed her. She had spoken with suppressed pain and difficulty, but her words had never once lacked the weight of honesty. He felt, or rather she made him feel, that he had heard a real confession, almost awesome in its completeness and its trust. He knew the risk she felt she had taken, had been obliged to take, and was grateful.

"Thank you," she said softly, breaking into his thoughts, "for not laughing or calling me crazy."

He stared at her face, turned toward him, her chin nestling on her upper arm, but its features were blurred by shadow. He stared at her, trying to find the right words to say, words that would reassure her and tell her that he appreciated the trust she had placed in him. He wanted words that would convey the sense of privilege he felt, the holiness of this moment, the respect it woke in him. He wanted words for all this and more, but as she turned her face from him again, as though resigned to the engima of his silence, the only words that came to his lips were simple but adequate. "I love you," he said. "I love you."

It was not until she watched the main TV broadcast later that night that Georgia learned of the second murder. She stared at the screen as though mesmerized. There was a head-on picture of Chiswick House, the camera panning slowly to show the sweep of the grounds, finally coming to rest on the already-too-familiar police tarpaulins and tapes. She must have been there hundreds of times. She remembered one occasion in particular, when Mark was small, remembered it pictorially, just as though it were a part of the broadcast. Mark chasing after a round yellow ball, his bare legs pumping to outrun his father, who deliberately held back, pretending to be puffed. The little boy's legs tangled with the ball in their eagerness, set him falling, rolling down the slope, his father spurting after him, scooping him up, tossing him toward the sky. . . . At which point the picture froze, their two laughing faces silhouetted against the sun. Father and son. She shuddered at the idea of that place, their special place, being defiled by another child's death.

She got up and went out into the corridor, tapped on the bathroom door.

"Mark? Are you all right?"

" 'Course."

"Don't stay in the water too long, love. I don't want you to catch cold."

"All right."

And it was not until she was sitting down again, looking at but not taking in the jumpy credits of an arts-magazine program, that she made the connection. What had Steve said last night? He had said that he went for a stroll before going to the hospital. That's right. He stopped on the way back from Richmond to go for a stroll in the grounds of Chiswick House. She remembered clearly feeling a silly pang of envy because it had been so long since they had been there together, and the mere mention of the place seemed to evoke something she had cruelly lost. Her heart jumped, and she turned her head toward the window, stared at it as though it were uncurtained and she could see down the railings where the first boy had died. Coincidence, she told herself. It could only be coincidence, of course.

Leigh hesitated, but only for a moment. It was a token gesture to her private self, an acknowledgment that she had thought about this and accepted the implications. At the same time she admitted that it had been bound to come to this; it was inevitable. Then, working together, they began to peel off each other's clothing. There was no urgency, no scrabbling and tearing, no passionate haste. This was a ritual unveiling. They worked toward a state of nakedness with mutual delight, their hands lingering, exploring, discovering. His body pleased her, hers him. They explored with hands and mouths, fitting together like pieces of a puzzle. They were animals, too, scenting each other, exploring the fleshly terrain of each other. It was necessary to know the texture of her hair, his skin, to taste and smell and feel entirely before they could join. Leigh felt herself become fluid. The contours of her body altered. He did not enter her or she engulf him, yet both these things happened at the same time, at the right instant, so that it felt like a mutual melting, a fusion. He did not take his time but found hers and made it his own. It seemed to Leigh that her hands, resting on his back, grew into his flesh. Her tongue in his mouth became his tongue in her mouth. Softness and hardness became one as they cried out together in a single, satisfied voice.

Afterward they did not speak. Steven slept in Leigh's arms, she rested peacefully in his, until all that had not been said and faced irritated her mind, tugged her into a lonely anxiety. She tried to resist, to push it all out and away, but it too was a part of what had just passed between them, whatever they would become together. Leigh understood this and accepted it.

When he woke, smiling, dawn was throwing a ghostly pallor into the room, and Leigh, knowing she must take the first step not to banish the dream but to tie it securely to reality, said, "Hadn't you ought to go home?"

"No." He laughed a little, rolled onto his back, stretching his arms extravagantly. "My wife threw me out."

"Seriously?" Leigh let the doubt show in her face and voice.

"No, not really," he admitted, his grin fading. "She said if I went yesterday I wasn't to go back."

"Because of me?"

"Not really. We'd been fighting all night, most of the next morning. I will have to go back, but it's in the cards, my leaving, I mean. She's having an affair with her boss."

Leigh pursed her lips, thought that this knowledge ought to make her feel better, and then realized she did not feel any guilt at all.

"I don't feel guilty," she told him.

"Of course not."

"You probably will."

"No. How could I? Not about you."

There was a temptation then, as she laid her head on his chest, to slip back into the dream, hide for a while longer, but his stomach rumbled, making them both laugh, and Leigh said they must get up. Neither of them could remember when they had last eaten. She showed him where the bathroom was and pulled on an old, loose nightgown and padded into the kitchen to make breakfast. It started to rain, streaking the kitchen window and turning the room dark as she cracked eggs and sliced bread and thought that it was not an auspicious morning but that they would make their own weather, if her luck held.

"Not only can I not remember when I last ate, but I'd completely forgotten why I came here." Nude, he encircled her waist from behind, kissed the side of her head.

"Put the light on will you?" Leigh asked.

"You're right. You do keep this place warm," he said, turning the switch and filling the room with a harsh neon flicker, which gradually settled to a smoother, shadowless glow. "Okay if I don't get dressed yet?"

"Fine. Tea or coffee?"

"Tea. I'll make it."

She showed him where the pot was, and he stood beside her, waiting for the water to boil.

"What was all that about yesterday? You never told me."

"No. There wasn't time."

"Well, come on. Or are you really a sorceress? Have you changed me into something? Do you always hypnotize your lovers, Ms. Duncan?"

"Don't joke about it," Leigh said. "Please."

"All right. But what was it all about? What happened to you? God, you scared me."

"Steven, not now. It's very complicated and difficult, and I don't know how to tell you, anyway."

"Tell me what? You sound scared." He touched her arm, persuaded her to look at him. "You must tell me," he said, his eyes searching her face.

"Not now . . ."

"Yes, I insist."

"Did you know another boy was murdered Saturday, at Chiswick House?"

"No." A look of pain crossed his face but he remained puzzled, holding her, making her look at him. "But what's that got to do with me?"

"I don't know. At least I'm not sure yet."

"So? What?"

"Don't you remember anything from when I put you into a trance?"

He frowned. "I don't know. I haven't really tried."

"Well you must, later," Leigh said briskly, turning back to the stove. "We'll talk. Tonight if you can make it?"

"I want to know now. You frighten me."

"Steven, please, it's too complex. Anyway I have to prepare you first."

"For what? God, you make it sound like a surgical operation or something. Leigh—" He grabbed her arm but she shook him off angrily.

Looking at his stricken, worried face, she realized that there was no way to prepare him, that eventually she would have to risk his fear, his unbelief, his anger, and all that that might do to their feelings for each other. It was too soon. She deserved more time, but he was grimly determined now, had to know. It would be like cracking an egg, she thought, and she had better do it now.

"Please, whatever you do, don't laugh."

"Go on."

"I believe that you're in telepathic communication with someone. To put it simply, I think your headaches, your loss of memory are caused because someone else, occasionally and perhaps involuntarily, takes over your mind. It's a phenomenon that has never been proven or studied. Until a few days ago I thought it was just a hypothesis."

She stopped then as Steven let out a great burst of laughter. He leaned against the counter, his body shaking with the force of it. He laughed until tears ran down his face. He kept trying to speak but fresh waves of laughter prevented him. Calmly, Leigh switched off all the burners and walked quickly out of the room, his laughter following her and making the day bleak and frightful.

\* \* \*

Georgia lay and watched the day start. Of course she did not believe that Steven had had anything at all to do with either of the murders. It was unthinkable, and yet she kept thinking it. It was pure chance, *chance* that the first boy had died outside this very flat, that Steven had visited the place where the second had been killed. Of course he had not been out that first time. He was only wearing his robe when she found him standing at the window . . . looking down at his handiwork? Had he hit her to prevent her seeing? Out of fear of discovery? But he had been with her, sleeping beside her. How long before she had missed his body, felt the cold that woke her and set her anxiously searching for him, afraid that he had somehow discovered her relationship with Roger and was grieving or angry? How long before his leaving the bed and her waking? Long enough to slip out into the night? No. She did not believe for one moment that Steven had or could even think of such a thing.

She made herself get up even though she felt bone tired. Movement, the start of the day's routine, would provide a distraction from these whirling, crazy thoughts, these unfair, obscene and macabre thoughts. She went to the bathroom, careful not to disturb Mark, swallowed a couple of aspirins with a mug of water. She looked dreadful and she felt sick. She would not think about it anymore. She had more important worries to keep her sleepless. It was loneliness, confusion, and depression that made her prey to such thoughts. Her life was a mess.

As she stood in the kitchen, afraid to put on the radio, to hear more details of the second death, her hand immobile on the lid of the kettle, one thing seemed absolutely clear to her. From the black torment and shameful ugliness of her night thoughts, one good thing had emerged: she had reached a decision. She would not take Steven back. When he turned up, when eventually he deigned to come home, she would make it absolutely clear that he must move out. She had to be on the safe side. She could not take risks. Although she did not believe for a moment that Steven was a murderer, despised herself for even thinking about it, Steven would have to go. It was sensible, necessary. She had made up her mind, and that was it. She did not have to give reasons. There were reasons enough, already spelled out. She just had to make sure that Mark was safe, that was all.

She lifted the lid of the kettle and turned the tap on full, splashing herself. She was glad that she had made up her mind . . . and nothing would change it.

Steven felt that he had been catapulted into madness, a madness that was not his or of his own making. He found himself thinking in terms as ancient as they were alien. He had spent the best, the most important night of his life only to have it dashed from him in the morning. To drive the point home, Georgia had thrown him out of the flat. Steven understood about crime and punishment, the wages of sin. But he did not believe in sin and certainly could not describe what had passed between himself and Leigh by that name. Yet he was punished, first by her madness, her wild babblings about telepathy and he really did not remember what else, and then by her terrible cold remoteness, telling him to go. And on top of that, Georgia's decision. Coming so fast, one on top of the other, they were unavoidably connected in his mind.

In seconds, everything had changed. When he had pursued Leigh out of the kitchen, his nudity had suddenly diminished him. He'd felt ludicrous. He had become an embarrassed man, hopping on one leg to get his pants on, while Leigh turned her back on him, cold and remote. He saw but did not understand why his laughter had driven such a gulf between them. Perhaps that was the nature of the species? Perhaps it was all his fault for believing in such fantasies, for having allowed himself to be drawn into Leigh's. He had needed a rude awakening and he had got it both from her tense anger and unconcealed impatience to get him out of the flat and from Georgia's set face and harsh voice when, later, he had gone to the flat to change his clothes.

"I've been doing a lot of hard thinking, Steve, and I've reached my decision. I want you to go, now. I've got to have time, space to sort myself out. I can't do that with you here. I get too tense, too nervous. Of course you can come to see Mark; phone me. We'll work something out, but please just pack what you need and leave now."

But for Leigh, he might have fought her unilateral decision or felt some palpable regret. After all, the curtain was coming down on fifteen years of his life and he felt powerless to stop it. That was the sum total his shattered emotions could come up with, and he felt cheated as well as punished.

When later that same morning, Heather, Dr. Zimmer's receptionist, called his office and asked him to stop by around noon because the doctor had received some of his test results, he did not at first know what she was talking about. He agreed grudgingly, wondering how on earth that mattered now. But going to Sonia Zimmer's office, making some show of interest seemed like a conscious attempt to get back into his own life, to wipe out the weekend that had fractured it, everything.

Sonia Zimmer sat, businesslike as ever, behind her desk, her white coat open, leafing through her notes on him.

"Mm-hm. Sit down, Steven. X rays fine. Cardiogram excellent. Your eyesights deteriorating. Nothing to worry about," she said, peering at him owlishly through her own heavily framed bifocals. "You should have another test in six months. Will you fix that?"

"Yes, sure," he said. "Could that be the cause of the headaches?"

"Maybe. But usually with eye problems one experiences a duller, regular kind of pain. More like a tension headache, located in the forehead region. No, I tend to rule that out, which leads me to the bad news."

"Oh?" He almost wanted it to be dreadful, something cataclysmic that would blot out his present worries.

She slapped a sheaf of printout paper, regularly folded, down on the desk where he could see.

"Your encephalogram is a bit crazy. Probably a machine malfunction. The girl should have spotted it at the time."

Steven stared uncomprehendingly at the more-or-less-even pattern of zigzag lines that suddenly erupted into a wide band of crossed and muddled ones. The lines seemed to have been etched with incredible energy, as though something (the machine?) was trying to erase something (his brain?). He looked up at Sonia, who smiled.

"This is impossible," she said, pointing the tip of a pencil at the thickest mass of muddled lines. "You must have it done again. I've called them. They can fit you in at four-fifteen."

"Does it really matter?" Steven asked.

"It most certainly does. What's the matter with you today? You seem more depressed."

"Well, that's about it. I didn't have a very good weekend, to put it mildly."

"Domestic trouble?"

"Something like that."

"Oh well, Steven, if you need a shoulder to cry on . . ."

"Thanks. But I guess it'll sort itself out."

"I hope so. Meanwhile, keep the appointment, please. I'll have the rest of the tests tomorrow or Wednesday. We can discuss the new EEG, then too. I've told them to make it priority."

"Thanks." He did not relish the thought of having all those little electrodes fixed to his scalp again. He had thought last time that it was like a process from some horror film in which the villain attempts to burn out the hero's brains.

"Don't brood, Steven. Try to cheer up. It's amazing what a shift of attitude can do. I'll get Heather to buzz you as soon as we have these results."

He thanked her again and went out. He knew all to well about shifts of attitude. One moment you were adjusting to the biggest and most important adventure of your life, and the next you saw a crazy person to whom you could not possibly relate.

Partly to deny his confusing thoughts and fears, he went straight to the pool and quickly changed into his trunks. Even his body felt alien to him. But it had pleased her, and suddenly all the months of effort, swimming, dieting had taken on their true meaning. It had been for her, not Georgia, as though his body had known that she must come to claim him, but that it must first undergo this ritual honing and cleansing.

These thoughts made his stomach turn. They would not be acceptable in a wet, dreamy adolescent, let alone in a grown man. He flopped awkwardly and ungainly into the water, all grace gone, and swam furiously, punishing himself.

It was all some sort of weird turn-on for her, he supposed, the hypnosis and the strange, exhausted reaction afterward. The whole process was patently some unpleasant ritual necessary to her. God alone knew what she had done while he was "out."

Then, he remembered, with pin-sharp clarity, lying on a bed, looking at a ceiling in a strange, green light. His clothes undone, awry, a terrible feeling of guilt . . .

He plunged his head beneath the water. She had undone his pants while he was asleep, had done something to him? He remembered that wet stickiness at his groin. Well thanks a lot, he thought angrily. At least you might have let me in on it. Afterward, he realized, he had not felt acute physical desire for hours. He had lain beside her, watching her rest, and then had listened to her fantastical tale of mystery drugs and psychic powers, and he had been quite content, happy even. Well, that wasn't natural, not for a man to lie so close, so intimately with a woman, such a beautiful and desirable woman, without wanting; unless, of course, he too was in postorgasmic lethargy, his body demanding time to recover and recharge. He was beginning to get the measure of her psychic powers, all right. *Drug* was the operative word in her wild story, the one he now pounced on eagerly. He'd read a little about America's so-called drug culture. Probably she'd been high on something, spaced-out all the time. A zombielike predator, her mind and senses so scrambled by drugs that the only way she could enjoy sex was by surrounding it with spurious rituals and power games. Didn't she say herself that she "tripped out"? Jesus, what kind of fool was he? She filled him with loathing. He thought how Georgia would laugh if Georgia ever found out. Leigh was a freaked-out junkie, a chemical dependent, a bitch. But he'd not been entirely wrong with his pathetic thoughts of sorcery. She was a latter-day Circe, one who used drugs for charms and men like pigs.

His anger felt good, revivifying as he toweled himself dry. He blamed Georgia. He would never have been so blind, so stupid, and so vulnerable if she hadn't put him under such intolerable pressure. He was glad to be out of her life. As for Leigh, well . . . It was his duty to alert the hospital to what she was—a tripped-out nymphomaniac. God, he pitied any patient of hers. His anger gave him his appetite back. Dressed, he hurried to the cafeteria and loaded his plate with all the starch and fattening foods he had denied himself for months.

He would be gross. He would be anything he wanted. He was his own man.

The day crawled by. Leigh got through it on what she privately called "autopilot." It was by no means the best seminar she'd conducted, but at least she had managed to hang in there, make a show of concentration and concern. Then she had lunch with Dr. Rathbone, a nice, avuncular man, who seemed genuinely interested in working with her. Afterward, she saw his patient and cheated on the assessment. She hated doing it, she hated eavesdropping, as she called it, but it was either that or be seen to fail, be incompetent, indecisive, and unprofessional. She "read" the man's mind, tuned into his thoughts while seeming to listen to his loquacious and devious statement. She gave what she thought and hoped was a reasonably competent first assessment and asked for a second consultation before writing a final, detailed report. Rathbone seemed to like what he mistook for her professional caution.

She only had herself to blame. She knew what she was risking, what she almost certainly was getting into, and her clear duty now, to herself and to her colleagues, was to get her own act together. She could and she must blot Steven Cole right out of her mind. It would be as though it had never happened. In time she would stop hurting. In time, she might even believe in involuntary telepathic communication as a mere hypothesis again. She told herself this even as she hung around in the corridor outside Dr. Zimmer's office. She had been downstairs to the flower shop and was carrying a small pot of African violets as a gift for Heather. But she did not go in. She walked up and down, waiting, telling herself she was crazy, playing with fire, and that she had to let go of this obsession: it would destroy her.

But her pulsebeat stubbornly quickened when she saw Dr. Zimmer come out of the office, calling some instruction over her shoulder to Heather, and stride away down the corridor. It was now or never, Leigh thought. Or she could just deliver the plant and go home, forget all about it. She opened the door cautiously, peeped in. The room was empty, just as she had hoped and perhaps known that it would be. She knew for certain that the pile of folders standing beside Heather's desk, awaiting filing, contained Steven's notes. The door connecting Heather's office with Dr. Zimmer's was ajar, and Leigh could hear the receptionist moving around in there. She walked to the desk, making no noise, and set the plant down. Then, keeping an eye on the open door she flipped through the pile of folders until she found his. She didn't even feel guilty. The EEG was on top. She did not need to lift it out. Dr. Zimmer, she assumed, had folded it at the telltale section, had probably puzzled over it. Leigh longed to, even considered removing it, but a glance was enough. She closed the folder, tidied the stack.

"Hello? Is anyone there?" she called, leaning over Heather's desk to adjust the plant.

"Oh, hello." Heather came out of the other room, smiling.

"I just wanted to thank you for your kindness the other day and to apologize for scaring you. I hope you like plants." Leigh stood back, aware that she was acting and doing it rather well. Maybe she would feel guilty later.

"Oh, that's lovely. You shouldn't have. You're really very kind."

"So are you," Leigh said warmly. "I really appreciate *all* your help."

Jane Paget was silent and rather grim faced as she fitted the electrodes to Steven Cole's skull, skillfully parting his fine dark hair and altering the position of his head with a light but firm pressure of the hand. Dr. Zimmer had a reputation for being something of a dragon, and Jane Paget was still smarting from the dressing down the doctor had given her. She would admit that she had perhaps skimped on her check of the printout in order to meet Dr. Zimmer's request for speed, but she was not incompetent, and she knew there was nothing wrong with the machine. All the other EEGs she had done that day were fine, and she had made all the usual checks. But as far as Zimmer was concerned the buck had to stop somewhere and Jane Paget had been elected.

It was not really surprising that some of her resentment was directed at Steven, but if he noticed it, he ignored it. When all the electrodes were in place and secure, Jane went to the machine, checked it, ran a test, and then told Steven, "Hold very still now."

She was, as specifically instructed, using a different machine, and as the printout began to slot rhythmically into the collecting tray, she noted, rather smugly, that everything was in order.

"Very still," she repeated automatically. "Won't be long now." It was a routine formula she always said to reassure the patients and keep their concentration focused. It was amazing how difficult people found stillness, and for a moment she thought Steven Cole must have gotten up off the couch and started to dance a jig. One glance, however, showed that he was lying exactly where she had put him and keeping quite still. Even so, the recording pens flew over the paper, scratching a pattern every bit as confused and extraordinary as that of the first test.

"Just a minute," she said, believing that there *must* be a malfunction. She stopped recording, ran a routine check on the machine. All was perfectly normal. But when she switched it on again, the same wild activity was immediately recorded. Jane stared incredulously at the machine. There was nothing wrong with it, but what it was recording was impossible. She was experienced, had been in this job three years, and she knew that no brain could produce that amount of activity. Something cold seemed to brush against her spine. She switched the machine off.

"Can you hang on a minute, Mr. Cole? I just want to check something."

"Not another malfunction?" he asked, grumbling.

"No . . . no . . . Just hang on a minute, will you?"

She was not going to risk another carpeting from Dr. Zimmer, she vowed, as she hurried out of the clinic and into her cubbyhole of an office. It gave her a feeling of satisfaction to pick up the phone and say, "Dr. Zimmer? Jane Paget here. I've got Mr. Cole on the EEG now, and I think you'd better come and have a look at the results for yourself. Yes, right now if you don't mind."

When she hung up curtly, she was actually smiling.

Steven hardly ever used the hospital staff bar. It was too noisy and virtually no one he knew ever went there, but that evening all the things he hated about it provided a sort of protective wall between him and his problems. He knew that he ought to make an effort to find somewhere to stay: his hastily packed bags were still in the car, and he had no idea where he would spend the night. It seemed rather late now to wish himself on friends, no matter how hospitable they might be. They liked to be given notice, time to make up beds, redistribute children to create room for visitors. The trouble was that all his friends were known in common with Georgia, and he could not face heart-to-heart discussions, not even with the best-intentioned. He wondered what, if anything, Georgia had told people. If she had kept it to herself he did not want to be the bringer of bad news. In fact, he rather liked the idea of being homeless, footloose and fancy free. He looked around the bar as though seeking an opportunity to test and exercise his new freedom. He could be like those young students over there, without a care in the world, free of responsibility, opportunities stretched like a carpet before their charmed feet. He wasn't too old. He finished his third double with a gulp and immediately felt the effects of it. He'd better watch it. He needed to relieve himself, too. He'd do that and then have one for the road and then he'd find a hotel or something. He knocked against the table as he stood up, making his empty glass slide from its coaster. He set off for the men's room, weaving slightly, pleasantly amused by the careful effort required to set one foot evenly in front of the other. Somebody held the swinging door for him, and he felt a burst of true gratitude for such courtesy. Then he was in the lavatory and could not remember why he had come there. He must be a little drunk, he thought. It would be a good idea to sit down. He felt a little wobbly at the knees. There was only one place he could sit down, and so, staggering a little, he bolted himself into a cubicle and sat down heavily, his head in his hands.

There was no pleasure in waiting. The rain fell in steady curtains, so that the few people who passed his hiding place did so hurriedly and often shielded under umbrellas. He could not stand still but paced restlessly, concealed from the road by the high back wall of the Fitness Center. Its only windows on that side were long narrow strips set immediately below the roof to prevent peepers into the gymnasium and changing rooms. He waited in spite of the rain, which made his clothing soggy and bad smelling, although he risked a chill and sensed that tonight his vigil was probably in vain. The possibility made him angry. The notice was there for all to see, taped to the larger and more traditionally placed windows of the building's facade: BOYS' JUDO CLASS 8:00 P.M.

The perfect opportunity, spoiled by the rain, the well-lit highway onto which the building faced, with its bus stops and new housing development. He hoped against hope that one at least, knowing like him of the gap in the railings, which separated him from the pavement, would cut across the rainswept recreation ground where the trees dripped a second rain and the earth was turned to mud. He waited, his anger mounting with frustration and dying hope. He paced, grinding his teeth, moving his hands in his pockets. The right pocket hung lower with the weight of the knife he longed to use. He had planned it exactly, had drawn lines on pictures of boys, had practiced with a sharp needle on innocent paper.

He waited until he heard the regular creak and slam of the street door, heard rapid, padding footsteps and young voices calling to each other. He moved then from the back wall of the building to the dripping shelter of a group of trees. From there he had a view of the glistening pavements, slick in the lights of passing cars. Two boys went by, sports bags slung over their hunched shoulders, their hair damp from the locker room showers or the rain. All those that passed were in groups of two or three, sometimes more. The lights in the gym behind him went out. Soon all the lights would be turned off and the caretaker would lock the building for the night and cycle slowly away. Knowing this his anger coiled into tension, became a bad taste in his mouth.

The door creaked and slammed again. His heart quickened when he heard no key turn in the lock. Risking his own safety, he pressed a little closer to the railings where the lights of a passing car might reveal him. The boy came slowly along the pavement and beautifully alone. The man's heart stopped, seemed to rise into his throat. A terrible joy came with it, stilling his twitching busy fingers. The boy stopped in a pool of lamplight, which showed his water-darkened fair hair, his maroon bomber jacket with the collar turned up against the rain. He put down his bag suddenly and squatted to tie the sodden lace of his black-and-yellow training shoe.

Hope surged. The gods were kind after all. And the man did something he had never done before. He whistled softly to attract the boy's attention. The boy looked up, looked around, saw nothing, and returned to his shoelace, making a secure double bow. The man whistled again, a blackbird calling through the rain, and this time the boy's keen ears pinpointed the direction of the sound. His pale face turned to the patch of deeper shadow beneath the trees and, curious, picking up his bag, he walked toward the railings.

## "N<sub>ooo!</sub>"

Steven flung out his arms. His fists banged against the metal partition walls of the lavatory cubicle, making them boom and rattle. His cry of fear and pain added to the din. His hands slipped from the cold gray walls. He did not know where he was. Voices came to him. Voices thick with alarm, shouting instructions, inquiring. He turned wildly in the confined space. Slowly, as the pain and panic subsided, he recognized the door and fumbled open the catch.

Two young medical students, their faces pale with shock, caught him as he stumbled out of the cubicle. He could not make out what they were saying to him. He pushed them away, retreated back into the cubicle, his stomach turning to liquid; he knew he was going to be sick.

They were very kind, the students. They waited and, after he had washed his face, helped him back into the bar and fetched a brandy for him. Since he could not explain to them he let them think that he had been roaring drunk. He realized, with a dull feeling of loss, that there was only one person to whom he could explain or rather recount what had just happened to him. One of the students offered to drive him home and Steven remembered that he did not have a home. He said no thanks, he could manage quite well. Let them think him mad, a prey to fits and seizures. They might be right for all he knew. The brandy, taken in small sips, calmed his stomach, revived his nerve. As soon as he decently could, he thanked the students, bought them a drink, and made his way out of the bar, holding himself erect and walking with deliberate steadiness.

* * *

Leigh did not immediately answer the bell. She went instead to the front window, pulled back the curtains a little, and looked down. Through the rain she recognized his car, parked across the road, under a streetlight. She let the seconds pass, grow into an interminable minute before Steven stepped out from the shelter of the porch, his face turned palely up to the window. She let the curtain fall back into place.

She did not want to let him in, was afraid where it would lead. She had washed her hands of him. But she also thought it likely that he had been drinking, and when he pressed the bell again, keeping his finger on the button, she feared that he would disturb the neighbors, perhaps start shouting up at the window. Her mind was made up; she ran down the stairs, left her own front door open, and put on the hall lights. He was leaning against the side of the porch and looked to be on the point of collapse. It seemed to cost him a great effort just to raise his head and look at her with desperate eyes.

"Please, can I come in?"

"I don't think so."

"Please, I've got to talk to you."

"No, really, I don't think—"

"For God's sake . . ." His voice rose hysterically. Leigh sensed rather than saw a movement at the window to her right. It would be even worse to have a scene on the doorstep, in eye and earshot of the people downstairs. "Please, just let me come in," he said, obviously making an effort to get his voice under control.

Leigh stepped aside, wordlessly inviting him in. She closed the door and watched him climb her stairs like an old man, pulling himself up by the bannister. She followed, closing and locking her own door, fitting her pace to his. At the top he paused, hanging on to the bannister, swaying a little. She hurried then, afraid that he might lose his balance and fall back down the stairs. She supposed he was drunk, and anger flared in her. He went into her sitting room and fell rather than sat on the old-fashioned sofa. Leigh put on more lights and stood looking down at him. His lips had an unpleasant grayish tinge and were pulled down at the corners by deeply etched lines.

"You'd better have some coffee," she said.

She had made a fresh pot half an hour ago, and she stood

quietly in the kitchen, waiting for it to heat up. She would feed him coffee, sober him up, and get him out of here. In order to do that she had to keep her mind completely detached from him. She had to blank him out, hear only his words. She poured the coffee, hot and strong and black, and added brown sugar, which would be good for him whether he liked it or not.

He was sitting forward, his hand dangling between his knees. She held the mug out to him.

"Careful, it's hot."

"Thanks."

He took the coffee and set it aside, stood up and pulled off his damp raincoat, draping it across the plump arm of the sofa. Then he sat again, as though exhausted. Leigh moved to the chair in which she had been sitting before he rang the bell.

"It happened again," he said. "That's why I had to see you."

"What happened again?" she asked without warmth or noticeable curiosity.

"I don't know." He shook his head and reached for the coffee, held it as though to warm his hands against the china.

Leigh refused to prompt or lead him. If something had happened, let him find his own way through it. By laughing, he had rejected her and all her talents. In the telling, if he could tell it, he might understand. She picked up the book she had been reading and closed it, marking her place with the flap of the dust jacket. She heard the rain beating against the window as Steven gingerly sipped the coffee.

"I went to the bar," he said, speaking slowly and in a quiet voice, as though marshaling his thoughts anew for each sentence he spoke. "I had several drinks, too many. I knew I was drunk but not incapable. I went to the loo. I felt very weak, tired. I had to sit down, and then . . ." His voice tightened, threatened to veer out of control. He paused, drank some more coffee.

"Crazy as this may sound, I was standing outside in the rain. God it was wet. I can still feel it." Without knowing that he did so, he hunched his shoulders as though to make himself small against the rain. "Only it wasn't me. *He* was waiting. I know the exact place. Waiting. Walking up and down. Restless, unable to keep still. And I knew what he was waiting for, what he was going to do. I felt it," he said, lifting his eyes to hers. They were haunted, almost blind with shock.

Leigh did not move, did not help him. "There was a boy," he went on at last, his voice shaking now. "He stopped to tie his shoelace. And the man . . . he whistled, whistled to the boy . . . like this." He made a soft, low whistling sound. Its very ordinariness struck a chill in Leigh. She could almost see if for herself, the dark and the rain, the vulnerable boy being whistled to. She clasped her hands tightly together, refused to imagine any more.

"The boy got up and went toward him, where he was standing. He was going to kill him," Steven said. "I could feel the weight of the knife in his pocket and . . . and . . ."

Even the despair in his voice as he spoke these last faltering words did not prepare her for the sobs that followed. He covered his face with one hand, fumbled to set the mug on the carpet with the other. He cried openly and bitterly, as though he was a child and lost. Leigh waited for the storm to pass, knowing it would and that it would help him. She got up quietly and went into the bedroom, came back with a box of Kleenex, which she placed on the sofa beside him. He sniffed, mumbled his thanks. She sat down again, not wanting to embarrass him. He helped himself liberally to the tissues, mopped his face and blew his nose several times. Then he took a noisy gulp of coffee and said, "Sorry . . . I'm sorry about that."

"It's okay. You needed to." She paused, forming her next question carefully. "You said that it had happened *again*. Tell me about the first time."

He shook his head but not to deny what she asked. Playing with a tissue, shredding it between his fingers, he spoke between sniffs and swallows.

"Waiting again. Under some tree . . . It was lighter, dusk maybe. A boy with a soccer ball, chasing a soccer ball . . . It isn't so clear. The boy came toward him through the bushes. And then . . . no, I can't, it's not clear."

"And the time before that?" Leigh asked quietly.

"No." He shook his head from side to side, very definite. "Those are the only times. Nothing else."

"And the headaches?"

"Bad again. I didn't know where I was. I behaved like a maniac, hitting out at the walls of the lavatory. Christ."

Leigh waited for a new spasm to pass. She offered more coffee, but he shook his head, refusing it.

"I saw your EEG this afternoon," she said.

"Oh? How did you manage that?" It was a mechanical response, spoken without real interest.

"By a cheap trick, of which I'm not very proud."

"It's no good anyway. They had to do it again."

"Oh? How did that go?"

Steven shrugged. "I don't know. The technician sent for Dr. Zimmer. They had a look at the printout, and then Sonia said it was fine."

"I don't believe her," Leigh said, snapping out the words. But she did not blame her, either. She would not want to believe what she saw, even if she comprehended it. And she certainly wouldn't want to be the one to tell Steven. Who would, Leigh thought miserably.

"What does it matter anyway?" he asked, leaning back on the sofa and closing his swollen eyes.

"It matters. It proves what's happening to you. At least to my satisfaction," she added.

He opened his eyes and looked at her. Leigh was afraid. Everything depended on this moment and on him. If he could admit it now, she could help him. If he denied it, threw it back at her . . .

"You mean what you said . . . about . . . what was it? Involuntary telepathic communication?"

"Yes."

"I . . . don't understand."

That was something, she thought, far better than an outright denial.

"Your EEG shows massive bursts of activity, almost unbelievable. Since you are not dead of a brain hemorrhage, there is only one possible explanation. At those moments, the machine records the brain waves of two people, two separate people. If it is possible to unscramble the separate lines—and frankly I doubt that if is—then I am certain they would show two distinct patterns overlapping, and I'm afraid one of them is very disturbed indeed."

Steven continued to stare at her and to remain, outwardly at least, quite calm.

"How is that possible?" he asked at last.

"In one sense it isn't. In another, it's long been accepted as a hypothesis that two people could so link mentally, telepathically, as to provide this sort of proof, but it's never been done. I think now that the basic error was in our assumption." Warming to her subject, Leigh leaned toward him. She was the professional, explaining to a slow student. "We've always thought that such a phenomenon, if it could occur, would happen to two people who were naturally very close. Twins, for example. It never occurred to us that it might happen between total strangers. Unless," she said taking a calculated risk, "you know who the waiting man is?"

"No." He sounded appalled. "Of course I don't." He leaned forward, his face growing paler. "Wait a minute. You believe there is someone, a man . . . there is someone other than me?"

"Definitely."

"Oh, thank God. I can't tell you what a relief—"

"That's what I tried to tell you this morning. Someone who can reach you, enter your mind just as, probably, you can his."

"I thought it must be me. I thought I must be—"

"No," Leigh said with quiet conviction. "You must never think that. Whatever happens. Steven, this is not your doing. You are not to blame. Do you believe me?"

She almost reached out to him but drew back her hand before he noticed the gesture. He stared at her, his eyes less haunted, almost gentle.

"You said my name . . ."

"Well of course."

"No, I mean it makes me feel . . . real. It makes me feel safe for the first time this evening."

"Do you believe what I just said to you?" she said insistently.

"I want to. Yes."

"Then it will be all right. We must find a way to control it, for you to learn—"

"We?" he asked quickly, interrupting her.

"I'll help you, if you'll let me and if you want me to. I'd

better also say that I think I'm the only person, at least right here, who can help you."

"Please, please help me."

His look, his voice pierced her front. She felt her professionalism waver.

"We'll talk in the morning," she made herself say. "I must think what's best to do, how to tackle this. You're too tired now, anyway. You've had a bad time. Only, Steven, you must promise me one thing."

"What?" He looked at her with a kind of devotion that scared her a little.

"You mustn't go back on this. You mustn't persuade yourself that this is all some kind of fantasy or bad dream. If you doubt me, change your mind about what I've told you, then I can't help you and I can't handle what it does to me personally. Before I can do anything, I have to be sure that you understand and believe."

"Of course."

"And no matter how much it hurts you, I want you to remember what you saw and experienced. I want you to remember that man and everything you can about him. You must never deny his existence or think that he is you. Promise me."

He nodded and then said, as though the realization had just come to him, "He's a murderer, he's the one who—"

"Yes. We know what he is, what he does. Now we have to find out who he is and how to stop him."

"But—"

"No. Not now. I don't know yet myself. I have to work on this. Tomorrow. Look, I'll come straight to your office and we'll work something out. Right now, you're very tired and I . . ." She picked up his coat and held it out to him.

"Can I stay here?" he asked, avoiding her eyes. "Georgia really has thrown me out. I swear."

Slowly, she let the coat drop. He looked at her with an almost pleading expression, and this time it was she who looked away.

"As long as you stay right there," she said firmly. "I'll fetch you a blanket."

* * *

Leigh was dozing lightly, her mind circling and worrying to find ways of helping him, when she heard Steven blundering about the sitting room. A crash suggested that he had knocked something over and was followed by a muffled curse or cry. She got up at once, hurried into the hall just as he found the light switch and put it on.

"What's wrong?" she asked.

He had knocked over a little magazine stand and was in the act of righting it.

"I'm sorry. I didn't mean to disturb you."

"It's okay."

He was fully dressed, and although he did not look rested, his skin was a better color beneath the dark peppering of stubble on his cheeks and chin. He picked up his raincoat, which, it seemed, he had been using as an extra bedcover.

"Can't you sleep?" Leigh asked, trying to keep her mounting anxiety to herself. "Has something happened?"

"I'm going to the police."

Leigh relaxed a little, realizing that she had been afraid that the man had made contact again, was dragging Steven off somewhere into a danger she could not yet combat and which he, she was sure, did not even suspect.

"At this hour?" she said, more to calm him than because it mattered.

"Yes. I should have gone last night. I just didn't think of it. Why didn't you suggest it?" He struggled into his raincoat and came toward her. Leigh remained where she was, effectively blocking the doorway. Now she went farther into the room and closed the door behind her. "What are you doing?"

"Steven, wait, just a minute."

"I must go."

"What for, Steven? What are you going to tell them?"

"What I know, of course. They might not even have found that boy yet."

"Stop right there, okay?" She held up her hand as though to hold back his rapid speech. "Just listen to me. The police will not believe you. And if you mean the boy you 'saw' last night, you don't even know that he's dead."

"He was going to kill him. I *know* it."

"But you didn't actually see him do it, did you? Or were you holding back on me?"

"No, I told you everything." He looked at her, puzzled. She could see that she had planted a seed of doubt in his mind.

"If you go in there reporting a murder that maybe hasn't even been committed, what conclusions do you think they'll draw? And what will they think if you *are* right? Have you thought about that?"

Slowly, he understood what she was getting at. Understanding dawned on his face and robbed it of color.

"Oh my God," he whispered.

"Exactly. The truth is, Steven, you know too much and not nearly enough. And as policemen, they're going to say that only one person could have known what you know."

"The murderer," he said, his voice hoarse with shock.

"Or an accomplice," Leigh added, nailing the point home.

He turned away, groping for a chair with his hands like a blind man. He sat down and put his head in his hands, shaking it a little. Leigh stood beside him, close but not touching.

"Thank God you woke. I nearly . . ." He turned his face up to her, his eyes flinching with fear.

"You'll have to be so very careful," she told him gently. "First we've got to find out more about him. You can, Steven. I'm sure you can. Only you."

He shook his head to show that he was confused and doubtful.

"But if he did . . . if that poor kid is lying out there . . ." He looked grief stricken at the window.

"Okay," Leigh said, her mind leaping to a decision. "At first light we'll go there and check it out for ourselves. You know the place? You can find it?"

"Yes. But what if . . . if there is something there?"

"I'll report it. I'll say I was out for a walk or something. I'll say I found it."

"You could make them believe," he said, grasping at a straw of hope. "If you came to the police with me, they'd believe you."

She shook her head slowly, negatively.

"It was hard enough to make you believe," she reminded

him, "and you had every reason. Back home, maybe, with the backing of the Agency I work for, but here, where nobody really knows me . . ." She shook her head again. "No chance."

"I don't think I can just do nothing," he said.

"But you are going to do something. We're going to check. And when we've done that we're going to lick this situation, get enough evidence or knowledge to take to the police. If you could just find out who he is, where he lives."

"How could I do that? Don't you think every policeman in London is trying—"

"By contacting him," Leigh said excitedly. She sat down opposite him, reached out and took his hands, held them tightly in hers. "Listen to me, Steven. So far it's all been running his way. He contacts you, whether by design or accident we just don't know. But when I put you into trance maybe, just possibly, you did make contact. No, listen, you must try to understand. Think of it like this. Think of him as a radio mast, okay? A transmitter. And you're the receiver. Somehow he can switch on the current and *wham!* you're there, seeing what he's doing and feeling. Well, what we've got to do is make you into a transmitter, find a way for you to call the shots. You do see, don't you?"

"Yes," he agreed reluctantly. "I suppose. Only I don't want to do it. I don't want to go near him. He's evil."

"I know. I know. But you have to. For your own sake and for theirs—for the kids, Steven."

He nodded again, seemed close to tears.

"I thought Georgia was making too much fuss about Mark, you know, being overprotective. Last night I realized, understood I suppose, what she saw from the start." He pulled one hand free of Leigh's, wiped a tear from his eye.

"Mark?" she said softly. "He's your son?"

"Didn't I tell you?"

"I guess we . . . there wasn't much time. I seem to remember I did most of the talking. I should have thought." She let go of his other hand, drew back.

"It bothers you?"

"You have other children?"

"No. Georgia can't . . . not anymore."

"I'm sorry."

"I'm so confused, Leigh. Yesterday I thought I hated you. I mean I really worked up all sorts of crazy thoughts about you. I was angry, I suppose."

"Don't tell me. I don't want to know."

"I just feel I owe you an apology."

"Okay, and me too. I ought to be able to handle other people's unbelief by now, but I can't. I was sore at you. My pride was wounded, I guess. I should have handled it better, anyway."

"I shouldn't have laughed. You warned me. You know, I think I was more scared than amused. The idea of someone else being able to get inside my mind . . ."

"Don't."

"I'm sorry. I didn't mean you."

"I know."

"So, where do we stand now, Leigh? I feel like I'm on a crazy seesaw or something."

She straightened her back, as though about to speak, then changed her mind. She got up and walked slowly to the window, stood with her back to Steven, staring at the closed curtains.

"I don't know, Steven. I think it may be too complicated for me, either of us to handle right now."

"I'm sure I love you," he said. "That's why I wanted to tell you about yesterday, why I feel bad about it all." She did not say anything but went closer to the window, lifted a corner of the curtain and looked out. "What are you doing?" he asked, irritated by her silence, her distance from him.

"Seeing if there's any sign of light yet." She let the curtain fall, turned back to face him. "Because that's the important thing, Steven. First we've got to deal with your problem. After that, we'll see."

He wanted to argue, to beg her for some sign, some token of commitment or feeling, but he knew she was right. Unless he was, himself, free of this killer, what could he offer her?

"There's a couple of hours to dawn," she said. "We better get some rest."

"Please, stay with me."

"Steven, you're tired out . . ."

"Please!" He held out his hand, and she had no choice but to take it, hold it close in both of hers.

"All right, Steven. I'll stay with you for a while."

Steven drove through streets which, because of the purpose of their journey, seemed ominously empty. It had stopped raining, but the lead-colored sky threatened more. Leigh felt how tense he was, how reluctant to go on, but she knew that he had to go through with it and that she must observe him with professional detachment, whatever they found.

"There it is," he said, pointing as they waited at a red traffic light.

Leigh looked at the small urban enclosure of grass and trees. Its main entrance was angled to the corner formed by two main roads and consisted of an imposing Victorian archway. It resembled a scaled-down copy of the Marble Arch.

"But it's closed," she said, spotting the ugly, out-of-period gates that filled in the arch.

"Oh I don't think they ever open that entrance," he said, engaging the gears and steering left. "There's a little gate up here, right next to the Fitness Center."

"Oh."

"I'll have to turn off here and park," he said.

"Sure."

They had passed a row of winter trees, a few bushes, railings. Beyond that was a sweep of green turf, churned up by soccer cleats and puddled with the night's rain. She waited, rubbing her hands together against the cold and the damp while Steven locked the car. In silence they walked together not knowing whether they should link arms or hold hands or stay awkwardly apart.

"This it?" Leigh asked, looking at the new peak-roofed Fitness Center. Steven made a sound that she took to be confirmation. He was looking at a bright red poster, garish with shiny black letters: BOYS' JUDO CLASS 8:00 P.M.

"Come on," she said, with more cheerfulness than she felt. "Show me."

Neither of them commented on the obvious absence of the police, cordons, tarpaulins, and all. Steven did not know how to interpret this negative evidence, and although she did, Leigh could not tell him.

"He walked up and down along the back there, see, and then went into those trees there. This is the lamppost where the boy stopped."

Leigh looked where he pointed, examined.

"And then the boy walked where?"

"Over there, toward the railings where the branches dip down."

"Come on," she said, taking his arm. "We'd better look."

They went through the small open gateway, stopped for a moment to look at the blank rear wall of the Fitness Center with its strip of inaccessible windows, then Steven led her to the right, a short distance along the path, and pointed dumbly to a spot beneath the trees. There was nothing there, the imprint of feet in the soft earth, perhaps, but no signs of a struggle. And there would have been a struggle, because he would have needed to drag the boy through the small gap in the railings. Certainly there was no body.

Steven said, "He wouldn't have done it there, would he? Far too dangerous. He'd have pulled him in and . . ." His voice cracked, and she pressed his arm against her side.

"Don't."

"It feels weird, like being here and yet not . . . knowing that he was right there and yet I—Where was I, Leigh, do you know that?"

"In the hospital," she answered calmly.

"Can you be sure of that?"

"Absolutely."

"I don't see how you could know."

"Because you told me and because I believe you."

"Then what does he want with me?"

"I don't know," she said truthfully. "Perhaps nothing. Perhaps he's not even aware . . . Come on, it's cold."

"No, we must look." His eyes went immediately to the bottom of the path, to where the shrubbery grew thicker beside the stone gateway. That would indeed be the best place, she thought, but there was nothing there. There was nobody anywhere in the recreation ground. Either the murderer had failed last night or had carried his victim elsewhere. She shivered, and not this time from the cold. "Come on," he urged.

"No, Steven. There's no need. There's nothing here."

"How can you possibly . . . ?" He began angrily, but stopped when he saw her calm and quite-certain expression. His mind turned a sort of cartwheel.

"I can see, Steven. I have 'looked,' 'searched.' I can't explain it any better to you. If he were here, I could lead you straight to him. Just be glad that he's not." Her voice was troubled and weary too, as though she had explained this so often that she was bored with it and the disbelief, the arguments that were bound to follow. She sighed. "But since you have to check for yourself, go ahead. I'll walk round this way. It'll be quicker if we split up." Without waiting for him to agree, she turned back toward the Fitness Center.

He stared after her, saw the uncharacteristic droop of her shoulders, the slow futility of her pace. But he could not take something as important as this on trust. He turned too, in the opposite direction, took a few brisk steps toward the shrubbery, and then halted. But if he was to believe her, care about her as much as he intended and needed to, it had to begin with such trust. He turned around again and ran after her.

"Leigh, wait, Leigh."

"Yes?" Alarm clouded her face as she turned to him. "What is it?"

"You're right," he said, putting his hands on her shoulders. "I believe you. I don't need to check."

He saw then her face come fully alive for the first time since he had met her. Her guard was completely down, and her eyes shone; her mouth curved in a smile of complete happiness, making him want to cry out that she was beautiful.

"Oh Steven, Steven." She threw her arms around him, hugged him. "Thank you for that."

He held her tight and warm, drunk on her scent. The world and all its cares dropped away for a moment. Their eyes met, and he knew that she would let him kiss her.

Footsteps thudded toward them. Leigh turned her head to look. A young man brushed past them, jogging.

"Good morning," he said, grinning.

Leigh answered happily, waved to him.

"Oh dear," Steven said.

"Why? What's wrong?"

"He's a junior intern at the hospital," Steven told her, tucking her arm through his and leading her toward the gate. "Tongues will wag, as they say."

"Let them," she said, tilting her chin defiantly. "You don't care, do you?"

Her face was still shining, and her happiness disarmed him.

"No," he said laughing. "I don't."

"Oh, Steven, I feel so good. You make me feel so— Hey, do you know what I want?"

"No." He shook his head, puzzled and amused.

"Is there somewhere we can get breakfast? A great big unhealthy English breakfast? Please?"

She was a little girl, he thought, and the intensity of her happiness spoke most eloquently of how little she had known, how few of these moments had been granted to her.

"As it happens," he said, "there is the very place, a real workman's café just up Munster Road there."

"Well come on. What are we waiting for?"

"The car?"

"Leave the car. I want to walk. I want to work up my appetite, and I bet I can eat more than you."

"You're on."

Laughing, she hugged him quickly, then grabbed his hand and ran off, pulling him after her.

Any woman walking into the crowded café that morning would have been an object of attention to the all-male clientele; a woman as handsome and striking as Leigh almost started a riot. Her response, after a quick double take, was to burst out laughing and shout a general "good morning." In fact, Steven was more surprised than she, for he had never been out before with a woman who, through no effort of her own, automatically turned heads. She sat down at the first available table, and Steven, pulling out the chair opposite her, asked her if the place was all right.

"Sure," she said happily, pulling off her woolen hat and shaking out her hair. Its color and thickness were inevitably greeted by more murmurs and stares. Leigh looked calmly around the room, made eye contact with several of the men, her expression cool but amused. This had the effect of quelling them. They avoided her eyes, switched their attention back to laden plates and tabloid newspapers. From then on, though she remained a center of attention, they were not intrusive. "Is this counter service or waiter?" she asked, reading the permanent menu that was written large on a square of yellow card fixed to the wall.

"I expect you just yell," Steven said, and, as though on cue, a man at the table behind him did exactly that.

"Two more teas over here, Arthur, when you've got a minute."

"Two teas," the portly Arthur repeated and then, catching Steven's eye, said, "What about you, guv?"

Leigh ordered eggs, bacon, sausage, fried tomatoes, and fried bread.

"You've won the bet," Steven informed her. He could only face two poached eggs on toast.

"Maybe I won't be able to eat it all," she said, "though I certainly feel as though I could." Her expression changed as she saw little worry lines form around Steven's eyes and he began to fiddle nervously with the salt and pepper shakers. "What's wrong?" she asked, covering and stilling his hand with hers.

"I was just thinking . . . What have we proved?"

"Only that if he did kill the boy, he didn't do it there. But I think we should assume he didn't. Maybe the boy got scared and ran off. After all, there were railings between them."

"I'd like to believe that."

"You should. It won't do any good worrying about what might have been. And if he did do it somewhere else, we'll hear soon enough."

Steven nodded, but he did not look convinced. The man at the next table suddenly folded his *Daily Mirror* and picked up his cup. Steven leaned across the narrow aisle and asked if he could have a look at the paper.

"Sure, mate, be my guest. Nothing in it, as usual, 'cept old Maggie Thatcher giving the Common Market a right bollocking again. Poor buggers."

Leigh observed his face as he scanned each page. There was

nothing, not even in the late-news column. Steven handed the paper back.

"Okay now? Will you at least hope that I'm right?"

"Yes, I will. Sorry." He yawned as Arthur slid their plates onto the table and asked what they wanted to drink.

Leigh started on her breakfast with gusto, her appetite every bit as huge as she had thought it was. Steven, yawning frequently and trying to conceal the fact, only picked at his soft eggs.

"You don't absolutely have to go in to work today, do you?"

"I don't know. I hadn't thought. I don't suppose the whole place will fall apart if I don't."

"Okay, listen. I'm your doctor right now and I say you should go straight back to my place and get some sleep. In fact why don't you take a few days off?"

"Oh no, I couldn't do that. I'd only get bored."

"Steven, you won't have time. When you're rested I want you to start writing down everything you can remember, every detail no matter how small. Will you do that for me?"

Too tired to argue, he agreed.

"But that won't take me very long," he grumbled.

"I mean both 'contacts,' Steven, and then we have to start work in earnest. It'll be much easier if we have time. Don't you see that?"

"I'll think about it," he promised. "What are you going to do?"

"I'll go in. And I'll see if I can rearrange my schedule so that I can spend more time with you. Do you want me to tell somebody you're taking the day off?"

"No," he said quickly, not wanting to fuel the fires of the hospital gossip. "I'll phone."

Leigh nodded. She did not want to push him, not then. Too much pressure when he was tired and confused might make him doubt again, back off. She finished her breakfast.

"Look, a clean plate. And I feel like I'm going to burst."

"I don't know how you do it," he said.

"Maybe being happy makes me hungry."

He smiled, but it was only a wan sketch of the real thing.

"Okay, come on. Let's get you home before you fall asleep over those eggs. Shall I drive?"

"If you like. Perhaps you'd better," he admitted.

They paid for their meal and left the café. The rain had started again, and they hurried to the car. Steven drowsed as Leigh maneuvered the unfamiliar car through the tightly packed traffic and did not even notice the woman, standing in the rain, waiting for a bus to take her to work, who stared in shock and anger at the passing car.

"I saw him, I tell you," Georgia insisted, raising her voice angrily. "It's so bloody unfair. *I* need the car. *I*'ve got to get Mark to school, myself to work. *I* need it, not him. What's he need it for? Just to go joy riding with some fancy bitch."

"Oh come on, Georgia," Marion said. "It's not that bad. All right, on a rotten morning like this, I can see it must have been galling—"

"You can say that again."

"But it's your pride that's hurt. It's pride talking now."

There was a note of tetchiness in Marion's voice, which was becoming almost painfully familiar to Georgia. She had heard it in Roger's voice, and with Mark it seemed to be the only tone he had when speaking to her. Not that he did too much of that anyway. He was sulking. But she was afraid of that tone, the frequency with which she heard it, and she did not want to think about what it meant.

"Well, he's got to let me have the car. It's the least he can do."

"You haven't heard from him?" Marion asked, pushing food around her plate. Georgia's anger tended to quench her appetite.

"Not since Monday morning. That's another thing. You'd think he'd have the decency to phone, if only to see if we're okay. He could speak to Mark at least."

"It's only been five minutes, Georgia," Marion said, trying to be reasonable, "and you could always ring him."

"Why should I?"

"Well, you threw him out."

"Because he's having it off with . . ." She could not think of a suitably vicious noun for the woman she had seen driving *their* car that morning, and the other reason she had thrown Steven out was something she wanted to forget. If she ever let that slip out to anyone they would hate her or think her mad. She felt ashamed enough without having her nose rubbed in it. But even so . . .

"What was she like? Did you see her?"

"She was driving, for God's sake. Driving *my* car. No. I couldn't see her really. She was wearing one of those silly woolen caps."

"Like mine?" Marion said, touching the woolen hat she wore, pulled down over her ears.

"Oh Christ," Georgia said. "I'm sorry. I'm becoming a bitch, aren't I?"

"No, not really," Marion said, pushing her plate away and lighting a cigarette. "You're just hurt and angry."

"He's never been unfaithful before. I'd swear to it."

"But you have," Marion pointed out. "And that's what all this is really about."

"Oh, I know. You're going to say that this . . . girl . . . means nothing. I've driven him to it. He's just getting his own back or crying on her shoulder."

"Well, it might be true. You could ask him."

"Never. I don't care."

"Oh, come off it, Georgia. You're not stupid. Don't act it."

"I don't know," she sighed. "I just don't know anymore."

"How are things with Roger?" Marion asked carefully, flicking ash from her cigarette.

"About the same. I don't dare ask him to the flat yet. Mark's barely speaking to me, so God knows what he'd be like with Roger. And I can't get out—"

"Don't you dare ask me to baby-sit for a boy Mark's age," Marion said, that tone returning to her voice.

"Well, at least there hasn't been another murder. That's something I suppose."

"And Mark's a sensible kid. If you tell him to stay put while you nip out for an hour."

"Well it might just be possible if I had the car," Georgia moaned.

"Roger's got a car. He could collect you, take you for a drink." Georgia shook her head impatiently, refused to look Marion in the eyes. "Oh no, don't tell me . . ."

"What?"

"You haven't told Mark."

"No."

"Oh Georgia!"

"Don't keep saying that. I will. It's just a matter of time. He's upset about Steve going. Anyway, what am I supposed to tell him? I don't know what I'm doing."

"Excuses. You know you ought to tell him the truth, prepare him. I told my two the truth, right from the beginning."

"You weren't having an affair."

"No, and if I had been I'd probably have felt just as guilty about it as you do, with my kids anyway."

"Oh Marion. What am I going to do?"

"I don't know, love. I only wish I did."

It was dead easy to play hooky from school. The trick was to go to afternoon registration and get your name ticked off, then, instead of going to your first class, you hid in the boy's room and slipped out the back gate as soon as everyone had settled down. He didn't really know why he did it that afternoon. Certainly not to go somewhere, have a good time with his friends. He hadn't even asked Ian Cadwallader to cover for him if old Chokko, the physics teacher, asked where he was. Mark had done it before, of course, but only once and for a lark. Usually he liked school. Right now he liked school a hell of a lot more than he liked being at home. Home was dreary and depressing. He preferred his parents' fights to Mum's solitary misery. He missed his dad and wanted to know where he was.

It was a dismal day to be out on the streets with nothing to do and nowhere to go. Once outside the gate he turned his head and looked almost nostalgically at the brightly lit classroom windows of the school, but having left, he couldn't very well go back in. He dug his hands in his parka pockets and set off down the road, toward the park. At least it wasn't raining, but it was cold and damp, and the sky looked like it could fall on top of your head any minute.

He crossed the main road, slipping between honking traffic, and turned down by the tennis courts. Too late he realized that some neighbor, someone he knew might spot him and tell his mum. He should have used the other gate, but it was too much trouble now. The pavement was slick with wet leaves, and he walked slowly, his eyes fixed on the ground. He didn't really care if someone did tell her. It was all her fault anyway.

Somebody bumped into him, someone hurrying out of the telephone booth that stood about halfway down the road. He wouldn't have been angry, but the sight of the phone booth gave him an idea. He had some money somewhere. That was another thing. He hadn't had his allowance this week because she'd forgotten to go to the bank. If he'd had some money he could have gone to the pictures or something. From the clutter of his various pockets he fished out a handful of coins, among which was a five-pence piece, enough to make a phone call.

He felt quite excited as he dialed the hospital number, pushed his money into the slot, and asked for his father's extension. It rang and rang. He was about to give up when a woman answered.

"Mr. Cole's office. Can I help you?"

"Oh, yeah. Can I speak to Mr. Cole please?"

"I'm sorry but he's not in today. Can I take a message or would you like to speak to someone else?"

"No. No thanks. It's personal."

He put the receiver down, stared at his own face in the cracked square of mirror. He should have asked, of course, or left a message. Why wasn't he in? Was he sick? Supposing something had happened to him? For the first time, as he entered the park through the large gates, he considered that his mother might have been lying to him. Maybe she did know where he was, what he was doing.

He didn't know why people split up. They just got to hate each other, he supposed. Rock stars were always going off with other girls, and so had Dave Underwood's dad, he remembered. That's why Dave and his mother had moved away. Well, he was damned if he was going to move, change schools, and lose all his friends just because . . . Only he couldn't imagine his dad going with another woman. It didn't make sense. His parents just were, were together, always had been and always . . . Only now they weren't. But his dad wouldn't. Surely he wouldn't? He remembered how he'd gone on and on about Goldie Hawn when she was in some special on TV, remembered his mum saying, "I don't know why you just don't go and live with Goldie Hawn and give us all a bit of peace."

And he'd said, "A change would be a fine thing."

But that didn't mean anything. That was like watching Raquel Welch on TV and wondering . . . Or looking at the girls in those sexy magazines Ian's brother kept under his mattress and no one was supposed to know about. His mum went on about Paul Newman but she didn't even know Paul Newman any more than his dad knew Goldie Hawn. So it couldn't be anything like that. Could it? It had to be just that they hated each other, just like he was beginning to hate them for messing everything up, ruining everything.

The rain started again, driven by gusts of wind from the river. He started to run. His bag, slung over his shoulder, bounced against his back. He stood morosely in the mouth of the tunnel that passed under Putney Bridge approach and watched the rain fall. A couple of old women took shelter there, too, moaning on about the weather and the price of things in the shops. When the rain slackened a bit, he climbed the steps to the road and turned down Fulham High Street. All the cars and buses had their lights on, making it seem like night, much later than it was. He had to think up something. There was still more than an hour until the end of school. He felt his latchkey in his pocket and wondered if he dared risk it.

He shouldered open the door of The Amusement Palace, pretending not to notice the sign that said LOITERERS PROHIBITED. He was a loiterer, he supposed, because he had no money to play the machines. He stood and watched a black kid, wearing a Rasta hat, play and lose at Space Invaders. When the kid moved on, Mark fiddled with the machine for a bit, imagining that he was really scuppering ship after ship. There wasn't anything else to do. The rain was falling relentlessly now, seemed to have set in for the night. Mark shrugged and left, slowly. He'd have to go home. One good thing about his dad taking off with the car was that his mother couldn't collect him from school anymore. And if she got home early or old Mrs. Thomas downstairs saw him and stopped him, he could always say they'd been sent home because one of the teachers was out sick. It was a risk but one he would have to take.

Now that he had a purpose he hurried past the dirty little garden place where tramps and other creepy characters gathered, staring at the passersby with their blank eyes, like dead people. He hated that place, always had. He slowed a little and twisted his face to look over the scrubby old bushes at the benches. The rain had driven them off, in search of shelter, all but one. An old man, very military looking and well turned out—not a tramp at all. An upright old man who sat beneath the dripping trees, his gloved hands clasped on the top of an old-fashioned cane, leered at Mark, beckoning with his pale eyes. The boy began to run then, skidded round the corner into Park Road and headed for home as fast as his legs would carry him.

Bertie Page had often likened the practice of clinical psychology to the "art" of detection and, as he left the meeting called by Dr. Zimmer late that afternoon, it was with the sense of being hot on the trail of something juicy. Representatives of the major hospital departments had been at the meeting, and in turn they had pored over and commented upon Steven Cole's extraordinary EEG. Page himself had had the least to say, but it had carried as much weight as his colleagues' contributions. They were baffled, dealing in guesses and hypotheses. The only certain conclusion was Zimmer's own: that the headaches Cole complained of were certainly caused by these phenomenal electrical charges.

Page had said that the brain-wave patterns, if indeed they were an accurate record, would lead him to suspect a deeply disturbed personality. As to their cause and periodicity, he would guess at a sudden, massive upsurge of emotion—fear, perhaps, or anger. Something sufficient to increase the electrical output and dramatically alter the pattern. He had sat out the rest of the meeting almost in silence, making a tent of his fingers and nodding his head now and then in sage agreement. What had set his curiosity alight was the fact that Cole had taken the day off and had left a phone number at which he could be reached in case of emergency. But the hospital would have his home number on file. Cole's excellent secretary— Page had once tried to steal her from Steven—would know it as well as her own. So why would Cole leave another number?

Under the pretext of taking a second considered look at the EEG tracings, Page had seen the number Zimmer had evidently noted in its margin.

"Perhaps I could take this and study it more carefully?" he had suggested. "You never know. I might come up with something." A pleasant little plan was already forming in his mind.

No one else wanted it. Indeed, they were rather glad to pass it over, let someone else attempt to unravel it. He carried it back to his office like a prize and went straight to his confidential filing cabinet, which he unlocked with a small key attached to a watchless gold chain he wore looped across his bulging belly. The number Cole had given and which Zimmer had scribbled on a corner of the printout was indeed Leigh Duncan's. He smiled happily. Just as he had thought. Then, his smile slowly fading, he spent several minutes reading through Leigh's personal file before buzzing his secretary and instructing her to call Miss Duncan and have her be sure to see him before she left.

Since Leigh was only in the next room, she tapped on his door seconds later, just as he was settling into his creaky chair.

"Ah, Leigh. How prompt."

Her eyes went at once to the EEG prominently displayed on Page's desk. She immediately made her face into a politely blank mask.

"You wanted to see me?"

"Indeed I did. Do sit down. Something very interesting has come up. I've been to a meeting with Dr. Zimmer, Dr. Pargetter and several other senior colleagues. About this." He pushed the pile of paper toward Leigh, his small eyes delightedly narrowed on her face.

She looked at it, made a show of inspecting it. What seemed to leap out at her and burn itself into her mind was her own telephone number, faintly penciled on one corner.

"Most unusual," she said, refolding the sheets and pushing them back toward Page.

"Isn't it? And it occurred to me that it might be right up your street," he said, giving his beard a little tug, "given your special interests."

"Oh? What interests are those, Dr. Page?"

"Do call me Bertie, dear. It's so much cosier."

Leigh acknowledged this with a slight bow of the head.

"What special interests?"

"Why your interest in the paranormal for one," he answered blithely.

"You think this might be evidence of paranormal phenomena?" Leigh asked. The note of incredulity in her voice was quite genuine. She had not thought that Page could so easily overcome his prejudice against the subject—a prejudice he had made abundantly clear at their first meeting—and reach an accurate conclusion.

"Frankly, no, but it would be a worthwhile avenue of approach, don't you agree? Exceptional evidence perhaps requires exceptional methods of investigation. And we must make use of your . . . er . . . special talents while you're here, mustn't we? That's if you have the time?"

Leigh pulled the printout firmly back to her side of the desk. She was itching to get her hands on it but did not intend to let Page know it.

"I'll be pleased to take a look at it for you," she said. "Did the meeting reach any conclusions?"

"No. I personally offered a quite interesting hypothesis."

"Really? I'd be delighted to hear it."

"I stress," he said, visibly flattered, "that it is only a hypothesis but . . ." He went on to repeat his comments on a deeply disturbed personality, a sudden upsurge of emotion causing intense electrical discharge. "I had rather hoped you might be able to throw some instant light on the matter," he concluded, smiling.

Leigh was excited. He had hit on something she had missed. It began to fall into place. She lifted the pile of paper onto her lap.

"I said," Page repeated, his voice less benign, "I had rather hoped you might be able to enlighten us at once. Just a crumb from your vast personal experience."

"Oh, why?"

"Well partly because—and I'm surprised you didn't ask this—it is the EEG of our friend Steven Cole."

"So I saw," Leigh said, pointing to the adhesive label

bearing Steven's name and hospital number fixed to one corner of the top sheet.

"Ah, yes, of course." Page shifted in his chair, fitted his fingertips together to make a pyramid, and stared at her.

"May I take this home with me?"

"Certainly."

"Then I'll let you have it back with my comments in the morning."

"I must remind you—I'm sure it's quite unnecessary, but nevertheless . . ."

"Yes?"

"We do have one very strict rule here. You must keep this information entirely to yourself. All records are strictly confidential and must on no account be shown to anyone, including and especially the patient."

"The same practice applies in my own country, Dr. Page."

"There you go again, my dear. Bertie. Bertie, please."

"I'll try to remember."

"And of course it would be a serious breach of professional ethics if one doctor should withhold any information germane to a case from another. We are often called the new priests, as I'm sure you know, but we, thank God, are not bound by the confessional."

"I'm aware of that, too," Leigh said.

"And you have nothing to tell me?"

"No. Not that I can think of. But it seems to me—please do excuse me if I'm wrong—that you are trying to tell me something."

Their eyes locked. A certain smugness pinched Page's lips, half lost in the jungle of his beard.

"Perhaps I should tell you, in confidence and as a matter of professional ethics, that my colleagues feel that Mr. Cole must have a brain scan immediately . . ."

Leigh opened her mouth to speak, to blurt out that really it wasn't necessary, it would show nothing. She clamped her mouth shut.

"Do your best to persuade him, won't you?"

"If I get the chance," Leigh said. "Now, if that's all?" She stood up, hefted the weight of paper under her left arm.

"I think so. Do you?"

"Just one observation if I may, Bertie. You are right to remind me of my professional responsibilities, but my personal ethics are entirely my own affair. I assure you I'm keenly aware of the possibility of a conflict of interests. Should that arise, the welfare of the patient will always come first with me."

Bertie Page could have hugged himself as he watched her walk coolly to the door. Lucky patient, he thought, to be put first in Miss Duncan's affections. For he had no doubt that that was what she meant. He tugged at his beard. He loved a bit of gossip. The secret doings of others were endlessly fascinating to him, especially when there was an element of danger involved. And the arrogant Miss Duncan was certainly putting herself in professional danger, if not personal. He would so enjoy observing her helpless little struggles in the tangled web. It was such dramas and the gossip they generated that made his little world go round.

After he had slept, bathed, and shaved, Steven sat at the table Leigh used as a desk and began to write down, as she had asked him, everything he could remember of the "contacts." He hoped that it would at least prove therapeutic, much as he found that writing reports for his job always clarified and focused thoughts that had seemed depressingly vague when he reluctantly set about the task. And something like that did begin to happen, though it was much more exciting. Steven did not know, in any conscious sense, where the "memory"—if that's what it truly was—came from, but he slipped into the grip of it, afraid only that he could not move the pen fast enough to get it all down. Afterward, he felt drained but better, as though he had gotten rid of some poison in his system. His excitement remained as he read it through, increased when he speculated on what it might be and mean.

As soon as he heard Leigh's key in the lock, he rushed to the top of the stairs and waved the foolscap pages at her.

"Here, you must read this. I think it's important."

She was carrying a large briefcase and a bag of groceries. Steven apologized and helped her to set them down.

"You certainly look very pleased with yourself," she said, smiling. Because she was still anxious and annoyed from her interview with Page, she welcomed the distraction of his eagerness. The EEG and Page's insinuations could wait.

"Please, read them."

"Okay, okay. How about opening that bottle of wine and letting me take my coat off?"

She began to read even while she got out of her heavy wool coat. This was new evidence, material Steven had suppressed or forgotten. It did not make pleasant reading, but it activated her own excitement. He had made contact and he could retain a memory of it. There was no other explanation. She forced herself to be calm, cautious. By itself, out of context, this oblique account of a man lying on a bed, surrounded by paper, his clothes undone was sordid and trivial but put together with his other "memories" it convinced her that she had been right al along.

"Well? What do you think?" Steven leaned over her shoulder, a glass of wine in his hand.

"Sh. Let me finish. I'm nearly through."

"Sorry." He paced up and down waiting for her verdict. "Well?" he almost shouted when she let the pages fall into her lap.

Leigh smiled and raised her glass.

"I think we should drink to our first success."

"You think that's him?"

"I'm sure of it. Unless you've got a whole posse of unwelcome visitors in your head. Oh, sorry. That wasn't exactly tactful."

"Go on, never mind."

"When I put you in a trance, I lost contact with you. You were able to tell me about the boy with the soccer ball, just like it was really happening. Then I lost you. *This*," she said triumphantly, slapping the pages he had written, "is where you went. You made contact yourself. You must have. Because if what Page said is right—" The telephone rang, interrupting her. "Hell. I'll get it." She thrust the pages at Steven and went to the phone. He looked at them again, could have kissed them with relief because she had confirmed their meaning. A breakthrough. Something at last.

"Hello?" Leigh said.

"I want to speak to Steven Cole," an unknown female voice demanded. "And don't tell me he's not there."

"Who is this please?" Leigh asked, feeling afraid suddenly.

"This is his wife. Who the hell are you?"

"A friend. I'll get him for you."

Something in her voice cut through Steven's excitement. He looked at her anxiously. She held out the receiver to him.

"For you. Your wife."

He looked scared, guilty even, she thought, as he took the receiver from her hand.

"Georgia?"

There was no mistaking the hysteria in her voice.

"Look, Steve, I've absolutely got to have the car. You had absolutely no right to just take it like that. I want it back and I want it now. And I want you to come round here anyway. It's Mark."

"Mark?" he said, alarmed. "What's happened to him?"

"Nothing. It's just that he's . . . Oh well, you'll have to know sooner or later. He's been truanting, and when I tried to talk to him he was impossible. He was so rude and belligerent. He called me terrible names, Steve, and I just can't cope, not with him on top of everything else."

"All right. I'll see what—"

"You're his father. You've got to discipline him. I just can't have this."

"All right. I will. I'll talk to him."

"Now. Tonight. And bring the car and just make up your mind you're going to leave it here, because my life is just too complicated. I've absolutely got to have a car."

"All right, Georgia. I get the point. I'll be round. Just hang on till I get there."

"Don't let me down now, Steve. You owe me this much."

"Yes, Georgia. I'm going to hang up now. See you."

The phone made a little *ting* as he replaced the receiver. He found it difficult to look at Leigh, was relieved to find that her face was turned away from him.

"I'm sorry about that."

"How did she get my number?"

"I don't know. Oh yes . . . I gave it to Gwen this morning when I rang in, just in case there was an emergency. She must have gotten it from her."

"It doesn't matter. You're going there?"

"I have to. Mark's playing up. They've had a row. Georgia can't bear rows with him. They tear her apart. Anyway, she insists that she needs the car for some reason."

"This is important too, Steven," she said, gesturing with her glass to the pages.

"I know that." He shrugged. What was a man to do?

"Will you be coming back?" she asked, her voice and body tense.

"Of course. I'll be as quick as I can."

"Okay. I'll get to work on this, the rest of the stuff you wrote, and then . . ." She got up, collected the papers together, and carried them to the desk. She had not told him about the EEG yet, the idea Page had given her. All that, she supposed, would have to wait. But where had all the excitement gone, that's what she wanted to know?

"I'm sorry," Steven said again. "But I really had better go."

"Sure." She tried to smile, but it looked more like a grin of irritation. "I guess these things are always messy."

"I fear so. Well, I'll . . ." He did not finish but went out of the room, got into his raincoat. She heard his car keys jingle. " 'Bye, then. I'll be as quick as I can."

"Sure. And good luck."

I am not cut out for this, Leigh thought as she heard the front door close behind him. The other woman. Borrowed time. All the old clichés crowded into her mind. She poured herself more wine, refusing to remember how much she had looked forward to sharing it with him. The role didn't suit or fit.

"Stop it," she said aloud, and took a deep drink of the warming wine. He would be back. And meanwhile there was work to be done. Thank God there was always work to be done. She crossed the room with determination, picked up her briefcase, and carried it to the desk. And even if the savor had gone out of it, the buoyancy, it would come back. It always did. And that would see her through.


Georgia greeted him red faced and sullen, demanded to know if he'd brought the car and then hurried away to the window to check that he had told her the truth. Steven thought it best to leave her, tapped on Mark's door and went in.

His son was lying on his bed, a pillow cuddled in his arms.

"Hello, Mark."

"Dad!" He sat up, his eyes shining, and then, too quickly, embarrassment and resentment dulled his expression. His features set hard against his father.

"So, how are things?" Steven asked, removing his coat and

looping it over Mark's robe on the back of the door. "Mm?" he prompted when Mark did not reply. Steven sighed, pulled a chair up to the bed and sat. "We're not going to get very far if I'm the only one talking."

"She sent for you, not me. It wasn't my idea."

"Well, I gather you've been skipping school and disobeying your mother. She's very upset."

"And of course you believe her."

"I haven't got much choice until you tell me your version."

He rolled over onto his side, away from Steven, pummeled the pillow into shape and propped himself on it.

"Why did you go away?"

"Your mother asked me to. We've not been getting along and—"

"She's got someone else."

"Yes," Steven said carefully. "She has."

"Well, what are you going to do about it?"

"I don't know."

"You're just going to let her?" He twisted his face around to look at Steven. His eyes were angry and hurt.

"Is that what's upsetting you? I thought all this was about—"

"Look, okay, I took off this afternoon. I just felt like it, right? Then I came back here, and she comes in early with this other man, Roger North. Then the school rings up and says 'Where am I?' They would. No one else ever gets caught. It's always me. And she goes crazy at me, and I told her she didn't have any right because . . ." He turned away again.

"Because what? Come on. Spit it all out."

"I saw her kissing him good-bye. She admits it."

Steven sighed, wondered how to begin.

"That's the first you knew about . . . Roger North, this afternoon? Your mother didn't tell you?"

He shook his head fiercely.

"She just brought him back here like he was . . . you."

"I'm sorry, Mark." Steven reached out and put his hand on Mark's shoulder. He shrugged it off.

"Don't," he said.

"I'm sorry you had to find out this way, but since you have

you'll just have to face up to it. I know it's a shock, difficult for you to understand, but—"

"Why don't you put a stop to it?" he demanded.

"I don't think I have the right, Mark. Even though we're married and have responsibilities to you and each other, we're still free agents. Georgia has the right to choose someone else if she wants. Perhaps she isn't happy with me anymore. She might need Roger more than me."

"Or me."

"I'm sure that's not true. I'd bet anything on it." Mark shrugged dismissively. "We don't always show the people we love how much we love them in a nice, loving way."

"Crap."

"Look, what I'm trying to tell you is that when you yelled at your mother or whatever you did, it wasn't because you hate her—"

"It was. I do."

"It was because you were scared and hurt. You gave her a bad time because you love her. And she you."

"Well, if that's true, what about you? Who are you shouting at?"

"I've finished my share."

"So you're just going to walk out and leave us. You're going to let him walk all over you."

"No, I won't do that. I promise you. Your mother and I have to decide what she wants to do and how we're going to sort it out between us."

"Well, I'm not having anything to do with him. You'd better remember that. She'd better tell him."

"Okay."

Steven waited, watched his son, who plucked at the corner of the pillowcase as though trying to unpick the stitching.

"I think I'd better go and talk to your mother now." Mark ignored him. "Look, I know you feel bad, but no more playing hooky from school, all right? You know it's dangerous with these murders—"

"Don't you start on about that."

"Your mother's right. Now promise me. You'll only make things worse for everybody by going to pieces. We need your help."

"Huh."

"Look, I'll talk to you again later, when you've had time to think about it."

"Please yourself."

"Mark, I've moved out of the flat, but I haven't abandoned you or left you."

"You never said good-bye, you never left a phone number."

"I'm sorry. That was wrong of me and it won't happen again. I'll leave you my number and—"

"You needn't bother. I can look after myself."

"Good. But just in case, eh?"

Mark shrugged.

"I'll see you later." Steven stood up and went to the door, taking his time, giving Mark a chance to say more if he wanted, but the boy remained turned away from him, plucking at the pillowcase.

Steven closed the door and waited for a moment in the hall. He felt so much, such a confusion of emotions, that he felt numb. Anger at Georgia. Guilt about and pity for Mark. He thought of Leigh and saw her for the first time as a deadly complication. And the reason he needed Leigh, the other reason . . . It all seemed crazy, unbelievable here in these familiar surroundings, which were no longer hospitable. He wanted to smash his fist through the dark green wall, and he wanted to turn his back on it all, just walk away. But he could not do that. He braced himself and walked down into the living room where Georgia sat in her usual chair, fingers drumming on the arm, one leg crossed over the other, her foot tapping impatiently at the air. Steven glanced at her then turned away to pour himself a drink. He really needed one.

"So, she's American, is she? Or is it Canadian? Never could tell the difference."

"American, yes," he said, capping the Scotch bottle with hands that shook.

"What's her name?"

"Leigh Duncan."

"And how long has it been going on?"

"Georgia, I didn't come here to discuss . . ." He waved his hand, brushing it away. "I brought the car. I've talked to Mark. A fine mess you've made of it, I must say."

"Me? Don't you dare criticize—"

"He's upset because he found out about Roger North. Why the hell didn't you tell him, prepare him or be a bit discreet?"

"As discreet as you, driving bold as brass down Fulham Palace Road—"

"What are you talking about?"

"I saw you. *Her* driving *my* car while I stood in the bloody rain getting wet through. My God, Steve, if that's being discreet!"

It seemed so trivial he couldn't see that it was relevant.

"Oh that," he said.

"Yes, that. It's all right for you."

"No, it isn't all right for me, but I'm not going to argue the rights and wrongs of it now. You called me here because you couldn't cope—"

"I can cope. Don't you worry. I can cope better than I ever did with you on my back."

"Good. Then why don't I just leave you to it?"

"That's right. Take the soft option. Just walk away, like you always do. Oh, you're so bloody soft."

"Stop it, Georgia. Just button your lip for once. I've had it. I've had it up to here." He chopped at the top of his head with the side of his hand. "I've got too much on my mind."

"Her, you mean."

"No, I mean me, other things. So let's just sort this out calmly."

"Oh? And what do you propose?" She pushed past him to get herself a drink.

"I've told Mark not to walk out of school again. I've promised to tell him where he can reach me, and I intend to tell him he can do so at any time. And I'll make sure I see him regularly, too."

"Oh, will you? Well I just might have something to say about that."

"No doubt you will, but you can't stop me, and if you try too hard you'll forfeit every scrap of love that kid's got for you. I'm warning you. This is your fault, Georgia. No one else's. Now I suggest you think before you make him any more unhappy."

"You bastard."

"So you frequently say."

"Soft bastard."

"Okay, that's it. I'm getting out of here before I . . . Oh, to hell with it."

"Before you what? Hit me?"

"I only wish I could, Georgia, so don't tempt me."

"Hah!"

He put down his glass and went to the desk, rummaged through it for a pen and paper.

"And what did you tell him about you and Leigh? I suppose he approves of you."

"I haven't told him anything."

"And you blame me?"

"Georgia, it's not as simple as that."

"No, of course not. I forgot. Nothing ever is simple for you."

He sighed, willed himself to be calm.

"If I knew how to make you understand, I would try. Look, I'll move back if you like, for Mark's sake and so that we can try to settle this mess amicably, without screaming at each other all the time. But if I do that, if you want me to, I shall still have to see Leigh professionally, because something is happening to me, something I can't control."

"It's called lust, Steven. Surely you remember the name, even though you haven't been putting much of it my way these last few years?"

"You see? It's impossible to talk to you. You're just a bitch. You're so angry you explode. And I don't know why or how to help you. And right now I don't even have the time."

"Or the inclination. Go on, be honest."

"Not much, no." He turned aside to the desk, wrote Leigh's address and telephone number on a square of blue paper.

"So what is this 'something' that's happening to you?"

Steven straightened his back, tore the piece of paper from its pad and folded it.

"If I thought there was a chance you really wanted to know, would listen and try to understand—"

"All right. Try me. Since I'm always at fault, give me a chance to redeem myself." She sat down, crossed her legs, and flicked something from her skirt.

"I don't know," Steven said. How could he find the words? How could he expect her to understand? If she did, if by some miracle he could communicate this to her, would it not do more harm than good? He shook his head and crossed back to the old washstand to pour himself another drink. "You?" he said, offering the bottle.

"No." She held up her drink. "I'm fine."

"You know those headaches I've been having? You remember how I couldn't remember anything the night I hit you?"

"I'm not likely . . . Sorry. Yes, yes I remember."

At least she was making an effort, he thought, and he knew that she could when she wanted to. It was just that she seemed to have lost the habit, and that made him sad.

"Well, it's happened again, twice. On Saturday and again last night. Only now, with Leigh's help, I'm beginning to remember, and what I remember is so awful and so . . . Oh it's hopeless. You wouldn't believe me anyway."

Georgia was stunned. It was as though they'd never had the rows, as though the years had rolled back and she could *see* him again, could care for him as she had forgotten how to do.

"Please," she said. "Go on. Tell me. I won't jump down your throat."

"I'll try." He sat down on the couch, tried to find and lace together the right words. "Each time it happened—these blackouts—has been when the murders happened. You remember that night?"

"Oh my God." Her glass slipped from her hand, bounced, the whisky splashing across the carpet. The glass rolled toward him, clinked against the metal leg of the coffee table.

"What's the matter with you?"

Her face was white with an almost greenish tinge. Her eyes were wide and terrified, her lips bloodless.

"I think . . . you're not going to tell me that you . . ." The last word was a scream, cracking the air. For a split second Steven did not understand, and then, when he did, he thought that anything he had ever felt for her, even the memory of it, which for a moment it had seemed just possible to grasp and hold on to, died.

"No, of course not," he said in a dead voice. "Leigh

thinks I'm in telepathic communication with the man, the murderer. That's all."

He could not look at Georgia. In a way it did not matter what she thought or said. She made a funny noise, a sort of smothered cough, which might have been a cold, bitter laugh. After what seemed a very long time, she started to speak, "I . . . I . . ."

He heard her get up. Briefly, as she stooped to pick up her fallen glass, she entered his field of vision, but her hair swung across her face, hiding it. He saw her legs pass, heard her open the whisky bottle and pour.

"Well, I'll give her ten out of ten for originality," she said at last in her scratchy voice. "My God I will."

The tension snapped, and Steven felt himself slump, physically and spiritually, defeated. Somehow, he hauled himself to his feet. As though living in a dream, he put his glass down on the coffee table and straightened up. She was leaning against the washstand, one arm crossed over her bosom, the other holding her glass inches from her lips.

"I'll give this to Mark," he said, surprised to find that he still held the slip of blue paper in his fingers.

"You're mad. You must be. You realize I could get a divorce like that?" She snapped her fingers. "I could even have you certified."

"I didn't even expect you to believe me," he said, "but at least I told you. It's the truth. Or as near to it as I can get at the moment. And I'll admit that I think I am very much in love with her, too, but that's irrelevant right now, because I am, somehow, in some way forced to know what is going on in that man's mind, and if you think that's funny or a symptom of madness or that someone would make it up, then I don't know what to say to you."

"Get out," Georgia hissed. "Just get out of here and stay away from me and my son. I won't have you here." Her face was terrible. He realized that he had never seen pure hatred before and that it looked a lot like pure fear.

He walked up the steps.

"Did you hear me?"

"I'm going."

"Don't you go near Mark." She started after him, but he

was already at the door and she could do nothing to prevent his going into the room.

Steven took down his coat from the back of the door.

"I'm off now," he said. "Here's my address and phone number. You can ring me or come round anytime."

Mark said nothing, just sat on the edge of his bed staring mutely and miserably at his father.

"I said 'out.' I want you to go. Do I have to call the police and have you thrown out?" Georgia shrieked from the doorway.

"Don't, Mum. Don't."

And then Mark was hugging him, clung fast to him, weeping. Steven cupped the back of his son's head with one hand and rocked him while he felt his own heart break.

Georgia said, "That's enough, Mark. It's all right now. Dad's got to go. Haven't you?" She looked at him, simply scared now. "Come on." She pulled the boy away from him, and he went willingly enough to her arms. Steven nodded his head and left them.

This was an entirely different kind of waiting, more active, a kind of search. He wanted to avoid the rain after last night. He still felt bitter, coldly angry about that wasted time. The frustration, the sense of being cheated was like a malignant tumor gradually gnawing away at his mind. Such feelings made him daring, for this place had never figured on his list of chosen spots. It had always been a possibility, of course, because so many young boys were to be found there, some as inmates, others as visitors. Some, he knew, misused the place as a sort of club, hanging around the Tea Bar, ogling the nurses in their thin white uniforms. He'd read about it in the local paper when they'd tried to tighten up on security, ban the boys. But now, as he passed the crowded, noisy Tea Bar, he spotted a group he knew had no legitimate business there. Saw their leather jackets and tight, patched jeans. One caught his eyes, stared at him in a challenging way, and he ducked his head as though to smell the large bunch of chrysanthemums he carried like a staff of righteousness before him.

Steven had his car keys in his hand, was bending to unlock the door when he remembered he'd promised to leave it for Georgia. He snatched his hand back guiltily, tensed for her scream of accusation. He even looked up at the big window, but she was not there, was still comforting Mark, of course, patching up their quarrel. Their relationship, tested by these present difficulties, would eventually squeeze him out. He went round to the back of the car and unlocked the trunk, took out his umbrella, and slammed it shut again. He had forfeited Mark's respect, he knew that. Henceforth Mark, too, would no doubt think of him as soft. Yet only a short time ago he had longed to smash Roger North's face in—a course of action Mark would no doubt thoroughly approve. The force of anger he had felt at that time had scared him, made him doubt his own sanity. Where had it gone now? As he trudged slowly down the long road, anger was the last thing he felt. Guilt he felt in plenty. Guilt toward Mark and what he was doing to him, about the whole situation he had allowed to veer out of control. And despair for his life, his family, for Georgia, who had become a bitter parody of her former self. And for Leigh, whom he scarcely knew and was perhaps using.

Maybe Georgia was right. He was mad, mad to allow himself to believe so quickly and easily in Leigh's theories and explanations. After all, he did not know her, had not even made any attempt to check out her claims to be psychic. But that morning when she had told him there was no body in the recreation ground, no need to search it, it had been impossible not to believe her. Perhaps he had been enchanted, was no longer himself but her creature, laboring under a spell.

One thing was certain. He could not go back to her, not yet, not with all this on his mind. He had to get something sorted out and stick to it. That seesaw he had mentioned to Leigh was rocking crazily to and fro, throwing him up and sweeping him down until he felt dizzy. He had to make one decision and stick to it, otherwise he would drown.

He had reached the old wharves, now stripped of their storage vats and ancient industrial machinery. In their place stood the skeletons of new public housing. When it was completed there would be a riverside walk right along here. One stretch was already open, ran along the front of the expensive block of private flats that reared ahead of him. He turned off the road, took a narrow path beside the flats, which brought him in a few moments to the river walk. It was colder there because less sheltered. The wind drove the rain in from the river, splashing. The path was lit by lamps set in the pathway itself, this underfoot lighting augmented by lamps, which stood about waist high at regular intervals. The effect, Steven noticed as he walked, his head bent under his umbrella, was to light the lower part of the body, leave the face and torso in darkness. It was an odd effect, he thought, as he saw, some way off, a disembodied pair of legs coming toward him. They moved fast, silent in soft shoes. Training shoes, he saw, the currently preferred footwear of young men and boys. The jeans were spattered dark and wet by the rain. There was an impression only of shoulders hunched against the weather—a boy out walking in this lonely place, all by himself. Steven stopped, his heart thudding. The boy came on, came closer, his legs scissoring through the pools of light and the scant shadows. And out there somewhere, perhaps not very far away, was a madman, a murderer. The boy's footsteps sounded now, splashing as Steven moved toward him. It was his clear duty to warn him, tell him. But then he faltered, mesmerized by the boy's rapid, confident approach and the sudden intense, smoky smell of chrysanthemums.

*Balls of color, soft color. Soft, feathered balls, lemon, bronze, and lilac. Outline smudged, blurred, held too close to the eyes. And beyond them, growing clearer, coming bright and sharp into focus, through a glass wall or watery window, shapes moving about, colors. White. The stark white of a nurse's uniform. Plaids. Colors. Children moving around, milling about. A television set ghostly gray in a corner. A card game spread on the floor. Warmth and the smell of chrysanthemums. A nose pressed to the glass, looking. Always outside, waiting.*

*Then a boy coming like a savior down a long corridor. Fair hair glinting in the overhead lights. Dressing gown flapping open, slim body in pale blue pajamas. Checked slippers on small, slim feet. The creak of the door opening. The boy looking straight ahead not seeing the figure lurking back there in the shadows, his blood throbbing and pounding. The boy frowns, puzzled, seems to shrug and pushes open another door, which sighs closed behind him. MEN it says in clear black letters on a silver-colored plate. The door closes the boy within, all blond and blue, and the man steps forward, the bouquet held high in his hands.*

*"Excuse me. Are you looking for someone? Visiting time's nearly over, and you've been standing there such a long time," a busybody nurse says, shattering his purpose.*

Steven's knuckles grazed against rough brick. Below him was a black swirl, lights stretched and refracted, turned to liquid sunspots on the viscous surface of the heaving river. Grainy brick scratched his flesh. The edge of the parapet wall, which bounded the riverside walk, bit sharply into his thighs. A noise made him turn his head to the left. His umbrella lay on the path, open, its spikes scraping on the bricks as the wind caught it, threatened to blow it away. With his head swimming in pain, he stumbled after it before the wind snatched it. Water ran from his hair into his eyes. Rain beat on his face. He stooped, feeling dizzy, feeling the pain crack through his skull, and saw the boy in wet jeans who had passed him unnoticed, pause at the far end of the path, staring back at him, this strange man who had lost his umbrella. He snatched it up just as the light caught the training shoes and rain-darkened jeans. As he straightened up, struggling to raise the umbrella above his head, a gust of wind bellied it and tried to drag it from his grasp. Then he saw another boy, *striding carelessly, dressing gown open, flapping behind him, blue pajamas, checked slippers. Black-and-white checked slippers. Houndstooth check. Soft soles padding on the shining parquet.*

The hospital.

He hung on to this as the vision—he could not call it anything else—faded and he stared at the empty pathway, at the rain forming silver curtains in the lamplight. The pain returned, sharper, several small jolts, as though to nudge him. He turned around, fought the pain. If the night had been clear he would have been able to see the tall central tower of the hospital above the roofs of the houses. But tonight there was nothing. He stared into the storm, into black nothing, trying to hang on to the one cogent thought he had—the hospital—telling his legs to run, eat up the ground, get there in time.

* * *

Leigh glanced at her watch, paused for a moment, thinking, her pen tapping at the spread sheets of Steven's EEG. He was bound to be a while, and she would save hours if she could just run this damn thing through a computer. Even if it didn't yield anything conclusive, it might serve to impress dear Bertie and get him off her back.

As she dialed the hospital number, she started to compose a note to Steven. When the switchboard answered she asked for the computer center and got a pleasant-sounding young man on whom she did not hesitate to use her charm. Her guess had been right. At this time of day there was some computer time free, and although she didn't really have any authorization . . .

"Look, you can ring Dr. Page at home. I have his number—"

"No, go on. I'll take your word for it, seeing as it's urgent."

Leigh promised to be right over and hung up, bundled the EEG into her briefcase, and made for the stairs, grabbing her coat on the way. With any luck she could catch a taxi. She pulled on her woolen hat and ducked into the rain. There wasn't a cab in sight.

Around the back of the hospital was a good place. Still shaken by the start that nosy nurse had given him, he sought the empty places and shadows back by the central-heating plant and emergency generators. All this was hidden away behind the smart, modern facade. Rain lashed through the pools of weak lamplight, danced in the headlights of a car drawing out of the parking lot. A fat black woman stepped out of a side entrance, probably reserved for staff, and scurried away through the rain, squealing when she inadvertently stepped into a puddle.

This entrance was just a narrow glass and metal door, designed not to break the strict geometric pattern of the rear facade. It opened onto a long corridor, rather dimly lit, which led into the bright bustle of the Emergency Room.

A red-headed freckled boy walked down the corridor, pale from his ordeal there. He wore a thick padded bandage on the middle finger of his left hand, the whole arm raised in a temporary sling. There was the heady smell of blood about him. Behind him was the starched white figure of a nurse.

The man stood back, could not hear their voices, heard the squeak of the unoiled door as the woman opened it, pointed, said something to the boy, who stepped out into the rain and darkness. The woman stood for a moment, whitely silhouetted in the doorway. She raised her hand, waved, then leaned out, shuddering, into the rain and pulled the door toward her, closing it.

The boy was alone, nursing his injured finger, keeping his head down as he hurried toward the back gate, and so he did not see the man poised in the black shadows, a sodden bouquet of chrysanthemums clutched to his chest.

Steven was running, his umbrella abandoned somewhere behind him, running through a world of water, not always sure that he was running. Sometimes it seemed that he was watching himself running, and sometimes there was an impression of stillness, as though he had floated free of time and place, was waiting, endlessly waiting until the pain came again, stronger than before. And it felt as though his head must explode, did explode.

He saw . . . *the pale face of a boy, eyes bulging, swollen tongue flapping between blue lips. Saw clothing torn from his body with a senseless, disproportionate strength. Saw pale flesh laid bare, the point of a knife tracing patterns on that flesh, scored lines beaded with little globules of blood that grew larger, burst, flowed together, a trickle of crimson, a stream. Saw the pale lemon ball of an in-curved chrysanthemum flicked and then stained dark red with blood.* Saw through the muzziness of pain, in disconnected images, until the pain itself became a blaze of red and ceased, leaving him running through honking, hooting traffic, through lights and people, running toward his own terror.

The computer broke the most clotted parts of the EEG down into two distinct and separate patterns. Faced with this evidence, proof, Leigh felt no excitement or pride at being proved right. She stared at the analysis, but her mind dwelt on something else, something she had overlooked in her eagerness to explain and prove the hypothesis of involuntary telepathic communication. The EEG could only show what was happening at the moment of the test. It could not record memory or

146

recollection, what had been. Therefore, the evidence lying so starkly before her could only mean that the man must be more or less permanently in touch with Steven. She had a sudden flash image of a small and deadly figure, a little black manikin, locked into the labyrinth of Steven's brain. A caged animal. Suppose he became desperate to get out? She made herself reject and erase the image. This was no time for fantasy. But the image made her heart race. Steven didn't know that the man was always there? She caught her own breath with shock at the enormity and terribleness of the thought that formed, focused, made her want to scream. Supposing there was no other man, that these two distinct tracings, the one permanent, the other periodic and sporadic, were evidence of a split, a Dr. Jekyll and a Mr. Cole? Supposing she had duped herself or allowed herself to be duped because he was in some parts and aspects of himself a good and attractive man?

But she knew he was not a murderer. She had "read" him. Surely he could conceal nothing from her? These other thoughts were rooted in tiredness, exhaustion. She looked at her watch and realized that Steven must have returned ages ago. The thought of him waiting anxiously for her was suddenly not pleasant. What she had thought was like the aftertaste of poison in her mind. She had no need of doubt, did not know how to handle it. She had always been able to verify the truth of other people. And Steven, by the abilities and evidence she had always trusted, was not a killer, *was* the confused victim of a telepathic accident. There was a crumb of comfort here. The maniacal killer's brain *had* shorted, and Steven simply happened to be in the way.

Shaken, but feeling a little better, Leigh collected her papers and loaded her briefcase. Steven had to come up with some explanations, be made to acknowledge, if necessary, the man's presence at times other than when the man found fulfillment or whatever it was in the slaughter of boys.

Wearily, she said her good-nights, thanked the young man who had helped her, and went down in the lift to the ground floor. The last straggling visitors were leaving. The hospital was settling down. Nurses went around switching off unnecessary lights. Each ward withdrew into itself. Outside the rain was falling even more heavily, as though some maniac force wanted to drown the world or wash it right away. Leigh almost understood such a force. Her clothing was still damp from her journey to the hospital, and she could not face another drenching. Instead she joined a short queue of others, also intimidated by the storm, waiting for taxis.

She stared across the formal garden that fronted the hospital and scanned the busy road for an approaching cab. Suddenly there was the squeal of tires, an angry hooting of horns. Through the blaze of light made dazzling by the rain, she saw a figure emerge, running wildly, heedless of the traffic, everything. He leaped up onto the slightly raised lawn and ran, weaving and staggering, toward the corner of the hospital building. Everyone was watching his crazily determined progress now. He was drunk or berserk, they said. For a moment, Leigh agreed with them. The man ran on, grimly sticking to his chosen path, apparently unaware of the shallow, artificial pool that blocked his way. His foot struck the low, brick wall, and he pitched forward with a cry. It was then that she recognized him, knew that it was Steven, even as he fell headlong into the water and lay quite still.

Later she was to be amazed by her own calm and presence of mind. She grabbed the arm of the man immediately ahead of her in the queue and tugged him along with her as she ran across the lawn toward the pool. Two men were approaching from the road and they got to him first. One waded into the shallow water and raised Steven's head and shoulders. The other hauled on his legs. Leigh and the man she had plucked from the queue bent and helped to take the weight of his sopping body.

"Please," she panted, pushing Steven over onto his back and raising him, propped against her lap, "go to Emergency and tell them to bring a stretcher. Quickly."

One man set off at a run. The others crouched on either side of them. She wiped water from his face, bent close to him to speak his name. He coughed suddenly, and one of the men helped her to raise him to a sitting position. Steven brought up a little water, coughed again. Leigh put her arms around him, put her lips close to his ear.

"It's okay now, Steven. You'll be okay now."

He turned his blank, stunned face to her: his skin had the cold, wet texture of fish.

"Leigh?"

"Yes. It happened again, didn't it?"

She watched his face crack with the pain of she knew not what memory. She tried to help him, to hold him, but he pushed her away.

"Go . . . you've got to . . . go round the back . . . there . . . For God's sake hurry!"

Only Leigh's ability to see beyond his face, hear more than his voice, enabled her to understand so quickly. All her instincts were to stay with him, see him safely taken into the hospital, but she grasped images, blurred but so horrible that she understood and had to act on his desperate urgency.

"Stay with him till the stretcher comes," she said, and stood up, her feet slipping a little in the mud.

He called something after her, but she did not catch it. She hurried through the rain, pushed past the crowd of people who had gathered to gawk and speculate, hurried to the corner of the building toward which, she remembered, in the split second before he tripped and fell, she had known he was making a beeline. A terrible dread seized her as she passed the brightly lit windows of the hospital and turned, hesitantly, into the darkness of the service area. She slowed her pace, walked aimlessly for a moment, summoning all her courage. She took shelter in the ambulance garage and stood very still, breathing deeply until she felt calm enough to close her eyes and let her mind roam free, searching. She let it slide into shadows, probe locked buildings, empty spaces, until, with a little cry of shock, she "saw" it.

Packed into the angle formed by two walls was a body, the blood washed clean from it by the relentless rain. Clothing torn from throat to groin folded back to display white skin still bleeding in places, but the blood was instantly diluted by the rain. Only the groin was a black pulp of blood and severed flesh.

Her inner eye moved on like a camera to where a bunch of flowers lay, battered and bruised, their florist's formality scattered and undone. Soon they would be tramped underfoot by those who would come to find him, and perhaps they would not immediately notice what Leigh would never forget: what remained of the boy's sex was fastidiously arranged among the bloodied flowers.

". . . mutilated body of a young boy was found last night in the grounds of a London teaching hospital at Hammersmith . . ."

Georgia bumped against the breakfast table in her anxiety to reach the little radio on top of the refrigerator, turn up the volume.

"Watch it," Mark protested as tea slopped into his saucer.

"Quiet, listen."

". . . third such killing in the area in little more than a week. Our reporter Jake Shawcroft spoke to the police inspector in charge of the investigation."

"Detective-Inspector Gurney, can I ask you if you are linking this latest death to that of the other two boys in the district recently?"

"Definitely. I'm afraid we have a maniac on our hands."

"Could you tell us why you link these cases?"

"Geographics, age and sex of victim, and certain . . . er . . . stylistic similarities, about which I can't reveal any details at present."

"Do you think there's any chance that this 'maniac' as you call him, or indeed her, will strike again?"

"I'm sorry to say that seems to be a very real possibility. Such a person is obviously unpredictable, but we must assume that he will at least try to murder again."

"I understand these murders are particularly gruesome. In the light of that, do you have any advice to give local residents?"

"Certainly I do. I want to appeal in the strongest terms to parents of all boys between the ages of eight and eighteen to be particularly vigilant. And to the boys themselves: keep off the streets at night. If you must go out after dark, go with a friend, keep in groups. Keep to the main streets. Use public transportation if your parents can't drive you or collect you. Above all, use your common sense. Remember there is someone in the Hammersmith, Fulham, and Chiswick area who has already killed three young boys. Don't assume it won't happen again, and don't assume it couldn't happen to you. And I'd like to appeal to anyone in the area who might have noticed something, no matter how small or unimportant, to contact their local police station. Even if you only thought you noticed something suspicious or a bit out of the ordinary, contact us."

"Thank you very much, Inspector. This is Jake Shawcroft for IRN in Hammersmith, returning you to the studio."

Georgia turned the volume down until the voices became a low background rumble. She leaned across the table, her face inches from Mark's.

"Did you hear that?"

"Yes."

"Did you take it in? Did you understand what the man was saying?"

"Yes. Don't go on." He put another spoonful of cereal into his mouth and munched loudly.

"He's told you. I've told you. Your father's told you. Now I want no more arguments about being taken to and from school. I want to know where you are every minute of the day and night. Understand? If I'm ever late, you go back into the school and wait there. And you are never, ever to go off by yourself again. Do you understand?"

"Yes, Mum."

"Good."

The telephone rang.

"Damn," Georgia said, moving to the door. "Now you just remember."

Mark rolled his eyes toward heaven and helped himself to a piece of toast.

"Yes?" Georgia said into the telephone.

"Mrs. Cole? It's Gwen here, Mr. Cole's secretary."

"Yes. Hello, Gwen. What can I do for you?"

"Well, it's really . . . Look, I hope you won't think I'm interfering, but I thought you ought to know that Mr. Cole was admitted to the hospital last night."

"What?"

"He was admitted—"

"Yes. I heard you. What's wrong with him?"

"Well, I'm not sure. I haven't been able to speak to the

doctor yet, but the sister on the ward says he was admitted with exhaustion and suspected concussion. It's nothing serious, but they want to keep him in for observation."

"Oh, I see. What happened, do you know?"

"Well, I understand he fell. He fell into the pond."

"The pond?"

"Yes, you know, the one outside the hospital, with the Henry Moore sculpture in the middle."

Drunk, Georgia thought. Fleeing from something? The boy was found in the grounds. Steven fell in the grounds. Coincidence again?

"Mrs. Cole? Are you still there?"

"Yes, sorry, Gwen. Look, thanks for telling me. I'll pop in and see him after I've taken Mark to school. Will they let me see him?"

"Oh, I'm sure . . . I'll tell Sister you're coming, if you like."

"Thanks. Thanks a lot, Gwen. I really must go now."

She put the receiver down quickly and stood by the telephone, trembling inside.

"What was it?" Mark called from the kitchen.

"Nothing," she answered automatically. There was no point in telling him. She made up her mind decisively. If she told him he'd only worry, want to come to the hospital with her. When she had found out more . . . She went to the kitchen doorway. "I've got to make a call before I go into work, so hurry up and get ready."

"It's not time," Mark pointed out.

"You'll just have to be early for once. Hurry up, now, I'm going to get ready."

In her room she stared at her pale, strained face in the mirror, too shaken and preoccupied to get on with the business of making up. Coincidence—three times in a row was too much for any person to believe without question. What should she do? Go to the police? The inspector on the radio had said anything, no matter how trivial . . . She tried to remember exactly what Steven had said, that cock-and-bull story about telepathy. Could she make that square, somehow, with the fact, the admitted fact, that Steven had been each time in the vicinity of the murder? If there was a connection, she could not grasp it. She did not want to see him. Her doubts, her suspicions released her, surely, from any wifely concern. But Steve could not, would not— How many wives, she wondered, had coasted along on such assertions of faith? How many had made themselves literally blind rather than face the fact that the man they loved, had spent their lives with, was a— The Yorkshire Ripper's wife, for example: had she truly never suspected anything? But the other doubt returned, told her such comparisons were odious. Steven was not like that.

"I thought you were in a hurry. I'm ready."

"Yes. Just a minute." With shaking hands she pulled her hair back, twisted an elastic band around it, and reached for her lipstick.

Dr. Yussef, who had examined Steven on admission, did so again before going off duty, this time in the presence of Sonia Zimmer. Afterward, they held a case conference in Dr. Zimmer's office. She also invited Dr. Page, who in turn brought Leigh along. Concussion, Yussel was explaining, had been considered because the patient appeared to have struck his head in the fall. However, happily, both he and Dr. Zimmer felt now that this could be ruled out. They felt that he needed rest, should be kept under observation for twenty-four hours, but there was nothing physically wrong with him apart from a few bruises and abrasions.

"You were there, I understand," Dr. Zimmer said, looking at Leigh through the upper crescent of her bifocals. "Do you know what happened?"

"I was waiting for a taxi. Suddenly I saw him running toward the hospital. He seemed not to notice the pond. He tripped against the edge, the little parapet, you know, and fell. That's all I saw."

"Had he been drinking, perhaps?"

"I smelled nothing. Did you, Doctor?"

"No. No sign of alcohol," Yussef agreed. "Certainly not to excess."

"Then what was he doing, running like that?" Dr. Zimmer asked.

"I don't know," Leigh said, avoiding Page's eyes.

"There have been some difficulties at home, domestic pressures," Dr. Zimmer said, flicking through her notes. "I suppose that might have something to do with it."

"I'd like to show you something," Page interrupted. "I asked Leigh here to run a computer check on that EEG you gave me yesterday. Here are the results."

Leigh had had no choice but to tell him what she had done, show him the analysis, and now she did not even care that he passed her idea off as his own.

"You see? Two distinct patterns. Or apparently so."

"Yes, yes," Dr. Zimmer said impatiently. "The unusual activity and the continuous tracing, which we may presume to be Cole's, yes?" She paused, looked at the others in turn. They nodded. "Right. And the activity increased with these periodic, separate tracings. It's as though we have two subjects, yes? Now how can that be?" She looked at Page who, with a smug expression, looked at Leigh. She became aware of all their eyes on her.

"I don't know," she said quietly. "I ran it through the computer. That's the result. I can't explain it."

"Extraordinary," Dr. Zimmer murmured. "Well, does anyone have a suggestion?"

"Yes, I do," Leigh said. "I think you should do another EEG. At least we could check that the continuous tracing matches a new one. That would confirm that we have a basic pattern to go on."

"Mm. I agree, absolutely. Dr. Yussef?"

"Sure."

"And while we have him here, we'll do a complete brain X ray on the scanner. I felt that was imperative before and now . . ." Dr. Zimmer shrugged. Page murmured his agreement. "So, thank you all. I think that's the most we can do for the moment. I'll make the necessary arrangements and keep you informed."

Leigh hurried out of the room ahead of Page, anxious to avoid his questions. Even though she knew he guessed she was going straight up to the ward where Steven lay in a private room, she did not want to fence with him or be forced to confirm her intentions. She had not slept. What she had "seen" and had later heard confirmed when a routine security check discovered the boy's body had kept her awake. She needed to know what Steven had "seen," "experienced," but there had been no chance to talk when she had looked in on him earlier. She got out of the lift and walked on to the ward, smiled at the sister who was sitting at the desk, working on a chart.

"Mr. Cole's very popular this morning," she murmured.

"Oh?" Leigh said, smiling.

"His wife's just gone in."

Leigh's smile faded. She turned around briskly and left the ward.

Fear more than concern made her gentle. He was propped up on the sloping part of the bed, wearing a hospital gown. There was a lump on his forehead, some bandage across the knuckles of his left hand. He looked very tired, seemed to have difficulty opening his eyelids when she spoke his name.

"Steve? What's happened?"

He moved his head as though to shake it.

"Well, how are you feeling?"

"All right. A bit . . . shattered."

She came closer to the high bed, wanted to touch his hand but was afraid the gesture might be rejected or misinterpreted.

"Can I . . . can I ask you something?"

"Yes."

"Did you know there's been another murder?"

His eyes rested on her face. They were weary, not guilty or in any way scared. He nodded his head once. He had asked, of course. One of the nurses had told him about it, and later, he thought—his grasp of time was hazy—Leigh had confirmed it.

"I know this isn't the time or . . . But I've got to ask. After what you said last night." Georgia's voice shook, threatened to become shrill. She got it under control. "Did you have anything to do with it?"

She waited, hating herself yet watching his face intently for the slightest telltale flicker, but nothing changed except, when he answered, he closed his eyes.

"No, Georgia, nothing. And please don't make me tell you that again."

"You were in the grounds. They said on the radio the boy was found—"

"Round the back, in the service area."

"You do see that . . . all these coincidences. Oh Steve, I don't want to ask you—"

"It's all right. I understand. You must believe me, though. Whatever happens, you must believe *in* me. You did once," he reminded her, opening his eyes. "This has got nothing to do with me. I swear on my life."

"Nothing at all?" she asked, fearful now that she had gone too far but unable to stop herself. She had to know, be absolutely sure.

"I knew that it was going to happen," he said quietly. "Can you believe that?"

"Then why didn't you—?"

"Stop it? I was trying. That's how this happened." He raised his eyes, indicating his forehead.

"Oh Steve . . ." She sat down and began to cry. She cried quietly, dabbing at her eyes with tissues taken from a box on his night table. She was weeping, he thought, for the dead boy and perhaps, he hoped, out of relief. "I'm sorry."

"It's all right." He closed his eyes again.

"You knew because of this telepathy business, you mean?"

"Yes."

"I don't understand."

"I know. I can't explain it to you now, perhaps never."

"But what are you going to do, Steve?"

That was too complicated as well. Even trying to think about it made his head ache, not with the sharp convulsions he had learned to dread, but with a steady, general throb that had its source and center in the lump on his forehead.

"Not now," he said. "I can't. I'm too tired. Head aches."

"I'm sorry." She stood up, leaned over him and unnecessarily straightened the bedclothes. "Steve?"

"Yes?"

"What should I do about Mark?"

His eyes opened at once, and his face showed clear anxiety.

"You must keep an eye on him. Don't let him go out or anything. You were right. Please, promise me." He took her hand, gripped it tightly.

"Yes. Of course I will. I meant, is it all right for you . . . for him to be with you?"

He turned his head away, released her hand. The question was too painful. He saw the depth of her doubts and felt sick and then angry. Angry at her and at the man who had driven this obscene wedge between him and his wife and son.

"I'm sorry. I shouldn't have . . . I'm so worried, Steve. There's so much I don't understand and— I had to ask."

"Yes," he sighed.

"I'm sorry. I don't enjoy—"

"It's up to you, Georgia. I can't do anything more to convince you. Only you can decide whether you believe me or—"

She swallowed against the threat of new tears. "I want to. Look, I'd better go. You ought to rest. I . . . can I bring you anything? What do you need?"

"Nothing. I expect they'll let me home soon."

"Home?"

"Well, out, anyway."

"I see. Oh Steve, what are we going to do?"

She pressed her hand to her mouth and nose, turned away to reach more tissues. Sister came in just then, took in the situation at a glance, and said that Georgia should leave now.

She bent over him again, touched his hand.

" 'Bye, Steve. Don't worry. I'll take good care of Mark."


"What on earth's the matter with you?" Roger spoke in a low voice, as though through clenched teeth, and he kept his head bent to his desk where a sheaf of letters awaited his signature.

Georgia looked through the glass of his office into the outer one. Marion was doing her obvious best to distract the speculating girls, though Georgia's eyes briefly engaged with Tracey's. She immediately looked away, busied herself with the sheet of paper rolled into her typewriter.

"You came in late, your work's all gone to pot. I can't make an exception of you, Georgia. The others notice." He glanced up angrily, not at Georgia but at the women in the other office. "And I never get to see you or touch you."

"It's not my fault," she said, feeling desperate, unable to cope with any more pressure. "Since Mark saw you—"

"I told you that was a damn fool idea."

"All right, okay."

"You'd better take some time off."

"Steve's in the hospital."

"Oh. What's wrong with him?"

"I don't know. He says he's . . ." The enormity of what Steven claimed, of what she had been about to blurt out, clogged on her tongue. Her readiness to tell Roger, to use it as an excuse for her lack of concentration, lack of time for him, frightened her. Did she believe Steven then and pity him? She closed her mouth, stared at Roger's bent head, knowing that she must look like a little girl waiting for the headmaster to make time to reprimand her.

"Well? What does he say?" He looked at her with eyes that, it seemed, had never been soft with love, warm with desire for her. His look reduced her to a minor irritation.

"It doesn't matter," she said. "It was just an idea."

"Well, you'd better take a few days off. I'll authorize it."

She wanted to say, Don't push me away. Help me now when I'm more confused and scared than ever.

"I'm sorry, Georgia, but it's best," he said, softening his tone a little. "I'll ring you this evening."

She nodded her head.

"Is that all? Do you want me to go now or . . . ?"

He wanted to say, Well, you're no use to me here, we can cope better without you, but he remembered in time that there was another Georgia, another way of feeling about her.

"You look done in," he said. "Yes, go now. We'll cope somehow. Make some excuse to the girls."

"Don't worry. I won't compromise you," she said with a ghost of her old anger.

"I don't like it any more than you do," he said crossly, "but you've got to think of staff morale as well as of you."

"Yes." She turned on her heel.

"Georgia?"

"Mm?"

"This illness—whatever it is of Steven's—does it make any difference to us?"

She paused, turning the question over in her mind, remembering only what he had said, that he had known and could not stop it, and trying to imagine how that must feel.

"Yes," she said at last, "I rather think it does."

As she opened the door she thought that she had said it more in the hope of hurting Roger than because she was sure it was true, and then she *was* sure. Yes, it did make a difference: it taught her something about need.

True to her word, Dr. Zimmer sent for Leigh as soon as she had the result of Steven's third EEG. Leigh was glad to find her alone in her room. Dr. Page was holding a clinic and Dr. Yussef was off duty, she explained. Then she watched Leigh speculatively and in silence as she examined the new tracings.

"Perfectly normal, wouldn't you say?" Leigh said, folding the sheets back in order.

"In comparison with the others, yes. You don't sound particularly surprised."

"Oh, I wouldn't say that. Relieved, I guess."

"You care about him, don't you?" Leigh looked away, her resentment at being asked such questions clamping her mouth into a narrow stubborn line. "I'm not Bertie Page, my dear. I'm not vicariously curious, and I can keep what I know to myself."

"Is it relevant, what I feel?"

"It might be, if you are very attached to him."

"Let's say I could be, but right now my main concern is with what's happening to him. I want to help him." Leigh looked frankly at Dr. Zimmer, who nodded that she understood or perhaps believed.

"Is it possible to split oneself so cleanly into two separate persons?"

"It's not easy, but I think I can lick it."

"Good for you. And what do you think is wrong with him?"

"What do you? You're his doctor."

"I would like to think, in the light of this"—she touched the new printout, aligned it with the straight edge of her desk— "that my original thought was correct."

"A mechanical malfunction?" Leigh said scornfully.

"You obviously think not."

"Do you, really?"

"Of course not. I said I would like to . . . prefer perhaps. Well, we shall have to be patient and see what the X rays show." Leigh avoided her magnified eyes, remained silent. "You wouldn't care to make a guess?"

"Nothing. The brain of a perfectly normal adult man. At a guess," she stressed.

"I hope you're right, naturally, though it will rather return us to—how do you say?—to square one." Leigh nodded to confirm the phrase, but said nothing else. "I have seen a great many strange things, and heard of them, too," Dr. Zimmer said, leaning back in her chair and turning a pencil elegantly between her long fingers. "I worked in Africa for five years after I qualified. I learned there that machines and the best, most rational diagnoses in the world are not infallible. I learned to respect mysteries."

"I'm sure it must have been fascinating. I'd like to hear about it sometime."

"But now you want to tell Steven the good news. Well, I won't detain you. I've prescribed a sedative, by the way. He was very tired after the tests. You might find him a little sleepy."

"You mean I can tell him about the EEG?"

"You have my permission. If you think it is good news, of course."

"Don't you?"

"I don't know. I'm a person who mistrusts extremes. I don't like things to be all crazy haywire one day and so apparently normal the next. It makes me suspicious."

"There must be an explantion," Leigh said guardedly.

"Indeed there must. And you know something, Leigh—I may call you—?"

"Oh yes, sure, please."

"I think you will find it."

"Thank you. Does that mean I can count on your support?"

"Tacitly, yes. And you will always get a fair hearing from me, no matter how bizarre your explanations may sound."

"I appreciate that very much." How much did she know or suspect, Leigh thought? She looked at the doctor, wondered if she dared probe, quickly read her mind. It seemed unfair, an underhanded trick. Dr. Zimmer stood up abruptly, dismissing her.

"I have a ward round in five minutes. Go and see Steven. And may I give you a piece of advice? Be cautious with but not alarmed by our friend Bertie. He's not completely harmless, but he isn't lethal, either."

"Thank you," Leigh said and found herself smiling easily for the first time since she had left Steven in the rain, had "seen" the corpse of the child who should have been running around free, not slaughtered for a sick whim. She shuddered.

"What's wrong?" Sonia Zimmer asked at once, pushing her spectacles up onto the bridge of her nose.

"Oh, nothing; just a goose stepping on my grave."

Dr. Zimmer frowned.

"And why should that disturb you, I wonder?"

She stooped over his bed, touched his shoulder gently, and spoke his name. He opened his eyes and stared at her for a moment as though through a fog. Leigh recognized the signs of fairly heavy sedation. Then he took her hand and squeezed it, smiled at her in an unfocused way.

"Hello. How are you?"

"I wondered when you would come. I want to tell you something."

"I'm sorry. There hasn't been a minute." She did not want to mention Georgia's visit, not unless he did. "I've got good news. The EEG, the one they did today, it's perfectly normal. No sign of—"

"I know."

"Who told you?"

"That's what I wanted to tell you. Leigh . . ." He gripped her hand more tightly. His expression was uncertain with the need to make her understand and believe. "He's gone."

"Gone? How do you mean?"

"I can't explain it." He shook his head impatiently. "Everything's . . . vague. I just feel there's no contact. He's not there. It's like . . . I don't know how to explain it properly. It's just a feeling. You know the old joke about the man who keeps hitting his head against a brick wall, and when someone asks him why, he says because it feels so good when he stops? Well it's like that—it's stopped. It's like I've had a dull headache for weeks, not enough to be consciously aware of, but suddenly it's stopped."

"When did this happen?" she asked, holding his hand in both of hers, wanting to believe him.

"While I was waiting on the gurney for the EEG. Suddenly it was like something snapped. It feels weird."

As though the other man knew and was frightened, she thought, sensed that, through the rogue tracings of the EEG, they were getting too close to him, too close for comfort. She saw again, mentally, that little black manikin turning and twisting in the myriad channels of Steven's brain.

"I don't care how or why," Steven said drowsily, "just so long as he's gone. My head's my own again."

"I'm glad," she said. "Would you know if he came back?"

"Yes."

She wanted to say that she feared he would or that if he did not Steven would have to find him, but she knew this was not the time. At least it confirmed what the computer analysis had made her realize: that contact was in some ways permanent, although dormant except at times of—

"What are you thinking?"

"Nothing that can't wait. You must rest."

"They gave me something."

"I know. Just to help you rest. Tomorrow, I guess, you'll be able to come home."

"To you?"

"If that's what you want."

"More than anything. Now I'm . . . I mean now I can think for myself. I can make plans."

"Sh," she said, pressing her finger to his lips. "Not now. We'll see. You rest now."

"I love you, Leigh."

"I know."

"And you . . . you'll . . . ."

She bent over him and kissed him lightly on the mouth. He lay, smiling up at her, his eyelids closing with tiredness.

"Sleep well," she said. "I'll see you first thing tomorrow."

"I'll be a new man," he promised.

"The old one will do."


Taking Mark to the hospital that evening seemed to Georgia an act of ritual daring, like spitting in the face of a malevolent god. She would have done anything to avoid it, could not suppress the flutter of panic as she followed him through the revolving doors into the lobby. For all she or anyone knew, the murderer could be lurking there among the motley crowd of patients and visitors, officials and staff, and persons without discernible purpose. She was parading her son, offering him up as a tantalizing potential victim. It was all she could do not to take his arm, drag him away before he could become infected by the aftermath of slaughter, that indefinable something that must linger in the atmosphere of a place where violent death has recently occurred. But she did not dare. Mark's rage and anxiety when she had told him about his father's hospitalization had shaken her badly. Nothing would pacify him but that he should see for himself, make his own assessment of his father's condition. So, when they reached the ward, she let Mark go alone into Steven's room, more as a test of her own faith and courage than because she wanted them to be alone together. The staff nurse warned them that he was sedated, and she obviously approved of only one visitor at a time. She was chatty, reassuring Georgia that he would definitely be able to go home tomorrow. Georgia managed to smile and say nothing. She wanted to ask the girl if she knew anything about the murder, the investigation, which might have been kept out of the papers and news bulletins, but she did not dare. To do so would be to tempt fate even further. She became restless, watching the other patients and their visitors, and was relieved when the nurse said she thought that was long enough, why didn't Mrs. Cole go in now, just to say good-night?

Propped on his pillows, Steven looked gray and tired, but he greeted her more or less pleasantly.

"The nurse says we must go now," Georgia told Mark. "Dad's got to rest. Do you want anything?" she asked Steven.

"No. No thanks."

She did not want to mention his impending discharge in front of Mark or give him an opportunity to raise the subject.

"Come along, then, Mark."

His farewell to his father was curiously formal and restrained. Georgia was uncomfortably aware of his eyes on them as she hesitated, then touched Steven's hand and wished him good-night.

Mark was silent all the way home, and although Georgia felt

better once they had left the hospital, she was content to devote herself to her own thoughts.

"Well, that wasn't too bad, was it?" she roused herself to say once they were safely inside the flat.

"I suppose not."

"What did he have to say to you?"

"Nothing much."

She began to make herself a cup of tea.

"Mum? Why can't you and Dad . . . you know . . ."

"I don't know the answer to that," she said honestly. "We need time, both of us."

"For what?"

"To decide how we feel, I suppose, how hard we're prepared to try."

The telephone interrupted her, and Mark started toward it.

"Let it ring," Georgia said sharply, guessing it was Roger and knowing that she could not speak to him just then.

"But it might be Dad, it might be the hospital." He stood uncertainly between the phone and the kitchen doorway, obviously itching to answer it.

"All right. But if it's for me, say I'm out."

He looked puzzled but went to pick up the receiver. After a moment, she heard him say that she was out and hang up without saying good-bye.

"It was for you," he said over his shoulder as he made for his room. "Him. He said he'd ring back."

"Next time, just let it ring," Georgia said, and turned to look at the kettle, her eyes filling with tears.

The days following Steven's release from the hospital were the strangest he had known until then. In one very important respect his life returned to normal: the piercing, spasmodic headaches ceased altogether, and his conviction that the contact was broken, that the man had gone from him, persisted and increased. Around this sense of freedom, of being himself, a feeling of well-being would have formed had it not been constantly offset by his circumstances and what he began to call Leigh's obsession with his "telepathic accident."

He could not pretend otherwise than that he was camping out in Leigh's less-than-convenient flat: nothing was permanent, nothing resolved. About their relationship he felt perpetually frustrated and came to recognize that Leigh used his contact with the man as an excuse to avoid discussing or defining their personal life together. At times he understood and sympathized with this, seeing that from her point of view it might balance the unresolved muddle of his marriage. He avoided doing anything about that, contenting himself with guarded phone calls, mostly to Mark, to whom he had relayed the good news that the X ray had shown nothing, no tumors or malignant growths that might explain his headaches or so much else about which he remained silent and afraid. He did not want to force any issues. If he felt guilty about it, he salved his conscience by thinking that Georgia needed this calmer time to assess her own feelings and wants: the ball was in her court, and he was happy to leave it there. The sum effect of both relationships was to make him frequently feel irrelevant. He clung by a thin, compromised thread to his son but played no meaningful part in Georgia's life, while Leigh increasingly made him feel that he was relegated to the passive end of a case history.

At first he had found some residue of interest and excitement in the subject, was able to accept and, within the limits of his understanding, confirm her theory about the EEGs. Yes, the second and separate patterning of the first two tracings seemed to prove that contact existed, and his present sense of being on his own, free of intrusion, which was perhaps exemplified by the absence of the headaches, seemed to confirm this. And again, yes, it did make a kind of sense that he only became conscious of the contact when the man felt some extreme of emotion, when the electrical discharge from his brain became powerful enough to pierce the barrier of Steven's separate identity. About the third element in her theory he felt less sure. He could not explain why, while he was passively wired to the machine, such extremes of emotion should have occurred. But her suggestion that the man had somehow "known" what was happening to Steven and feared discovery when the third EEG was to be done seemed to him almost ridiculously farfetched, perhaps because he resisted the idea of such "eavesdropping" being possible. In the face of these doubts, Leigh argued that it was some such knowledge that had made the man "withdraw" just before the third EEG.

"So what are you saying? I should have an EEG every week to scare him off?"

"I don't want you to scare him off. I want you to find him and hang on to him."

And that was the thorn in their common flesh. As the days passed and there was no hint of contact and, more importantly, no more murders were committed or reported, all Steven's instincts prompted him to leave well enough alone, let sleeping monsters lie. He wanted to learn about Leigh, put his house in order, retreat—if she insisted upon that word—into normalcy. He noted for the first time an aggressive tenacity in Leigh, a certainty on her part that it was a matter of pride, perhaps even a mark of his manhood, that he should be in control. He counterargued from a scant but persuasive knowledge of other psychopathic killers. Was it not true that such people sometimes only killed until their sick appetites were sated and then withdrew, became to all intents and purposes sane and ordinary people, leading unremarkable lives? Why should not that be the case with this man? He was satisfied now. In time, surely the police would trace and capture him. Why should Steven risk flushing him from his cover or, worse, risk forcing him to kill again? Leigh balanced this by supposing this present time to be an interlude, a rest period, if Steven preferred, and when the desire to kill again seized the man, Steven would be as vulnerable and as helpless as he had been before. He should grasp the advantage now, arm himself so that he could fight when the time came.

"If it comes," he persisted. "You can't know that."

"It's every bit as likely as your cockamamie idea he's gone into voluntary retreat. You are not dealing with a rational person, Steven. Can't you get that through your head?"

"Now wait a minute. You're not being so rational, either. If you're right and he was scared off by the EEG, then he must know that he can contact me. He must be aware of the ability. Now if he's sensible enough to withdraw because of something as small and subtle as an EEG, if he has that sophistication of knowledge about what is happening to me, then he's going to make damn sure he stays 'silent' or whatever you want to call it. He'll kill again if he wants to, but he won't involve me."

"And that's okay by you, is it? Let him slaughter half the kids in London as long—"

"That's not fair. That's not what I'm saying at all."

"Well it sure sounded like it."

To that Steven had no answer, only a nagging sense of guilt that she was right. But he did not want to be manipulated.

"Anyway, if Page is right about the moments of extreme emotion, he may not be able to control it. It may be out of his hands. Contact might just happen, without either of you willing it. And then where would you be?"

"No worse off than I was before."

"Anyway," she said, attacking on a new front, "I'm not sure he is conscious of it. I see him more as a totally instinctive person. Okay, sure, he can lead an outwardly normal life when he wants to or perhaps is allowed, but deep down he's instinctive, impulsive, a person who has gone beyond the moral and social barriers. He isn't rational. Now—wait a minute, please—if he's always had this ability or even if it's only an integral part of his 'madness,' his instinctual side, it will seem quite normal to him. He'll sense things maybe and act instinctively on those promptings. What I'm saying to you, Steven, is that you have the advantage of rationality. You know what's happening. I don't want you to be passive, Steven, at the mercy of his instincts. I want you to be in the driver's seat, for your own sake and for all those kids he might—damn it— kill. And I believe now is the time for you to move. I believe he's vulnerable because temporarily satisfied. His guard's down. I'd stake my life on it. Now is the time to contact him and get a hold on the situation. Won't you try, at least?"

As a result of this and, to Steven, seemingly countless similar arguments, all of which led to the same impasse dressed in different guises, he allowed Leigh to put him three times into a trance. He had been scared at first, less so each time the experience yielded nothing. He felt only that he had slept, slightly and without much benefit, but he brought nothing back, no memory of dreamlike images. Did that not prove that Leigh was wrong? He was only the receiver, perforce passive. He was not a transmitter and never could be. The man had gone, had finished with him, perhaps was dead himself. Had she not heard of murderers who, after an orgy of killing, took their own lives? It was possible. Anything was possible.

"You don't want to do it," she accused. "You're not trying hard enough because you're scared. Deep down in you there is a terrible fear that you really do have this ability, and if you ever accept that and use it it will make you some kind of freak. Deep down you're scared that you will discover that some part of you has an affinity with this man. You just don't want to face that."

"Would you?" he shouted at her, because she voiced an unspoken truth he had refused to examine coolly. "I don't remember that you found it so easy to be 'different.' I seem to recall you felt pretty sorry for yourself."

"But I've learned to live with it."

"Then why don't you use your fantastic powers to find him? Go on, you can read minds and see through walls. You bloody well find him. You're the one who's so keen on it all. You do it. And for Christ's sake stop using me like a piece of medical equipment."

Later he apologized, and she acknowledged that there was some truth in his accusation, but it was not something she sought or wanted to stress. Later still they made love for the first time since Steven had come out of the hospital. Until then, Leigh had held him at arm's length, diverting all attempts at intimacy into a discussion of his "problem." They made love, and it was good, but not as good as it should have been, as they both knew it could be. The rift of anger was healed between them, but the issue itself remained like a cold hand shivering their flesh.

"Suppose I can't," Steven said. "Suppose I can never do it. What will you make of me then?"

"You can. You're a latent."

"A what?" He laughed.

"That's what we call people who have abilities, paranormal talents, but never admit it, never seek to acknowledge or use them. If they become aware of them, by an accident, they suppress them, explain them away. Latents have phenomenal powers of suppression. I'm bad for you, Steven," she said sadly. "You'd better know that. If we had met under different circumstances I would have been able to handle it. I'd be the last person on earth to make a latent aware, but you were already in contact and I couldn't ignore that. I still can't. And that's why I lean on you so much. I have to."

"And what wonders am I capable of?" he asked, deliberately teasing her to distance himself from this latest confusion.

"I don't know, and it doesn't matter. You can handle whatever it is."

"All right, but just tell me this. If I am able to contact the murderer, if I can do what you want and somehow we come through it all, what then? What will I mean to you then?"

"You will always be very dear to me."

"What future will we have?"

"That's not for me to say, is it? You have a wife and child. I can't help you with them."

"You could. If you said you loved me and wanted to be with me—"

"I can't say that either. Like it or not, Steven, you are a 'case,' and in many ways it's best that you remain one. It would be easier, but not so sweet." She leaned over him, tracing the contours of his face with the tip of her finger. "I have to split myself in two. It is possible," she asserted, remembering what she had said to Sonia Zimmer. "But one side has to lose out. And when I lose, you lose, too. Before I met you I'd more or less accepted that I would always be alone, that people like me can't ever make a lasting relationship. Now I want to so much but I know that I can't, dare not. Not yet. I can't forget or pretend I don't know that you're linked to that man, and I am scared that it will destroy you if you do nothing about it. If I can help you to save yourself, then we'll have to start over. We'll have to see."

Her words were like a cold wind, chilling his body. He drew her closer, for warmth and comfort.

"Can't you see the future? Can't you tell how it will all turn out?"

"No, Steven." And even if I have some vague and desolate idea, I would never tell you, she thought. "Like everyone else I have to live for the moment."

"Then let's do that. Let's take what we can and—"

"And when he comes back?"

"You're so certain he will?"

"I'm so scared he might and that I might lose you because you're not prepared."

"What do you want me to do?"

"You know. You *can* do it."

"It's like a trial, isn't it?" he said, pushing her away from him and sitting up. "Faint heart never won fair lady, and all that. Deal with this and then . . ." He turned to her, pleading with her.

"We'll see," was all she could say.

"I don't have any choice."

"You can leave now. You can walk out of here and never speak to me again. I wouldn't blame you. I'm not good for you."

"I'd included that possibility when I said I had no choice."

"Oh Steven."

"I do love you."

"I know it. And I wish I could make magic. Then I'd make you happy."

He lay down again, drew her into his arms.

"Then you'd better put me into a trance," he said. "I'm going to try to win you, no matter what the cost."

Outwardly there was nothing different, nothing to distinguish this trance from the several others that Leigh, with an almost fatalistic premonition of failure, had put him into lately. He sat on the sofa facing her, his body relaxed, his eyes in repose. Out of habit, Leigh reached out and switched on the portable tape recorder. His nose twitched, the nostrils flaring as though taking in some exotic or precious scent. He wriggled his bottom on the seat, raised his hands in front of him to a position about level with his shoulders, then let them fall again passively. All these movements Leigh noted down, but her pen became still, frozen over the note pad when he let out a low, amused chuckle, followed by a sigh of near contentment. She moved closer to him, willing him to make the next step, to speak. The sigh again, accompanied by a slight movement of the shoulders, then he began to speak in a low, monotonous voice, spoke rapidly but without inflection.

"Three boys are dead, and an uneasy peace, like an

impending thunderstorm, hangs over the London borough of Hammersmith and Fulham. There is a sense of waiting, of dread. As the bereaved mother of one of the young victims said last week: 'Every time I pick up a newspaper or switch on the news, I hold my breath, waiting to hear that some other mother's heart has been broken.' This woman, like the other residents of the borough, lives in fear. These people know they harbor a monster in their midst, an insane, evil child-killer who has already claimed three lives in a manner that has shocked and sickened even the most hardened police officers. And the police guardedly admit that they fear the murderer will strike again.

"Who's this man? What is he like? Where does he live?"

Steven's voice broke off there, and he began to laugh. The sound made Leigh's flesh crawl. His laughter sounded warm and natural. She longed to slap him, to slap his face as one would a hysteric's, but the laughter subsided. She remembered when he had imitated for her the man's soft, calling whistle. The laughter, also ordinary, unremarkable, was even more chilling. He shook his head as though to acknowledge his amusement, settled deeper on the sofa, his lingering smile fading.

"Someone must know. This is the cry you hear most often as you walk the streets of this ordinary district that has become the setting for a nightmare. The parents of the victims, the ordinary people in the street, even the police constantly repeat: Someone must know who and where he is. And that person, if they chance to read this, should know that they are as guilty as the maniac who has slaughtered and mutilated three adolescent boys.

"In an exclusive interview, Detective-Inspector Gurney admitted that the police are stumped. Like some monstrous creature in a horror thriller, this man can apparently come and go at will, commit his obscene crimes, often in public places, and vanish without a trace. Repeated appeals to the public for information, no matter how slight, have so far only yielded one nugget. An unnamed boy has reported being approached by a man, but we understand he was not able to give the police a full description. Fortunately, the boy concerned had the presence of mind to run off before the villain could strike. But this near miss only reinforces the wariness of the community.

"This maniac must be found. And when he is, the full punishment of the law must be visited upon him. The bereaved parents and brothers and sisters of the three victims speak with one voice, echoing a cry that has for too long been ignored by those we put in power: Bring back capital punishment now. And before trendy do-gooders and leftist so-called humanitarians begin to shout these tragic people down, let them remember that hanging is too good for those who prey on the bodies and lives of young boys poised on the threshold of life."

The clipped recitative of his voice ended in another sigh. In the following silence Leigh heard the soft hiss and whir of the tape recorder beside her. A newspaper report, obviously, but not one taken from either of the two fat Sunday papers Steven had gone out to buy earlier and which lay now picked apart into sections about the room. Which paper then? Steven moved again, making himself more comfortable. She sensed that an alien presence or atmosphere had gone from the room. It had spoken with Steven's voice but somehow altered or borrowed it, she thought. It made her feel uncomfortable. The excitement she felt from contact having been made again was offset by the power and directness of the communication. Steven had been used, she felt sure of it, would probably remember nothing when she brought him out of the trance. Her perceptions of the man altered, shifted, in some ways grew closer to Steven's. He was indeed clever, was perhaps showing off his powers, taunting them. Maybe she had been wrong to nag Steven into trying. He stirred suddenly, and she pushed her doubts and speculations aside, stopped the recorder and set it to rewind. Then she leaned toward Steven and said his name.

"When I count to three, Steven, okay? You'll wake up. Here we go then. One . . . two . . . three."

He woke as from an ordinary sleep, a nap, stretching. He looked at her, saw that she was worried.

"Sorry," he said. The tape recorder clicked off, attracting his attention.

"You don't remember anything?"

"No."

"Listen to this." She pressed the Play button on the recorder and moved to sit beside him, holding his hand.

"You got something?" he asked eagerly.

"Sh. Listen."

The voice spoke. Steven stood up and adjusted the volume control.

"Hey that's me. Isn't it?"

Leigh shook her head to indicate that he should be silent, listen attentively. He sat down again and this time reached for her hand. His fingers gripped her tightly when the laughter came. The unmistakable note of genuine pleasure and amusement was horrible, more so than any ghostly wailings or cries of terror. She felt his whole body tense, and he whispered something inaudible through his teeth. But as the voice began to speak again, he stared fixedly ahead of him, slowly pulling his hand from hers. She watched, more nervous than clinically observant, as he reached his hands to his head, clutched it. When the voice ceased, dying again on that last sigh, he did not move. Leigh remained still beside him until the hiss of the tape recorder became unbearable. She stood up and switched it off.

"Steven?"

"Sh. I'm getting something."

"What? Wait!" She turned the tape recorder on again, setting it to record. "Which paper, Steven? Can you see which paper he was—"

"*The Mail*. Pictures of all three boys. Fuzzy pictures. Holiday snapshots, school photos, that sort of thing."

Laughing at them, they both thought. Steven groaned, pressed his knuckles hard against his temples.

"No." He shook his head and let his hands drop. "Nothing else."

"Wait." Leigh picked up the notes she had made at the beginning of the session, scanned them. The gesture she had noted, the raising of the hands, was suddenly comprehensible. It was the gesture of a man raising an open newspaper. She saw Steven as a puppet suddenly, his body and mind manipulated. It was horrible to think of him so, and she pushed it to the back of her mind. "You wrinkled your nose," she said. "Was there a smell? Can you remember?"

Again he shook his head, then concentrated, sniffed.

"Cabbage," he said with surprise. "Yes, a strong smell of cabbage, overcooked . . ." He frowned with the effort of trying to recapture more.

"That's good, Steven. Very good," she said quietly.

"No. Nothing else. It's hopeless." The note of defeat in his voice was raw and pitiful.

Leigh switched off the tape recorder.

"No, Steven, that's good. Not only did you make contact but you remembered."

"Good?" he said, scornfully. "Oh yes, terrific. Now we know what paper he reads and that he overcooks his greens. Do you realize how many people read *The Mail* and eat cabbage for Sunday lunch?"

"Now wait a minute; stop right there. How do you know he does the cooking?" He stared at her blankly. "Come on. You said *he* overcooked the greens. How do you know?"

"I don't. It was just a . . . I assumed . . ."

"Try, Steven. Please," she pleaded, her voice throbbing. "Just relax . . ." She did not dare to move, not even to switch the tape recorder on again. She remained still, hunched toward him as his eyes became blank, unfocused. He seemed to see through her, through the walls beyond her. His hands gripped his knees in a pose she had never seen him adopt before. There was something square and military about the set of his shoulders. A nervousness emanated from him. He pursed his lips, moistened them. He slapped the palm of his right hand against his knee, as though impatient, as though trying to make some important point.

"Mummy used to make a lovely Yorkshire pudding," he gabbled. "Every Sunday. Oh, I used to look forward to that. I do miss it," he added pathetically, and his eyes returned to Leigh's face, became aware of her, confused.

"No," he said, his shoulders slumping, rubbing his hands together. "I'm sorry."

Leigh straightened up, put her note pad on the table.

"Steven, tell me something?"

"What? I can't try anymore. My head hurts."

"No. About yourself. Did your mother make Yorkshire pudding on Sundays?"

"Sometimes, why? What an extraordinary—"

"Only sometimes?"

"Yes. If and when we had beef. Only with beef."

"Did you particularly look forward to it? You know, was it a special treat or something?"

"Not really. To be honest, she wasn't very good at it. It was always too heavy. Georgia makes a much—" He stopped himself. Georgia's name was still an embarrassment, a potential danger between them.

"You're sure?" Leigh insisted.

"Well of course I am. God, I ought to know about my own mother's cooking. What is all this?"

"You said, 'Mummy used to make a lovely Yorkshire pudding. Every Sunday. Oh, I used to look forward to that. I do miss it.'"

"That's ridiculous. A, it's not true, and B, I haven't called her 'Mummy' since I was in short pants."

"No, I guess you wouldn't."

"So . . . ?" She smiled as she saw understanding dawn on his face. "I said that?"

"Yes."

"I wasn't even in . . ."

"No. Don't you see, Steven? You've done it. You got through to him. Oh Steven . . ."

She hugged him excitedly, but he was unresponsive, rigid against her embrace.

"Steven?"

"I had to . . . to put it all away before Mummy came in."

"What? Steven . . ." Her voice was thin with panic.

"No. It's all right. I'm just remembering. That time, you know, what I wrote down, remembered?"

"Yes?" she said, nodding eagerly.

"It was the word *Mummy*. It reminded me. That time he thought . . . he was scared . . . he had to put it all away before Mummy came in."

"Oh Steve . . . That's terrific."

"Is it?" He stared at her bleakly.

"Yes of course. It shows you can remember, it's all there, locked in your mind."

"And you want to let it out?"

"Well sure, we've got to put all the information together and build up a portrait. Then we can go to the police." Her words seemed to bounce off him as though he were deaf or had cut her entirely out of his consciousness.

"Do you know what it was?" he asked, "what he had to put away before Mummy came in?" His voice was sick with loathing.

"No."

"Pictures of boys, obscene pictures." He turned his head away in disgust as though he could see them again and could not bear to look. "He was—"

"Yes, yes, I know. It's okay."

"I don't want to remember such things. It makes me feel filthy." He stood up wiping his hands against his thighs as though they were soiled, slimed with some disgusting substance.

"It's not you, Steven. Hang on to that."

"How do you know?" he demanded bitterly.

"Because I do." She put her arms around him, would not let him pull away. "Oh please, please trust me, believe in yourself. We're getting there, Steven. We've really broken through. And it will be all right, I promise you."

He stared at her.

"No more," he said. "I can't. Now now. I want . . . I want to have a bath."

He pushed her almost roughly aside, and she watched him go, pulling his shirt out of his trousers as he hurried toward the bathroom. She had to let him go, did not know what else she could say to comfort him. Besides, she had to get it all down now, while it was fresh in her mind. If she could piece it all together, these fragments might spark other memories, put flesh on the skeleton. Steven would understand, he had to. Someone had to get their priorities right around here, she told herself angrily as his bath water began to rattle in the ancient plumbing. What are you doing? she asked herself, pulling herself up short. But the answer was clear and obvious. My job, she answered, sitting down at her desk and picking up a pen.

It was a cold, overcast morning, the sort that could no longer pass for the tail end of autumn. Winter had come with a vengeance, Roger North thought as he reluctantly left the warmth of his car and stared across the frosted wastes of Wandsworth Common.

He felt leaden and dull and more than a little impatient as he spotted Georgia's car and saw her profile through the windshield, her gaze fixed anxiously on a distant soccer game. He rapped lightly with his knuckles on the roof of her car before stooping and opening the door. He slid in beside her, leaned to kiss her cheek. The kiss was perfunctory, a social greeting without depth, and they both knew it.

"God it's cold," he said, rubbing his hands together.

"Thanks for coming," Georgia said. "I know this isn't your idea of how to spend a Sunday morning."

He thought longingly of his ideal—the heavy Sunday papers spread over a warm bed, a breakfast tray, an attractive woman to share it all with, lightly and easily. A lazy bath, a pub lunch washed down by several pints of sharp bitter. Instead, here he was attending a junior-league soccer game.

"I couldn't think of any other way to see you, and I had to," she said.

"Do you do this every Sunday morning?"

"No. Steve used to, sometimes. It's just that with these murders . . ." Her eyes passed him by, were fixed on the field where Mark scampered and ran, yelling with the others. "I've never seen so many parents turn out before," she said.

"Maybe you should all be grateful then. Maybe the murderer is unwittingly fostering family ties, encouraging more participation, narrowing the generation gap or whatever."

"I don't think that's very funny."

"It wasn't meant to be. It was a perfectly serious sociological observation."

"Then it was in bad taste."

"Sorry."

He tried to stretch his legs, but the seat, adjusted to accommodate Mark, was too far forward and his knees struck against the dashboard.

"Am I to come back to work?" she said, her eyes cast down

to the red Fair Isle gloves she wore, her hands knotted in her lap.

"If you feel up to it," he answered noncommittally.

"Apart from anything else, I need the money . . . now."

"Oh, you'll be paid. I said you were on compassionate leave."

"It's not just that. I need something to do."

"Well, as you like."

"I thought we ought to talk first, outside the office." She glanced at him. He was staring straight ahead, appeared to be examining the dark blue hatchback parked immediately in front of them with great concentration.

"Why haven't you been answering your phone?" Roger asked.

"I told you, I needed time to think."

"It's not much of an affair when you can't even talk. Not seeing you—"

"That was your idea," she reminded him.

"I had to think about my job, and yours." He defended himself.

"Well, I needed to escape the pressures—"

"And has that worked? Have you decided something?"

He looked at her, demanding an answer, but she only shook her head. He thought she was going to cry. After a time she said, "It won't work. It can't, can it?"

"I'd better tell you that I could never take on all this." He waved his hand airily in a gesture that was meant to embrace the parked cars, the spectators, the boys raucously chasing a soccer ball. Georgia saw the movement but did not immediately understand what it meant. "I am just not cut out for it. It makes me impatient, restless. I feel trapped by all this. Damn it, I don't want to spend my Sunday mornings in the cold, stomping up and down to keep warm, watching a game that seems to me as boring as it is pointless."

"I used to feel exactly the same," she said quietly. "Before I met you. Oh, I don't mean just the sports but the whole thing. I was sick of the sameness of it all. Shopping, meals, cleaning. It's a very narrow life. I felt trapped."

"And now you don't?"

"God, yes. But there's a reason for it now. I see that.

Perhaps when Mark's a bit older it will be possible for me to break out, do something else, but now I really don't have any choice. He's my responsibility."

"Yours and Steven's."

"But definitely not yours."

"No."

"I should have realized . . ." She turned her face away, wiped what might have been a tear on her glove.

"I didn't ever know that it would come to this. When it did I . . . I tried. I would like to be . . . No, that's not true. I wish I were the sort of man who could fit into your life, but I'm not, and it's not true to say that I want to be."

"You should have told me."

"I was prepared to try to make it work, somehow. You didn't make any conditions when we started. You took what was there without question or hesitation."

"Some people would say you tricked me."

"Then they would be wrong. I made no promises. Georgia, I wanted you. I still do. In my way I love you. It's just that I'm not prepared to put up with all that loving seems to entail. I can't understand why it can't just be fun, uncomplicated. Why ruin it with . . ." He shrugged, looked at the common again, the snake of stationary cars. "I suppose you think that's very immature."

"Not really. No more so than me. Marion was right. I did hope you were some kind of knight in shining armor, that you would carry me off . . ."

He laughed. "You must admit there's something incongruous about the thought of a teenaged boy thrown across the saddle while his mother hangs on behind. There wouldn't be much room for the knight, would there?"

"I suppose not."

"It's a lovely thought, though," he said gently, touching her arm. "In my way I'm just as conventional and comfort seeking as you."

"A nice warm woman in your bed, without complications."

"Something like that," he admitted, and took his hand away.

"I'd better go and watch," Georgia said, unfastening her

seat belt. "I don't feel comfortable, even with all those people around."

"So, will you come back to work tomorrow?"

"Perhaps not tomorrow. Can I ring you?"

"Take as long as you like."

"I won't make a fuss or anything. You needn't worry."

"I know." She reached for the door handle, and he caught her hand and drew it back. "What will you do now? Will you and Steve . . . ?"

"I don't know. I don't think so. I don't know if we can."

"I'm sorry."

"So am I."

"I wish we could . . . just once more. You're very special, Georgia."

"No. I'm a classic case. A married woman, approaching middle age, feeling sorry for herself. When I was a kid, I always hated being told to count my blessings."

"Me too."

"You'd better go now. I don't want Mark to see you. And I must . . ." Her eyes were drawn back to the field. Roger leaned forward and kissed her on the lips. Georgia took the kiss, permitted it, but she kept her hands clenched together in her lap, refused to release any of the feelings he could still inspire. "Any one of them," she said, when he withdrew, looking at her with a sadly puzzled frown, "could be the murderer. That's what I keep on thinking. That's what's so terrible about it all. Suddenly nothing's safe. Everybody is a potential monster. He could be there, right now, among the crowd, one of the referees even. What better way to get access, time to choose?" She turned away, opened the door. "I'm sorry, Roger."

He got out and they faced each other over the roof of the car. Georgia avoided his eyes, locked her door, then walked around the car; he stood back to let her lock the other door.

"Well, I'll see you then. I mean it—take your time, but you will be welcome back."

"Thanks."

They stood, not looking at each other, not really wanting to part.

"Walk me to my car," he said. "It's just down there."

"No. I've got to go . . ."

She never finished the sentence. Stumbling a little, she left the pavement and hurried across the open ground. After a moment she started to run. Roger sighed and turned toward his car. He'd passed a pub about half a mile back. It was almost opening time.

"It'll do you good," Leigh said. "Besides, it's something *I* want to do, lunch in an English pub, a walk by the river." She swung out of the room, all activity. Steven felt too dispirited to argue, let himself be caught up in the wake of her energy and enthusiasm. He certainly had no wish to spend the day picking over the scraps of what had happened, dreading the moment when Leigh would insist or trick him into trying again. It was a good idea to get out, close the door on it, leave it all locked in here.

And once outside, strolling the pavements in the crisp Sunday air with Leigh on his arm, he began to feel lighter and better. She was chattering as he had never known her to do before, the sort of relaxed and inconsequential talk that required only a minimal response from him and was soothing. He saw another facet of her personality, an aspect that was kept in check by their present preoccupation. She was momentarily the girl she might have been, the woman she yet might be able to become. He felt sad and grateful to her. Too often he blamed her, resented the way she pushed him toward the man, horrors he could do without. He saw, as he watched her animated face and heard the lilt of gaiety in her voice, that it was no fun for her either. Much that she had said to him lately began to make sense. Too often, as well, he was passively content to be fascinated by her, to perceive her as an exotic creature rather than as a woman, complex and, in the full and best sense of the word, ordinary. He wanted to tell her all this but did not want to break into the flow of her happiness and freedom from care. As though to complement and enhance her mood, the sun suddenly broke through the clouds.

"Excuse me, just a minute, okay?"

They had reached the pedestrian tunnels that traveled beneath Hammersmith Broadway. He noticed his surroundings as she darted away from him, into a newsstand. Light traffic hissed across the elevated section of the road between the Odeon and the eastern entrance to the underground station. Across the road Catholic families filed from St. Augustine's, all dressed in their Sunday best. The children's clothes in particular had the formal air of the 1940s or '50s about them: a little girl in a smaller version of her mother's green tweed coat, wearing an odd little hat; a boy in a double-breasted suit and polished Oxford shoes.

He found himself staring at the boy. It was as though his eyes had developed the equivalent of a zoom lens. The boy stood out sharply from the chatting, milling crowd. Steven shook his head to correct this slip and trick of his eyesight. At the same time he remembered what Sonia Zimmer had said about getting his eyes tested again, how he would probably have to wear glasses. Bored, the boy strayed through the open church gates, stared at Steven from the opposite pavement. He had light brown hair, thick and glossy, freshly washed. His skin had the soft flawlessness of youth, marred only by the faint down of an emergent moustache on his upper lip. His eyes looked at or toward Steven with a frank inquisitiveness; they were light colored, probably blue. There was something disturbing and fascinating about the boy, something Steven did not put into thought or words. The formal suit seemed too tight for him, to confine his body. He should be dressed in looser, casual clothes, or running naked. . . . Steven caught himself on the edge of a disturbing act of imagination, then became aware of the traffic crossing and slicing his vision of the boy, who was suddenly the correct distance away and in perspective. He turned and walked back to his parents. Steven realized that Leigh was again by his side, leafing through a newspaper. She caught his eye, smiled, folded the paper, then stowed it in her tote bag.

"Which way?"

He pointed silently, let her take his arm, hugging it in both of hers.

Leigh was quiet as they passed under the elevated roadway, passed another, Protestant, church, set in a cushion of green and graves. She had scanned the article sufficiently to verify that it was as Steven had "recited" it, had seen the pictures of the three dead boys, and she assumed that Steven must know that's what it was. There was no need to mention it. They turned down toward the river, the sun dazzling to the eye, and descended to the mall.

To Steven everything seemed gray and dirty. He did not think about the boy or the trick his eyesight had played. Instead he concentrated on the knowledge that he was not alone. He was in control of all his faculties, without headaches or any visual evidence of the other presence. But it was there, a cloud in his mind, a dulling of his mood that made him irritable and depressed at once. For example, he noticed the press of people and the unpleasant smell as soon as they entered the pub. Under the beer and the spice of cigar smoke, he could smell their sweat. He was tempted to use his elbows too sharply as he forced a passage to the bar.

"You okay? Look, there's a space there," Leigh said.

Somehow they had acquired drinks and veal-and-ham pies on beds of crisp lettuce and tomato. Leigh squeezed behind a small table fashioned from a barrel and smiled happily at the dancing fire, which Steven glimpsed between the legs of a group of standing men. Flesh bulging against cloth, the play of muscle and tendon, the soft bulge of sexual organs. He felt sick at the rank rottenness of the human mind, of people. He watched Leigh unwind scarves and shawls, watched her remove layers of clothing until her breasts hung pert beneath a blue sweater, jiggled as she leaned forward, raised her glass in a toast that was, what, mocking? The lager was cold and sharp and acid on his tongue, like bile. In profile, as she turned toward the fire, he saw one perfect nipple silhouetted, thrusting against the wool. The old words *harlot* and *Jezebel* came into his mind. Cramming food into her mouth, flakes of pastry adhering to lips that sucked the seeds from a half tomato, she was suddenly repulsive and ugly to him. He pushed his own plate away, disgusted.

Through a mouthful of food, shouting above the roar and grumble of voices, Leigh said, "It's good. You should eat."

"I'm not hungry."

She leaned forward, breasts swaying, to pick tidbits from his plate, fumbling them into her mouth, sucking her fingers clean.

He took their glasses to the bar to escape her, not because he wanted another drink. A young man, elbows propped on the bar, his backside stuck out in invitation, was being served ahead of him. Steven stared through the skintight jeans, imagining, no, seeing . . .

"Lager is it, mate?"

"Yes. Please."

"Pints?"

"Yes. Please."

The barman, bare arms coated with thick black hair, glanced at a regular customer, indicating Steven with his eyes. We've got a real crazy here, his look said. Foam dribbled down the side of a glass. The barman slopped it away, beads of amber sticking to the hairs on his arm. Steven paid and carried the glasses back to Leigh. A man bending to tap out his pipe on the fire grate bumped against him. The contact burned. Leigh held a piece of pie to his mouth, wheedling. He shook his head.

"Oh, but it's so good."

She popped the food into her own mouth, then leaned back, patting her stomach. Her mannerisms disgusted him.

"Let's get out of here."

The smell of smoke and stale beer stifled him.

"But you haven't touched . . ."

He did not wait for her. He stood up, pushed the pipe smoker aside, and barged his way to the door. He missed his footing on the three steps down to the mall and slipped ungainly, having to jump to regain his balance. He stood there, filling his lungs with clean air, panting like a man who has jogged a mile. Children, attracted by the carousing adults, or left outside while their parents drank, played on the wide flagged space in front of the pub—little girls hopscotching, a boy flying a toy airplane. An older boy, one foot cocked against the river wall, sat astride a flashy yellow bicycle with narrow whitewall tires and dropped handlebars. He dashed a cowlick of dark hair from his forehead and bent to grip the handlebars. Steven's eyes were drawn to the patch of exposed skin between the waistband of his jeans and the tail of his sweater. Such pale skin, milk smooth, unwittingly exposed. The boy twisted, leaned lower to check the leather straps on his pedal, and the space of exposed flesh grew.

"That wasn't a good idea, huh?" She stood in front of him, wrapping a scarf about her neck, muffling her chin. She took his arm, thus moving out of his line of vision, followed the direction of his fixed gaze. The boy straightened up in the narrow saddle, reached behind him with unconscious grace, to hitch down the welt of his sweater. "Steven?"

"Let's walk," he said, tearing his eyes from the boy, forcing his suddenly reluctant feet to move.

"Okay. This way?"

She turned him up river, steering him like an old man or an invalid, hugging his arm as though he were a prisoner or someone she could not trust to walk safely alone. He tugged against her grip so that she fell against him, her weight unbalancing him. That moment, as they tottered and swayed together like quarreling Siamese twins, the boy chose to push off from the wall, bear down hard on the raised left pedal and turn his sleek bike in a tight arc. He stood on the pedals, making a sprint start, head down.

"Look out," Leigh said and threw her weight against Steven. He stumbled. The boy applied efficient brakes, sending the back wheel into a skid. The front wheel grazed Steven's shin. The boy got one foot on the ground, the bicycle angled between his splayed legs.

"You bloody young fool. Why don't you look where you're going?" He dragged his arm free of Leigh, kicked at the bike.

"Hey, watch my spokes."

"Don't you know better than to ride on the pavement? This is for pedestrians, not stupid hoodlums."

"It's allowed," the boy shouted.

Steven pounced then, caught him by the front of the sweater just below the throat and pulled him toward him. In his fright, the boy dropped the bike with a clatter. For a long time Leigh would remember the tick and whir of the back wheel uselessly turning, the shiny spokes sparking the sun into cruel lances. The boy pushed against Steven's shoulders, his face deathly pale.

"I'll teach you a lesson, you bloody young thug."

"Steven." His name was torn from her. She tried to

interpose herself between them, but the bike made it impossible to get close enough. She saw the white of Steven's knuckles, the stretching of the sweater, which threatened to snap or burst open. "Leave go, Steven. Stop it." She yelled at the top of her voice, managed to grip the boy's arm and pull him back. He hopped on one foot, trying to clear the bicycle, failed and fell against her. Startled, Leigh stepped back. It seemed that Steven would never let go. The sweater, still gripped in his fists, stretched and held the boy like a fish caught in a net. Then Steven threw the boy from him, and he fell onto the flagstones with a cry of shock and pain.

An old woman, passing home from church, and several men from the pub gathered around them. The two little girls who had been playing hopscotch stared with saucer eyes. Leigh knelt down beside the boy.

"Are you okay? I'm sorry. He didn't mean it. Are you hurt?"

A man in a yachting-club blazer and silk cravat picked the bicycle up by its crossbar, carrying it as though it weighed nothing, to prop it against the river wall. The boy, fearing the theft of his new and precious machine, scrambled up. One elbow stuck grazed and red through a tattered hole in the sweater.

"My bike . . ."

"The bike's okay, son," the man said. "What about you?"

Leigh desperately scanned the crowd for Steven, saw him walking away fast, up river, his hands pushed into his pockets. She got up, touched the boy on the shoulder.

"I've got to go after him. Are you sure you're okay?"

The boy nodded, close to tears, and clasped his elbow with a wince. Leigh ignored the questioning, complaining voices clamoring around her, and fished in her bag.

"Look, take this, for the sweater. I'm so sorry." She pushed a five-pound note at the boy's hand, saw that the knuckles, too, were skinned. "Please, see he's all right," she said to the yachting man. "I have to go after him."

"I'd leave him, darling, if I were you," another voice said behind her. "Let him stew. Come and have a drink with me." He touched her arm proprietarily.

"Leave me alone," she said, pushing him. The yachting

man nodded, put his arm around the boy's shoulder. "Thanks." To the boy she said again, "I'm so sorry."

She went running after Steven, calling to him, knowing that he must hear her steps. The path narrowed, seemed squeezed between the water and a row of high-walled, expensive houses. He stopped, and Leigh, telling herself to be careful, slowed her pace, approached him slowly.

"Steven? Please . . ."

"Go away," he said, his voice harsh and bitter. "Leave me alone."

"No, Steven, please. Let's walk—"

"I said leave me alone." He swung around then, his face blazing, broken, nerves jumping, his eyelids blinking rapidly. "I don't want you near me. Get away from me or . . ." A spasm seemed to seize him, to twist his features into a look of surprise, a snarl of rage. He never completed his threat but turned and strode away from her. Leigh's calls died on her lips. She watched him until a bend in the path carried him from her sight. She turned, undecided, looked back toward the pub in time to see the boy scoot away, mount his bike, and ride off.

"Steven, be careful," she whispered, knowing that she had to follow him.

She forced herself to run to the point where the path curved a little inland, then slowed, wanting to keep a cautious distance between them, if possible to follow without being seen. But it was she who could not see him. Rounding the bend the towpath broadened again, stretched before her toward a distant, misty bridge. Among the few people passing to and fro along the path there was no sign of Steven's bent head, hunched back. Pulled by a tug of dread, she went to the low river parapet, her heart thudding jerkily. The tide was in, the river high, lapping blackly at the weed-slimed wall. A pair of mallards bobbed on the waves, their golden eyes turned greedily toward her. A piece of wood, part of a splintered fruit crate, edged its way between them. Relieved but still worried, she sank down onto the wall, her eyes lulled and fascinated by the rhythm of the river.

Here she was huddled on a brick parapet in the cold, knowing that Steven, the man she loved, was not himself and had slipped beyond her caring reach. The boy with the bike had been the trigger to a rage as ugly as it was uncharacteristic. It had not been Steven but the aftermath of the man's insane anger, breaking over him in waves, sweeping him away. She got to her feet, hurried through an alleyway between two buildings, and emerged into a narrow street where another pub, this time with its back to the river, spilled its customers over the pavement. Right or left? Either way the road stretched blank with his absence. A T-junction led deeper inland, and she peered in that direction but saw nothing, no one that was Steven. She had lost him. Let him go, a voice inside her said. Let him go now. You're better off without him; you said yourself you were bad for him. Let him go. It won't hurt as much as you think, and not for long in any case. I can't, she answered and turned back in the direction of home, to where he would know to find her, if he wanted her.

At some point he climbed the wooden steps of a pedestrian bridge that passed across a railway line, two dye-straight silver tracks passing beneath him, curving gracefully away to a distant infinity. He stopped on the bridge, staring first at the high gray walls with their decoration of over-familiar graffiti. He stared at the scratched words with a sense of loss and despair, then raised his head to look over the bridge, to gain an unexpected bird's-eye view down onto a housing estate. The sky above was dark and darkening even more. Two youths worked on a car to the sound of harsh pop music. The pain cracked and fizzled through his brain, blinding him, causing him to stagger on the bridge. His hand slipped on the smooth gray metal, landing on a stippled row of rivets. His mind turned again, exhausted, sick. *He stared down from his perch, half concealed behind a loop of green curtain, stared down, the angle foreshortened, over the plumed heads of a crescent of girls. He ignored the boys, whose bodies were tense with desire, which spilled from their eyes and stiffened the shameless muscles in their groins. In olden days they would have been beaten to cool the fever of their lust, sent to bed supperless, their wrists thonged to the head of the bed that they might avoid sin, that they might grow strong and pure.*

"Pure," she said, expelling her breath with each hiss and

*crack of the cane.* "*Pure. I'll make you pure. I'll make you into a man. You'll go mad, touching yourself down there. I'll cut it off, you'll be better off without it. I'll make you pure. I'll beat some goodness into you if it's the last thing I do. Come away from that window. You haven't got any friends. You've never had any friends, never will have any. Nice little boys don't want to be friends with dirty, filthy little boys. Come away from that window.*"

The world washed blind in green. His hand splayed between the cool nipple rivets on the bridge parapet. He swung his head, felt the vertiginous pull of the track below him, felt the sweet promise of silver death. His eyes sought footholds, handholds, measured the distance. It would be so easy to climb the parapet. And he pushed away from the temptation, staggered. Ahead of him, blurred and swaying as though detached and blown by a strong wind, the rough wooden steps with their protective strips of metal stretched down, beckoned. Gripping the handrail tight, he pulled himself along the remains of the bridge, forced his clumsy feet down, shuffling, one tread at a time, both hands gripping the rail. He did not dare to look left or right or up. Look down. See the toes of your own shoes, the ground getting nearer, standing steady under the feet. Safe and seeing the tatty row of sad shops, seeing them with his own eyes, with Steven Cole's eyes?

A motorbike roared past, its wind brushing him, dabbing his face; it snarled into the crescent to bring the boys running, splashing their Sunday trousers with mud. He walked toward them and did not know, as he put one foot with growing confidence in front of the other, if he saw them with his own or other eyes. He didn't *know*.

He just remembered passing the boys as they crowded around the bike. After that everything was blank until he found himself on a main road, watching the first swollen raindrops become stains on the pavement. But it was a different kind of blankness, one which, he knew, did not veil lost events. This was the blank of shock or rest, the mind's autonomous need to recuperate from the onslaught on the bridge. What he had seen and, especially, felt there was all too clearly rememberable, a plague in his mind. He took shelter in a doorway, miserably watching the rain spots stretch into ribbons. When he saw a bus approaching, its lights shining through the premature darkness, he made a dash for the nearest stop and wildly flagged it down. On the upper deck, he trembled in a window seat and bought a forty-pence ticket from the taciturn conductor, uncertain as to where the bus was going and not caring either. At least it was warm on the bus and perhaps safe.

It was too soon to make sense of what he remembered, attempt to piece the fragments into a coherent narrative. The shot remains of his sanity would not permit that yet. He knew that he had had a glimpse into hell and that hell was the ordinary world seen from another angle. Perfectly innocent people and events—a boy standing outside a church, Leigh eating, a group of boys whiling away a Sunday afternoon— became sick and ugly, inspired thoughts of destruction and lust. He remembered with a mental wince how he had wanted to smash the boy on the bicycle, had needed to see his flesh discolored, spoiled with bruises and cuts, his white bones broken as though the pale skin and wholesome flesh were but a facade.

It was the boys that got to him most, the feelings he felt or perceived when he saw them from that other angle—rank devils, rotten vessels, their flesh starting to stink, their minds moving toward insanity. They were perceived—he chose his words with extreme caution, watching himself for any slip, the least proof of involvement—with a lust that was unprecedented in his experience. A lust compounded by anger and guilt to such an extent that the mingled emotions were knotted into an indivisible skein. Had he ever known even a hint of a lust like that? He knew he had not, could assert that. But he knew it now, and the knowledge brought bile to his throat. And could he ever lust for a child of his own sex? That was the grain of sand that scratched at his conscience. What had Leigh said? That he feared some deep affinity with the man, something he had suppressed and . . . He began to sweat unpleasantly. It was so easy to say no, he had not, could not, and yet the memory of recent events brought him an intimate knowledge of such desires, a knowledge he wanted desperately to believe he had only shared, borrowed, or inherited but which, nonetheless, tainted him, altered his perception of the good world.

The man, he thought, leaping toward reason, wanted to destroy in order to possess, possess in order to destroy these boys he watched and brought blatantly and terrifyingly to Steven's attention. When he thought of *boy* for himself, it was Mark who was imagined in his mind. Mark was loved, cherished, but somehow rendered eternally sexless by their relationship. Or did that only prove the strength of the incest taboo, he wondered, unconsciously torturing himself? When he thought of those other boys his body withered and he felt only disgust. Not at them but at the way he was forced to observe and comprehend them. He did not think he was guilty, but once you had looked on the face of hell and drawn its bloody stench into your nostrils, you were never entirely innocent again.

The bus drew up opposite Harrods. Steven got up suddenly, ran to leave the bus before it lurched on again. He left because his thoughts had made the bus unclean. He watched it withdraw, enjoyed the feel of the rain-freshened air on his skin, drying his unnatural sweat. He felt better, more himself, had found a sense of proportion that seemed strong enough to bear him up until the next round. Yet he felt like a man who was convalescing from a long illness, a man of bruised mind and tired body. The longing for his bed, peace and safety and quiet, was suddenly irresistible. He crossed the road and joined the short queue at another bus stop. He had decided to go home.

Replete with Marion's food and comfort, Georgia dragged a protesting Mark from a game of chess with Fiona, Marion's patient daughter, insisting that it was already seven o'clock and he still had to finish his French homework and have a bath before bedtime. She felt curiously cleansed by her decision to part from Roger, and warmed by Marion's common sense and sympathy. Who knew what fresh pain and infection the morning would bring, but at least she felt able to get through the night. It wouldn't be easy, none of it would, but from her present calm she could see beyond the storm of doubt and unhappiness that was to come, would assail her, and she saw herself walking intact out the other side. If only she could hang on to that when the pain of missing him and hurt pride and loneliness came to batter her. And then there was also, perhaps, the hurdle of the return to work to be cleared. How to face him, feel the touch of his fingers as they exchanged documents, without trembling or breaking into a spontaneous smile? How could she bear the smell of his tobacco and aftershave, of *him* without feeling wanton?

"Mum, did you leave the light on?"

She was standing in the road outside the flat, locking the car up. Mark was on the pavement, his sports bag clutched to his chest like the comforting teddy bear of his infancy.

"What?"

"Look, up there."

She followed the direction of his nod. The big window with its fine view glowed in the half-dark with a golden radiance. In a split second she could identify which lamp it was: the one just inside the room, the one that stood beside the steps on the left as you entered. Of course she had not left it on. Why would she leave a light on when they had left the flat at nine-thirty that morning? What it must mean—a burglar—caused her heart to trip.

"Mark . . ." He was gone. She saw the heavy swinging door bounce open, shut, open, and the light, operated by a time switch, came on to illuminate the stone stairs. "Mark," she screamed. Damn the boy. She ran around the car. He had a key. She ran up the path and leaned her weight against the door. She could hear him above her, on the next landing, pausing to push home the next time switch. "Mark."

"What?"

"Don't go in there."

"Don't be silly. Come on."

"Mark, do as I say." She stumbled up the stairs, almost falling. Only fear and a sense of urgency enabled her to snatch her balance back in time. "Mark . . ."

"Maybe it's Dad. Do you think he's come home?"

She hadn't thought of that. But no, he wouldn't . . .

"It must be a burglar. For God's sake . . ." She reached their landing just as he was putting his key in the lock, balanced on one foot to squeeze the cumbersome bag against his raised thigh and free arm. "Don't, Mark."

"It's all right. Nobody's broken in. Look."

The door indeed stared back at her, unscratched, unsplintered. But they might have picked the lock or slipped it with a piece of plastic, could be in there now, cornered and desperate, waiting to spring. She leaped forward and pushed him away, just as the door swung open under its own weight.

"Ow! Now look what you've done."

Off-balance, Mark had dropped his bag, spilling the contents on the landing. A mud-encrusted soccer shoe rolled down the stairs—*clop, clop, clop*.

"Honestly, Mum, you're bloody impossible," he said, scooping a towel and muddy shorts back into the bag.

Her heart thudding, Georgia ventured into the flat. The kitchen and bathroom doors were partly open, the others closed. No other lights shone but the faint spill from the sunken living room. She felt for the hall switch and snapped it down. Behind her she heard Mark descend the stairs two at a time to retrieve his shoe.

"Who . . . who's there?" Her voice was small and scratchy, did not carry.

"That won't scare anyone," Mark sneered from the landing behind her. "Let me . . ."

"No." She moved forward, determined to be brave, at least to protect her son, if necessary to die and give him time to escape. He came thudding behind her.

"See?" He said triumphantly. "Honestly . . ."

She felt weak, had to lean her weight against the wall. The lamp by the door left Steven in shadow, dozing on the sofa. Mark dropped his bag with a crash.

"Hello, Dad."

"Go and close the front door," she said automatically. "And take that bag into the kitchen."

"In a minute."

She went down the steps.

"Steven?"

She crossed the room, put on more lights. He wasn't dozing. His eyes were open, blank and staring. His face had a lifeless look, like a mask in which the eyes darkly glittered.

"Steve? Are you all right?"

She did not want to go too close to him. He had looked this

way, she remembered, in the second before he hit her that night. Dead looking, like this, as he swung around in response to her touch and raised his hand. . . .

"What's the matter?" With a thump Mark jumped the steps into the room. She thought that Steven's eyes flickered, moved toward the boy. "Dad?"

"I don't think he's—"

"Is he asleep? Hey, Dad—"

"Don't touch him." Something in her voice frightened Mark into stillness. He looked from his strangely immobile father to his mother's pale, anxious face.

"What's the matter with him?" he asked, his voice dropping to an instinctive whisper.

"I don't know. I just think we should—"

"Dad?"

"Steve? Steve, can you hear me?" She dared to go a little closer, stooping to see into his face. He did not move or acknowledge them in any way. For a moment, Georgia doubted that he was even breathing, but then she saw the shallow rise and fall of his chest, and he blinked rapidly, three times. "Steve?"

"Mum? It's spooky. What's wrong with him?"

"I don't know. Just be quiet."

"Is he ill?"

"Mark!"

Again his eyes seemed to move toward the boy, but Georgia could not be sure. She went to Mark, forcing a courage she did not feel.

"Come on."

"Where? What are you—"

"I think we'd better call Dr. Campbell."

"All right."

She put her arm around his shoulders, and for once he did not protest. Georgia steered him toward the steps, wondering if she dare close the door and lock it. Where was the key anyway? Mark started up the steps ahead of her.

"I did have a friend anyway. I did, I did, I did."

They turned together, their faces slack with surprise. Georgia felt Mark press close to her. The childlike repetition of the words was curiously at odds with the flatness of his tone.

"I always had him, always. He was always there. It was just that she couldn't see him. No one could see him. Only me. We did naughty things together." He laughed softly, a little nervously.

"Mum?"

"Sh."

"What's he saying? Why's he sound so funny? Mum . . ."

"Mummy couldn't know. She couldn't. No one knew. He was mine, my secret friend. He was always there, always, whenever I was alone. There he'd be, waiting for me. I'm a poet and don't know it." The laugh again, more expressive than the flat reel of words, a secret, giggling laugh. "He started it, not me. Standing there, showing me, saying, Come on, come on, let's. Dare you. Double dare. Dare you to show me yours."

Mark caught his breath and then burst out laughing. His laughter was amused and frightened, too.

"Mark." She pushed him.

"Well why . . . ?"

"It was only a game, a game. He never got beaten. It was always me. But he started it. It wasn't fair."

"Mum?" Mark started the word on a rising inflection which threatened to break, become a scream. It pierced the cold and horrible fascination, which held Georgia tight in its grasp. She shook herself.

"Come on," she said, herding him up the steps, into the corridor.

"I don't understand . . ."

Neither did she, but her mind was tense with suspicion and fear. Steven's odd voice sounded again behind her, but she did not try to make out what he said.

"Why's he talking to himself like that?"

"Where's that piece of paper he gave you, with his phone number?"

"Why?"

"Where is it?" She caught his shoulder and shook it.

"On my desk."

"Get it."

He obeyed her instantly, galvanized by the force of her tone, or perhaps he was simply glad to have something to do, to distance himself from the madness he heard and could not comprehend.

Georgia crept back to the doorway. He was unnaturally still.

"In the bath sometimes he would when she wasn't looking. In my bed at night. Couldn't stop him. Didn't want to, more like. Not my fault, not my fault. Don't beat me, Mummy. I won't do it again."

"Oh my God . . ." Georgia said, appalled.

"Here . . . here it is, Mum." Mark waved the slip of paper at her.

"You come with me, stay by me." She grabbed his wrist as he, curious, moved back toward the living room. He let himself be pulled down the hall. "Now just stay there. Don't move. Don't you go near him."

The voice rumbled on, disembodied, muffled by distance. Georgia's hand shook as she dialed the number. She thought perhaps she had misdialed, but then, with an explosive click, the number started to ring, rang again, and once more before a voice answered.

"Leigh Duncan."

Mentally, Leigh had stopped waiting long before the telephone sounded, but her body remained tensed, expectant throughout the long hours. At the first shriek of the bell, her body was up, leaving her mind momentarily behind. In the space of those three short rings she thought that he was dead, injured, had been picked up wandering the streets mad, was a murderer.

"This is Georgia Cole, Steve's wife—"

"I'm sorry, he's not here right now."

"I know. That's why I'm calling—"

"I really can't talk to you now—"

"He's here. Steve's here and I—"

"With you? Is he all right?"

"If you'd just let me speak!" Georgia snapped. "He's sitting here talking. I can't make any sense of it. Talking to himself, I mean, in a funny voice. He doesn't respond to me or our son. I don't know what to do."

"Why did you call me?"

"Steve said . . . he told me about this telepathy business. He said you were helping him. I thought—"

"Okay, here's what you do. Don't disturb him, don't try to stop him or bother him in any way. Have you got that?"

"Yes."

"Then—do you have a tape recorder? If you do, put it on, near him. It's important we have a record of what he says, if possible."

"Mark has one."

"Fine. I'll be right over."

"Should I call a doctor?"

"No. Do nothing. And . . . um . . ." Leigh hesitated, wondered if what instinct prompted her to say was a terrible betrayal, but she decided that she had to risk that. "Mrs. Cole? Keep your son away from him." She heard the sharp intake of Georgia's breath and spoke over it before she could question or argue. "So, don't disturb him, and get what he's saying down on tape. I'm on my way."

Georgia stared at the humming receiver, was reluctant to put it down as though it were some kind of protective talisman.

"Telepathy? Who were you talking to?"

"A friend of your father's. Go and get your cassette machine, quickly."

"What for?"

"Please, Mark, this is important." She didn't know why. Part of her thought she must be mad to take that woman's word for it, to demean herself by rushing to do her bidding, but another part said it didn't matter, nothing mattered as long as . . .

". . . bad. All boys are bad. Oh yes. That's the truth of it. Once you see that . . . It's a shame, a crime of nature but . . ." The voice trailed off in an implied shrug. Georgia went quietly down the steps. Steven seemed unchanged, as remote and eerie as before.

Mark brought his cassette recorder, and she took it from him and placed it on the corner of the coffee table, as close as she dared go to Steven.

"How do you work this thing?"

"Oh Mum . . ." He bent over the controls. She wanted to hold him protectively, glanced nervously at Steven. "The batteries might be a bit low."

"Never mind. Hurry."

"What are we doing this for anyway?"

"Is it going?"

"Yes."

"I could never make her understand that. Didn't dare, that's the truth of it. In later years, well, it wasn't something we wanted to talk about. But I wish I'd told her, before the end, that I understood, that I saw how bad they all were, the boys, how they got up to more and more mischief."

"Come away, Mark."

"What's he talking about?"

"Never mind that. Just come away." She shoved and harried him out of the room. "I don't want you to hear that. Look, why don't you have your bath?" He would be safe in the bath, the door locked.

"I want to know what's going on."

"I don't know. You see how he is. This woman says we're not to disturb him. She's coming over."

"What was that about telepathy?"

"I don't know, Mark."

"I don't know, Mark," he mimicked her shrilly. "You never know anything; you never tell me anything."

"It's the truth. You know as much as I do. Now please . . ."

"I want to be with Dad. You can't stop me. If he's ill or something . . ."

"Yes, that's it. He's ill. Something to do with that bump on the head, I expect. You can't stay with him. We mustn't disturb him."

"I won't disturb him. I'll—"

"Oh for God's sake, Mark, stop it. I can't take any more. Please, please go to your room or take a bath or something, but stop. Just stop."

She could not fight him anymore. She leaned against the wall, trembling, trying not to cry. She watched his stubborn face become sullen, then resentful.

"Please," she whispered, pleading with him.

He stared at her, and though she could see that he was debating with himself, she could not guess at the arguments. Whatever they were, reason won. He went past her to the door of his room.

"Just don't forget, it's my tape recorder," he said, a pathetic parting shot, and he went into his room, slamming the door.

Georgia let her shoulders slump, closed her eyes, took several deep breaths. She only became aware of the silence when she heard pop music coming from Mark's room. She looked down the corridor to the living room. Her eyes fastened on Mark's bag, and she made herself go and pick it up, seeking comfort in routine. She held the bag, listening, but there was no sound from Steven. If he had stopped talking, she thought, maybe he was himself again, but something prevented her from peeping into the room to check. She did not want to see. She carried the bag into the kitchen, leaving the door open, her eyes traveling every other second to Mark's door. She unpacked the bag automatically, sorting the contents into piles. Part of her stood back and watched herself, laughed at her habituated reliance on routine, demanded to know what the significance of a pair of dirty soccer shorts was at a time like this. She suddenly remembered tales of her maternal grandmother, how at the height of the Blitz she had refused to go to the communal air-raid shelter at the end of the street until she had cleared the table and washed the dishes, as though to leave the house tidy for destruction. Perhaps it was something in the genes, passed down through her mother, that made her put Mark's kit into a warm soak, spread a sheet of newspaper on the floor, place his muddied shoes tidily upon it. Maybe she was mad, would eke out her days in some gray institution, endlessly tidying. The doorbell rang, startling her. She dropped the towel she held, stared at it heaped on the floor. The bell rang again, demanding attention. Nervously, she put a hand to her hair then, hearing Mark's door open, the music sound louder in the hall, she moved.

"Turn that down, Mark. Stay in your room."

"Who is it?"

She opened the door.

"Hi. I got here as soon as I could. Where is he?"

Georgia did not look at her, stood back, mutely inviting her in. She had only an impression of Leigh's height and that she seemed to be swaddled in many layers of clothes.

"Straight ahead," she said, closing the door. "Mind the steps," she added.

Mark was staring openmouthed after Leigh as Georgia began to follow her.

"Who is she?" he whispered, obviously impressed.

"The lady who can help your father. Now, please, just stay in your room."

"What's she going to do? Is she a doctor?"

She waved him silent with a flap of the hand.

Leigh was standing quite still, staring at Steven. The double aura flickered around him, all shades of blue with a black heart.

"He's been like that all the time?" Leigh asked curtly, not looking at Georgia.

"Yes."

"How long?"

"I don't know. Um . . . we got back around seven-twenty, maybe half past. He was already here. Just as you see him now."

"But talking?"

"Off and on."

"You got the tape recorder; good."

"I don't think he said much after . . . since we put it on."

Leigh went to it, looked at it.

"What are you going to do?"

"Wait. There's nothing else we can do right now." She began to remove her scarves and loose coat. Georgia saw that Leigh was beautiful and hated her for it.

"I want a drink," Georgia said. "You?"

"No, thanks." She sat down without asking permission, in Georgia's chair, and seemed to compose herself very neatly. The aura was already fading a little. She leaned forward, concentrating hard. What she "read" was a jumble: guilt and a sense of righteousness, a terrible weariness that was Steven, she guessed, could only guess because the mind she touched and perceived was incoherent, like the scream of static from an untuned radio. She withdrew as though burned.

Georgia poured herself a neat Scotch and sipped it gratefully.

"That's all?" she said. "You're just going to sit there?"

The black was draining from the aura, seeping away like the lifeblood of one of his victims. The blue grew paler, settled. Leigh turned off the tape recorder.

"Can you remember anything he said before you called me?"

"I . . . I don't know. It wasn't . . . It didn't make any sense. I was too worried, preoccupied . . ."

"Maybe it'll come back to you later. I'd like you to try to remember and let me know. It's important, or I wouldn't ask."

"Can you explain all this to me?"

"Later . . . Sh . . ."

Steven sighed, moistened his lips. His eyelids closed at last. Both women watched him intently, but only Leigh saw the aura fade to a pale suffusion of light, concentrated around his head and shoulders.

"Steven? Wake up now, Steven."

"He wasn't asleep," Georgia protested.

"It'll probably seem like that to him, though. Please don't do or say anything to alarm him. Steven?"

He stirred, rolled the back of his head against the couch.

"Come on now, Steven, please."

He opened his eyes and saw her, saw her in the wrong room, his world jumbled and patched wrongly together.

"It's okay now, Steven."

"Steve?" Georgia came forward. His eyes swiveled to her. For a moment it was almost comic as he stared from one woman to the other in amazement. He pushed himself up so that he was sitting straight, tried to speak. The words came out as a groan, and he squeezed his eyes shut, put his hands to his head. Leigh got up and went to him, touched his shoulder.

"Headache, Steven?"

He nodded, painfully. "What are you doing here?" he asked.

"I sent for her," Georgia answered. "I didn't know what else to do. You scared me."

He tried to focus on her, but her face melted under black waves of pain.

"He can't talk right now," Leigh said. "Can he lie down somewhere?"

"I suppose so . . ."

"Home," Steven insisted weakly. "Take me home."

"You are home," Georgia told him sharply.

"You're not fit. You must stay here for a while, rest up. If he could, please . . ." she said to Georgia.

"All right." She put down her glass and went along to the bedroom, put on the lights, drew the curtains. Leigh helped him to stand, supported him along the corridor.

"Do you have any sedatives?" Leigh asked Georgia as she helped Steven onto the bed, *their* bed. "Sleeping tablets would be fine."

Georgia crossed to the dressing table, picked up a small plastic container. She did not want this woman in her room, taking charge, giving orders. She thrust the pills at Leigh.

"That'll do. Some water?" She bent over Steven, pulling off his shoes. Georgia wanted to scream at her to get out, leave him alone, but she made herself go into the kitchen. Leigh dropped his shoes on the floor, looked for something to cover him with. Mark stood in the doorway watching her, his face pale and worried. His features, Leigh realized with surprise, were a perfect blend of Steven's and Georgia's, and they blended well together.

"Is he all right now?"

"Sure," she said, glancing at Steven to see if he reacted to the boy's presence, but he remained still, locked in pain and tiredness. "He's going to take a nap."

"Is he going to stay here?" Mark asked.

"Tonight, yes."

"Out of the way, Mark. I told you . . ." Georgia pushed him aside, a glass of water clutched in her hand.

"Help me, please," Leigh said, trying to raise Steven. He groaned again, attempted to push her away. Georgia leaned across the bed. Together they managed to raise him. Leigh fed the pills into his mouth, and Georgia touched the glass to his lips, urged him to swallow. Gently, they lowered him down again.

"Is there something to cover him with?" Leigh asked.

"If you'll leave me for a moment," Georgia said stiffly, "I'll see to it."

Leigh hesitated, saw and felt Georgia's resentment. She nodded and walked out of the room.

"And you, Mark," Georgia said. "And close the door."

Mark followed Leigh down into the living room, watched as she picked up her outer clothes.

"Is my dad really going to be all right now?"

"Yes, I think so. The pills will help him to sleep. He's very tired and has a bad headache."

"A hangover?"

"No. Though it probably feels a little like one." She smiled at him.

"Who are you?"

"My name's Leigh. And you're Mark."

"How do you know?"

"Your father told me. Look, I think I'd better wait for your mother."

"Yes. Do you want a drink?"

She did now, badly. She wondered how Georgia would react and then remembered that she had offered one earlier.

"I would if you think your mother won't mind."

He shrugged.

"What do you want?"

"Do you have any gin? With tonic?"

"Easy." He began to prepare the drink, then said, "You'd better say how much. I haven't done this very much before."

"You're doing fine. That's great. And lots of tonic, please."

He brought the glass to her, carrying it with studied care.

"Thank you. Cheers. You'd make a great bartender."

"Are you a friend of my dad's?"

"Yes. I work at the hospital."

"Has he been staying with you?"

"Yes. He didn't have anywhere else to go and—"

"Is he going to stay with you again?"

"I don't know, Mark. You'll have to ask—"

"That's enough, Mark." Georgia came down the steps. "It's time you had that bath. Now." She picked up her drink and looked at Leigh.

"I hope you don't mind? Mark offered, and you did say earlier . . ." Leigh indicated her glass.

"Of course not. Go along now, Mark. I want to talk to . . ." She did not know what to call her.

"Leigh," he said.

"Bath," Georgia said fiercely, pushing him toward the door.

"Oh, Mum . . ."

"No arguments. I'll see you afterward."

He went, dragging his feet. Leigh called good-night to him, and he responded with a quick, shy grin that was somehow achingly reminiscent of his father.

"He's a fine boy," Leigh said.

"Yes. Well, you'd better sit down."

"I'll go if you like. I just thought I ought to . . ."

I undressed him, I put him to bed, just as though he had come home roaring drunk, Georgia thought, and all the time I thought of you, your hands on his body, taking him away from me, perhaps driving him mad. Leigh picked up the thoughts, drank, trying to shut them out.

"We'd better talk," Georgia said.

"Very well." Leigh sat down.

"Just a minute." She went to the door. "No dawdling now, Mark," she called, then pushed the door almost closed. "Now, I'd like you to explain what is going on. What has happened to my husband? What is all this? And where do you fit in?"

Choosing her words carefully, Leigh took the questions more or less in order, explaining in the simplest and clearest language she could muster. Georgia listened, her doubts, swings of belief and rejection, chattering unspoken in Leigh's mind.

"The object of what we're trying to do now is to get Steven in control of this situation. By that I mean that he should be contacting the man, taking the initiative. Hopefully he will learn enough from that for us to be able to identify the killer, or at least have something concrete to take to the police."

"Wait a minute. Why Steve? Why does this man pick on Steve?"

"I honestly don't know. I suspect it's an accident. Steven just happens to pick up on the man's wavelength, so to speak."

"That's a bit farfetched, isn't it?"

"It's the best I can do."

"All right. And is Steve in contact with the man now?"

"Yes. In a limited way he has been. Who was contacting who tonight I can't say, not until I've talked with Steven and listened to the tape. May I take the cassette away with me, by the way?"

"Yes." Leigh opened the machine and took out the cassette. "And you . . . you know about this sort of thing? This is your work, is it?"

"I'm psychic myself. I specialize in helping people to adjust to their psychic abilities, and I study, scientifically, the bases of what is generally called the paranormal."

"Are you saying Steve is?"

"No, but I think he could be. He's what we call a latent, someone who has suppressed or never noticed what powers he has. I suspect they have something to do with, play some part in, making him a suitable receiver."

"Then there could be others?"

"Undoubtedly."

"So why did this man pick Steve? Or put it another way. Why didn't someone normal, ordinary, get in touch with him?"

"I've told you, I don't know. Maybe we never will know the answer to that."

Georgia stared at her, her mind whirling in confusion. It could not be true, but as Leigh had already suggested, what other explanation was there?

"Look, I'm very tired and it's getting late. I'm sure Steven will sleep now, but if you should need me . . ." Leigh stood up, reached for her coat.

"Just a minute," Georgia said.

"Look, you need time to digest this."

"You haven't answered my other question. Where do you fit in, personally, I mean?"

"I don't know that either. I can't pretend that ours is an exclusively professional relationship."

"Steve says he loves you."

"I know."

"And you, what do you feel?"

"Very confused, if you want the truth." She put on her coat, wanting to make it clear to Georgia that she had no intention of prolonging this conversation. "The important thing is to help him through this. I have to do that, if he will let me and if you will."

"I? What say do I have in it?"

"You could have quite a big say, I guess. I hope you'll be on my side, for Steven's sake."

"I can't promise."

Leigh inclined her head, accepting.

"Well, thanks for the drink and listening to me. Thanks for calling me, too. That couldn't have been easy."

"I panicked."

"You did right."

"How do I know? This might all be some figment of your imagination."

"Look, Mrs. Cole," Leigh said, her voice hardening. "All my life people have thrown that at me. There's nothing I can do about it. I can only ask you, everyone, to take me on trust. But before you make up your mind, consider this. Steven's in danger, real danger. His mind could crack completely under this kind of pressure. If the other man gets too powerful, he might even be able to manipulate Steven into acts. . . . He might be able to control what Steven does as well as what he sometimes sees and thinks."

"Does Steve know this?"

"I haven't told him in so many words, but he's no fool. So, whatever you think about me, remember this: who else do you know who can help him? If you care about him—and I think you do, a lot—then give me a chance."

Georgia scrutinized her, searching her face for some sign of cunning, gloating duplicity. What she saw was an honest face, open and tired with the effort of always being stretched on the line.

"And you'd better understand this. I'm going to fight for him. I want him back, and I mean to get him."

"That's your right," Leigh said quietly. "Just make sure there's something to get." She flung a shawl around her shoulders and crossed the room. Georgia followed her, wondering whether that was a threat or a warning. Leigh steeled herself as she passed the bedroom door, would not allow herself to look, to check on him. She could not, must not cheat. If there was to be a battle, she must fight with ordinary weapons. "You'll remember . . . you have my number. If anything develops, call me, no matter what time."

"I think I can cope," Georgia said, stiff with her own desperate dignity.

"Good-night, then."

"Good-night."

Georgia closed the door behind her and bolted it. Turning, she saw the bathroom door standing open and realized that she had forgotten about Mark. There was no light in the bathroom, but a reassuring strip showed under his door. She opened it. He had fallen asleep, comic book still open and propped on his knees. With a sudden rush of love and gratitude, she tiptoed to his side, removed the comic, turned him over and settled him, arranging the covers over his shoulder. He stirred uneasily, but she soothed him with a light kiss. By some miracle, the essential components of her world had come together again, were restored and fitted into the old, familiar pattern. It was Leigh Duncan who was out in the cold, she thought.

It was not like waking at all, but a gentle transition from one state to another, like a curtain slowly rising on another perspective of time and space. He was quite calm, liked the darkness on his eyes. He had no need to see, knew this room like the back of his hand, as they say, every nook and cranny of it. Was content to listen to the heavy thud of his own heartbeat pumping the blood around the circuits of his body.

The carpet was soft and familiar beneath his feet. He moved with less force than a breath of wind, without noise, a part of the darkness. The door handle was hard beneath his grip, the mechanism well oiled, turning perfectly in silence. Feeling the mute walls, finding each door in turn, listening, ear pressed to the wood. The sound of breathing, the smell of sleep seeping through the cracks. The odor of flesh and sweat. He went in, a ghost in the night, a slight stirring and thickening of the dark. The imagined stench nearly overcame him, the rank reek of a body corrupt, lying completely relaxed, open and vulnerable. He could make out the shape of it, the quilt kicked back, saw it as tones and tints of gray. He drew closer and closer and bent, breathing through his mouth now so as not to smell. The weight of mercy was heavy in him. He could almost feel sad, almost. . . . He reached out, touched cotton, touched flesh, his fingers seeking . . . almost burned by the warmth of rotten flesh.

"What? Who . . . ?"

A flurry of movement, a carelessly flung arm caught the side of his face, making him recoil.

"Dad? What time is it? Dad?"

Mark, one hand still resting on the lamp switch, stared at his father through a haze of too-sudden light, leftover sleep.

"What is it? Dad?"

Something made him cringe from the reaching fingers. His legs thrashed, tangled in the quilt. His elbow struck the bookcase on the other side of the bed, sent a loose pile of books thudding to the floor.

"Don't! Get off! Dad, don't!" Mark lashed out to knock the outstretched, rigid arms away. Suddenly he felt himself falling, but threw himself over so that his hands would strike the floor first.

More light threw the scene into sharp and terrible relief.

"Oh my God. Mark."

Georgia would always remember it. Steven bent over the bed, holding the boy as though he weighed nothing and mattered less. But her cry and the sudden rush of her movement toward him made him loosen his grip just a little, sufficient for Mark to kick out with his legs and slide out of view, onto the floor on the far side of the bed.

Georgia did not speak again. A scream was locked in her throat, choking her. She saw her own hands as though through a magnifying glass, saw her sharply filed nails reaching for his flesh and his terrible blank eyes. She went for the eyes. She felt the prick of stubble and the wax of flesh. She heard him catch his breath in surprise. A look of simple horror came over his features. If he had not put up his hands she could have torn his eyes from their sockets. He covered his face, not fighting her, but backing away. She began to hit him then, swinging wild slaps, bunching her hands into fists to beat him with. At each blow she heard her own breath leave her body in a growl. Somehow they were moving, dancing toward the open door. The sight of it drove her on. She even kicked, the blow paining her bare feet more than him, and the pain too spurring her on. She rained blows on his back and head, and suddenly he was stumbling away, into the darkness of the corridor. Her torn nails snapped against wood and suddenly, with a crash, she sealed the door, leaned her weight against it while searching for a key, a bolt. There was neither.

"Help me. Help me, quickly."

Her fingers were bloody and slipped on the heavy stripped-pine chest of drawers. She could not get a grip on it, succeeded only in rocking it to and fro.

"What? What are you doing?"

"Push. For God's sake!"

Mark ran around the other side of the chest and leaned his weight against it. The chest of drawers slid forward, caught the tailing hem of her nightgown beneath it. As she stepped away it tore, and she threw herself onto the chest, then rammed it home against the door. She stumbled back, panting, tearing her gown again, and then saw her son's deadly pale face staring at her.

"Mum?"

She could not speak. She held out her arms to him and he came to her, not into her embrace but to take her arm, steady her. She sank onto the bed, panting with the sound of sobs. Mark sat beside her and clumsily put his arm around her heaving shoulders.

"It's all right, Mum. It wasn't him. Honestly, it wasn't him."

She stared at him, her face working, trying to speak, but she could only make another sob and bury her face in his shoulder, hugging him to her for dear life.

Mark slept, curled onto his side, his arm curved across his eyes against the light Georgia was too scared to turn off. She huddled under a corner of the quilt, his bathrobe around her shoulders. She sat upright, legs drawn up, sucking at her torn and bruised fingers. The resilience of the young impressed and touched her: how could he sleep and yet how glad she was that he did. Perhaps sleep would heal some of his wounds. For herself, it was out of the question.

They both had listened to him, stumbling around the flat beyond the barred door. Mark wore a worried frown but said nothing. He must have drifted off to sleep before she heard Steven weeping brokenly and pacing up and down the corridor. She had looked at Mark then, afraid that this show of emotion might move him to pity, but he was already asleep, and she had turned him onto his side, settling him. The sounds of misery outside seemed entirely fitting, an extension of her own mood. She grieved with the sounds, let them serve for her own tears. Then silence followed, and at last—she had lost all sense of time—she had heard the front door open and close with a final, familiar click. She suspected a trap, of course, a trick to lure them out of safety into something she could not name and dare not imagine. She did not move, and the silence continued, grew and slowly became comforting.

Now there were cracks of daylight showing at the curtained window, and the lamplight was diluted, became pale and dusty. She considered what she must do. Could she shift the heavy chest by herself, get out of the room without waking Mark, or should she take him with her, seeking safety in numbers, being there at least to protect him? She put out the lamp and eased her cramped limbs from the bed. Quickly, she tugged back the curtains and looked down into the central well of the building, up at the overcast sky. The windows of two other flats were brightly illuminated. She saw a man hunched over a plate of cereal, eating his solitary breakfast. In another a woman moved back and forth, cooking. Could she call to them for help maybe? She went to the door and eased a corner of the chest away from it. Working systematically, applying herself to the task, she was able to create a space just large enough for her to squeeze through. She stared at it. She would risk going alone. Steven would need to apply a lot of force to push the chest farther into the room if he was determined to get in, and that at least would give her time. At the very least she would be able to get the front door open, scream. She took a deep breath, gathered Mark's robe closer around her, and silently turned the handle of the door. In the hall she stood listening to her own heartbeat, the hairs on the back of her neck prickling unpleasantly. All the doors stood open. The bathroom was closest. She pushed the door wide, snapped on the light, holding her breath and straining her ears to see if that sound had carried and roused him. Nothing. The bathroom was empty, still untidy from Mark's bath. Suddenly, she desperately needed to use the lavatory but did not dare, not yet. She went to the kitchen, pushed the door inward, put on the light. Again nothing. Now she had to retrace her steps, leave the haven of the front door behind her. She crept toward her own bedroom, certain now that this was where he would lie in wait. She was tempted to slam the door shut in the hope of buying precious seconds to get out or back to Mark, but, her nerves screaming, she made herself go in. The rumpled bed and the closed curtains looked sinister, created imaginary hiding places from which a maniac might at any moment leap. She ran to the window, tore back the heavy curtains, and in the gray light saw that the room was harmless and empty.

"Thank God," she whispered.

She shrugged Mark's robe from her shoulders and put on her own, cuddling into its familiar warmth. She found her slippers too, and slid her cold feet into them. Only the living room now, the most dangerous place of all. The steps were a disadvantage, and a person could easily hide behind the door, unseen until she was vulnerable. She made a plan, forming in her mind where the main light switch was, calculated how she could reach it from the steps. She imagined that a cold and terrible hand would fasten on her wrist as she leaned into the dark, felt for the switch. When the light came on she jumped back and peered through the crack made by the hinged side of the door. Nothing. But behind the couch or a chair, anywhere . . . She stood just inside the room exploring it with her eyes and did not find him. There was only one hiding place left—the curtains. They were full and long and could conceal him, though surely his feet must show beneath the hem, and there were no feet visible, nothing. She let out her breath in a gasp of relief as she swept the curtains aside and let in the gray light of a normal winter morning. The car stood below where she had parked it last night, and an early jogger padded into the park, blowing with the effort.

He had gone.

She began to shake. The need to use the lavatory was perilous. She turned from the window and saw, set out neatly on the coffee table, his door keys. She stared at them in disbelief. As though they might be a chimera or trick of her imagination, she bent to touch them, felt the hard metal and sharp edges. Then she ran from the room, the length of the corridor and bolted the front door.

He really had gone, and he could not get back in.

She wept softly with relief as she hurried to the bathroom.

A sleepy doctor attended his face without question or visible curiosity. The nurse who assisted him showed a similar lack of interest. Their silence and indifference proclaimed that they were used to such sights, no longer felt surprise at the city's wounded, walking in at all hours of the night. Beyond the little cubicle made of curtains, Steven could see the derelict drunk sleeping it off and the pacing, twitching girl who periodically demanded a pain-killer and constantly was told to be quiet. The doctor scrubbed his cheek and dabbed it with stinging antiseptic, then fixed a light gauze dressing over the wound, telling him to keep it covered for a day or two. He explained that the dispensary would not be open until 10:00 A.M.. Did Steven want to come back or take a prescription to his local chemist?

"What is it?" Steven asked.

"Just an antibiotic in case of infection. You're not allergic to penicillin, are you?"

Steven shook his head.

The hospital was old and shabby, obviously decaying. Steven wound his way through the long corridors, back to the road. He must have walked there, though he had no memory of doing so. The stinging pain of his raked cheek and the alarmed look a young man had given him served to rouse Steven, prompted him to take his bearings and seek the old hospital with its peeling Emergency Room. Now he stood outside again, the prescription in his hand, watching the streetlights pale with the onset of dawn. He set off in the general direction of the West End, prompted by the instinct to get as far away from his home and everyday surroundings as possible.

The unavoidable fact of the matter was that he had wanted to kill Mark. *He* had, not some unknown, faceless other. His eyes pricked, and if he had had any tears left, he would have wept again. As it was, he walked dry eyed, bent under the burden of this knowledge. He was his own Draconian judge and jury, and he found himself guilty, without extenuating circumstances. And there was no mercy. He would be his own executioner, too.

Leigh woke to the unfamiliar emptiness of the flat. She felt uneasy, felt that something was wrong. Many times she had experienced similar feelings, and consequently they did not panic her. On this occasion she did not need to seek for the source or subject of her foreboding. It was Steven, or the other half of his double aura, his possessor.

Before going to bed, she had played and transcribed the cassette Georgia Cole had let her take from the flat. It had not been an easy task. Some music, presumably recorded by Mark from the radio, was interrupted by Steven's bland and featureless voice. It was difficult to make out, because the voices of Georgia and Mark, standing closer to the microphone, overlaid it. At other times, Steven's voice dropped to a whisper, became almost inaudible. She had played it over and over, filtering out their voices, straining to catch his whispers. What she had was:

. . . made her understand that . . . truth of it. In later years, well . . . talk about . . . before the end . . . the boys, how they got up to more and more mischief, became corrupt, evil. . . . She didn't understand that it was never my fault. Because of that I could forgive her in the end. Should have told her, before she died. Failed in my duty, as a son. Of course I forgave her. I loved her so much and I never wished, not for her to die, no. Even though I knew if she did, when she did, I would be free . . . [Inaudible] I tried to turn a blind eye, shut him out, my friend, growing like me to man's estate. The naughty hair on the body [laughter] . . . get close to him again but he was gone, not there. It's very lonely. I wish I could find him again, my friend, the one she couldn't see and so did not believe in. It would be all right now. I have a feeling he must be out there somewhere, if only I could reach. . . . If I could find him I wouldn't have to do . . . what I want . . . so much . . . I keep myself occupied of course. I have my little treats, fill up the time nicely thank you. . . . But I want, I want . . . (4 mins. 35 secs. silence) It's their fault not mine. They ask for it. I don't do them any harm. They're better off. They say I'm bad, but that of course is absolutely ridiculous, laughable. . . . They're blind. Don't want to see, more like. No standards. Lack of discipline. They all need a good dose of the cane, and now even the teachers are for banning it.

I'd line them all up in a row, yes I would, line them all up and make them bend over, and then swish, swish, swish, swish with the cane. [Laughter] I'd beat it out of them like she beat it out of me. Oh yes indeed. That's what's required. Only I worry sometimes that beating's not really enough, not enough for them. . . .

Leigh let the transcript fall, sickened by it. She knew it almost by heart anyway, and a picture had now formed in her mind, a profile. But where was he? How could they get him to show himself? How much more of this could Steven take? Her instinct was to push on, increase the pressure if necessary, force the whole thing to a climax, but right now she did not even know if Steven would come back. Perhaps she had already lost him. Georgia had meant what she said last night, and Leigh recognized a formidable opponent when she saw one. So perhaps her uncomfortable feeling was no more than the premonition of loss and loneliness.

When she had washed and dressed, swallowed a cup of coffee, her stomach refusing any food, she packed all the evidence she had into her briefcase. This, too, was the prompting of something she did not yet understand fully. She had a feeling she might need it, had better keep it by her. Then she rang Steven's number. She did not think Georgia could object to this one call.

"Hello?"

"This is Leigh. I wondered how Steven is this morning."

"I don't know. He's not here."

"Oh."

"He . . . he attacked Mark last night."

"What? Why didn't you call me?"

"What could you have done? Anyway, there wasn't time. I had to barricade the both of us in his bedroom . . ." Georgia's voice cracked.

"Where's Steven now?"

"I don't know and I don't care. He left. I hope he's in hell. He could have killed Mark . . ."

"I'm sure . . . Look, try to remember, it wasn't him, not really—"

"If anyone says that to me again, I'll scream."

She hung up or rather slammed the receiver down with a force Leigh could well sense even at the other end of the wire. She put her own telephone down slowly. Her forebodings crystallized, became clear. I warned her, she thought. I told her to keep the boy from him. Stupid woman. Then she felt sorry for Georgia, and guilty. She should have stayed, should never have left Steven, should not have assumed that he would sleep, be free of the man. She had exposed him to the very thing he most feared. It would set him back. And it meant that the man was still in control, manipulating him. She felt almost daunted at the prospect of persuading Steven to go on now. All his instincts would prompt him to withdraw, run away. If he hadn't cracked already.

She hurried then, knowing that she must see him as soon as possible. Why hadn't he come to her when he left the flat? It was a bad sign that he had not. Maybe he'd gone to the hospital . . .

But he wasn't at the hospital. It had always been a vain hope anyway. When he still hadn't shown up by noon, she became very afraid indeed.

The only questions were how and where? He examined them sitting in a dirty café drinking cup after cup of stewed and scalding tea. His death was inevitable, a given fact. Raising his head momentarily he saw a man pass, carrying a loaded plate of greasy food. The sight threw a switch in his memory. Leigh had sat opposite him, making little murmurs of appreciation as she'd eaten her enormous breakfast, a look of pure contentment on her face. Then he recalled what she had said to him, another time.

"Whatever happens, Steven, remember it isn't you."

He shook his head, groaned aloud. The handful of other customers in the café, which felt damp with steam and smelled of rancid cooking oil, ignored him. They were used to eccentric displays, for this was a haunt of down-and-outs.

"It isn't you, and you can get in control. You can do it, if you really want to."

He could not abide the thought of her, not now and in this place. He could only guess at what damage he had already done her, what further harm he might wreak if he went on living. He finished his tea and bought another cup from the youth at the counter. His thirst seemed unquenchable. Leigh belonged, with everything else he cared about, on the other side of life, from which he had debarred himself. He pushed her out of his thoughts. But something stirred in him, a little coal of anger, which slowly leant a new perspective to his plan and hardened his resolution.

He realized, as he waited for the tea to cool a little, that his flight had been partly motivated by a hope of escaping the man. Using Leigh's "transmitter theory," surely if he got far enough away from him, the contact would snap and cease, or simply fade out in a murmur of static. It seemed to him vain to wish for such things, but he acknowledged that the impulse had been there, mixed in with the need to protect his son and his sanity. And the last few hours he had been himself, free of that appalling influence. Now he considered that perhaps he had been wrong to seek to escape the man. If there was one thing that would lend some dignity to his death, it would be to contact and destroy his tormentor. The idea quickened his blood a little. After all, the man had brought him to this ugly pass and he deserved as well as craved some kind of revenge.

Where was he, where was he now?

He went out into the streets again, to a world inhabited by human flotsam on a sea of litter, junkies queueing restlessly for their matutinal dose of slow death. It would take courage of course, but he thought he had that kind of courage, or could at least find it. It would require him to look directly into the face of hell, to enter fully into that other world the man inhabited, but that seemed impossible, even right. After all, it stretched all around him now that he had learned the trick of seeing. He had, from the moment he had entered Mark's room, accepted his rightful passport to this world. It was the other that scared him, that he could poison with his simple presence. Perhaps that was all Leigh had ever meant, that he should enter fully into it, not hang back, not insist that such things could not happen, least of all to him, should not walk in fear of whatever it was that bound him to the man, attracted the man to him. The last barrier was down. He had attacked his son, yearned for his death: what more did he have to lose? And so much to gain.

"Come on, you bastard, where are you?" he muttered in a

dry, cracked voice. In hell he would find his adversary and embrace him. And then it all would be over.

Tired suddenly and cold, his head beginning to ache, he turned into the warm and scented lobby of a cinema. It was still so early that the cashier was counting out change, stocking the register. She paused, looked up, and gave him a ticket without comment. He made his way into the empty, ill-lit auditorium and found a seat at the side, close to a burning radiator. He would need strength as well as courage. He closed his eyes and slept.

"So, you are postulating someone with a very disturbed childhood—sexual repression, beatings, an imaginary friend, yes?"

"Yes," Leigh said eagerly, to hide her anxiety. Any moment now she expected Sonia Zimmer to peer in that owlish way of hers through the upper part of her spectacles and dismiss the whole thing with a "tut" of impatience.

"The mother would appear to be dead, and you argue that this was the trigger, what released him into . . . action."

"Right. The evidence suggests or leads me to guess, maybe, that after the traumas of childhood and adolescence particularly, somehow they stayed together, the man wrestling with his resentment, guilty about his longings and essentially juvenile sexuality, wanting to lead his own life but incapable of doing so. Maybe through guilt or a sense of duty. Now he is only able to realize himself, his sexuality, in a context of guilt and punishment. Maybe every time he kills he's killing himself, the 'naughty' boy he was, trying to propitiate her, even beyond the grave. He's killing the child his mother beat, perhaps in an unconscious attempt to cancel out the guilt he associates with his sexual desire for his victims. He says somewhere—"

"He says?" Dr. Zimmer interrupted. "Don't you mean Steven says?"

Here it was then, the crunch, the collapse of the fine theory. Stand back, watch it, don't get hurt, don't cry.

"I told you, no. It's Steven's voice but the other man's using it. The words, the thoughts, the situation—they're not Steven's."

"How do you know that?" She pounced, bright eyed, accusing.

"It's true I don't know so much about his background, but you only have to know the man . . ." Leigh heard herself about to protest too much and too generally. She stopped.

"Fortunately I do." Sonia Zimmer turned and took a folder from the table behind her. It was green and marked CONFIDENTIAL. "Steven Cole was assessed when he came here, like everyone else. This is his personal dossier. Unless he is the most consummate liar—"

"He isn't. I know he's not," Leigh interrupted. Sonia Zimmer's head came up sharply. She stared at Leigh but did not ask how she knew. She did not need to. Instead she seemed to accept what she said.

"I'm inclined to take your word for it. It bears out my own experience. In which case you are right. These are not the words or thoughts of Steven Cole per se, not as we know him, anyway."

"Well then?" Leigh's hands were opening and closing in her lap, and she could not control them.

"This is all very impressive," Dr. Zimmer said, removing her glasses and tapping Leigh's notes and profile with the tortoiseshell earpiece. She pressed the index finger and thumb of her right hand to the bridge of her nose. "You are to be congratulated."

"I didn't come here for praise . . ." Leigh protested.

"When you write this up and publish it, it will do your career a lot of good. Let's be practical."

"I'm not sure I ever will. I don't think I want to. Besides, that's not the point."

"No. What is? Why have you shown me this?"

"You said I would always get a fair hearing."

"And have you not?" She slipped her glasses on again so that her eyes were magnified, boring into Leigh.

"Yes, yes. Look, last night he attacked his son. I don't have any details. His . . . wife was too upset. Now he's missing. I don't know what to do, Dr. Zimmer."

"Ah . . . I see." Sonia Zimmer stared down at her desk, her hands folded together in front of her face. "You would maintain, of course, that it was not Steven who attacked his son, but Steven motivated . . . er . . . prompted by the man?"

"Yes. I believe he can manipulate Steven. Or so take over his mind that Steven is temporarily helpless, literally does not know what he is doing. There have been times when he hasn't known, afterward, whether he or the man was responsible."

"And what are you afraid of now?"

"What he did last night will appall him when he's himself again. I fear what that might make him do."

"Suicide?" Sonia Zimmer said in a tone that implied it was cowardly not to face everything, spell it out.

Leigh nodded. She could not bring herself to say the word, dare not in case, just by being spoken, set free on the common air, it might somehow bring the possibility closer.

"Most of all I'm afraid . . . that without help, the will to combat the man, Steven will be forced or tricked into doing something . . . that he might kill."

The word hung between them, trembling the air. Leigh could not look at Dr. Zimmer. In fact she closed her eyes, as though to blot it all out.

"In that case," Sonia Zimmer said in her familiar matter-of-fact tone, "whether I accept every part of your theory or not is scarcely relevant right now. I accept the possibility you speak of. Obviously that must be prevented—"

"But how?" Leigh cried, desperate.

"He must be found and helped . . . or restrained."

"You've known him longer than I have."

"But not as well, I think."

"Where would he go? Have you any ideas?" She held her breath, willing the doctor to come up with something, no matter how slight or indefinite, but she only shook her head.

"No. I have no idea. You could ask his wife, but . . . my dear," she said, her voice deepening, "you can find him. Surely, you of all people."

"How?" Leigh said again. It was a cry of frustration and denial.

"You possess ways that are . . . not given to all of us, I think. Use them."

"How can I in—what is it—eight, twelve million people?"

"I would have thought, if a person loves someone enough,

the bonds must be very strong, and anything, the most daunting task, is possible. Is it not so?''

"I don't know."

"I fail to see what other alternative you have."

"Perhaps I don't love him enough."

"Is that what frightens you?"

"What if I do?"

"Ah well . . . Who can say? You could always report him as a missing person, of course."

"And set the cops after him? No."

"Well then, what other choice do you have?"

"I don't know. I must think about it."

"You said to me before that it would not be easy to divide yourself into two, but you thought you could manage it. I suggest that you have, quite properly, stressed the clinician, the professional side of yourself to the detriment of the human. Perhaps all that is required now is that you forget all this''— she waved her hand at Leigh's notes—"and concentrate on the heart."

She knew it and she did not think she could do it, could bear to do it.

"I don't know."

"That is my advice. I don't give it lightly, either."

"I appreciate that."

"So . . ."

"You've been very kind, very helpful. I'll have to think about it."

"I don't envy you but I do sympathize. I will be here if—"

"Maybe he'll just come back, when he's calmed down," Leigh said with a false brightness. "I guess I'll leave it for today. He might come back tonight, when he's gotten over the shock."

"It's a possibility, of course. And what else do we have to comfort us and get us through each day?"

Leigh looked at her but she could not sustain the clarity and certainty of Dr. Zimmer's stare. They both knew what she had to do, but Leigh still shrank from it, afraid.

"I'll think about it," she repeated, and she hoped it sounded like a promise.

*   *   *

In spite of the keys left on the coffee table, Georgia spent the morning finding a locksmith and then overseeing his work. She did not care that the new matte gray locks gave the place the despairing look of a fortress. The noise of sawing and hammering woke Mark, whom she had let sleep in, and he seemed quite pleased to be given the day off from school. When the locksmith had finished, she fed Mark lunch and asked him for the hundredth time if he felt all right, was sure he wasn't hurt. He had a bruise or two, but he felt fine. Tiredness enveloped her. She knew that she could sleep at last and that she had to. She checked the new locks, settled Mark in front of the television, and crawled gratefully into the cold, unmade bed, where she fell asleep at once.

The sound of voices woke her. One voice, she realized as the fog of her exhausted sleep receded, was Mark's, followed by the *ting* of the telephone receiver being replaced. She must have slept deeply not to wake when it rang. She heard Mark come down the hallway, go into his room. It was warm in the bed now, and she wanted to stay there a while longer. It was getting dark and she hadn't shopped, but the Indian supermarket stayed open late. There was no hurry. She lay dozing, drifting, thinking. Her head felt as though she had drunk too much, but without the pain of a hangover. What would she do now? The sensible thing, she thought quite calmly, would be to go away somewhere, take Mark right away until . . . She wasn't ready yet to think about the future, what might happen. But where could they go? All her friends were in London. Money was a barrier anyway. She only had a few hundred pounds in her current account and she could not rely on Steven being able to support them. It was safer here anyway. She knew the terrain, thought almost happily of the new locks on the old door. There were people she could call on, friends and neighbors. And she had to think of Mark. His education was important. She didn't want him falling behind at school on top of everything else. She would have to go to see Mrs. Machell, the headmistress, explain that if Steven should turn up they were not to let Mark go with him, on no account. And how would she explain that? She ought to contact a lawyer, put things on a formal basis. Mark would be her life now. She would have to look out for him unaided, and it would be easier on him if things were settled.

"Mum? Are you awake?"

"Mm."

He came toward her, carrying a cup of tea.

"Oh, darling, how lovely. That's just what I need." She sat up, patted the edge of the bed, inviting him to sit down. As he set the cup down beside her, she realized that he was washed and dressed. "You got dressed," she said, surprised. "Why? There's no need."

"Mum, can I ask you something?"

"Of course." She felt light and indulgent. If he wanted some favor, she would grant it and if, as she expected, he wanted to talk about last night, the present situation, she felt equal to the task. "What is it?"

"Can I go and see Dad?"

Her heart contracted as though squeezed by a cruel and mocking hand. She lifted the cup and saucer onto her updrawn knees, trying to buy time, to find the right words.

"No. I'm . . . afraid you can't."

"I've got to see him."

"No, Mark, it's out of the question. After last night I'm surprised you—"

"It wasn't him, Mum. I know it wasn't."

"Don't be silly. I saw him. I pulled him off you."

"I know." He sounded miserable but not afraid. "I can't explain, but I saw him before, before you came in, and I know it wasn't him. Honest."

"I'm tired and upset and I don't want to argue with you, Mark. I know what you've been through and how you must feel, but for your own sake you can't see him."

"Please, Mum."

She took a sip of the tea, which was weak and had too much milk in it. She smiled and said it was lovely. Then, to change the subject, she said, "I thought I heard you on the phone. Who was it?"

"It was me." He hung his head, tracing with one finger the pattern on the quilt cover. "I rang Dad at the hospital. He's not there."

"Well then," she said, feigning a relief she did not feel, "how can you possibly go and see him?"

"I've got his address," he said stubbornly. "You know."

"I scarcely think he'd want you turning up there," she said dryly, thinking of Leigh Duncan.

"He said I could go any time."

"That was before he . . . Anyway, he knew I wouldn't let you."

"Why not?"

"Because he's . . . oh, never mind that now. Look, why don't you go and watch TV or something? I'll get up in a minute, and then we'll get something nice for supper."

"I've got to see him. It's important."

"And I've said you can't."

"Why not?"

"Because he might hurt you."

"He won't. Anyway, I'm not scared."

"But I am."

"Mum . . ."

"No, Mark, and please don't whine."

"I'm going anyway. I don't care what you say. I only asked you because I promised I wouldn't go out by myself."

"No, you mustn't." She put the teacup aside and gripped his arm. "You know you mustn't."

"Well if you won't drive me—"

"I can't go there. I don't want to see her."

"Who?"

"That woman, Leigh Duncan. Anyway, she said he wasn't there."

"Why? What's wrong with her?"

"Nothing. Go away now. I want to get up."

"Tell me."

It snapped then, her temper, and with it came a temporary relief.

"All right. Since you're so keen to know. Your precious father, the one who half-killed you last night— Yes, he did. Don't make faces at me. He could have killed you. Anyway, he's living with her. She's his mistress. He says he's in love with her."

She swept the quilt aside and climbed out the other side of

the bed. It was better that he knew. If he knew he might stop asking questions, understand that she had to behave this way.

"I don't believe you," he said. "He wouldn't."

"Don't be ridiculous. It's time you grew up and realized your father's no hero. On the contrary—"

"You're only saying that because you've been . . . because of Roger North," he shouted. "You're just trying to make out he's as bad as you. And even if he is, you started it. You ruined everything. You drove him away with your rotten bloody boyfriend. Now you're just saying that out of spite, to put me off. I know he's not like that, and he didn't mean to hurt me. I know."

"Mark . . ."

He ran out of the room. She started after him, wondering if she was strong enough to prevent his leaving, but he ran into the living room, slamming the door.

Was it true or was it just that if you threw enough accusations, some of the guilt stuck? From his point of view it probably was true. He hadn't noticed the years leading up to her affair with Roger. He'd been cushioned, protected, had taken her for granted, just like his father. He only saw the mess when she tried to find a little happiness of her own. She looked at herself in the mirror, pulled a wry face. She'd cast herself as the wicked lady, and so Steve had become, in Mark's eyes, the knight in shining armor. She was tarnished; he was pure. She could see it, understand it even, but it wasn't like that. She was not mad. No. She stopped herself, bit her trembling bottom lip until it hurt. She had to remain calm, be reasonable. Her anger and hurt were her business, not Mark's. If Steven was all that she dreaded and feared, then she would have to support Mark through the shock when the time came. Mark would never believe her, would always think that she was trying to blacken Steven or trying to turn her son against his father. He would have to learn the hard way, and she would have to be there to help him through. In the meantime she had the right, the sacred duty to protect him, and he would have to see that. That was it, she had to be calm, use reason. No more anger or sniping.

She brushed and tidied her hair, got dressed quickly. She could do it. She would not be provoked. She went into the kitchen and checked the refrigerator, the vegetable rack, then she got her car keys, new door keys, and shopping bags ready. Finally she went into the living room.

Mark was curled on the sofa, tossing a small rubber ball into the air and catching it rhythmically. He did not look at her. She sat at the other end of the couch, not trying to touch him or comfort him.

"I'm sorry, darling, I shouldn't have said all that. I should have broken it to you gently. It's true, but I shouldn't have put it like that. I'm very sorry. I don't want to turn you against your father, and I swear I won't. But you can't see him yet. He's ill, not in control of himself, and he might try to hurt you again. You must understand that I can't let that happen, can't risk it. I really can't. Please try to understand."

The ball slapped against his palm, was tossed again, slapped again, and that was all the answer she got.

"I want you to know, too," she went on, taking a deep breath first, "that I'm not going to see Roger North anymore. That's all over. I told him on Sunday. So you needn't worry about that."

He still said nothing, still threw and caught the ball. Georgia sighed.

"I've got to go to the shops. We haven't got anything to eat. Will you come with me, please?"

He shook his head.

"Then promise me you'll stay here. You won't try to go out?"

"No. There's something I want to see on TV in a minute."

She hesitated, remembered her resolution, and stood up.

"Okay. I'll only be a few minutes anyway. Is there anything you particularly fancy?"

"No. Thanks."

He got up, pocketed the ball, and crossed the room to switch on the television set.

"I won't be long then," she said and made herself go, collect her keys and bags and negotiate the new, unfamiliar locks. Outside she hesitated, considered the consequences, and knew that she had to do it. She stooped, inserted the key, and turned the new deadlock from the outside.

* * *

London was indeed the capital of hell: Hell City, Hellopolis. Steven walked through spilled neon light, his face changing color with those around him—white, green, pink. People pushed and shouldered him aside. The air smelled of beer and rotten fruit pulped underfoot. He saw a body stretched on an abandoned market stall, a bottle clutched like a baby to its breast.

Somewhere in this filth and dreadfulness was the man he sought.

He pressed back from the crowd. He could not be a part of this, and yet he had to be. He tried to concentrate, to get his bearings. Across the street a purple sign winked at him, on and off. GAY. GAY. GAY. As he drew closer, jostled by young shoulders hurrying on strong legs to their doom, two other words, respectively red and white, flashed in synchronized rhythm with the purple. PORNO. CINEMA. Beyond the sign that stained his face and hurt his eyes, beyond the dusty bead curtain was a small carpeted shop. ADULT VIDEOS. GAY BOOKS AND MAGS. A man sat at a counter watching a silent television set, listening to the tribal thump of radio-muzak. The man flicked a glance at him, returned his eyes to the television, which presented its bellied back to the room.

*He went into a shop blinking in the bright light after the dark outside. The wire baskets, stacked near the door, had blue plastic handles. His nose revolted at the smell of curry and spices. Sweating with temper, he squeezed between the perilously stacked shelves. He'd bet the bread was stale, would not touch the so-called fresh-baked, unwrapped loaves, which had been pawed and handled by the unclean, so that their crusts visibly crawled with germs and poisons. He squeezed a sliced loaf in its plastic sheath, felt the bread contract and spring back like foam rubber. That at least was clean and reasonably fresh. He dropped it into his basket, muttering to himself. A waft of cold air rose from the freezer cabinet, cooling his flushed face. The garishly colored packets danced before his eyes until they all seemed to melt together into a cabinet of vomit. He leaped as though burned when a slim Indian stood beside him, extended a delicate wrist into the mess, gold bangles jangling. He knew they claimed the beads and bangles, the plastic bracelets with their tinsel flowers,*

*were part of some religious observance, but he knew other-*
*wise. He saw them stripped of all but their gewgaws, flaunting*
*their copper bodies, lasciviously inviting. The Indian spoke to*
*him, dared to speak to him, and the man shook his head,*
*pushed past him, pushed his lean body hard against the cold*
*metal of the freezer cabinet. A cackle of laughter sounded in*
*his head: That'll cool his ardor.*

A cackle of laughter sounded from the radio, insane, inane.
The man behind the counter reached out and turned the volume
down, his eyes glued to the TV screen. Steven flipped the
pages of a magazine. A nude youth adorned its shiny cover,
which caught the light and dazzled it into Steven's eyes.

*The Indian boy was touching himself, thought he was*
*secure, unseen in his little wooden box behind the till. An acid-*
*green bracelet with a green and white rosette adorned the bony*
*wrist that moved the bad hand on the pouting groin. The man*
*moved forward, quickly, an arm of vengeance, bringer of*
*wrath. The boy looked up, rested his guilty hand on the cash*
*register before him and smiled. The man held himself back,*
*aloof. The boy lifted the man's purchases one by one and rang*
*their cost up on the cash register, where each figure showed in*
*digital green. The man watched as the boy turned away and*
*bent, his rump flaring so that he saw the tight lines of his*
*underwear bisecting his buttocks beneath cheap and too-tight*
*trousers. It was an invitation, an act of aggression that dazzled*
*his eyes. . . .*

. . . Bare buttocks obscenely spread, dazzled his eyes.
With a feeling of disgust Steven thrust the magazine from him,
shuffled to the curtained doorway, and burst through into night
air, which cooled the sweat on his face. He stood shaking on
the pavement.

I almost had him then, he thought. Where are you, where?

*Going back home in the dark, lacing with swift and certain*
*steps the pools of lamplight one to another. The plastic bag of*
*purchases bumping against his calf. Stomach churning, de-*
*manding food. Badly sweating from the ordeal, heart thud-*
*ding.*

"Hey, mister . . ."

*A boy detached from the shadows, hands in his pockets,*
*shoulders hunched, demanding a light, pulling a battered pack*

*of cigarettes from his pocket, putting one between his lips,*
*smiling . . .*

A young man smiling, pushing himself free of the tiled wall
against which he leaned. Smiling, standing straight. Smiling at
Steven, who looked around him nervously, recognized the
milling, noisy concourse of Piccadilly Circus Underground
Station. A young man with dark red flashes in his hair coming
toward him, swinging a rolled umbrella, smiling.

"Hello. Got a place?"

Steven moved quickly, pushed him away, butted him with
the side of his arm, his shoulder. The young man staggered,
turned and ran off, startled. Pushed him not to hurt him, no,
not to hurt him, but to save him, to save him from . . .

At ten Leigh picked up the telephone and called Georgia again.

"Yes?"

"I'm sorry to bother you . . ."

"Oh, it's you."

"Have you seen Steven?"

"No. And I don't want to."

"He didn't show up at work today and he hasn't been here.
I'm worried."

"Then you're a fool."

"Look, do you think we should report him missing, to the
police?"

"You can do what you like. I'm—"

"I thought it would be better coming from you."

"Listen, I don't want anything to do with it. I don't want you
to keep on calling me."

"Have you any idea where he might be? Friends, someplace
he—"

"I told you. I hope he's in hell."

And she hung up. Leigh started to dial again, annoyed, but
decided it was hopeless. For herself, she couldn't set the police
on him, not in his condition. If they found him, which she
knew was a long shot, under what circumstances might they
find him? It was a risk she could not take. Yet she had to find
him.

She would try. What Sonia Zimmer had said, advised really,

was engraved on her mind. If she loved enough, if she dared to love him enough . . .

She went into the bedroom and stretched out, on the bed in the dark, fully clothed. A little light filtered from the hall through the door, which stood ajar. She closed her eyes. She knew it was hopeless this way. Her range was short. She had to be pointed in the right direction, so to speak. A few yards from the scene of the murder at Chiswick House, in back of the hospital, or in the empty recreation ground, she could do it, but when he might be miles away, in another town even, or dead somewhere . . . The best she could do, probably, was to "enter" the flat below or the house next door, and the idea of such spying, being a secret intruder, was repugnant to her. Anyway, she knew Steven wasn't there, wasn't close.

She sat up suddenly, like a jerked puppet.

What if Georgia was lying to her? They had patched things up somehow? In return for her forgiveness, Steven might have promised not to see or communicate with Leigh. Georgia would answer the phone, freeze her out while he licked his wounds, holed up in the safety of his own home. Safety? With Mark there? She scoffed at the thought, did not believe he could be so stupid. But the thought would not go away. Could she reach so far, as far as the flat?

She lay down again, made herself relax, then collected her energy together and let her mind go, imagined it bursting like a shooting star out into the inhospitable night. Nothing. *Steven.* She concentrated on his name and face. Like a rubber ball her mind bounced back bringing her only a headache. It was no good, hopeless. Perhaps if she went to the flat, stood outside by the park railings . . .

There was another way, of course, what Sonia had really meant, if she was honest with herself. To do it certainly required the commitment, the absolute, total commitment Sonia had spoken of, demanded of her, in a way. The memory of that last trance was still with her, smudged and painful. She did not want to do it again, but if there was no other way, if she loved him enough . . .

She saw herself standing alone, someplace she did not recognize, a dream place, and Steven's back was resolutely turned toward her, walking away from her. She knew that he would not look back.

That was it then, what she feared. Oh come on, she chided herself. Could it be any worse than this? She was alone now, and she knew he needed her just as surely as she knew that in her "vision" he did not. The present could alter the future. She had to believe that. If she reached him now, helped him when he most needed it, perhaps he would not walk away. If she failed him now, who could blame him? If she didn't love him enough she deserved to lose him. That's what Sonia had meant, what her own powers had just shown her.

She tossed her head miserably on the pillow. I can't. I'm afraid. Then you deserve to be lonely, a freak cut off from other people except in the safety of your clinics, your rationally proscribed world. You're afraid to let go, be spontaneous, get hurt, hurt yourself. You deserve to be alone. *No.*

She unbuckled the strap of her watch with trembling fingers, held it up, swinging and dangling before her. It flashed in the light from the hall. I'm afraid to find him dead. That's just another excuse. If he is you'll have to know sometime and live with it. It will be partly your fault, either way. This way you might be able to save him. She swung the watch again, her arm aching. Silently, as the flash of light from the gold casing of the little watch pierced her eyes, jabbed at them, she screamed his name.


The hotel was not very clean, but it was all Steven could afford. He lay in the bed, fully clothed, not daring to trust his skin to the gray sheets and rough, sour-smelling blankets. Periodically, the room throbbed with the passing of an underground train. The vibrations set a loose pane of glass rattling. The gray-and-crimson patterned linoleum was cracked and peeling. Beside the bed was a bald patch where countless feet had stood in transit, going to bed, getting up. He did not dare to turn the light off, although the scorched plastic lampshade gave off an unpleasant, metallic odor. The wall opposite the bed was only a thin partition through which music and male voices sounded. He looked at the shabby furniture. Beneath each piece balls of gray dust moved like ghostly mice scuttering in slow motion whenever a subway train passed.

He closed his eyes and the light burned red through his lids. There were thousands of supermarkets in London run by Indians. He could think of five or six within walking distance of the flat. It would be like looking for a needle in a haystack, and even then who was to say the man went there regularly, that it was near to his home? Try as he might he could not recall the exterior or any other identifying feature from his bizarre dream or vision. If he pressed too hard, he saw the boy moving from the shadows again, asking for a light, and thus he entered the man's sick thoughts, and he could not bear any more of that. He had entered hell, and he would again, but if he went too far, lost that last vestige of control . . . Thank God he had the presence of mind to push that young man away. The boy emerging from the shadows, asking for a light. No. The young man at the subway station, who had approached *him*. He and the man, he thought, stood on either side of a dark mirror—the mirror in the room was cracked and gave back a disjointed, out-of-kilter reflection of the room—their visions of each other blurred and muddled. A boy came out of the night shadows on one side of the mirror, asked for a light, stuck a tube of tobacco in his mouth, and on the other side, a young man approached with a rolled umbrella and an inviting smile.

Which was which? Who pushed which boy away? He could no longer tell. What had happened to the other boy?

The pain came then, squeezing his brain tight, forcing his eyes open onto the sordid room, blotting everything out. He had pushed the young man in the subway station away, had run away from him, run here like a hunted animal, to huddle in the cold and light. Was it not allowed to ask the fate of the other boy, then? He felt the sluggish stirrings of excitement. If it was not allowed, that was good, wasn't it? The man had wanted to show off his other victims, had wanted to share them, gloatingly. So the boy with the cigarette must be safe.

Steven realized that he was staring at the cracked mirror. He felt calmer, better. Not mad, not guilty. The boy was safe. There was a crumb of comfort in it, perhaps enough to permit sleep, face another day in hell. How many more could he stand? How many?

He turned over and pressed his damaged cheek into the hard pillow. He had forgotten to get the prescription filled or to buy more gauze. He had left the wound uncovered after washing his face and tried to remember how it had looked or if he should worry about it.

Perhaps he did sleep, or doze at least, drifting, his mind blank if not peaceful. For when the rattle of the next train disturbed him and he heard someone coughing behind the partition, the room seemed a better place, lighter, cleaner and there was a faint trace of lavender in the air. He sniffed and thought of Leigh, could almost imagine that she was lying beside him, holding him, giving off the lavender base of the scent she always used and said she could not buy in London and was running out of. He could imagine that she smiled at him and loved him and wanted him to sleep, rest so that he would be strong for what lay ahead.

She was shivering. Her teeth chattered despite the usual high temperature in the flat. Her clothes were damp and unpleasant with perspiration, sticking and clinging to her as she moved from the bed to the window, trying to get warm again, unable to believe that it was day at last.

So she had failed.

She stared out over the backyards of suburban London, so ordered and ordinary. Frozen washing flapped awkwardly on a cold line; a cat prowled homeward for breakfast milk. But as Leigh stared, her eyes pricking with the threat of tears, she touched a well of peace and cold contentment in herself. It was gray and cold and somehow sterile, but it was free of tensions, held no terrors. She frowned, trying to remember when and where she had experienced this sensation before, this sensation of having succeeded, achieved, for what it was worth.

Then she did not know whether she had succeeded or not. The terrors crowded in again, a spoiling slime. They drove her from the window, into the kitchen where she set coffee to heat.

Spike had gone away once, had been called home where his father was dying. He was very distressed, and she had been unable to comfort him. He had not called, but she had understood why. Then, in the morning, the first they had spent apart since their love had become a force between them, binding and stifling, he *had* called, to thank her. To thank her for lying with him that night and for comforting him. He had smelled her perfume, he had said, had almost been able to see her. She had no knowledge of it herself but as he spoke, his voice crackling over long distance, she had touched and experienced that cold, comforting well in herself. She had been at peace. And now again she felt it.

The coffee boiled over.

He was waiting for the traffic lights to change, stamping his feet against the cold, when he saw the placard screaming at him.

WEST LONDON BOY MISSING
POLICE SEARCH

He ran across the road, grabbed a paper from the pile, scanned it, looking for the story, not understanding why the paper seemed to lead with something else, a murder.

"That's seventeen p., guv."

He glared at the newspaper seller, angered by the interruption, understood what the man was trying to tell him only when, impatiently, he thrust out a soiled, mittened hand. He dug into his pocket, pulled out a handful of change. The coins scattered everywhere, bounced and tinkled on the pavement. He ran, knocking into people, chasing a rolling silver coin. The man yelled at him as though he were taking off without paying. He crouched low, blocking the pavement, collecting up his money. He saw legs passing him, stepping round and over him. Nobody stopped, nobody helped, not even the seller, who regarded him with a sort of leer. Somehow he had dropped the paper too, and somebody trod on it. He snatched it up, looked for more coins.

"My, we are in a state, aren't we?" the man said as, shaking, he counted out the coins.

"It's all the money I have," he said. "It's all I've got."

The man shrugged, turned away to hand a paper to a woman, who looked at Steven as though he were unclean. He hurried away, into the nearest underground station entrance,

237

and leaned against the tiled wall. The echoing voice of a singer, accompanying himself on an ill-tuned guitar, announced that a hard rain was gonna fall.

YOUTH MURDERED was the black banner headline. At the foot of the page was a photograph, blurred, of a young boy, the head cropped from the body. The caption below it read: *Craig Kingly, the missing boy.* Missing or murdered, which? He shook the paper, forced himself to read through the dirty footprint. To read slowly and calmly.

A massive police hunt disrupted busy Soho this morning after the body of a youth was discovered in a parking lot off Frith Street. The body was discovered by Mr. Alfred Payne, a parking lot attendant from Mill Hill, when he reported for work this morning.

The partially clad body is believed to have multiple stab wounds. Police at Savile Row have not yet released the victim's name but a spokesman confirmed that the young man was known to the police and worked as a male prostitute out of Piccadilly Circus.

Below this, in bold type, was

**The Scandal of London's Rent Boys—pg. 7**

There followed an asterisk, indicating the start of a separate item.

*Police investigating the recent murders of young boys in West London today expressed concern for fourteen-year-old Craig Kingly, who disappeared early last night. Craig, who lives on the Western Estate, went out to call for a friend at about 7:30 P.M. and has not been seen since. Police are appealing for anyone who may have seen Craig to come forward. Fears are growing that he may be the latest victim of the violent sexually motivated murderer who has already killed three times. A spokesman said it was too soon to comment about a possible connection between the Soho and West London killings but confirmed that Hammersmith police would be conferring with colleagues at Savile Row later today.

Both sides of the mirror came together, fused.

I didn't do that.

*I didn't do that.*

He bunched the paper together, tore it without meaning to. The smudged picture of the boy stared up at him.

*Hey mister . . . Got a light?*

The body in the parking lot, only a short distance from where he stood—was it that of the young man who had approached him, smiling, carrying a rolled umbrella? I didn't do it. I didn't have a knife.

*I didn't do that.*

He dropped the paper as he swung around, heard laughter. There was no one there, yet the voice had sounded in his ear, just as though the speaker stood behind him, looking over his shoulder.

*I didn't do that,* sounded inside his head.

"Where are you? Where?"

The laughter was distant, fading like smoke on the air. He began to walk, kicking the paper aside. A gust of wind lifted it and flattened the picture of the boy against the tiled wall for a moment. He stared at it, horrified.

*. . . stared at the boy's pale face where it lay against the wall.*

The paper fell to the ground as the wind died, and was trampled underfoot.

*. . . bent and struggled to loosen the belt pulled tight around his neck, pulled and yanked at it, causing the head to roll, as though being shook, saying no. Wished the tongue did not protrude in that ugly way, thick and blackened. Got the belt free at last and stared at the livid welt, a necklace of dull red and blue staining his skin. Touched it with his gloved fingers. The true colors. Not the pure white, milky white of his outward appearance. In his true colors now. Red raw and blue bruised. Nodded sagely, contented. There, you see. Wound the belt around his hand, a neat coil, and dropped it into a black plastic bag. Moved away. Bent, picked up the boy's underpants from the floor, held them almost tenderly, inspected them for signs of sin and corruption . . .*

"Are you all right? Excuse me, but are you all right?"

The woman's face was out of focus, funny. He closed his

eyes, feared to see the boy's dead face form out of hers, feared some new trick, new torment.

"Here, let me help you."

Steven let her take his arm and lead him. He felt the air grow warm.

"Sit down, just for a minute."

He sat on a bench with people going by, staring, staring. The woman's face loomed again, worried beneath blue-rinsed hair.

"Shall I fetch an attendant? Do you want a doctor?"

"No." He shook his head. Her concern, her kindness made him want to weep.

"Well, if you're sure you'll be all right . . ."

"Yes. Thank you."

"You looked so poorly. I thought you were going to keel over right there."

"Thank you."

"Are you going to get a train? Can I help you down to the platform?"

"Yes. Thank you."

"Where do you want to go?"

"Hammersmith."

"Have you got a ticket?"

"No."

"You wait there then. I'll go and get one."

He wept, the salt tears stinging the wound on his face like iodine. He knew he did not have enough money for the fare, knew that he was exploiting the woman's kindness, was moving back into hell, away from her. But he had to. It seemed as though she had been sent, to make this last journey possible for him. There was nothing he could do about it but accept and weep. Her kindness would survive, perhaps she would even understand. She came back to him and asked, "Feel up to it now? Come along then."

She helped him through the automatic ticket gate and on to the escalator. As they traveled down, she pushed his yellow ticket into his pocket, saying, "There you are."

He could not even thank her. The tears were streaming down his face, and his throat felt as though a rock had lodged in it.

"I'd come with you only . . . Oh dear, you are upset. Are you sure you'll be all right?"

The train came in, rattling from the tunnel. He moved away from her, unable to speak, wanted to throw himself beneath it, onto the gleaming rails, but then the doors opened, people jostled him, and he was inside, sitting down, people staring at him. He found his handkerchief and mopped his face. The scratches felt tender. He hardened his heart against the woman and those who stared. He stared them down, shunned them. A man on the other side of the carriage pulled a rolled newspaper from the pocket of his jacket and shook it out. The boy, Craig Kingly, stared at him, disembodied from his gray memorial photograph.

. . . *touched the flesh of the boy's thigh. His flesh had had a pinkish tinge, like the first surprising blossom of spring. Was like silk not wax. Dead white wax skin. Ugly. Turned the boy fully onto his back, arranged the stiffening arms by his side as though lying to attention. Lied. Told lies, bragging and boasting, of course.*

A match flared, its sudden flame hurting Steven's eyes. The paper lay across the man's lap. He sucked at a cigarette, exhaled a cloud of smoke, shook the match and dropped it dead to the floor.

. . . *smoking, at his age. Boasted about it. Light-fingered, too. Stealing from the shops. Sweets and cigarettes. Sweets to rot their teeth, cigarettes to poison their lungs. I told him. You're poisoning your system. You should be taking care of your body. Pure in heart and mind and body. Do you keep yourself pure? Smoking's one thing. You can always cut that out. But other things, the other. He laughed. Laughed in my face. A filthy laugh. Abused me. Me. A torrent of filth. You need the badness whipped out of you, I said. I've a good mind to put you over my knee and take your trousers down and give you a good spanking. The things he said then. Evil things, disgusting. Not true, either. None of them true. I'm not*

. . . *Tug the legs straight, neatly aligned. Look at him, just one last time. Innocent as a lamb. Just the mark around his neck where the belt went. Take your belt off, I said. I'll use that. I'll teach you to think such evil things, say such filthy things to me. No blood, not a spot. No mess. Everything nice and clean. He was a clean boy. Smelled nice, clean. I said, be a man. I'm not going to hurt you. It's for your own good. Not going to hurt you. Rolling the boy over now, gently, keeping the limbs together. The lacerated buttocks, red weals, a scribble marring the flesh. And over again and over again. There. Looks so pure now, pure and peaceful. Didn't hurt you. No. Wrap you up now, put you to bed. Folded the edges of a white sheet over the body, wrapping it tightly around. Nice and snug. Lifting him, a white bundle. Hardly weighs a thing. All wrapped up nice and clean and safe. Now we'll just pop you into Mummy's nice big bed where you'll be safe and free of temptation. There we are. The sheet wrapped so tight you can't touch yourself, can't move. Lying in her big bed, incapacitated, waiting in the cold dark. There you are. All safe now. All tucked in. In Mummy's nice big bed. Stooping gently to kiss the cold forehead. Don't you put your tongue out at me. Don't you dare. Where's my stick? I'll give you such a thrashing . . .*

A stick rapped sharply against his shin.

"Sorry. So sorry."

A blind girl was waving her white stick from side to side. Someone reached her a helping hand, guided her to a seat.

"Sorry, so sorry."

*You'll be sorry. You'll go blind.*

Blundering blindly up from his seat, he squeezed through the doors as they closed. Standing there, standing on the cold platform shaking, panting . . .

He retraced Sunday's route: the mall, the area behind the river's wintery frontage. He did so under some compulsion he did not dare to name or analyze. It was like walking against himself. Each step was the result of a battle, and if he once allowed himself to consider where and why he was going, he would be lost. His courage would fail. He would turn tail and run. He tried to keep all thoughts of the man out of his mind, for his own sake and so as not to alert, forewarn his quarry. Since he left the tube train there had been the equivalent of silence, no tricks of vision. What he saw was just the blank world of winter with its heavy sky and biting cold. In spite of this he sweated with the effort to keep moving, go on.

At the foot of the railway bridge he almost gave up. He was afraid of that urge to jump, afraid of what he was approaching.

The urgency went out of his purpose, and he sat on the lower steps, staring at his cold hands. He did not know how long he loitered there. Then two women crossed the bridge with loaded shopping bags and passed him. They paused on the pathway, looking back at him, whispering together. Their suspicion and fear made him realize that he must not draw attention to himself, not here and in these circumstances. He stood up, tried a wan smile that pulled his scarred cheek painfully. With any luck they might take him for a drunk. He made himself mount the steps and hurry straight across the bridge, his head safely down. He took the second flight at a run and landed panting on the firm ground.

It was the fourth shop along from the inverted bowl of the Western Estate, flanked by a newsagent and a closed-down, boarded-up dry-cleaning store. The faded sign said V.K. AND D. PATEL.

He ran across the deserted road and pushed into the shop. There was the pile of blue-handled baskets, the long freezer cabinet, the smell of Indian food. Packed shelves leaving too narrow gangways. Behind the cash register sat a plump Indian woman, a white overall buttoned tight over her sari. Perhaps alarmed by his stare of dumb recognition, she said something, and a young man came slowly down the aisle, slim, with gold bangles whispering at his wrist.

"Can I help you, sir? Can't see what you want?"

He shook his head, stared at the youth's face. The other, the boy who had stood behind the cash register, of course, would be at school or at lunch. The Indian's smile faded.

"No. Sorry."

He hurried out, turned toward the estate. He knew now, was certain. A green curtain tweaked back, looking down. Green curtains. He stood on the frozen mud that was intended to be a green hillock and stared up at the rows of windows, searching, searching.

"Hey, you. You looking for someone?"

Two uniformed constables were coming toward him, slow and purposeful. How big they looked when you were afraid.

"You looking for something?"

"No. I . . . was just wondering if it was going to snow."

He indicated the sky with his eyes, knowing he must seem inane. "It looks like snow," he added, stressing the obvious.

"You live around here?"

"What you done to your face?"

"No. I . . . had a fight."

"Who with?"

"My wife, actually."

One of them laughed, the other frowned.

"Looks like she won."

"Where do you live?"

He gave the number and street of the hotel but not its name.

"What you doing here, then?"

Inspiration came to him.

"I fancied a walk by the river, but it was too cold. I'm lost, really. Can you tell me the way to Chiswick High Road?"

The two policemen exchanged a look. One shook his head slightly.

"Where were you last night?"

"Mm . . ." He made a pretense of remembering. "Home. Didn't go out."

The slightly shorter of the two policemen—they were shrinking as his confidence returned—thrust something at him.

"You haven't noticed this lad hanging around anywhere, have you?"

It was a bigger, glossier version of the photograph printed in *The Standard*. Craig Kingly was squinting a little against the sun, wore a short-sleeved shirt, open at the neck. Steven shook his head even as he wanted to say, he's here somewhere, wrapped in a sheet, in a big double bed behind green curtains. His eyes moved toward the nearest block of flats again, nervously. The green curtains he remembered from his last visit here, but only now was their significance clear to him.

"You sure you're not looking for someone? You know someone lives around here?"

"No. No. I've not seen the boy, sorry."

"All right. But don't go hanging about around here. This lad's missing and we've got our hands full."

Was the killer watching now, laughing to himself even as the smaller constable turned and pointed out the direction Steven should take, explained how to reach the main road? And if so, why was he silent, why didn't he make his presence felt?

There was nothing to do then but go, follow the instructions he'd been given. He saw other policemen as he went, knocking on every door, showing copies of the photograph. What would happen when they reached *his* door? What would he say? Or would he refuse to answer? Had he already slipped away, leaving the dead boy in the big bed?

"Where are you, damn you? Where are you? Why don't you answer me?"

There was only silence and emptiness beneath the traffic's roar. It was like that time in the hospital, before his third EEG. The man had gone, gone into retreat, gone from him. He had failed.

It was her locking the door on him that did it. He made up his mind right then. If she couldn't even trust him . . . Besides, he'd had enough. Everyone else was doing what they pleased, why shouldn't he? He planned it carefully, putting it off until he had a legitimate reason to take his sports bag to school. Into this he packed his track suit, sleeping bag, and warmest clothing, just in case. He left school just before the last period, when he was scheduled for gym. In the melee of the locker room it was relatively simple just to disappear. As he jogged along the side streets, he thought it was unlikely he would be missed until his mother came to collect him, and by then everything would be okay. He hoped.

He'd thought about nothing else, really, since Monday night. He knew his dad was not responsible for that scary scene in his bedroom. You only had to look at his eyes. Only he couldn't make her see that. It was like the horror films she despised and criticized without ever seeing, which he and his dad had always enjoyed. People did take funny turns like that, and he had to let his dad know that he understood and wasn't afraid and wanted to live with him, not her. Somebody always had to believe in the monster and befriend it, and when it was your own father . . .

What she had said about Leigh Duncan was equally important, perhaps even more so. He knew she was lying. He also thought she was lying when she said she'd finished with

Roger North. The important thing was that he had to know, had to hear it from his dad's own lips, and if he said yes, he did love her, was going to marry her, then he knew exactly what he was going to do. He was going to run away. He knew his dad wouldn't. When she was in that sort of mood, his mum would say anything as long as it hurt. He'd seen that trait in her character getting stronger and worse for years now. He supposed she felt bad about Roger North and spoiling everything, so she wanted to pretend his dad was just as bad.

He came to the back of the hospital, to the service road you could use as a shortcut through to the main entrance, but there was a security guard there, checking everyone, so he turned into the road that ran beside the big complex of buildings and made his way around to the front. He knew he had to be cool now, dead casual. He rode the escalator up to the first floor and went straight to his dad's office. Every step of the way he expected to be challenged, but nobody bothered him, and when he put his head around the door, Gwen looked up at him, looked puzzled for a second, then smiled.

"Hello, Mark. How are you?"

"Fine, thanks," he said, sliding into the room and closing the door. He couldn't remember her name. "Is Dad in? Can I see him for a minute?"

She looked worried then, almost embarrassed.

"No. I'm sorry, he's not."

He could see she was bursting to say something else, but she only fiddled with her typewriter.

"You're not expecting him, then, later?"

"Well I don't really know. I mean, well, the truth of it is, he hasn't been in this week."

"Oh. Okay." He shifted his bag from one hand to the other, trying to hide his disappointment. "It doesn't matter. I was just passing. I'll see him later. Thanks a lot." He got the door open.

"Will you? Oh, I thought . . . Just a minute, Mark."

"Sorry, I can't stop. Soccer practice." He forced a grin he knew could be charming, raised his bag a little and kept moving.

"Mark . . ."

" 'Bye. Sorry to bother you." He hurried to the escalator,

ducked around it and pushed open the door to the men's room. He was breathing heavily, not with the effort but with nerves. He didn't really want to face his father at Leigh Duncan's place. If she was there it could be awkward. He shook his head impatiently. But he'd been through all that, had accepted as part of his plan that he might have no choice. What he had to concentrate on now was that woman, his dad's secretary. She might have followed him, be looking for him. More likely she'd ring home, speak to his mum. But that was okay, because she'd have set off for the school by now. A man pushed the door open, and Mark looked out, scanning the brief glimpse of the lobby for any sign of Gwen. He could not see her. He put down his bag and washed his hands. There was a side door on the left of the lobby. If he used that and cut down to the back gate outside, there'd be less chance of bumping into anyone who might be looking for him. And they were only checking people coming in that way, not going out. He hoped.

As he left the lavatory, Mark trod on the man's heels, using him as cover, made a dash for the side door and got out into the cold air again without anyone shouting his name. So far, so good. He slowed down, made himself walk casually and calmly. If they stopped him at the gate he'd say . . . say what? That he'd been to X ray, to have his leg checked. Had hurt it playing soccer. Was on his way home now, straight home. But the gray-uniformed guard only gave him an old-fashioned look, did not challenge him. He walked straight through, turned left then right. From his pocket he fished the crumpled piece of paper and checked the address. He had a rough idea where the street was, near Barons Court Underground Station somewhere, so he set off in that direction, thinking that he would ask someone the way when he got closer.

Mum would go to the school, find out he'd gone, go crazy and ring the cops, he supposed. Or perhaps she'd come looking for him herself first. She'd guess where he'd gone. And she had the car. But he had a good start, and once he got to his dad it would be okay. Even so he started to run again and began to panic when the first person he asked for directions turned out to be a foreign woman who just shook her head and gabbled something he couldn't understand. He glanced at every passing car, expecting to see his mother's relieved and irate face. The next person he asked for directions knew the name of the street ever so well but couldn't for the life of her remember where it was.

"I'll tell you what, love. Go up to the subway station and ask the old feller there what sells papers. He'll know."

He thanked her and ran off again. He found the newspaper man, and he did know, and it was near, and he just kept running until he could see it, number fourteen. Two sevens. That had to be a lucky number. He was panting, flushed, and nervous when he reached the house. The streetlights were already on, and he saw that night was closing in suddenly. He crossed his fingers, just in case.

Her name was taped above the higher of the two bells. He pushed it hard with his thumb, huddled with his bag into the little porch. He pressed three times before it dawned on him that there was no one home. His spirits plummeted. He had not planned for this and felt very lonely. He rang the bell a fourth time, just in case.

She'd be back. She'd be home from work soon, and she'd know where his dad was. Perhaps his dad had popped out for a newspaper or something, would be back any minute. Only he couldn't wait around here in case his mum came looking for him. He had to keep moving, keep out of sight. He told his feet to move. They felt like lead. He'd telephone Leigh Duncan's flat. He'd walk down to Hammersmith Broadway and then he'd phone from the station. No, better, he'd go by subway. Less chance of being seen there. He could ride the trains until he got her. Or his dad might be back by then. Yes, that was it. He felt better already. It would be warm, too, on the trains. And when he rang she'd answer, or his dad, and they'd tell him what to do, and it would be all right then. Of course it would.

Mrs. Machell put down the telephone and turned to face Georgia Cole.

"I'm sorry. It looks as though Mark skipped the last period. He wasn't in gym."

"Oh my God. How could you . . . Aren't you supposed to look after the children?"

"We do our best, Mrs. Cole," she said, icily calm, though she felt far from it. "Now, shall I call the police or will you?"

"Yes, I suppose—"

"Unless you know where he might be?" Georgia's mind was frozen, refused to work. "He's got his own door key, presumably?"

"No. I had the locks changed. I didn't give him a new set."

"Then you'd better get back home."

"No. His father. He'll have gone to his father. We've split up. I was going to tell you this morning."

"And where is he, do you know?"

"Yes. I've got an address at home. I can't remember now."

"I think we'd better call the police, don't you?" Especially with that maniac on the loose, she thought but did not say.

"Yes, please."

Georgia sat down. She had to sit down. Leigh Duncan. What was the address, the phone number? She could see that piece of blue paper quite clearly in her mind's eye, but she could not recall anything that was written on it. Last night that boy from the Western Estate, now Mark.

"Yes," Mrs. Machell was saying in her calm, clipped voice, "there has been some domestic trouble. The mother thinks the boy may have gone to his father. She has the address at home."

So that was it: her life, her son, all reduced to that bland phrase "some domestic trouble." She felt dead inside, petrified.

In another world, Mrs. Machell said, "Yes. I will. No. Yes, indeed. Thank you, officer." She hung up. "They want you to go straight home, Mrs. Cole. There's a good chance that Mark will be there, waiting for you. If not, phone the address through to Fulham Police Station. I've written down the number."

"I'd better go there. It's in Barons Court somewhere, I'm sure."

"No, Mrs. Cole. Telephone by all means, but you must be at home in case Mark turns up. I'm sure he will. Otherwise, it's best to leave these things to the police once they're involved. Are you all right to drive or—"

"Yes, I'm fine. Of course I can drive."

"That's all right then. Here's my home number. You will ring me—"

"Yes. I must go now."

"Carefully, Mrs. Cole. We don't want an accident on top of everything else, do we?"

It was the curse of teachers, she thought as she ran across the darkening, deserted playground, that they always made you feel like a child and in the wrong. She should have known, should have suspected. He'd been too quiet, too docile. She'd persuaded herself it was shock, that she'd got through to him by speaking so calmly and honestly. She hadn't wanted to rock the boat, wanted to give him time to adjust in his own way. And all the time he was scheming and plotting. God, she'd kill him when she got her hands on him. Then she heard what she was thinking and tears welled in her eyes. Oh, please God keep him safe. Let him be there, on the stairs, waiting for me. Let him moan and grumble because I wasn't in. I don't care. I don't care. Anything, only please, please keep him safe.

He wasn't on the stairs waiting for her. And no matter how she searched she could not find the piece of blue paper. She searched everywhere, knowing that she was wasting precious time, that Mark would have taken it with him. She must ring the police. They could get Leigh's address from the hospital. She had to think, not give way to panic, the hysteria that rose in her, threatening to engulf the world in a tidal wave of screams and tears. She had to stay calm, like Mrs. Machell, think, do the right thing, when all she wanted to do was run, screaming his name into the night, to find him. Even as she thought this, saw herself doing it, her hand lifted the phone and dialed the number the headmistress had written down for her.

There was no answer when he phoned Leigh's flat from Hammersmith. It seemed already that he had been killing time for hours, seemed much later than it really was. Dispirited, he crossed the Broadway and bought himself a hamburger and fries from McDonald's. He would have preferred to stay in the bright warmth of the interior, but he felt on display, a sitting target in the bright lights, with only a plate-glass window between him and King Street. He set off again, eating as he walked, his bag slung over his shoulder. By instinct he moved into the back streets and in the general direction of home.

He had considered that he might end up on his own, if his father said yes, he was going to marry Leigh Duncan. He wouldn't stay then, couldn't, and there was no way he would go back to his mother, so he would run away. In a sense, that's what he was doing now, though he hadn't abandoned all hope yet. He would try to phone again later. She had to get home sometime. Unless they'd both run off somewhere together. The thought made him feel cold and lonely again.

"Mark. Hey, Markie."

His blood froze. His body wanted to stop, to respond to the call in the usual, innocent way, but he increased his pace. It could be someone else. His wasn't an uncommon name, after all.

"Mark, hey, hang on."

He started to run then, dropping his envelope of fries, which scattered on the pavement. He swung his bag from his shoulder and ran, the sound of heavy feet pounding ominously after him. He had to cross the road to get away, and that was when he saw them, three boys, older and bigger than him, moving purposefully from the shadowed yard of a block of flats to cut him off. One lad, a tall, rangy black boy, shouted something to his pursuers, one of whom yelled back "yes." He realized he had no hope against his interceptors so he skidded to a halt at the pavement's edge and turned, trembling, to face his fate.

"Bloody hell, what's up with you, Markie? Don't you recognize me?" The boy came on, two others trailing him. Maybe the police had been around, telling them to look out for him, stop him. Perhaps there was even a reward on his head. His eyes refused to recognize the gangly, unkempt youth who panted up to him. If his memory contained his name, some knowledge of him, it refused to yield it up. The black boy grabbed his shoulder, just like a cop, and he squirmed against the grip. "It's me, shithead. Bernie. Bernie Dakers," said the boy who had pursued him.

"Oh, Bernie . . ."

"I've got him, Bernie," the black boy said. "What you want him for? Gonna kick his head in?" The black boy's companions sniggered. One slapped his fist menacingly into the flat of his other hand with a smacking noise.

"No. Leave him alone. He's a friend. Ain't you, Markie?"

"Yeah," he said, struggling to catch his breath. "Yeah, sure, Bernie. I recognize you."

"What you take off for like that? Didn't you see us, back there, on the wall? Walked right past us."

"Sorry. I didn't . . ." He wriggled against the black boy's grip.

"Leave him, Elvis," Bernie said.

The hand, mercifully, was removed. A car came around the corner, down the road, and they all moved onto the pavement. The others stared at him. He kept close to Bernie, who had been in his class at school for a while, before he was thrown out for persistent truancy. Bernie, his slowly thawing mind reminded him, had a reputation, a certain street glamour.

"How you doing then, Mark?" Bernie clapped him on the shoulder like a long-lost friend.

"Great."

"What d'you run for?" This was Elvis, belligerent and gruff.

"Yeah, who's after you?" another boy asked.

"He was just shit-scared we was going to thump him," offered another, one of those who had chased after Bernie.

"No," he said. "It wasn't that. I never saw you."

"You been stealing, got something in your bag?" One of them tugged at his bag, tried to take it.

"Leave him I bleedin' told you," Bernie said. "He's all right."

The boy shrugged, stepped back.

"The fuzz might be after me," he said. "That's what I thought."

"What for? What you done?"

"Nothing. I'm sort of running away."

"What? From home?"

"Yes."

"Why?"

"It's a long story. I'm trying to get hold of my dad. I've got to phone."

"You wanna keep off the streets then," Bernie said, nodding sagely.

"We don't want no trouble, man," Elvis chimed in. "Tell him to piss off, Bern. We don't want the fuzz round here."

"They're only looking for me," Mark protested.

"I can't risk it, man. I'm already on probation. My old man'll kill me," Elvis babbled. They all looked up and down the street nervously as though anticipating a whole posse of policemen, batons drawn for the charge.

"Come on," Bernie said. "I'll walk with you a bit."

The others protested, yelled, called for Bernie to come back, stay with them. Mark felt almost tearfully grateful for his companionship and what seemed like loyalty. Bernie told the others to piss off, he'd see them later.

"It's all right," Mark said. "You don't have to come with me."

"I don't have to stay with them, neither," Bernie said. "I go where I please and with who I want," he added truculently, jerking his thumb at his own chest. "So, where you making for then, Mark?"

"I don't know, really. I was just walking around till I could ring my dad again."

"Ain't he at home, then? I don't get it."

It all came pouring out of him then. He'd told no one, not even Ian Cadwallader, and Bernie was the perfect recipient. His world was not rocked by separations, rows, divorces. Bernie boasted that he did not know who his father was. He listened, he sympathized, and he offered to mind Mark's bag while he tried to ring his father again from a phone booth.

"No go?" he said, cocking his head on one side as Mark pushed the door open wearily. Mark shook his head. "Come on with us then. I've got a good idea."

"Where?" Mark asked, scared and a little excited too.

"I been thinking," Bernie said, setting off at a lope up the long, straight street. "There's a place I know. Well, to be straight with you—you can button your lip, can't you, Markie?"

"Sure," he said, panting along beside the longer legs of his friend. "You know I can."

"Yeah, right. You never squealed on us at that stinking school. That's why I told that lot you were my friend."

"I am," Mark said. "Honest."

"You still go there?"

"Where?" Mark said, not understanding.

"That bleedin' school."

"Yes. Look, what about this place?"

"Oh yeah, right. It's a great place. Great. A place where we can get through the fence onto this building site. We go there to sniff, like, you know. We got stuff stashed there. It's great. You could stay there. It'd be dry, anyway."

"Hang on, Bernie. Where is it?"

"Bottom of Anchorage. Where all them new flats and stuff's going up."

"No." Mark stopped dead in his tracks, his bag bumping against his leg. "No, I can't go there, Bernie. I can't."

"Why the fuck not?" Bernie turned, lowering, his shoulders hunched aggressively.

" 'Cause I live in Anchorage, up by the park."

"Oh yeah. But that's neat. That's great, that is. Come on."

"No, Bernie."

"Look, you stupid nerd, who's going to go looking for you on your own bleedin' doorstep, eh? You gotta think, son. Use the old gray matter." He took hold of Mark's arm, forced him along. "You gotta get off the streets. You do wandering around Hammersmith bleedin' Broadway and they'll pick you up like *that*." He snapped his fingers under Mark's nose. " 'Specially now they got these extra patrols out, looking for that loony who's killing kids."

It made a kind of sense to Mark. At least it would give him time to think, plan. The mention of the murderer made him think what his mother would say if he was caught, and that clinched it.

"Okay, you're on."

"Terrific. It's the old wharf, see, near them gross old flats. They ain't pulled it all down yet. It's great. And we've made a hole in the fence through onto the building site. They've nearly done some of the new houses. You'll be all right there. Come on, let's leg it."

They ran together, at an easy pace. Mark began to feel good.

This was the sort of life he'd never shared, only heard about at school from kids like Bernie. It was a kind of life his parents deplored, kept him from. Kids running wild in the streets, having a great time. Well he'd show them. He didn't care about them anyway. Bernie knew more than they did. And he, Mark, was a quick learner.

Panting, they stopped on the corner. Bernie was laughing, trying to catch his breath.

"What's funny?"

"Nothing. Just feeling good, that's all. See," he twisted Mark round, faced him toward the old wharf at the bottom of the street. "We smashed the lights in, see, so's we can get in easy, without being spotted. Come on."

It was true. All the streetlights had been smashed at the end of the road and partway along Anchorage. It was dark and cold and very exciting.

"How do we get in?" Mark asked, peering through a lattice of wire to a wasteland of rubble, the shell of a half-demolished building.

"Over the gate. It's easy. We didn't even have to make footholds or nothing. I'll show you. That's the best bit, really. We didn't even have to break in, so nobody knows we go there. Come on."

Bernie lobbed Mark's bag over and then showed him how to climb. One foot on the main strut of the iron-and-wire gate, swing yourself up, grab hold of the top, get your leg over so you sit astride for a moment to catch your breath, and then you let yourself down easy. It was harder for Mark, being smaller, but he made it, sat on top of the gate, feeling like shouting for the sheer pleasure and freedom of it, laughing at the far black gleam of the river. Then he dropped down, bumped against Bernie, who giggled and pushed him away.

"We gotta give the signal now, see. Two whistles to show there's two of us."

"Why? Who else is there?" Mark's flesh prickled apprehensively.

"I don't know, do I? Some of the lads. Maybe no one. Come on." Crouched low, Bernie picked his surefooted way through the rubble and fallen masonry. Mark followed noisily, hopping and slipping. Bernie shushed him, told him to be still, then he straightened up and whistled twice, two fingers stuck in his mouth. A moment later an answering whistle sounded. "Come on, Markie," he said. "Move it."

"Miss Duncan?"

Leigh turned, a quizzical rather than a startled look on her face, just as she was about to fit her key in the lock.

"Yes?"

The man was young and tubby. He climbed out of an unmarked car. Leigh did not notice the uniformed driver.

"Police, Miss. Sergeant Patcham." He displayed his badge.

They've caught him, she thought. Or found him. She didn't want to know, didn't . . .

"Yes?"

"Case of a missing lad, Miss. Mark Cole. We have reason to believe he may have come here."

"Mark? Did you say *Mark* Cole?"

"Yes, Miss. Seen anything of him, have you?"

Her relief was very short-lived indeed. A reel of disturbing images spun through her mind.

"No, no I haven't. When—?"

"Do you think we might . . . er . . . go inside, Miss? There's one or two questions."

"Oh, excuse me. Of course."

She unlocked the door while Patcham spoke to his driver, then led the way upstairs.

"This is terrible," Leigh said, shaking out her gray hair.

"Oh, we'll find him, Miss. Never worry."

The policeman's cheerfulness was not reassuring. What about the others? What about Craig Kingly last night, she thought, but the sergeant was already launched into his routine questions, asking her to confirm or deny Georgia Cole's belief that Mark might come here looking for his father. Leigh agreed but tensed. She saw the next one coming, knew it was going to be awkward.

"And Mr. Steven Cole, Miss—is he here?"

"No. No he's not."

"Are you expecting him?"

"I'm not sure."

"Do you know where we can contact him?"

"Isn't he at home?"

"No, Miss."

"Then no, I'm sorry."

"I see." Patcham rocked on his heels a little. "But he has been here?"

"Yes."

"When did you last see him?"

"Sunday. I left him at his home, with his family."

"I see."

Do you? I hope not, Leigh thought to herself.

"Do you think it's possible Mr. Cole's missing, too, Miss?"

"Oh no, I'm sure not."

"But nobody seems to have seen him since Sunday."

"Look, I don't know how much Mrs. Cole has told you but—"

"I wouldn't worry about that, Miss. You just tell me what you know."

"I don't *know* anything. I was just going to say that Mr. Cole's been under a lot of pressure, has a lot on his mind right now. I sort of assume that he's gone away for a while to think things through."

"You 'sort of assume'?"

"I believe." I want to believe it. "I don't know."

"But you're not alarmed by this absence?"

"Oh no, no." Liar. You're terrified.

"All right, Miss Duncan. Tell me, do you think it's possible Mr. Cole may have taken his son, taken him away somewhere?"

"It's possible, I guess. And there wouldn't be anything wrong in that, would there?"

Patcham did not answer, but he pursed his lips in a doubtful way that made Leigh feel pretty sure Georgia had told him about the attack on Mark. Poor kid.

"If the boy turns up, Miss Duncan—"

"I'll keep him here, of course, and call you. And Mrs. Cole."

"That would be just what the doctor ordered, Miss." He grinned. "Oh, and the same goes for Mr. Cole, Senior, if you don't mind."

"Sure," she said. That wasn't a promise, was it? That was noncommittal.

"No need to see me out, Miss. I can find my way."

Leigh stood in the middle of the room feeling impotent and irrationally guilty. If she hadn't had that drink with Sonia Zimmer, if she had come straight home . . . Georgia must be going out of her mind with worry and might say too much. But if Steven had taken Mark, then everything had to be said. She stared around the room. There was nothing she could do here. She knew what she had to do.

All the boys seemed to be called Darren, except Bernie, of course, and Mark couldn't count how many there were because they kept moving around, and after he'd started sniffing they began to split into two, melt and flow into one another. They huddled together on a motley collection of old mattresses and car seats people had dumped over the fence once the demolition work began. These were arranged in a corner of a partly destroyed factory or old warehouse. Three walls and a part of the roof remained. A glassless grilled window opened onto the night. They had candles stuffed into bottles and old jam jars to protect the flames from the wind. The flickering light sent their shadows dancing. After three sniffs at the bottle of amyl nitrate they started him on, Mark watched their shadows detach themselves from their owners, perform their own jigs on the wall, get sucked up into the black sky, the night. The sniffing made him very relaxed and giggly. His sports bag made a good pillow. He listened to snatches of their whispered conversation. Often they were silent. Like shy animals coming to a waterhole at dawn, he saw them dip their faces one by one into the pool of light, sniffing from a plastic bag held tight to their noses. Afterward they were silent for a while or made little exclamations of excitement or pleasure.

"Come on," said Bernie. "Your turn."

He struggled up from his couch, looked at the plastic bag, not knowing how to manage it.

"Here, like this," Bernie said. One of the Darrens laughed. Bernie clenched the neck of the bag in his fist and held it to his nose, sniffing in sharp, noisy bursts. His face was palely radiant, slack with private pleasure. "Go on," he urged. "It's great."

"Great," Mark agreed dreamily before he'd even tried it.

It was pungent, acid, acrid. The fumes stung his eyes, made them bleary with a moisture that wasn't tears. Then his brain expanded, his mind rose like dough, pressing against the helmet of his skull, which seemed to split, to set his mind free, growing. The shadows were green, red, and beautiful blue. Somebody swore at him and dragged the bag from his loose grip. He laughed to see the colors, closed his eyes, and watched a whirl of sparkling stars, exploding shapes, like a video game gone multicolored crazy. He gave himself up to it, floating and spinning. Then someone was tugging at his arm, telling him to shut up and get down.

"What?" he said, sprawled beside Bernie, uncomfortable on the rubbly floor.

"It's the fuzz patrol boat. Always goes past about now." A sensation he would normally have identified as fear nagged but failed to take root in him. "They ain't on to us. It's the queers on the other bank. They've got a bleedin' great searchlight though, and you never know where they're gonna swing it."

"On some creep with his trousers down," a Darren said.

They laughed and huddled together listening to the distant throb of the boat's engine until it faded to a mosquito hum.

But the mood was broken, the effect worn off when they got to their feet again, dusting themselves down. A row broke out over the relighting of the candles. Two Darrens sloped off. Another suggested they go through the fence, onto the site, muck about. He waved an aerosol in their faces.

"Yeah, that's right," Bernie said. "Gotta find Markie a place for the night, ain't we?"

"Ain't you got no home to go to?"

"He's on the run. Come on. Bring some candles."

It was all a bit hazy to Mark. He tagged along behind them, encumbered by his sports bag. He wanted to sniff some more stuff, recapture that easy companionship they had all shared, passing the plastic bag and little bottle around. He stumbled over the littered terrain, shivered in the light wind from the river. The hole in the fence was small and low down. To get through you had to lie flat on your belly and wriggle. His bag got stuck, tore as a Darren yanked it free. Sharp ends of naked wire snagged at his clothes. Bernie pulled him through, cursing.

"Here . . ." Somebody offered the plastic bag again. He took it greedily, sniffed until the whole world seemed to drop away.

"That's enough. Jesus. Give it here."

The cold air felt like frost in his nostrils. He wasn't able to stand. Two of them supported him, giggling and flopping, and lay him on some smooth bleached boards that smelled of wood shavings and sawdust, like the carpentry shop at school. He lay there and watched the brilliant stars; they were Christmas-tree decorations, colored icicles gyrating through a spiked frame of rafters and incomplete walls. The stars fell one by one, entered his head, exploded.

Later, he heard the others talking, the voices punctuated by giggles and snorts as the bag was passed. Talk of a Darren and some girl, the things they had done together, how the others had watched. Their laughter said how great it was. Then Mark was standing up, weaving, needing to relieve himself. A frame stood in place of a door, and he staggered toward it.

"Hey, Markie, where you going?"

"Pee, got to pee."

"Mind how you go then."

"Don't splash your boots."

"Probably going to jerk himself off."

"What you wanna bring him for, Bernie? He's a nutter."

"Leave him be. He's okay. He's my mate. Here, give us a sniff."

The voices faded as he stumbled over tire ruts in the frozen mud. He loved Bernie, felt really warm and good about Bernie. He was as good as them, as free and wild as them, out for a good time. To prove it, he relieved himself giggling into the open mouth of a concrete mixer. Wait till he told them about that! They'd die laughing. When he'd finished he could not find the way back, and that struck him as very funny indeed. Laughing, he wandered into other half-built houses, which seemed to him like toys. In one, he found a skeletal staircase leading up to the sky. He climbed it on all fours and stood leaning against the serrated edge of an unfinished brick wall. Below him the river stretched and flowed, its surface reflecting back the stars like a fireworks display. He leaned far out toward it, looking for his own reflection.

A hand jerked him back roughly.

"There you are. What you doin'?"

"Come on, Bernie. I'm freezing," one of the Darrens said.

"Just a minute. Mark, look, there's your bag, right?" He dropped the bag with a thud on the planking. "I put a candle in it and some stuff, okay? I gotta split now, Markie."

"Bernie, I'm off," yelled one of the guys.

"Hang on. I'm coming. You wanna go farther along that way, see, up toward the park. They've got the roofs on up there. Be warmer for you. You understand, Markie?"

"Warm roofs, yeah?" Mark giggled, swayed.

"Come on. You'll bleedin' kill yourself up here."

Bernie tossed his bag down the stairs, led him down, holding his wrist tightly. Mark sat on the stairs, his head swimming.

Minutes, hours, a lifetime later his elbow slipped from his knee, struck painfully against the step he sat on, jerking him awake. He had a dull headache. His throat felt sore, and there was an unpleasant aftertaste in his mouth. He was also very cold.

"Bernie?"

Silence.

"Darren?"

He stood up, found that his legs were steady now. Too steady. He needed some more stuff, wanted to get high again. His head hurt.

"Bernie?"

He walked down the last few steps and struck his foot against his sports bag, lying on its side. As he bent to pick it up he realized that Bernie and all the Darrens had gone. He was alone, completely alone, and his heart was hammering painfully. He was afraid.

They came like monkeys, came out of the darkness, the shadowed wastes of the demolition site, and leaped at the old gate, making it rattle, its wire sing. He watched them cling and climb, swing their legs over, night horsemen for a moment before dropping down, training shoes slapping the pavement. They glanced around nervously, and he shrank back, melted into the wall he was already hugging.

This was not a place he had ever thought of as likely. He was en route to another spot, one he had cased and chosen in the long years of waiting. He planned to go there because he could not go home. Not yet. He could not risk waking the boy who lay so peacefully in Mummy's big bed.

The boys padded toward him through the dark.

"You reckon it's all right to leave him there?"

"Yeah, course it is."

"I dunno. He's only a kid."

"You should've thought of that earlier, Bernie. What you gonna do? Hold his hand? Sing him to sleep?"

"All right, shut up."

He moved then, stirred by what they said, the gift they had given him. He moved away from the wall, showed himself. One of them glanced at him, stared.

"Good night, boys," he said, almost tenderly.


Marion wrenched the door open. She could not be bothered with all those fancy locks, had left the door on the latch. Instead of the policeman she expected, or Mark, whom she prayed to see, a tall woman with a ruffled mane of gray hair stood there, staring at her with strange, almost creepy eyes. Instinctively, she closed the door a bit.

"Yes?"

"I wanted to see Mrs. Cole."

"You can't, not now."

"I'm Leigh Duncan. The police told me—"

Marion glanced over her shoulder, sensing Georgia behind her.

"Have you seen him?" She thrust Marion aside, flung the door wide so that it cracked against the wall. "Has Mark been to you?"

"No. I'm sorry. The police came. They asked me. Steven's not there, either. I told you . . ."

Georgia turned away, weeping, covering her face with her hands. Marion stared after her as she hobbled, broken, down the corridor.

"Perhaps you'd better come in," she said, looking at Leigh. "You see how it is." She shrugged, closed the door.

"I don't want to upset her any more."

Marion shook her head, motioned Leigh toward the living room.

"What do you want?" Georgia said, trying to shout but only managing a croak.

"I thought I might be able to help, do something. I don't really know. I guess I feel guilty."

"Where is he? Where's Mark?" Tears blotching her face, Georgia held out her arms helplessly, hands flapping. Marion went to her, cradled her against her bosom. "Why aren't you at home?" Georgia demanded, struggling with Marion. "What if he goes to your place?"

"The police are watching it," Leigh said. "I spoke to an officer in a car as I left. He said they'd keep watch until I got back or . . . Mark turned up someplace else."

"I don't want you here. What do you want?"

Marion tried to comfort her, sat with her arm around her heaving shoulders.

"They think," Leigh said, "Steven might have taken him off somewhere. Do you think that? And if so, where? There must be someplace you can think of, some place he might go?"

Georgia tried to speak, but only sobs came out, more sobs

and more tears. Marion held her tight, stroking her hair, murmuring to her as to a child. A little embarrassed, knowing she would get no answer until Georgia was calmer, Leigh went to the window. It was undraped, and she glanced down into the dimly-lit road. The river was a black sheen in the distance. The clear stars fretted her own ghostly reflection. A car passed slowly down the road, and the driver switched the headlights to high beams as the car approached the blind corner by the park gates. Leigh watched without registering until those same lights swept his body, showed him to her for a moment. She caught her breath, pressed her face against the glass.

"What is it?" Marion said, her voice tight with suppressed excitement or fear.

"I'm not sure . . . I . . ."

"What is it? Is it him?" Georgia ran toward the window, seemed about to throw herself at the glass. Leigh turned around, grabbed her arm, holding her.

"I think I just saw Steven down there. I'm sure I did." Georgia stared at her, mouth open, eyes stark with fear. "I must go see," Leigh said as she stepped around Georgia, began to run for the door.

"Steven?" Georgia said. Then she began to scream.

Steven knew that only death mattered now. He shuffled through the old remembered streets not out of hope or in search of comfort but because known territory demanded less effort. He had given up the struggle, failed. Only his own execution concerned him now. The river, blackly waiting, cold—it held the pretty face of death he sought and longed to embrace.

"Steven?" She did not dare to touch him. The aura was single but disturbing in its intensity and blackness. A fog of black flame seemed to bow his shoulders, threaten to engulf him. Behind her was a commotion, Georgia's strident voice, then Marion's calm and firm, leading her back inside. Leigh fell into step beside him. If he heard and recognized he was impervious to Georgia's anguish.

Leigh let her mind touch his silently, saw what he saw. He slipped through the cold water, his lungs clogging with it, limbs passive, refusing to swim or struggle. Her mind reached out to his: *No*, she told him fiercely, *you must not. No, Steven, no. I love you. I need you.* His mind stirred a little at this, sluggish like the fine silt at the bottom of the river. He stopped and turned his washed-out eyes on her. They slid across her face, not with the blankness she had seen before, but as though they were hollow screens with nothing behind them but the image of death. His despair defeated her. Her own sense of approaching loneliness seemed to spill from her and join with his. It was unbearable, a kind of dying. To avoid his eyes, she looked away, over his shoulder where the building site rose in jagged, uncompleted lines and shapes against the cold sky. Her mind tripped, went from her. She felt her vision alter and twist, and she saw him then, saw him in an empty, enclosed space, stalking.

"Steven." Her hands were on his hanging arms, shaking him. "He's there. He's right there. Steven, for God's sake, you've got to try. One last time. Do it, Steven. Do it."

He suffered her to shake him, to turn him around, propel him toward the chain link fence. Her tumbling words made no sense, were an intrusion on his quiet fascination with impending death. He shook her off, but hooked his fingers in the cold mesh and peered through.

Then he could feel him, tense with excitement and expectation, sliding through incomplete rooms that smelled of raw wood and wet plaster, feeling the rough texture of bricks and coarsely laid mortar. Climbing dusty stairs, the scent of his quarry in his nose. Could hear his breathing and feel his sweat of anticipation. Shared the tightness in the throat, the terrible prickle in the groin. Could see and not see a light flickering, the angle of a doorframe set emptily in a wall, a huddled figure shivering, turning its face to the doorway. And saw then with a clarity that pierced him, broke the caul of despair and cracked his heart.

"Mark," he said, and then again a cry of rage and pain: *"Mark!"*

He had found a good place, a room with a roof and two unglazed windows. If he huddled in the lee of the wall beneath the larger window there was some protection from drafts. He doubted that he would find a better sanctuary, was, in any case, too scared and tired to search farther. From his bag he took the

candle in its jam jar, the rattling box of matches Bernie had
provided. His fingers fumbled with the matches. The first one
went out. He shielded the second more carefully and touched it
to the blackened wick. The candle took just as the match flame
licked and blistered his fingers. He dropped it with a little cry
of surprise and pain. It was better with a flicker of light.

He sat, huddled over the candle, his hands cupped above the
meager flame, seeking a little warmth. In a minute he would
get his sleeping bag out. He would soon get warm, snuggled
down inside it. With the light to chase away some of the dark,
it wouldn't be too bad. In the morning early, he'd—

It wasn't so much a sound that made him start but a more
general sense of somebody near, somebody watching him. He
had difficulty swallowing. His head was still slow from the
solvent fumes he had sniffed, but he knew that someone was
there. He looked fearfully toward the black doorway, was sure
that he had heard a sound, a cautious slithering. The darkness
framed by the doorway was thicker, as from a human bulk,
approaching, casting its own impossible shadow. Then relief
flooded through him. Of course . . ."

"Bernie?" he said, starting up. "Is that you, Bernie?" Of
course it was. Bernie had come back. Good old Bernie. Had
come back to stay with him or take him to a better place.
"Come on, Bernie. You scared me. Stop sneaking about,
Bernie. Please."

The man stood in the doorway blocking it. The candlelight,
guttering in the cross drafts, was unable to reach his face.
Instead it gleamed on the shiny black gloves he wore, his hands
piously folded in front of him, still and waiting.


Leigh threw herself at the door, beat on it with her fists. She
did not realize that she was shouting. Below her, doors opened,
voices murmured.

"What on earth . . . ?" Marion stepped back, her face
ashen, as Leigh pushed into the hall.

"He's there . . . Mark . . . out there!" She pointed
wildly in the fancied direction of the building site. "The
police!" She went past Marion, fumbled at the telephone,
knocking the receiver, purring, to the table. "Steven's gone
. . . gone to get him. We must get help!"

As she dialed, Georgia came along the corridor, her hands slapping at the walls, seeking support. Leigh spoke rapidly, as calmly as she could. She saw Marion try to restrain Georgia, plead with her, heard her say, "At least put your coat on."

Georgia thrust her aside and ran out, down the echoing stairs.

"Yes, Anchorage Road. Please come quickly. He's there, yes. Please be quick. I can't explain, but I swear it's true. Oh, please just get over here quickly." She hung up to prevent their asking any more dumb, time-wasting questions. Outside she heard raised voices, neighbors demanding to know what was going on, Marion shrieking after Georgia. She had to go too, had to go and wait and see, even though she knew there was nothing anyone could do. It was up to Steven now. All up to Steven now.


"Mark!"

The shout echoed from another world, another time, a haven beyond reach. Mark tore his eyes from the impassive figure, looked toward one of the cold black windows, to the voice that called his name once and once only.

"Is that your name, then, Mark? That's a good name. A biblical name, Mark. Yes, I like that. But that isn't the point, is it? Anyone can have a good biblical name, but are they good? Are you a good boy, Mark?" The man moved as he spoke, carefully, with all the time in the world. Mark retreated, matching him step for slow step.

The man loomed over the candle, his shadow filling the room. Mark stared at the polished toe of his shoe as he paused for a moment before kicking out, knocking the jar over, dousing the flame. The jar rolled back and forth, back and forth on the floorboards with an eerily repetitive sound.

"We don't need that, do we, Mark? Don't want anyone to find us." The tone of voice was so reasonable that Mark almost found himself agreeing, but stunned by the sudden loss of light, he kept silent, shrank back again, retreated as the shadow came on until he felt the rough, unplastered wall pressing behind him.

"What . . . what do you want?" he said, inching to the left, toward the nearest window, his voice shaking.

"Was that one of your friends calling you, Mark? Was that Bernie?"

"I don't know."

"What were you and Bernie up to here this evening, eh? What have you been doing?"

Mark could see the window, the rectangle of paler darkness against the pitch of the room. Another few feet and he could call out, but the cry died in his throat as the man's torso filled the window, was silhouetted against the sky and the radiance of distant streetlights. Mark tried to remember where the door was, had to make a dash for it, run. His foot caught the unseen jam jar, sent it spinning across the room to shatter against the wall. He heard its gunshot crack as the man seized him, swung him around, and clapped a gloved hand over his mouth. His head was pulled sharply back against the man's chest. The leather-covered thumb pressed cruelly against one nostril while the palm completely closed his mouth.

"We don't want any noise, either, do we, Mark? We want to stay here quietly till they go away."

He struggled then, twisted, but the man's grip was like iron. Mark tried to kick, but his legs encountered only the empty air. The man laughed, a pleased little chuckle, then caught his breath and kicked out viciously, knocking Mark's legs from under him. They went down together, and the man's grip did not falter for a moment. His free hand caught Mark's arm and twisted it up toward his shoulder blade. The man knelt on one knee, pressing Mark into the floor as his finger slowly pinched his other nostril closed.

Steven scaled the gate with an ease and strength he had not known he possessed. This was a flimsy structure of wood and netting. As he swung himself up to the top, one of the makeshift hinges snapped and the gate veered inward. The force of it threw all of Steven's weight against the top spar, and the old wood cracked and splintered. Desperate, he jumped, landed awkwardly, and pitched forward, striking the frozen earth with enough force to drive the breath from his body.

Mark! Mark! his mind screamed as he scrambled up. Where? Where in this dark and jumbled place? He stumbled in the ruts left by truck tracks, over planks laid by workers for wheelbarrows. He darted into half-constructed houses, scrambled over low walls, ran from one house to another. Where? Where are you? He had to make contact now. Had to. How? Where are you?

. . . *that's better isn't it, Mark? You can breathe now. But if you make any noise* . . .

"Mark?"

He ran on, to more solid houses. He crashed into one, another, his footsteps echoing.

. . . *that's nice. You like that, don't you, Mark? You like that. Because you're a bad boy, a filthy boy. You haven't kept yourself pure. You've go to be taught a lesson* . . .

"No!" Steven shouted aloud. "Mark? Where are you?"

He blundered into the next house, paused, made himself be still, quiet, listening. He must use skill and cunning, his mind and ears. He was the rational one. They must make some noise. He flinched at the imagined sound of a struggle. He heard the wind, the lap of the river. Help me, help me, he prayed.

*A staircase, Steven. Upstairs. A room with a roof and two windows. A staircase, Steven. Hurry.*

Her voice was in the wind and lapping water. It soothed and spurred him on.

*I love you, Steven.*

He found a staircase, scrambled up it. Nothing. Oh God, nothing. He leaped from a point halfway down the staircase, dashed out into the night, into the next house and knew at once by the faint smell of candle wax on the air, that his search was over. He found the stairs just as a siren started, up river, wailing.

When Steven burst through the doorway, he passed through that dark mirror he had imagined, and he found himself on the other side. The wailing siren became his son's sobbing screams as, startled, the man released him, flinched back, drew himself up. There were other sirens, too, and voices, the sound of Mark dragging himself across the floor. Steven did not hear them, created his own silence out of the desire to kill. It was the purest sensation he had ever known, and he savored it fully.

The man shrank back against the wall, his arms hanging

loosely at his sides. Steven took his time, deliberately prolonging the moment in order to understand and preserve it. He was going to kill, cause the utmost pain he could imagine. He was going to put into practice all that his tormentor had taught him, all that he had shown him in hell.

The man did not defend himself, made no attempt to evade or escape Steven's approach. Steven hit him first, drove his fist deep and hard into his belly so that, with a gurgle of surprise, spent breath, the man doubled over, leaned toward Steven. He brought up his knee, felt it crunch against the man's chin, and as his head came up he punched again, knocking him sideways and back so that his head struck the rough wall. Then Steven gripped him by the lapels of his dark coat and drew him close, pulled him into a deadly embrace. His knee found the softness of the man's groin. The man cried out, almost a sexual scream of pleasure, and Steven shifted the position of his hands, pushed aside the lapels and fastened on the throat.

Light hit the room. One of the windows blazed, and beneath the dying of the siren he heard voices. He saw Mark in the light, pulling himself up into the window frame, shouting and waving. The light showed him the man's face as his thumbs found his windpipe and pressed.

Their eyes met and locked, and for a long, agonizing moment, they seemed to become one. Steven could feel it. His impulse to kill waned, just for a fraction of a second. The man's lips drew back in a smile of welcome and recognition. They had been friends, always, always would be. The man's smile said that he had found his friend, all he had lost, and his arms, finding some new, last strength, came up and folded about Steven's back in an embrace. Steven remembered his own death, how he had longed to die, and he pressed harder, making the smile stretch. He pressed ferociously, because he knew, with a clarity as bright and clean as the searchlight that remained fastened on the window, filling the room with brightness, that what he was killing was a part of himself, the part that made him one of Leigh's latents, the part, above all, that had allowed the man to befriend him.

He swung the man toward the light. His head cracked against the wall beside the window. And cracked again. He heard sounds as the man's face faded into the light—voices, shouts, screams close by. He dashed the man's skull against the jagged edge of the window and thrust him out toward the light, heaved with all his strength. He leaned out, his hands loath to let go, leaned out until it seemed that he must fall and someone was trying to pull him back, calling him. And he let go, saw the body turn and gyre, black coat flapping like a damaged wing, saw it strike something, and then disappear into the silky black water waiting below.

The spray thrown up by the body striking the water turned to crystal tears in the light, tears through which, when he turned, he saw Mark staring at him, saw that the son had seen his father kill, had seen the mirror smash so that they were one and separate. As he turned toward the doorway the broken shards of the jam jar crunched under his foot.

Several police cars and a fire engine blocked Anchorage Road. Their blazing lights were trained on the construction site. The noise of the sirens and squealing tires had brought the residents out into the street, where they gathered in noisy knots. Georgia was the focus of attention, huddled against Marion beside one of the official cars. The air crackled with the sound of walkie-talkie sets, echoing commands from the river patrol launch. Policemen swarmed through the open, broken gates, their heavy torches beaming through the night.

Leigh, standing apart, on the fringe of the crowd, watched an ambulance nose its way toward the impromptu blockade. She heard shouts from the building site, and a ripple of excitement or fear passed through the crowd. Some teenagers buffetted her as they pressed closer to the center of the action. She was detached, separate, outside it all—different. She had done her best, the best she could.

The crowd became restless suddenly and surged forward. A policeman with a megaphone talked them back, others pushed and herded them. Leigh turned, steeling herself, and looked toward the gates. She saw Georgia enter the light, Marion hesitating behind her, before she saw Mark. They ran toward each other, their voices mingling brokenly. And just behind came Steven. He looked older, disheveled, his clothing stained with dirt, the scratches on his cheek livid against the pallor. A policeman supported his elbow. He stopped at the gateway, bent his head to hear something a plainclothesman said to him. He nodded, then stared beyond the man to where Georgia and Mark clung together. It seemed to Leigh that he stood there a very long time, that time stretched unnaturally to fix every detail of the scene indelibly on her mind. Steven seemed to shake himself, then walked toward Mark and his mother. The boy turned, reached out for him, and Steven lay his arm around his shoulders, on top of Georgia's, so that they were linked together by the child. They all three turned away then, as one, but it was Steven's back Leigh watched until it disappeared into the shadows.

Encouraged by the police, the crowd began to disperse. The ambulance and the fire engine trundled away, unwanted. Gossiping, the crowd flowed around Leigh, broke up. Doors shut all along the street. Traffic was let through again, drivers and passengers craning to see what all the fuss had been about.

Standing alone on the pavement, Leigh acknowledged the landscape of her vision and noted only one ironic difference: in her mind's eye, Steven had walked away alone, not entwined with his family. She had overlooked that.

"It's all over," somebody said, straggling past.

"Yeah. Lot of fuss about nothing."

Leigh turned into their footsteps, pushing her cold hands into the deep pockets of her coat. Yes, it's all over. But for her it had not been for nothing, at least not entirely.

# EPILOGUE

The body that was fished with hooked poles from the river was identified by papers carried in an old, cracked wallet next to the man's heart. He was Arthur James Gossage of 88 Mayfield House, Western Estate. When policemen broke into the flat, which was still rented in his deceased mother's name, Ida Rose Gossage, they found the cold, naked body of Craig Kingly wrapped in a white sheet, lying on the bed in the carefully preserved room previously occupied by Mrs. Gossage. The boy had been strangled with his own belt, which was found, along with his other clothes and few possessions, in a black plastic rubbish bag in Gossage's cell-like, green-curtained bedroom.

Injuries to the head and throat of the deceased Arthur Gossage were attributed to the fight between him and Steven Cole, when the latter interrupted Gossage's assault and attempt on the life of his son. Lesions, abrasions and bruising to other parts of the body were commensurate with his subsequent fall from the unfinished house into the Thames. No charges were made against Steven Cole.

Arthur Gossage had lived for more than twenty years at number 88 Mayfield House, and neighbors described him as a shy, quiet man, devoted to his rather domineering mother. He had become more withdrawn after her death and kept himself very much to himself. Colleagues at Hammersmith Town Hall, where he had been employed as a clerk in the housing department, confirmed that he had been very distressed and "moody" after his mother's death and burial. But as time passed and more details of his crimes became widely known, he was endowed by those who remembered him with staring eyes and a furtive manner. Some neighbors suddenly recalled evidence of a foul temper, and many young people on the Estate swore that they had always found him "creepy."

Three days after the identification of Arthur James Gossage, a businessman from Glasgow was formally charged at Savile Row Police Station with the murder, in a Soho parking lot, of Alan Black, aged eighteen, prostitute.

Mark Cole became a fleeting center of interest once his brush with the killer and rescue by his father became known, and he tended to bask in the attention, bragging particularly about his father, whose actions that night he edited and exaggerated and came to believe. He still thought occasionally, and with repugnance, of the man's prying hand as they lay together in the incomplete room and it was so difficult for him to breathe properly. Sometimes these memories formed the basis of bad dreams from which he woke struggling for breath and with a feeling of shame. But everyone said he was young and the young were resilient, especially those who came from a good, stable, and loving home, as the Coles' undoubtedly was, now that Georgia and Steven had resolved their differences.

Georgia Cole never did return to her job, not because she continued to be afraid of her feelings for Roger North, but because she did not wish to be reminded of that time, and also as a mute declaration to Steven and her son that the affair was well and truly over. Mark's accusations had lodged in her mind, and she thought, increasingly, that Mark's narrow escape was now some kind of retribution, a warning at least, from which Steven had saved them both. By straying from the narrowness of her life, she had left the door open for chaos to come in. It was much easier, consequently, to forgive Steven than herself. Whatever dreadful suspicions she had harbored about him, whatever delusions she had labored under, whatever he had done with Leigh Duncan—and into none of these topics did she care to inquire—he was exonerated by saving Mark and restoring him to her. Steven was a good man, and she would never again think of him as "soft." For his part,

Steven promised that their life would be less ordinary, humdrum, bound by routine. They would get out more, spend more time together.

Thanks to Sonia Zimmer's intervention, Leigh's attachment to the hospital was smoothly and surprisingly quickly transferred to another in Cambridge. Bertie Page let it be known to all who would listen that the transfer was directly the result of her unfortunate liaison with Steven Cole, whose marriage had nearly been wrecked as a result, but to Leigh he was charm itself, even though his eyes and smug mouth contradicted his words and manner.

The night before she left for Cambridge, Leigh destroyed all her notes and tape recordings, every scrap of evidence that might have proved that involuntary telepathic communication was indeed a fact. She did so without regret. She felt raw, flayed by the whole experience, and the move to a new job, away from Steven, inevitably reminded her of Spike and their essential separation. She saw her life settling into a pattern and vowed to break it. She had been bad for Spike, bad for Steven, and she accepted that she must be alone, remain detached, and maybe in time she would begin to feel comfortable that way. Meanwhile there was her work, so much to be done.

Steven often thought of her at first. They had not spoken privately or personally since the night he killed Gossage and he had become Georgia's knight in shining armor. But as time went by and he took his family on a much needed and deserved holiday, she began to fade for him. She became his Circe again, someone he had dreamed, imagined, the fair face of a foul experience. Her memory was too painful, and he told himself there had never been any substance to their relationship, it was all due to extraordinary circumstances. As her magic waned, seemed illusory, so her beauty became merely extraordinary, even a bit odd.

As time passed he thought more and more deeply about Arthur James Gossage and came to believe that he himself had been, in some inexplicable way, the imaginary friend of that lost and abused child who grew into a monster. His sense of privilege grew stronger every day, as he continued to believe that he had killed absolutely that part of his nature that few men are ever forced to acknowledge. He took a spiritual, almost religious strength from that, and his anger softened. He could no longer hate the unwanted befriender.

# SHOCKING TRUE CRIME STORIES

**THE BEAUTY QUEEN KILLER**
by Bruce Gibney
The true account of a twisted mind and the killing spree that
horrified a nation!
☐ 42380-2/$2.95

**DISAPPEARANCES: TRUE ACCOUNTS OF CANADIANS WHO HAVE
VANISHED**
by Derrick Murdoch
The chilling reconstruction of fourteen missing Canadians who
have vanished over the last thirty years.
☐ 43198-8/$3.75

**EDWARD GEIN: AMERICA'S MOST BIZARRE MURDERER**
by Judge Robert H. Gollmar
The terrifying true story of the Wisconsin mass murderer—told
by the judge who convicted him!
☐ 42210-5/$3.50

**KILLER CLOWN**
by Terry Sullivan with Peter T. Maiken
The horrifying true story of a man convicted of more murders
than any other person in U.S. history!
☐ 42274-1/$3.95

**LADIES WHO KILL**
by Tom Kuncl and Paul Einstein
The true-crime story of the deadly women awaiting execution on
death row.
☐ 42494-9/$2.95

**THE PROSTITUTE MURDERS**
by Rod Leith
The true-crime shocker of Richard Cottingham, who killed and
tortured Manhattan prostitutes.
☐ 42281-4/$2.50

---

# LEWIS PERDUE

**THE TESLA BEQUEST**
A secret society of powerful men have stolen the late Nikola
Tesla's plans for a doomsday weapon; they are just one step away
from ruling the world.
□ 42027-7 THE TESLA BEQUEST                                    $3.50

**THE DELPHI BETRAYAL**
From the depths of a small, windowless room in the bowels of
the White House, an awesome conspiracy to create economic
chaos and bring the entire world to its knees is unleashed.
□ 41728-4 THE DELPHI BETRAYAL                                  $2.95

**QUEENS GATE RECKONING**
A wounded CIA operative and a defecting Soviet ballerina hurtle
toward the hour of reckoning as they race the clock to circum-
vent twin assassinations that will explode the balance of power.
□ 41436-6 QUEENS GATE RECKONING                                $3.50

**THE DA VINCI LEGACY**
A famous Da Vinci whiz, Curtis Davis, tries to uncover the truth
behind the missing pages of an ancient manuscript which could
tip the balance of world power toward whoever possesses it.
□ 41762-4 THE DA VINCI LEGACY                                  $3.50